Pippa Roscoe lives in Norfolk, near her family, and makes daily promises to herself that this is the day she'll leave the computer to take a long walk in the countryside. She can't remember a time when she wasn't dreaming about handsome heroes and innocent heroines. Totally her mother's fault, of course—she gave Pippa her first romance to read at the age of seven! She is inconceivably happy that she gets to share those daydreams with you. Follow her on Twitter @PippaRoscoe.

Millie Adams has always loved books. She considers herself a mix of Anne Shirley—loquacious, but charming, and willing to break a slate over a boy's head if need be—and Charlotte Doyle—a lady at heart, but with the spirit to become a mutineer should the occasion arise. Millie lives in a small house on the edge of the woods, which she finds allows her to escape in the way she loves best: in the pages of a book. She loves intense alpha heroes and the women who dare to go toe-to-toe with them. Or break a slate over their heads…

CP/4

TERMS OF THEIR COSTA RICAN TEMPTATION

PIPPA ROSCOE

CROWNING HIS INNOCENT ASSISTANT

MILLIE ADAMS

MILLS & BOON

DUDLEY
LIBRARIES

000003075978	
Askews & Holts	15-Mar-2021
AF ROM	£6.99
2CR	

Crowning His Innocent Assistant © 2021 Millie Adams

ISBN: 978-0-263-28236-8

MIX
Paper from
responsible sources
FSC® C007454

Printed and bound in Spain
by CPI, Barcelona

TERMS OF THEIR COSTA RICAN TEMPTATION

PIPPA ROSCOE

For Rani.
Because sometimes all you need is friendship
and laughter to put the world right again.

xx

PROLOGUE

SKYE SOAMES TOOK a deep breath that quivered at the back of her throat for a moment before she drew it into her lungs, hoping that her sisters hadn't noticed. Not for the first time she wondered what the three of them were doing in Norfolk on an unseasonably cold, grey miserable day, standing beside the coffin of a man they had never met.

She clenched her jaw against the cutting wind as it hit her like a slap. They'd been picked up from their small home on the outskirts of the New Forest by a limousine—neighbours frowning and whispering into their hands as they peered through white lace curtains, as if they hadn't had a lifetime of gossip already. But four hours in a car that glided over concrete had cocooned her and her sisters in a warm, contented state of confusion until they had caught sight of the stone church and the Gothic graveyard beside it.

They were here to…what? Pay their respects? To a man who had kicked out his only daughter at the age of seventeen and cut her off without a penny or word ever since? Because until today that was all they had ever known about their grandfather, Elias Soames.

Summer, her youngest sister, shifted on her feet and drew her dark wool coat around her middle, her face strangely pale against the blonde hair she'd pulled back into a messy ponytail. So very different from Skye's own brown hair, carefully wrapped into a neat bun, and just as different from the long vibrant, fiery red strands the wind whipped across Star's cheeks. A difference that came from each sister's father. Some might have called them half-sisters, but to Skye, Summer and Star there was nothing half about the bond between them. Star's hand came up to brush her Titian hair back, revealing startling green eyes sparkling with a sheen that looked suspiciously like tears.

'Star?'

'It's just so sad,' she said.

'We never met him. He abandoned our—'

'Ashes to ashes, dust to dust…' The words spoken by the priest cut through Summer's response as if in admonishment and another blast of icy-cold air trickled down Skye's spine. She shivered, not for the grandfather she had never known, but for another funeral, one yet to come. One that threatened to rock the very foundations of Skye and her sisters' lives.

Mariam Soames hadn't been able to attend the funeral because of her treatment schedule—if you could call sipping on herbal teas and CBD tablets treatment. Thanks to the postcode lottery that determined access to specific treatments on the NHS, they'd lost out. Big time. And it had only encouraged their alternative lifestyle living mother further into 'natural treatments'.

Skye had spent more midnight hours than she could count trying to work out how to fund the life-saving health care privately, or even a very costly move into another area where Mariam stood a better chance of treatment. But the housing costs in the nearest health region where that might happen were four times more expensive than what they paid now and, no matter the calculations, they just couldn't make it work. Besides, Mariam didn't want to move, she was focused on quality of life not quantity. Skye's heart twisted that she couldn't find a way to achieve both for her mother.

She looked up at the large house in the distance. Her mother had insisted that even had she been well enough she wouldn't have come. Mariam Soames had said all she needed to her father the night she had left Norfolk thirty-seven years ago.

Elias's lawyer nodded, announcing the end of the small service that marked the end of a man's life. No one else had been in attendance. Clearly Elias Soames had not been a popular figure in the community, leaving the mourners to number five, including the priest.

The lawyer walked them back to the limousine and chose to sit up front with the driver, effectively preventing any conversation until they reached the estate. Skye felt sick at the thought of her grandfather having enough money to fund his daughter's treatment and then some, and felt shame knowing her primary motivation for being here—the will.

Barely five minutes later the car pulled into a grand sweeping drive that took them towards their grandfather's home and Skye's jaw wasn't the only one in the car to drop.

It might not have had the grandeur of the estate from *Downton Abbey*—Summer's favourite TV show—but it wasn't far off. The sprawling ancient building revealed itself in glimpses as the car took the large twists and turns of the drive towards an impressive set of steps at the main entrance, which finally revealed the house in its entirety.

'Holy—' Star's curse was cut short by a not-so-gentle shoulder-shove from Skye, who had no wish to incur any further disdain from Elias's lawyer, Mr Beamish. But it had managed to draw a spark of something to Summer's grey eyes—a spark that had been absent for the last few weeks.

Skye stepped out of the car and was forced to crane her neck to look up at the glorious building. This was…

unimaginable. Her mother had walked away from this? There had to be…

'There are over twenty rooms in the main section of the house, but though the east and west wings have been closed off for quite some time now, they also boast a modest fifteen apiece. I'm afraid we have to hurry things along a bit,' he claimed, barely stopping for breath. 'You'll understand why shortly. Follow me.'

With that, he turned on his heel and disappeared into the bowels of the house. Skye and her sisters followed him down dark hallways with moth-eaten carpets, various pieces of antique furniture, sideboards on which sat china bowls of scentless aged potpourri and walls covered in old dusty paintings of ancestors Skye couldn't even begin to imagine. She saw her sisters' heads sweeping from side to side as if to take it all in. But Skye focused only on Mr Beamish as he led them into what was clearly the estate office. One of them had to keep their head on straight and focus on the situation. And, as always, it would be her.

He gestured for them to sit in the three chairs provided, facing the beautiful and clearly ancient wooden desk. Only when they had done so did Mr Beamish take his place opposite them. Skye watched as he pulled a raft of papers from his briefcase and began the formalities of the reading of the will. Whether it was exhaustion from the day's early start or the particular pitch of his monotone voice, she couldn't keep his words in her head for long and her mind wandered as freely as her eyes around the room. They caught on a large oil painting just behind Mr Beamish.

The image was quite startling, and she knew without a shadow of a doubt that she was staring at a portrait of her grandfather. He looked…mean. And miserable. And nothing like his daughter, who had more laughter, more love in her than she could contain, both traits often trailing in

her wake. Skye's mother might be flighty, might have little to no thought of practicalities and necessities, but she
loved greatly.

So different from the malicious intent in the eyes of Elias
Soames looming up behind Mr Beamish as he delivered
his last will and testament. And then her mind snagged on
what the lawyer had just said.

'I'm sorry…what?' she asked. Shock cut through her,
as if her body had reacted before comprehending what the
words had meant.

'As I said, Ms Soames. The entire estate will be yours,
on certain conditions. For five generations the entail known
as the Soames diamonds have been missing. Much like his
father, and his father's father before him and so on, Elias
had been desperately trying to recover them. The specifics
of his search are in this folder here,' he said, pushing the
folder only halfway towards the women. 'Before his death,
my client made the stipulation that you will inherit the entire estate—to do with as you will—on the condition that
you are able to retrieve the Soames diamonds within two
months of his death.'

Skye was speechless, her mind hurtling at the speed of
light through the possibilities this might mean. For them.
For their mother.

'So we could sell the estate?' Star demanded.

Mr Beamish nodded. 'If you find the diamonds, yes.'

'Is this even legal?' Skye asked, even while her mind
screamed, *I don't care!*

Mr Beamish had the grace to look embarrassed, but not
to answer the question. 'Should you fail to discover their
whereabouts, then the estate and the entire entail will revert
to the National Trust. I believe the deadline set by the will
fails to allow for enough time to contest the will. Further-

more, a legal battle would be costly and time-consuming and the two-month deadline is immovable.'

'But—'

Mr Beamish cleared his throat over Summer's protest and pushed on. 'A provision has been set aside for any expenses needed for your endeavours—expenses that I will be able to approve and release as requested. The last stipulation is that one of you must remain in residence at the estate for the entire two months.'

Mr Beamish sucked in a discreet lungful of air as if he'd had to force the words out in one go, no matter how distasteful he had found them.

'You can, of course, choose to refuse the terms, upon which the entire estate and entail will revert immediately to the National Trust. It is clearly a lot to think on. Rooms have been made available for your use this evening, and we will meet again in the morning to hear your final decision.'

With another firm nod, the man left with barely a goodbye—running for the hills, Skye thought. The room was silent until a gasp of horrified laughter erupted from Summer.

'Missing diamonds! How romantic,' Star said on a dramatic sigh.

'That's what you took from all this?' Skye demanded of her whimsical middle sister. 'Romance?'

'Yes! It's *so* romantic,' she insisted, even as Skye shook her head.

Summer had already pulled the thick file which promised to contain details of Elias's attempts to uncover the location of the Soames diamonds towards her from across the table.

'I can't take two months off. I have a job,' Skye insisted, already torn between practicalities and the possibility of what the terms of the will meant.

'A job from which you've never taken a holiday,' Summer said absently, already scanning through the pages of the file. 'Rob would give you anything you asked, and you know it. You just don't ask.'

'Well, it's not long until school's out for the summer,' Star pressed on, covering the need for Skye to respond to Summer's unusually blunt observation. 'I'm sure they'll let me take the rest of the term off. And Summer's just finished her degree so... Oh, this could be so much fun.'

Fun wasn't what Skye was thinking. She was thinking that if they did manage to find the missing jewels, then perhaps they'd be able to cover their mother's medical bills. Pay for even better treatment. And perhaps... But she stopped her mind from going there. Skye had never put much faith in wishes and prayers like Star had.

'If we found them, we could sell the estate...' Summer said. 'Or at least mortgage it?'

'A mortgage we'd never be able to pay back,' replied Skye.

'But how are we supposed to find jewels that have been missing since...?' Star said, ignoring the practicalities as usual.

'1871,' Summer said, glancing up from the folder for the first time.

'And, even if we did, how *would* we sell it?' Skye asked.

Summer looked away, as if considering. 'I might...know someone,' she said with a shrug of her shoulder.

'You might know someone who happens to have...what? Several hundred million in the bank to buy all this?' The look in her sister's eyes made Skye feel bad about her apparent scepticism. 'Summer—'

'I do,' she replied, ignoring the bite of Skye's words. 'It's a long shot, but yeah. And besides, we don't need several hundred million. We just need enough.'

Skye nodded in return. Just enough to cover Mariam's medical bills.

'Oohh, I love an adventure.'

Skye and Summer shared an eye roll over their sister's excitement.

'So, we're actually doing this?' Skye asked, tempering the unwanted excitement beginning to build in her stomach. She might have spent her life grounding her siblings to counter the airy dreams of their mother, but even she couldn't deny that there was something thrilling about the idea of going on an actual treasure hunt. It was a silly feeling, something that was almost naughty, as if it were a guilty pleasure her heart just couldn't deny as it thrummed quickly in her body.

When Summer and Star nodded, sharing looks of excitement and hope, just for once Skye allowed herself to imagine that this could be the start of a thrilling adventure.

CHAPTER ONE

Two weeks later, Skye was finishing up her final search of the last room in the west wing and decided, pulling cobwebs from her hair, that there was nothing thrilling about fruitlessly searching through decades of dust. Beamish hadn't been lying when he said the two wings had been closed for years.

By the time she pushed open the door to the library that had become the Soames sisters' base of operations, she found Star hauling a portrait that must have been nearly one hundred and fifty years old across the room.

'Should you be doing that?' Skye queried.

'Why not?' Tug. 'I thought—' tug '—that it would be good inspiration,' tug.

'Because it might be worth a fair bit of money?' Summer replied without looking up from the mounds of paper she had spread out on the table in front of her. Skye winced at the sound of the gilt frame scraping against the wooden floor as Star shoved it up against one of the many bookcases in the room.

'There. The last time the diamonds were seen. Catherine Soames' wedding portrait.'

All three of the girls repressed a shiver at the thought of their great-great-grandmother being forced to marry her cousin. Elias's research had been surprisingly detailed.

Then again, four generations of Soames men had been looking for the diamonds ever since they'd gone missing from Duke Anthony Soames's private chambers two nights after the painting had been finished.

'Well, they weren't in the west wing, just like they weren't in the east wing,' Skye said, filling them in on the results of her searches. 'Though, from the damage I've seen, I think Elias thought they were hidden in the walls because there are huge holes knocked into them, dust and plaster and God knows what else all over the place. Honestly, it looks as if Elias went at them with a sledgehammer.'

'Perhaps he was mad and that's why Mum didn't want to talk about him?' Star wondered out loud.

'Perhaps it ran in the family. According to the notes here, after Anthony had his valet arrested and imprisoned for the theft, he then decided that Catherine had hidden them, even if he couldn't prove it, or even understand how she might have done it,' Summer said, looking up from the file that seemed to be permanently glued to her hands.

'I hope she *did* hide them. He sounds like a miserable creature.' Smiling at Star's unique description, Skye flipped on the light switch. Although the library was a great place for them to gather, she didn't like how dark it always was.

Sinking down into one of the leather armchairs, she struggled to remain optimistic. Taking up the terms of the will had given them purpose, a goal, something to work towards for their mother. But two weeks in and it was beginning to seem hopeless. Not that she'd ever say as much to Star and Summer. They relied on her, they needed her to be the one to spur them on.

'I think we should move to another room,' Star said, the floaty material of her wide-armed shirt hanging low as she reached out to touch the old leather spines of the books. 'It makes me feel…hinky.'

'Hinky?' Summer asked with a laugh.

'Yeah…just wonky, somehow.'

Skye frowned. She'd never really noticed it before but, now that Star had said it, she knew what her sister meant. Skye tried to look at the room with fresh eyes, rather than ones that had seen it for more hours than she would have wished. The little library, the women's library, Catherine's library. The room had more names for it than any other in the entire estate and, even though it paled in comparison to the Duke's library, all of the sisters had preferred it here, despite the darkness which, now Skye was looking at it, must have had something to do with the—

'The windows!' Summer exclaimed, at the exact moment Skye had realised the same thing. 'The shelves on the left-hand side… I think…' Her words were cut off as Star ran out of the room into the hallway, peering back into the library, then disappearing off to the next room along and reappearing again.

'The room—it's smaller than it should be!' Star practically screamed and Skye tried to suppress uncharitable frustration at the sister who had most definitely taken after their mother in her sense of both romance and adventure. Skye felt a painfully familiar sense of longing that she was ashamed of. A longing to be more like them, a longing to join in with the fun. But then she would be even less like her father, whose serious, quiet, non-confrontational nature was so very different to Mariam. And she clung to whatever she could of her father because when he'd remarried he'd just seemed to get further and further away from her.

Pushing aside the stab of pain brought by her train of thought, Skye focused on what Summer was doing— pulling out some of the ancient tomes lining the left-hand shelves and piling them up on the floor.

'Skye, can you—'

'Coming,' she said, leaning into the thrill of possibly finding the jewels as a distraction.

'Star, these books are hundreds of years old, please don't just—'

The thwack of another large tome hitting the floor made Summer wince.

'Sorry, it's just so…'

'Exciting, yeah we get it,' Skye mumbled under her breath. Surely if this was the final resting place of the jewels someone would have found them by now?

Two shelves cleared, Summer was running her hand underneath the wooden shelves when all the girls heard a *click*. The central panel of shelves shifted forward. A streak of lightning-quick excitement shot through Skye and she could see it reflected on her sisters' faces.

Had they found them? Could it be that simple?

Pulling hard, the central block of shelves swung away from the wall to reveal a secret recess illuminated in the light from the window. Dust particles danced and swirled in the air, disturbed by the quick breaths of Skye and her sisters.

Summer reached in to retrieve a large bundle wrapped in an old leather sack, dark with age and slightly moth-eaten. As she carefully placed it on the large table the sisters each took a step back, watching it as if it were an unexploded bomb.

Star and Summer looked to Skye, who released the breath she'd been holding, shifted forward and parted the edges of the leather, revealing the contents concealed within.

Disappointment and guilt hit her hard and fast and Skye was instantly reminded of Christmases when her mother's gifts had seemed to be for anyone other than her. But as she looked at the pile of leather-bound books she was crushed that they weren't the jewels that would have made everything so much easier.

Summer took the top one in her hands, carefully, lovingly opening the cover.

'They're journals,' she said, a trace of awe in her voice.

Pressed into the middle of the pile of journals was a small framed portrait of a young girl who looked about five or six years old, around which was wrapped a chain and pendant, tarnished with age. Star took up the loop of silver chain, carefully unwinding it from the portrait, passing the wooden frame to Skye as she continued to study the unusual pendant. Turning the frame in her hands, Skye read the inscription on the back.

Laura, my love
1876—1881

The girl had been five years old. 'This must have been Catherine's daughter,' Skye whispered, overwhelmed by the emotion of discovering their family history and unable to ignore familiarity in the features of the young girl.

'She looks just like you did, Summer, when you were that age,' Skye said with a sad smile.

Summer blinked at her for a moment before turning back to the book in her hands. She cleared her throat a little and said, 'Look at this,' before offering the book for Skye and Star to read.

June 1864
Today was my coming out and everything and nothing was as expected. I know my duty. The need for me to make a match, given that Father has not a male heir. The risk that I should be married off to my cousin doesn't bear thinking on.

Skye sent Summer what she hoped was a comforting smile just as Star let out a peal of delight, her uncontained energy causing the journal in her hands to look slightly precarious. 'This one is dated 1869 and she's in the Middle East! She's talking about elephants and desert castles…'

'We should put them in date order and read them properly. They might contain information about the jewels,' Summer said.

'Why? They're just journals,' Skye replied, feeling bad for dismissing Catherine's memories.

'Journals that were hidden in a secret hiding place never discovered by any of the subsequent generations,' Summer snapped, before instantly looking so sorry that Skye rubbed her arm, letting her know it was okay.

Star ran the necklace through her fingers, holding the pendant close to her face. 'It's a strange-looking thing for the period.'

'And you know much about jewellery in the eighteen-hundreds?' Skye teased gently.

'No, it's just…so *romantic*.'

'What does the last entry say?' Skye asked Summer. 'It might tell us where the diamonds are.'

Checking the dates on the journals, Summer retrieved the last one and turned to the final page and let out a huff.

It has been two days since the wedding portrait and this is where I leave you. There are no shortcuts in life. Already I know that it is the journey, not the destination, that will matter most at the end.

As for my life now? That is for history to document. I chose my path and will make the best of it.

Go with trust and love, always,
Catherine

'Well, that's not cryptic at all,' Skye said.

Summer pulled another journal from the stack and scanned through the pages of neat handwriting—barely a word scratched out, the swirls and loops were pretty on the thin aged paper. Skye frowned when she noticed a letter underlined. Not a whole word, but just a letter. At first she thought it was a mark, a kind of ink blot, but then she noticed another and another.

'Are there any underlined letters on your pages?' she asked Star, who began to flick through the pages.

'Careful! These are over one hundred years old!' Summer scolded.

'See?' Skye said, holding out the journal to show her sisters. 'Here—' she pointed '—and here again. But not every page has them.'

'It's a code. It must be a coded message,' Summer replied with wonder in her voice.

Star sighed. 'This is going to take for ever.'

Hours passed and although admittedly the code was simple, with Summer reading out the individual letters and Star writing them down, there was little for Skye to do other than watch her two younger sisters, who she had almost singlehandedly raised. It had been Skye who had made them dinner and got them to do their homework, got them dressed and to school on time as her mother, more often than not, lost herself to a daydream, or a commune, or a whim. But in the last few years… Well, they were all older now and their lives were taking them in different directions and sometimes Skye couldn't help but feel a little left behind. A little as if she were no longer needed.

'I think I've got it,' said Summer with no hint of tiredness in her voice. 'Here…'

If you have discovered my message then I can as-

sume two things: that you are female, because no man would wade through the private fripperies of my youth, and that you are clever, to have found the journals. That alone makes you more worthy of un-covering the Soames diamonds than my husband.

He has always coveted them. And though society deems him worthy of my hand in marriage, I do not deem him worthy of them. They are the only part of the estate entailed to the female line and I will keep it that way.

Benoit Chalendar, a familiar name if you have read my journals, has the map to the secret passage-ways—the only copy.

'Chalendar? Why does that name ring a bell?' Skye asked, turning already to her laptop to put his name into the search bar.

'He's the guy Catherine's father commissioned to redesign the house after the fire.'

'What fire?'

'It was pretty bad—it burned down a large part of the original estate that dated back to the sixteen-hundreds. I think it happened just before the journals start. His name came up a few entries into the first journal,' Summer said, before returning to the message.

He is the first part of your journey, as he was the first part of mine. We loved—

Star squealed, 'I knew it!'

Yet it was as naïve as spring, though I would not have refused it for the world. He has promised to keep the map safe for you, no matter how long it takes.

Good luck, my child. I can almost see you as Laura would have been, brave, loving, intelligent—for you will need all those qualities and more.

Skye hit enter on her laptop, expecting to see the screen filled with pictures of a man from the eighteenth century, which was why she only took in a chiselled jawline, piercing blue eyes and effortlessly styled sandy blond hair. From *this* century.

'Ooh, nice.'

'Star,' Skye scolded, hating the way that her cheeks stung from a blush caused by exactly the same thought. 'This can't be right, though. He's…he's clearly…'

'Hot?' Summer teased.

'Yeah, but look… This says he's the acting CEO of Chalendar Enterprises. Now, I mean. Not then,' Skye replied, trying to regain control of her senses.

'He must be a relative.'

'He could be anyone,' Skye said, exasperated. 'It's been over one hundred and fifty years since Catherine wrote these journals. What are the chances that he—or whoever Benoit's descendants are—still have this map? And what does Catherine mean, "the first part"?'

'I don't know. It's going to take me some time to go through all these and write out any more messages,' Summer explained.

'Is that a Victoria's Secret model?' Star said, peering over Skye's shoulder, looking at the various headlines proclaiming *this* Benoit as Europe's most notorious playboy. 'Well, I know her—she's an Oscar-winning actress,' Star said, pointing to another one of his reported love interests. Well…not *love*, just 'interests'.

Skye turned back to his bio—the company name rang a bell in her head and then she remembered. 'Chalendar Enterprises—they make high-end building materials. I think Rob's mentioned them a couple of times,' she said, speaking of her boss, once again thankful for the construction firm owner's understanding as he'd let her take this time away from the office. Then again, as her sister had said, she hadn't actually taken a holiday since…since…had it really been five years?

'Is there a phone number for him?' Star asked.

'What—we're just going to call him and ask if he knows anything about a map?' Skye demanded.

'No phone number,' Summer said, looking up from her own laptop.

'Twitter?'

'You want to tweet him?' Skye asked, incredulous. 'What emoji would you use for map and diamonds?'

'There's a number for his office in Paris,' Summer said, reaching for the phone.

'Summer! We need to talk about how we're going to—'

Summer held up her hand, cutting Skye off. 'Hi, yes. I'd like to speak to Benoit Chalendar, please… Oh. Of course. But it's very important that I… Ah. Well, I have urgent contracts that need his signature.'

Skye felt her eyebrows at her hairline. *What are you doing?* she mouthed to her sister, who shook her concern away.

'I understand, but if these contracts aren't signed by Mr Chalendar, then a massive deal is going to fall through… Which deal?' Summer furiously typed on the laptop, anchoring the mobile between her ear and shoulder, staring at Skye and pointing helplessly at a list of companies Chalendar dealt with. 'Hold on one moment,' she said into the phone. 'What's the most likely "huge deal" that he could be making?'

'Are you insane?' Skye demanded. 'You want me to pick

a hypothetical business deal that a man I've never met may or may not be—'

'Just pick one!' her sister hissed.

Skye scanned the list of companies and saw one that did business throughout Europe and America and pointed.

'Hello?' Summer said into the phone. 'Thank you for holding—it's the Stransen Steel contract.' From the loud and clearly panicked reaction from the other end of the phone, it had been a good guess. 'Yes, I'll need an address for the courier… Costa Rica? Two days. Okay. I'll get that done. Thank you,' Summer said, disconnecting the call and tossing her phone on the table as if it had burned her.

'What did you just do?' Skye demanded.

'Found out where Benoit Chalendar is going to be. But he's only there for two days before he goes "off grid", whatever that means.'

'But shouldn't we find out what the rest of the journals have to say?' Skye asked.

'We don't have time. We have an address for Benoit that expires in two days.'

Star sighed. 'Costa Rica, how rom—'

'Don't,' Summer and Skye said at the same time.

Skye pushed back a strand of hair that had become glued to her temple. The heat was like nothing she'd ever experienced. Perhaps her sisters had been right. She should have dressed more…or, well, actually *less*, given the climate. But she'd wanted to feel in control when she met Benoit Chalendar. So the buttoned-up white shirt and grey blazer, over her jeans and favourite light brown Oxford brogues, had felt like a good idea. Had felt like armour. Until it had been punctured by an eleven-hour flight and a hard dismissal from the man's PA turned bodyguard. He might have looked like a Hoxton hipster but he had been completely immovable. Chalendar would not be seen.

Moisture hung heavily in the air, making it hard to breathe. Her stomach twisted into knots as guilt, shock and desperation clogged her mind. She'd been so stupid. She'd actually thought it might have been that easy. That the man would have agreed to see her. That he would have simply handed over the map.

She searched in her bag for her phone, feeling oddly vulnerable without the luggage she'd left at the airport, having decided to come to find Chalendar first rather than checking in to her hotel. Pulling out her mobile, she bit back the rising sob in her chest and called her sisters.

'What happened?'

Not, *How are you? Did you make it there okay? Was the flight on time?*

'He wouldn't see me. I'm so sorry—'

'Where are you?' Summer demanded.

'I'm outside the hotel, but it's useless.'

'Did you know that Catherine and Benoit had a mad, passionate affair?' demanded Star, as if they hadn't just failed at the first hurdle.

'Yes, I—'

'Skye, you *have* to speak to him,' Summer said, and the urgency in her sister's voice reminded her of exactly what was at stake here. Thoughts of her mother swirled like a mirage in the hateful heat.

'I know, but there's not much I can…' Skye trailed off as she saw a man emerge from the side entrance to the hotel and throw a massive duffel bag in the back of a Jeep. His height was what first drew her gaze. He must have been well over six feet tall but there was a litheness about the way he moved, as if he belonged more in the jungle than a five-star hotel. A honey-blond beard barely concealed chiselled cheeks and a well-defined jaw. It made him look rugged and arrogant, as if he didn't care what people thought. He turned her way and for a second she was caught in the beam of two startlingly blue eyes. An instant jolt ran across her skin and Skye told herself that it was only one of recognition. 'That's him,' she said, forgetting she was on the phone for a moment.

'What's him? He's there?'

'He was…' she replied as she watched him discard her as if she was below his notice and stalk back into the hotel. 'He's putting things in a car.'

'What, now?'

'No, he's gone back inside,' Skye said, exasperated at the running commentary she was having to supply.

'Get in the car.'

'What?' Skye demanded, panic rushing through her. At the thought that she'd miss him, the thought of what her sisters were now screaming down the phone at her.

'Get in the car, get in the car, get in the car!'

'I can't just…' Skye argued even as her feet were taking her towards the Jeep.

'Is it locked?'

'I don't know,' she replied, casting a glance around her to see if anyone was there to see her trying the handle of the door. Her pulse was racing and a sweat that had nothing to do with the heat broke out across her skin. 'No, it's not locked, but I can't just—'

'Skye, I swear, if you don't—'

'Okay, okay,' she hissed into the mouthpiece of her mobile. Cursing herself, and her sisters, she cast one last furtive glance around to make sure no one was looking. 'This is insane,' she hissed as she pulled open the door and slipped into the footwell of the back seat. A bubble of hysteria rose in her chest, threatening to shut off her oxygen supply. She reached towards the large duffel bag and pulled it over her, still firm in the belief that any second the Hoxton Heavy would find her and demand to know just what she thought she was doing. It was a good question. One she genuinely didn't have an answer to.

'Skye?'

'I'm in, I'm in,' she whispered. 'I have to go. I'll call you as soon as I can.' And with that last promise she hung up, wondering if she'd lost her mind.

'Où est elle?' Benoit demanded, looking around the foyer of the hotel. He didn't have time for this. His staff didn't have time for this. Or at least the rest of them anyway, he thought, glaring at his assistant.

'Je ne sais pas. Elle est partie.'

At least his assistant had the good grace to look shamefaced at not knowing where the woman he'd asked to leave had gone. Enough for Benoit to know it wouldn't happen again.

Yesterday one phone call to his assistant had upset the contracts team in two countries as they'd scoured through years' worth of Stransen Steel paperwork to find some apparently unsigned contract. He'd received more phone calls in the last twelve hours than he'd had in the last twelve weeks and he'd had enough. He was meticulous with his paperwork, as were the people he employed. This was Stransen's mess and they could deal with it.

'Alors...' Benoit had given this mystery woman enough of his precious time. 'C'est fait?'

'Oui.'

He left the foyer without another word to his assistant. Four days. He just needed four days of silence, of nothing. No emails, no demands, no company by-laws that forced him into things he never wanted to do.

He checked his watch. He'd wasted at least twenty minutes looking for this woman. Twenty minutes too long. He wanted to be at his home, the only place where he was truly shut off from the world of Chalendar Enterprises—and the axe that hovered over his head.

He'd given everything to the family company in the last fifteen years, but in the last two... He didn't need his great-aunt's warning ringing in his ears to know that he'd pushed himself and—clearly—the board too far.

Shaking his head and biting back a curse, Benoit simply could not believe that he was in this position. That was why he had to get away. To see if there was any way round the ridiculous by-law the shareholders were threatening to enact that meant he had to marry by his thirty-second birthday. Two weeks. He had two damn weeks.

His Great-Aunt Anaïs had tried to warn him, but the final straw had been when she'd mentioned his father. He was nothing like his father. *Nothing.* Before he'd died of a heart attack, André Chalendar had nearly bankrupted the company that had been in his family for more than one hundred and fifty years. And Benoit had brought it back from the brink, he'd made major deals, and so what if he'd immersed himself in a *little* mindless pleasure in the last two years? He was a healthy adult male in the prime of his life and he had healthy adult *very* male appetites. He was single—and would stay that way, no matter what the board of directors wanted.

Refusing to give in to the streak of fury burning bright, he closed the door to his Jeep gently and, turning the key in the ignition, he put the four-wheeler into gear and took the road out of San José. He needed to get to his house before the sun went down. Although the crime rate was low in Costa Rica, the roads at night were a different matter.

He turned up the volume on the radio and let the music

soothe him as he glided the powerful Jeep from the smooth motorways off towards the potholed jagged concrete roads that cut towards the rainforest. Four days of uninterrupted blissful isolation was exactly what he needed.

Thirty minutes into the journey he switched radio stations and almost smiled at the heavy base line pounding through his speakers, letting it ripple across his skin and vibrate deep in his chest, when something shifted on the back seat and, heart in mouth, he watched with horror as a figure appeared in the rear-view mirror. Shock caused him to swerve sharply.

He struggled with the steering wheel as it shook in his hands, his muscles tensing against the pull towards danger, and had almost regained control when the car hit a deep pothole which sent it careening off the road and fast towards a tree. He pumped the brakes, desperately trying to slow the car, to lessen the impact, to—

The bonnet smashed into the dense wooden trunk with an angry shriek of screeching metal and something white clouded his vision and exploded—a popping sound cut through his thoughts, pain sliced his temple and from somewhere he could hear the echoes of a high-pitched scream, realising only a moment later that it had come from the woman in the back of his car.

CHAPTER TWO

BENOIT PUT A hand to his head, where the sting of pain was more acute than throbbing and cursed when he saw the traces of blood on his fingertips. Fighting through the haze in his head, he twisted, ignoring the pain in his ribs, to make sure the woman was okay.

'Tu va bien?' he called, hoping that the stowaway in the back of his car would answer.

Nothing, no response. Panic began to build in his chest, outweighing any of his own aches or pains. He was ready to kill her, but first he needed to make sure she was alive.

'Es tu blessée?' His breath only escaped his lungs when he heard her groan. At least she was conscious.

'I don't think so,' came the feminine English-speaking voice from the back. 'I just need to—'

'Stop!' he commanded in English as he saw her reach for the door. 'You may have hurt your neck. Just…just stay there.'

Quickly checking himself over mentally, aside from the cut on his temple, a sore—but thankfully not broken—nose from the airbag and an ache in his side that didn't feel like anything worse than bruising, he wasn't too bad. His blood pressure, though, was a different matter. He was probably going to need statins after this.

He kicked at the door from where it had bent shut in the

crash and poured himself out of the Jeep. He opened her door and took in the sight of the dishevelled brunette crumpled in his back seat. Stifling a curse, he ignored the wide stare of startlingly rich brown eyes with a sheen that looked horrifyingly as if it might be tears if given the chance.

'I just want to make sure you're okay.' He leaned in and placed his hands either side of her neck, slender and long, the flutter of her pulse quick but strong beneath his palms. She stiffened but held her tongue as he gently pressed. 'Does it hurt?'

'A little, but I'm okay. Really, I am.' The second statement was stronger and, Benoit noticed, irritated. Casting a glance over the rest of her, not seeing any cuts but a whole lot more clothing than was appropriate for the Costa Rican jungle, the woman seemed to be faring much better than he was.

'Okay,' he said, leaning back out of the car. 'Then would you mind telling me who you are and what the hell you think you're doing in my car?' he demanded hotly.

She flinched and the sight caused him to step back. Adrenaline had spiked pinpricks into his skin but as it receded it left an anger he had to get a grip on.

'I needed to speak to you,' she said as she finally struggled out of the back of the car and onto the forest floor beside him. The woman wasn't tiny but she still had to crane her neck to look up at him. 'It's a matter of great importance,' she insisted, her eyes piercing him with a strange sincerity.

Taking her in with one quick glance, he genuinely didn't know where to start. Usually he wouldn't have given her a first glance, let alone a second one. She was attempting to smooth her shoulder-length brown hair into submission. Her body was entirely hidden by a pair of jeans that were neither skintight nor baggy, their only saving grace that they were a pleasant dark inky blue, a white shirt buttoned up to the collar, over which sat a grey blazer that did absolutely nothing for her skin tone. Then again, it was possible the pallor of her skin could be due to the accident. Or because she was English; it really could go either way at this point. Which drew him to her shoes. He didn't think he'd ever seen a pair of Oxford brogues outside of, well, Oxford. Benoit's lips pressed together against the curse that wanted to be let loose.

'Are you from Stransen? Is this about the contract?'

Her eyes rocketed up to his face and if her cheeks had been flushed before then the blush that rose to her skin was almost painful to see.

'Well?' he demanded.

'About that…'

'Yes?'

'It's not exactly… There is… Mmm…'

He watched as she stumbled over her words, wondering whether perhaps she had hit her head in the crash.

'There-is-no-contract,' she said, the words rushing out together so quickly that it took him a moment to mentally translate them.

'What do you mean, *no contract*?'

'Stransen. There is no unsigned contract. We needed to speak to you.'

Benoit paused for a beat that served only to fan the flames of his ire. 'Do you mean to tell me that you had nearly thirty members of staff searching through five years of contracts because you *fancied a chat*?' For once he didn't care that his voice had risen to a shout. Only her lips thinned and it was a look that reminded him a lot of Anaïs when she got annoyed at him and he had a sneaking suspicion that he might just have made a grave mistake.

Fire. That was what he saw when she looked at him next, turning her rich, smooth chocolate eyes to molten lava.

'I will not talk to you like this. You're in a mood.'

'Of course I'm in a mood,' he huffed out through an incredulous laugh. 'We're stuck in the middle of the Costa Rican rainforest, a ten-hour walk from civilisation, the sun is setting and the car is a write-off.'

'And when you're over your mantrum I will happily discuss what I came here to speak with you about.'

'Happily discuss? *Tu es folle.*'

'Did you just call me crazy?' she demanded.

He narrowed his eyes in suspicion. 'I thought the English didn't bother with French past GCSE level.'

'That's both a generalisation and offensive,' she replied, her imperious tone ridiculous given the circumstances.

'And true,' he said under his breath, realising quickly that they needed to stop sniping and get moving. Taking a deep breath, he held out his hand. 'Benoit Chalendar.'

'Skye Soames.'

He hadn't expected her handshake to be firm, nor for the touch of her skin to cause a snap of unwanted awareness in him. As she removed her hand from his, using it to shield her eyes from a shaft of sunlight he could see the lithe strength in her body, toned yet not overly, naturally healthy and not paid for like some of the women of his recent acquaintance.

'Do you have a phone?' he asked, even though he'd already calculated the chances of having a signal out here very slim. He looked away when Skye bent back into the car, her blazer and shirt rising a little over her backside, gritting his teeth against the shocking spark of a most definitely unwanted arousal.

'No signal,' came the response from behind him.

'Okay. Then we'd better—'

'And you? Does your phone have any signal?'

'I don't have one,' he said, bracing for her rather obvious and utterly expected response.

'What do you mean, you don't have a phone?' she demanded. 'That's shockingly irresponsible.' It was like getting told off by his elementary school teacher.

'I don't have to, nor will I, explain myself or my decisions to you,' he said, walking round what had been his favourite car and prising open the boot. 'Besides, we don't have time,' he said, reaching for his canvas bag and filling it with what they'd need. 'The roads out here are dangerous at night. Our best and only hope is to go. Now.' First aid kit, water, matches, the food he'd picked up at the market that morning. He eyed the bottle of whisky and decided it was necessary. For medicinal purposes, obviously.

He'd known when he'd started to leave his phone behind on these trips that accidents could happen. While part of the attraction was that he would be completely unreachable—no emails, phone calls or anything to do with Chalendar Enterprises—the other part was that it was a test. Of himself. To prove that he didn't need anyone. To know that he could survive using his own skills and his own mind. Of course it usually wasn't a hardship, with his home fully stocked with all his favourite foods and wines. And if he had to walk ten hours through the jungle to get there? He knew he was more than capable. It was Skye he wasn't so sure about.

He turned back to Skye, taking her in as her eyes swept up and down the road. 'Is that all you have with you?' he asked, nodding to her handbag. 'What's in it? Water?' Her face fell. 'Food?' he asked, and it fell a little more. 'Anything?' he demanded.

'No, I… I left my suitcase at the airport before checking in to the hotel because I wanted to see you before you…

left,' she said as if she hadn't just hidden in his car to go off to some unknown destination.

'Okay then. Let's go,' he said, hauling the packed rucksack onto one shoulder.

Skye frowned, feeling distinctly unbalanced and unsure. 'I don't… I don't think I should go anywhere with a stranger,' she said, instantly cringing against her own words. Had she really just said that? Maybe she *had* hit her head.

'So you want to stay out here on the road and just hope that a *different* stranger comes to your aid?'

'I have pepper spray,' she said defiantly and then realised she probably shouldn't have admitted it, if *he* was actually someone to worry about.

'Good for you. But this isn't England, the animals here bite and when they do they're poisonous. And that tightly buttoned shirt isn't going to keep them away.'

She couldn't help but self-consciously play with the button of the collar at her neck. 'What's wrong with my—'

'If you don't lose that blazer and undo a button you're likely to lose at least half your body weight in sweat in the next five minutes alone.'

Skye thrust her shoulders back as if readying herself for a fight. 'I don't know you. For all I know you could be an axe murderer!' She'd definitely hit her head and she definitely needed to stop talking. Because she was in complete agreement with the way Benoit was looking at her right now. She was crazy.

'You have no water, no means of making a fire, you have no means of signalling for help and no *real* means to defend yourself.' Her heart was dropping with each and every failing he found in her situation. 'You're dressed like a nun—'

'I'm sorry, I didn't realise you required a dress code,' she interrupted, glad to find something to be angry with him for because then she might not be so angry with herself for getting into this mess. There was nothing wrong with her clothing, she assured herself. But she *was* beginning to get quite hot. 'Would you have preferred sequins, a skirt that barely covers my behind and a pair of stilettos?'

'Personally? Yes. But for now? I would have preferred not to have a stowaway who caused me to crash my car!'

'It wasn't intentional!'

'Oh, so you *accidentally* fell into my car?'

'Yes! No. Sort of?'

'If you can't decide how you got into this mess, how on earth do you plan to get out of it then?'

'Walk,' she said, hating the way her shoulders raised into a shrug and her voice trembled, making it sound like a question.

Benoit stalked towards her in just two strides, took her by the shoulders and spun her so that she was facing up the road in the direction they had been heading in the car.

'This way, you'll reach the next town in about one hundred and fifty kilometres.' He spun her to face the opposite direction and she tried to focus on the road rather than the way his hands felt on her shoulders. 'That way, you'll reach the next town in about eighty kilometres. Good luck!' he said and stalked off the road and into the jungle.

'Where are you going?' she called after him, feeling for the first time a real sense of fear swirling in her stomach.

'Home,' she heard him growl over his shoulder.

She bit her lip to stop herself from calling him back. *Think, think, think.*

She could feel panic beginning to build within her. If she stayed she could be waiting for hours before someone found her. But if she followed Benoit into the jungle it would take her further away from…from… She shook her head. He had the map. He was the key to her mother's treatment. Her stomach twisted as if it had been punched, something she felt almost every single time her mother crossed her mind. He was the only choice.

'Wait.'

He stopped walking, turned slowly and pierced her with his bright blue eyes. 'Which one is it, Miss Soames? Am I an axe murderer or your salvation?'

She bit her tongue for the first time since she'd got out of the car and he seemed to nod as if he approved of her silence.

'Leave the blazer in the car. You won't need it,' he called out as he set off into the jungle.

Skye threw her blazer in the back of the car, mumbling to herself that if he wanted to have a Bear Grylls moment then he could at least have thought about bringing a satellite phone. But she instantly felt better once the thick layer of her blazer was no longer trapping so much body heat against her skin.

This wasn't who she was, she thought to herself as she followed Benoit through the thick jungle. She didn't get on planes and fly to unknown places, let alone follow strangers into jungles. She was a secretary, for God's sake. She had responsibilities—to her mother, to her sisters. She'd been responsible for them long before her mother had got ill. And would… She couldn't finish that thought.

She almost wished that they hadn't found the journals, that Rob hadn't given her the time off work. Because then she wouldn't be here, so far from everything that was even remotely familiar. Her stomach swirled and she felt a little nauseous. She didn't know what the rules were here, how to act…who to be. Alone with Benoit Chalendar, world-renowned businessman, a supposedly charming international playboy and a man who seemed as at home forging his way through the rainforest as he might be in a boardroom.

He was in front of her, forcing his way through the forest, and she couldn't help but watch the push and pull of his arm muscles rippling beneath his T-shirt as he sliced through another hapless branch. His movements were swift and efficient, his powerful body gliding ahead as if he was in his natural habitat rather than off the beaten path. All the while, heat and humidity pooled in her socks, causing her feet to slip and her shoes to rub. She was being eaten alive by mosquitoes and the sounds of her hand slapping against her skin punctuated the air as much as the thwack of the machete Benoit used to cut back branches from their path.

Hot, Star had said when they'd looked him up on the internet. *Yes*, her inner voice replied assuredly and accusingly—as if Skye had done nothing to feed her body's carnal appetites for far too long… *If ever*, it asserted scathingly.

Benoit Chalendar had been impressive online, but in person? Once the shock of the accident had worn off, and the minutes in the forest trickled into hours, she'd had time to really consider him…or at least the back of him, which was enough. He was wearing khaki cargo pants, which she'd never expected a French billionaire to wear, but they most definitely suited the situation. Strangely, having seen him like this, she just couldn't imagine him wearing some bespoke handmade suit and leather shoes. The idea seemed so absurd she nearly laughed.

The sound she'd made must have caught his attention as he turned back to her, a query painted clearly in those stunning blue eyes. And for a moment she just stared. His sandy blond hair was just a little longer than necessary, curling at the ends enough to make her want to reach out for them. He had a beard, closely trimmed to his cheeks but more than the designer stubble she saw on the backs of magazines at the office. More…masculine.

His nose was a little on the long side but it was challenging, daring the observer to find fault with it, when there was so much beauty in the rest of his features. She shrugged away the unspoken question and he went back to thrashing the foliage, and she went back to…

She hauled her gaze away from his backside and blushed. She barely recognised herself and blamed it on the situation. Because she hadn't actually checked out a guy in… Oh, she thought on a sad sigh, had it really been that long? And the sting of pain as she thought of Alistair, of how he had left, reminded Skye exactly why she had avoided men for so long.

When the first drop of water hit her arm Skye was genuinely concerned that it might have been a tear. But soon there were far too many to count. The heavens opened and in an instant she was drenched. She looked up to where Benoit was standing, beckoning her on with fast movements of his arm.

'Hurry,' he commanded, and this time she obeyed without question. Jogging along the path as best she could, she stumbled slightly when she caught up with him. The rain drowned out the sounds of her harsh breaths as he pulled her deeper into the forest. The huge deep green leaves did little to protect them from the downpour and as she chanced a glance at Benoit she saw that his hair had turned dark with huge drops of water falling from the curling ends.

Her feet were now squelching deep into the mud, her legs having to work even harder to fight the suction beneath her. Her jeans were clinging to her skin, the material stiff and rubbing painfully. A thin branch whipped out and caught her on the arm and she couldn't help the shocked gasp that fell from her lips.

He shouldn't have turned around, he told himself, trying to focus on the thick, rain-soaked foliage in front of him instead of what he saw in his mind's eye. Mud-covered, jeans-clad thigh and white, nearly see-through, shirt slick against a flat, toned stomach. It had taken a lot more than he'd care to admit to drag his eyes up to her face, but that hadn't been much better. She'd just swept her dark hair back, her eyes a little unfocused, mouth open just a little... *Dieu*. All he'd thought was that this was what she must look like when she'd been thoroughly ravished.

He ignored the rush of blood to his cheeks and other areas. It was the heat and the rain and the pace he was having to set. He cast a look back at her to see if she was following. He was surprised to find her keeping pace. Her head was down, concentrating on her steps, only a slight stress on one leg over the other.

He frowned. She hadn't complained once. She'd fought him, accused him of having a...what was it she'd said? He rolled the English word around on his tongue. *Mantrum?* He almost huffed out a laugh. Almost.

He thought fleetingly of what any one of the number of beautiful women to have graced his bed recently would have done in this situation. There would have likely been tears. No. *Definitely* there would have been tears. Maybe even some screams and not the good kind. He'd bet his life on a tantrum or two. But Skye Soames? She was nothing like those women. Not even in looks.

He'd not realised he had a type. Or at least he'd developed one since Camilla, now he thought of it. Just the mental use of his ex-fiancée's name left a bitter taste in his mouth. There was a good reason he'd taken up a penchant for statuesque blondes and his tastes would stay exclusively on those.

'Talk.' He didn't mean it to come out so harshly but she didn't seem offended.

'About?'

'What do you do? Where are you from? How you learned French,' he said as he slashed another branch with the machete. He needed a distraction. Clearly his mind wasn't to be trusted. There was a pause in which the sounds of the squelching mud beneath them and the roaring rain around them became a symphony and he nearly turned his head again but she started talking.

'I… I picked up a bit of French helping my sisters with their homework. And yes, it was GCSE homework,' she said, the confession lifting the corner of his lips. 'And I'm an office manager for a construction firm.'

'Which one?'

She huffed out a laugh. 'You won't have heard of it.'

'Try me.'

'R. Cole Builders.'

In that instant he realised that she'd been right. It was probably…

'It's a small company in the New Forest area.'

'That's where you're from?'

'Mmm-hmm.'

'What's it like?'

'Very different to this.'

'In what way?'

'Do you really want to hear about my childhood growing up in a two-bedroom rented house just outside of Salisbury with two half-sisters, a single mum whose greatest regret was missing Woodstock and an absentee father who started another family as quickly as was humanly possible?'

His feet had slowed, partly because he was consuming all the information she had just disseminated and partly because no one could have missed the echo of pain in her voice. He knew what that was like. Not wanting to talk about the past, parents or childhood. And he had no intention of pressing on that wound. Hers or his.

'I didn't think so,' she answered, misunderstanding his silence. Which was probably just as well. She'd be out of his hair and out of his life as soon as they got back to his house and she could call for help.

He gripped the machete in a tight fist, refocusing on the pathway in front and the sneaking suspicion that they might have gone off route.

Slash, slash, sweep. Slash, slash, sweep.

They couldn't be lost. He wouldn't allow it.

After five minutes of silence Skye was beginning to wonder if Benoit was lost. It wasn't that they'd passed the same tree exactly, but his movements had become a little…urgent. But perhaps that was a preferable thing to consider rather than to question why she'd just revealed painfully personal details to a complete stranger who was probably not used to more from women than a 'Yes, thank you, more please.'

She exhaled a long breath. She shouldn't have been so defensive. She *should* be trying to get him on side. But suddenly it had all felt too much—getting to safety, to a phone where she could call her sisters, to convince Benoit to give her access to the map, if there even was a map after all this time. She bit down hard against the urge to give in to tears. She wouldn't quit. Couldn't.

She followed Benoit into a clearing and came to a sudden stop, the sight before her cutting off her thoughts.

'Don't be deceived. It has a five-star rating on TripAdvisor,' Benoit replied cynically.

CHAPTER THREE

BENOIT STUDIED THE old plane wreck, relief thrumming through his veins. He was soaked through and he wasn't the only one. He'd seen the crash site when out walking on his previous visits and knew that it was too far away from the road to attract unwanted attention.

'Just let me go first.' He didn't mention that there might be things like snakes or poisonous spiders, but they were a real risk. He pulled a torch from his bag and ducked through the jagged hole in the side of the plane where the door had once been. Hitting the torch against the ceiling to scare off any animals, he checked behind what was left of some of the seating of the twin-engine Jetstream and scoured any other possible hiding places he could think of.

Satisfied they were gone, he tossed down the bag and assessed the situation. A fire would be possible—hard, but possible. Though he'd have to be careful what they burned because some of the plane's detritus could have chemicals in it. But there was enough dead wood scattered about for a good few hours of fire, hopefully long enough for them to at least dry off. Nights were dark and cooler than the days, but it would still be warm enough.

But it wasn't really the heat he was worried about. He had to get Skye Soames out of those wet clothes. The way the rain had plastered her clothes to her body was messing with his head and he couldn't afford to be distracted. He cast a look to where she stood outside, her hand at her forehead sheltering her eyes, waiting for his permission to enter, clearly trying to hide the shivers racking her body. Whether it was the cold from the rain, or fear finally kicking in after the crash and the thought of having to spend a night in the rainforest with a complete stranger, he suddenly felt guilty. And Benoit did *not* like feeling guilty.

He called her inside and set about making a fire, not missing the way she perched on the edge of a seat as if ready to flee at any sign of danger. Good. She was learning then.

The smoke from the damp wood wasn't pleasant, but trails of it were finding their way outside through the cracks in the broken windows. Once the fire took hold and the smoke began to clear, he saw Skye shift closer to the heat. The light caught on fascinating strands of red gold in the slowly drying tangles of her brown hair. Hair that rested just above the V in her white shirt, open enough for him to see a tantalising glimpse of…

Scratches. Little angry red lines and an alarming number of bites were already beginning to swell along her slender arms. He stood, not quite to his full height—the angle of the plane's cabin too low for him to straighten fully—and took her in properly, looking past the flare of his unwanted awareness of her to assess the damage the trek through the rainforest and the crash had done to her.

He cursed himself for not realising sooner and reached for the first aid kit in his bag. Opening it, he reached for the one addition he'd made to the small kit a year ago: a bottle of witch hazel. His Great-Aunt Anaïs had instilled a deep respect for the stuff since he and Xander had been kids getting into scrapes at the chateau in the Dordogne. Pushing back the dark thoughts that always followed memories of his brother, he turned back to see Skye twisting her hair in her hand and wringing out drops of water.

He had absolutely no idea why the image of her hair wrapped around her fist shot fire through his body, and if it hadn't been for her cuts and bruises he would have turned his back on her, walked out of the plane wreck and kept on walking all night if he'd had to.

'Here. You need to clean those scratches.'

She looked up at him, her mouth curved into a tight smile. 'And the bites,' she replied. 'I really am sorry about what happened. I must have fallen asleep in the car because I had planned to let you know I was there much sooner. But that's no excuse.'

She'd held his gaze the entire time and he was impressed. The few people he encountered who were inept enough to make mistakes and needed to apologise never met his eyes—instead scurrying to find someone else to blame.

'Let's just make it through tonight and we can figure out everything later,' he said, mentally counting down the hours until they could get to his home and she could phone for…for whatever or whoever would get her back home. He was still determined to rescue some of what would remain of his time in Costa Rica. Alone.

He pulled out a spare T-shirt from his rucksack and threw it to her.

'Change into that,' he said, immediately noticing the steel lengthen her spine at his command.

'What about you?' she asked, her eyes raking over the wet T-shirt plastered to his body.

His jaw clenched, one hundred per cent convinced that she genuinely didn't know what effect that was having on him. 'I guess I'll have to grin and Bear Grylls it.'

The swift intake of breath that followed him out of the wreck spoke of embarrassment and outrage. Good. Much better that than she have any softer feelings towards him. He placed their empty water bottles in secure places to catch the rainwater, while swearing to find out what she wanted as quickly as possible so that when they returned to the house she could leave.

Mortification heated her skin far more efficiently than the fire. The man must have hearing like a bat. He was the perfect predator. Eyesight, hearing, power, looks. Silently growling, she yanked her shirt down her arms and flinched when she heard a tear. She clamped her jaw together, just like she'd done as a child when she'd felt the threat of tears. She wouldn't cry. Not here. Not now.

She was fine. Her sisters were safe. Her mother was happy for the moment and things would look different in the morning. It was only a few hours. Nothing bad could happen in a few hours.

Peeling herself out of the wet jeans, Skye cast a glance around the wreckage of the plane, wondering who it had belonged to and whether anyone had made it out alive. She shivered at the thought. The thin shards of sky she could make out through the cracked windowpanes in the cockpit showed a deepening inky blue. The rain had eased off, but she could still hear the patter of it hitting the body of the plane, which was oddly comforting. Familiar. Unlike every single other aspect of this situation.

The fire had begun to give out some heat and if she hadn't been so hungry she might have fallen asleep. Instead, she hung her jeans, socks and shirt out to dry on various seats and twisted metal and was safely attired in his T-shirt when Benoit returned. Thankfully it was long enough to come halfway down her thighs. If she pulled it down by the hem.

She felt bad as she took in his rain-soaked clothes...until

he pulled off his T-shirt and then… All thought stopped. Seriously. He was rich. Clearly defined abs spoke of hours at the gym. This was no lazy billionaire playboy. The dips and grooves expanded and retracted as he reached for something from his bag and when she saw the protein bars in his hand she wasn't sure whether it was her stomach growling or her inner voice purring.

Purring? She *never* purred.

She slapped a cotton pad doused in witch hazel on the bite on her elbow and hoped that the sting would bring her back to her senses. He was digging in his bag with his back to her and for just a moment she indulged in watching the play of muscles in the shadows of the fire. He turned to her with something in his hand and she gasped.

'You're bleeding!'

He frowned, touching his hairline and pulling his hand away with fresh blood on his fingertips. 'It's nothing.'

'It's a head wound.'

'It's hardly a—'

'Sit down,' she commanded, channelling her feelings into anger at him for not saying anything. She swallowed her surprise when he actually did as she'd asked and ignored the wry raising of a single eyebrow.

She came around in front of the seat he had chosen, eyeing the cut that bordered his hairline, leaning and stepping forward slightly to get a better look. He tensed. 'I'm not going to hurt you,' she said, sounding as exasperated as she felt until she reached down to pick up the witch hazel and realised that she'd somehow stepped right in between his legs. Trying to ignore the sudden awareness of…*him*, his chest, his maleness, the heat coming off *all that*, she poured the clear liquid onto a cotton pad before reaching to lift a wave of hair, dark and slick with rain, away from the cut.

She squinted through the dim lighting in the cabin and saw a cut about two centimetres long but thankfully not wide. Cuts to the head always bled profusely, as she'd discovered early on with Summer, whose mind was always on a daydream rather than what was in front of her. And as her mother had a very different idea of what a medicine cabinet consisted of, Skye had become well versed in the use of herbal remedies, even if she'd always longed for proper painkillers and antiseptic cream.

'This is going to—'

'I'm not a—'

The word 'child' that would have come out of Benoit's mouth was cut off as she whacked the cotton pad onto the cut and instead she heard a deeply satisfying hiss. Only then did she realise she was close enough to feel it on her cheek, and somehow on the hairs on her arms and shivering down her spine and shockingly deep within her core.

'I'm surprised to find witch hazel in your first aid kit,' she said, trying to ignore the pull she felt to him.

'My great-aunt,' Benoit said. He continued to look straight ahead with an odd determined glint in his eye. 'She swears by it.'

Skye inspected the wound she'd been pressing on to see if it had stopped bleeding. It was definitely slowing. She took a slightly deeper breath and spoke to the air above his head. 'I'm sorry you got hurt in the crash and I'm sorry about all this.'

'You already apologised. No need for more.' His tone was clipped, but when he glanced up at her something sparked low, igniting quick and hard, rushing every inch of her body in one powerful wave. She'd never felt anything like it and when he lifted his hand upwards she thought for a crazy moment he was going to touch her, until he reached past her to retrieve the T-shirt hung up behind her and all that spark and energy turned harsh, biting and hot, twisting into embarrassment.

As Skye retreated, hiding behind a curtain of gently drying shoulder-length hair, Benoit cursed himself to hell and back. He had more finesse than that. But he'd needed to put some space between them before either of them did something they'd regret.

But for that moment, when she'd stood between his legs with nothing but his T-shirt separating them, his hands had fisted on his knees to stop himself reaching for the backs of her thighs, from running his hands up under the hem of the cotton top and palming—

Dieu, he felt as if his heart was about to explode in his chest. He hadn't been like this since he was a teenager. *It's just the situation*, he told himself. He needed food. And whisky. Not necessarily in that order. He reached for the apple he'd been trying to give her when she'd noticed the cut on his head.

'Here,' he said, catching Skye's attention before throwing her the apple. 'It's not the steak I was supposed to be having tonight, but it's better than nothing.' Leaning over and exhaling through the ache in his side, he retrieved the rest of the bag with the food he'd bought at the market this morning. It already felt like a lifetime ago.

He'd not bought anything substantial, knowing that his housekeeper would have stocked the fridge for his arrival, and certainly nothing that would have been affected by the heat and the journey. So really all they had were some nuts, savoury biscuits, bananas, apples and a few protein bars. It was hardly a feast, but it would get them through.

He divided the rations between them and turned to Skye, who now had one foot on the seat, her arm resting on the knee while the other long, smooth leg, shapely calf muscle and tiny ankle caught the firelight and his attention simultaneously.

Biting down on the apple, she was either the most skilled temptress he'd ever met or completely innocent and Benoit honestly didn't know which would be worse. He'd come to Costa Rica to get his thoughts in order. To figure out a way round the by-law. He honestly hadn't thought he'd need to, sure that the board would eventually back down. But they hadn't. And if he didn't find a wife within two weeks the CEO position would pass to his brother because he *was* married. Reflexively, Benoit gripped his fist, knuckles turning bone-white. No. He'd *never* let that happen. Not after Xander's betrayal.

Benoit had given everything and more to Chalendar Enterprises. When he was a child his great-aunt's words had sunk in and sunk deep. *'We have a duty to the past. A responsibility to bear for future generations to come.'* Benoit had felt the weight of responsibility of a company that had been in his family for over one hundred and fifty years. His whole life had revolved around it, studying applied science, mathematics as well as business, working through summer holidays while at university. He'd worked in every single department they had, learning from the ground up, understanding each part of the organisation. He'd brought the entire company back from the brink of bankruptcy. And the board wanted to enforce the by-law that meant he must marry because he'd had a bit of fun for two years?

But it wasn't just the board, was it?

The crunch of an apple being bitten cracked through thoughts of his great-aunt and brought Skye into focus. Just one day, he told himself. He just had to get through one more day with her.

He passed Skye her portion of the food before reaching for the whisky. He spun the lid from the top and took a large mouthful, swallowing the amber liquid with relish. It hit his near empty stomach like Greek fire and warmed him from the inside out within seconds. He put the bottle down and picked up the nuts, catching Skye's eyes gazing at the bottle on the floor.

'Would you like some?' he offered.

She tucked her bottom lip beneath her teeth.

Temptress.

'I've never actually had whisky before.'

Innocent.

She was giving him whiplash. She'd never had whisky? Who *was* this woman? 'Now probably isn't the best—'

She cut him off with an outstretched arm and a look in her eyes that made Benoit try not to laugh. She had the stubbornness of a mule and he had a feeling that if he didn't comply with her request she'd finish the whole damn bottle just to spite him. And that *wouldn't* be funny.

He passed her the bottle and watched as she took a conservative mouthful of whisky and then struggled not to cough as the alcohol burned her throat. For a second the memory of raiding Anaïs' alcohol cabinet with his brother as kids rose in his mind like smoke from the fire. Benoit's eleven-year-old self had been focused not on the illicit thrill of his first drink but making sure his little brother didn't get sick from it.

Skye finally coughed, shaking her head and flapping her hand by her cheeks as if to dry the big plump tears that he could see sitting in the corners of her eyes. Laughter rose unbidden in his chest and the attempt to stifle it made his shoulders shake, drawing yet another glare from Skye. He held his hand out for the bottle and she passed it back.

'It's not that funny,' she said when she had finally stopped coughing.

'No. You're right, I'm sorry,' he said so insincerely that she threw her apple core at him. Which he caught one-handed and tossed into the fire.

For a while silence descended as they each practically inhaled the protein bars, nuts and fruit. Benoit stuck his head outside to make sure that their water bottles were filling up. If they did finish the whisky the bottle could be re-filled with water if it kept raining. Not that it was a good idea to finish it.

Coming back to his seat by the fire, he reached for the whisky, only to find Skye sneaking another drink. He raised his eyebrow and she passed it back to him. He settled back into his seat, took a sip and said, 'So, Miss Soames. Are you ready to tell me why you stole into the back of my car yet? Am I over my "mantrum"?'

'You're not going to forget that, are you?' she asked, a slight trace of humour glinting gold in her deep brown eyes.

'Not any time soon, no.'

Skye fought to keep hold of that feeling. The gentle mockery had built between them, but reality began to bleed in just as the heat from the whisky burned out. She was torn between throwing herself on his mercy and telling him everything, or paying attention to the little voice in her head that said if she revealed everything then he'd have the power. The power to demand anything he wanted, because Skye and her sisters really needed that map. Her mother needed the map. And she simply couldn't trust him not to betray that.

'My sisters and I are doing some research into our family.'

Skye was glad it was dark and that the flames from the fire didn't give off enough light for Benoit to see that her cheeks were bright red. She didn't need a mirror, she could feel them. She'd always been terrible at lying.

'*Oui?* And?'

'And we thought that as your great-great-grandfather did some work on the estate in Norfolk he might have some…relevant documentation.' Oh, God…oh, God, she was making it worse. Perhaps she should just tell him the truth.

'You came out here for "relevant documentation" on an English estate?'

She reached for the bottle he'd left midway between them and took a rather large mouthful of Dutch courage. It tasted terrible but at least it made things a little…softer? Or was that fuzzier? She wasn't quite sure.

'You should probably take it easy on the—'

'Yes,' Skye said, nodding for emphasis, only that made the ground wobble a little. 'Relevant documentation. Very important. Benoit Chalendar has it.'

'I don't.'

'Not you. The other Benoit. Your great-great-great-whatever.' She could see that he was frowning at her and she groaned. 'He helped redesign the estate after the fire.'

'I know he went to England in the mid-eighteen-hundreds to explore the glass structures at the Crystal Palace before *that* burned down. He was hoping to help develop a stronger, cheaper way of creating reinforced glass. The research he did there laid the way for the future success of Chalendar Enterprises. But I never heard anything about an estate in Norfolk.'

'Of course you didn't.' She waved her hand as if he were an irritating fly, because he was being particularly irritating with all these questions and details. 'It was a *secret*.'

'What was?'

She had the sneaking suspicion that he was laughing at her, but suddenly it wasn't funny. It was important. 'The passageways in between the walls. They were a secret.'

She reached for the whisky, but Benoit moved it before she could take it. She shook her head. Never mind.

'Benoit Chalendar designed secret passageways in an English country estate?'

'Yes. For Catherine.'

'Catherine?'

'My great-great-grandmother. Or my great-great-great… I don't know. There are a lot of greats in there.'

She watched as Benoit ran a hand through his hair, continuing to stare at her. She wasn't explaining this very well. It was just that he was so handsome and it was hard to keep it all in her head. But, no matter what, she absolutely could *not* mention the Soames jewels.

'What are the Soames jewels?'

'Are you a mind-reader?' she whispered in shock.

'No. You said that out loud.'

'I shouldn't have said that!'

'Apparently not. Skye, I know you haven't drunk whisky before, but have you drunk *any* alcohol before?'

'Yes,' she replied indignantly, but perhaps the occasional cider didn't count. 'Anyway, now that you know—'

'About?'

'About the *jewels*,' she clarified, not quite sure why Benoit suddenly seemed not to be so clever at all, 'that Catherine hid in a secret room, locked with a special key, that only the secret passageways can get to. We need the map. Benoit has it. *Had* it? So we thought you had it. *Have* it.'

'You're on a treasure hunt?' The incredulity ringing in his tone jabbed at her.

'Yes. My sister thinks it's *so romantic*.'

'Really? Why?' Benoit seemed to be smiling at her now. With her perhaps? She wasn't quite sure.

'Because they were *lovers*.' She whispered the word as if it were naughty somehow.

Benoit was trying very hard not to laugh. He pressed his fist against his lips to stop himself from making the situation worse because Skye Soames was going to feel all kinds of bad in the morning. But then he was caught by the idea that his ancestor knew hers. Loved hers.

'Catherine's father asked Benoit to review the structural damage at the estate. He believed that a French tradesman would be "of little consequence" to his seventeen-year-old daughter. But he was wrong. Fathers usually are,' she confided.

But, rather than the conspiratorial tone he'd expected, there was more than a hint of sadness and Benoit remembered how she'd circumnavigated his question earlier.

'So Catherine fell in love with Benoit and he her.'

'Skye, he came home and married Adrienne.'

'Because he had to!' she cried. 'Catherine's father wouldn't allow the match and he sent Benoit away without paying him for the work he'd done on the estate. And then, after Catherine returned from the Middle East—'

'The Middle East?'

'She was forced to marry her cousin Anthony, who was horrible. Like, *really* horrible.'

She shivered dramatically and he decided that the unbuttoned Skye was very different to the buttoned-up one and couldn't help but wonder what had caused such a decisive split into the two parts of her character.

'And that's when she hid the jewels. And wrote the coded messages in the journals.'

'There are coded messages?'

'Oh, Benoit, *do* keep up,' she chided.

'And you think they're still there?'

'They have to be. We need them.'

'Why?'

Of all the questions he'd asked, that seemed to sober her instantly. 'I... That's not your concern. But we do need the map. We need you. Is it ringing any bells? Please?'

Alarm bells maybe, Benoit thought. But...actually, somewhere in the distant past there might have been something his Great-Aunt Anaïs had said. The thought remained intangible.

'And if I help you find this map, what do I get out of it?' he asked.

'I...' She seemed stuck on the thought. 'I have nothing to offer,' she said quietly.

Maybe. Maybe not.

'You should try and get some sleep,' he told her, fishing out some painkillers from the first aid kit and putting them close to the water bottle he'd been trying to get her to drink from. 'We've got a long walk ahead of us in the morning.' And doing it on a hangover would not be pleasant, Benoit thought.

Was Skye Soames really on a one-hundred-and-fifty-year-old treasure hunt? *Had* Benoit been in love with Catherine enough to keep the designs of the secret passageways of an estate in England for her? There was only one person who'd know. And the moment he got back to France in five days' time he'd find out. Because if he did have access to the map Skye so desperately wanted, then maybe there was a way to solve the problem of the damn by-law.

CHAPTER FOUR

SKYE SOAMES WAS never drinking again.

She told herself this every single time her stomach rolled or the pounding in her head became particularly acute. What was so great about it anyway? Snippets of her revealing *everything* to Benoit last night crashed through her mind. But, thankfully, she hadn't spoken of her mother's illness. She just couldn't shake the belief that it would put her completely at his mercy.

She was exhausted. She'd always thought that drunk people just passed out, but she couldn't even do that right. Oh, no. Instead of slamming into complete oblivion, her mind had kept racing with Technicolor fantasies of Benoit without his shirt on. In fact, he might not have had anything on in some of the more explicit moments where he'd—

'Are you okay?'

Skye squeaked in surprise, causing him to smirk, which just made her feel worse.

'No, I didn't sleep well.'

'Because of the alcohol?'

'Because you *snore*.'

The sound of Benoit slashing and sweeping through the rainforest came to a sudden halt and she looked up to find him staring at her in horror.

'I do not snore,' he said, sounding so indignant she couldn't help but laugh.

'Oh. You snore.'

'No one's told me—'

'You stick around long enough to have that discussion?' The words took her by surprise as much as Benoit from the look on his face and the racing heartbeat in her chest. Apparently, this was another symptom of the hangover. Or him. She still wasn't sure. Either way, he chose to ignore her question.

Skye flinched as she caught her already ruined shirt on a branch and heard another tear. Back in the plane Benoit had given her privacy to change back into her clothes from the day before and she now hated the pair of jeans that had once been her favourite. They were still covered in mud from yesterday. She'd have given anything for a clean top but that, along with a lot of other things, had been left at the airport with her luggage.

They'd been walking for three hours now and she hoped that there wasn't much more to go. At first she'd been fascinated by the steam rising from the ground of the rainforest, watching it dissipate in the heat of the morning sun. The strange bird calls, feathers fluttering high above them. But the swishing sound of Benoit's machete had now become commonplace and she was sweaty and uncomfortable. It couldn't be too much longer until they reached his home, could it?

She wondered what it would be like and imagined industrial steel and masculine chrome, so very different from her and her sisters' little place in the New Forest. There was space enough for Mum to stay there when she visited, but since Skye had been able to rent a place for herself and her sisters Mariam hadn't liked to be held down by the constraints of a home. She spent her time drifting between friends she'd met on the festival circuits, or other friends with alternative lifestyles. Mum had always been into alternative medicine, but her latest venture was candle magic. Skye loved her desperately, but couldn't see how a candle was going to magic her back to health.

But if she found the map in time, if they found the jewels in time, if the estate could be sold in time…

A branch slapped against her cheek, shock ricocheting through her, and she wondered if Benoit had done it on purpose. For a moment she'd thought things might have thawed between them, and she'd relished the exchange of whole sentences rather than the monosyllabic sparring of their first encounter. But there was a silence between them now that made her uncomfortable. It was so different from the constant noise of her sisters, or the irregular eruptions of the machinery on the building site where her office was in Rob's construction firm.

'So what are you doing out here?' she called out to Benoit.

'You have to ask?'

She sighed. 'No, I mean in Costa Rica. Why have you gone all…*mancenary*?'

'Okay, you're just making words up now.'

'No, it's like mercenary, but without the training.'

'Is this some new form of misandry? Putting "man" in front of a word and making it a term of abuse?' he replied, surprising her, from the look on her face. 'Because I don't particularly care for it. Having never disliked, mistreated or misspoken to, or about, women I'm not sure why you're directing this at me.'

'Did you say all that to get out of explaining why you're in Costa Rica?'

'Did you answer a question with a question to avoid providing an answer?' he fired back, despite the shock sparking in his chest that she'd called him on it. Because no one did that any more. He'd imagined her getting outraged, storming off in a huff and leaving him—as usual—not having to explain himself. Skye Soames, he was beginning to see, rarely did as he expected. But, from the look in her eyes, she wasn't going to answer so eventually he conceded, 'I'm not good in the morning without coffee.'

'You have coffee at the house?'

'Coffee, food, a shower.'

She groaned out loud, the sound making the hairs on the back of his neck stand to attention.

'I'll have the coffee, while eating a sandwich *in* the shower. So...you're here to...?'

Benoit wanted to growl, and not just because she was refusing to give up the interrogation. The thought of her in his shower... He purposefully shut the door on that mental image. She was completely off-limits. If not because of her obvious innocence, then most definitely because of the idea turning in his mind like a screw.

Map. Marriage. Skye. Map. Marriage...

Perhaps he could use her interrogation to at least test the waters slightly.

'To think,' he answered, shrugging a shoulder as if it was nothing. As if the weight of a multi-billion-dollar company and generations of Chalendar men didn't rest upon them. Easing into the subject, he pressed on. 'To get away. The shareholders of Chalendar Enterprises are threatening to enact a by-law regarding the CEO position.'

'Why?'

The simply delivered, innocent questions were beginning to grate. Partly because he knew where they were going.

'Because they don't like the way I conduct my personal life.'

'But if you're not hurting anyone...'

'There is concern about the more salacious headlines being attached to the company name,' he growled.

'It's none of my business,' Skye said, holding her hands up as if warding off any more details or more anger.

'It would be nice if the board saw it that way.'

'How do they see it?'

Benoit clenched his fist around the machete and slashed unnecessarily at the foliage either side of the path.

It wasn't really a case of 'they'. Benoit was one hundred per cent sure the board would have lost the game of chicken he'd been playing with them for the last two years. They knew they were onto a good thing with him as CEO and wouldn't really depose him and risk losing the obscene amount of money he brought to their bank accounts.

'The concern is that negative headlines could affect stock prices.'

You're becoming just like your father.

His great-aunt's words had been like a sucker punch. He hadn't seen it coming. It had dropped him to his knees. He felt it even now.

'Are they right?'

'What?'

For a moment he feared she was asking him if he *was* becoming just like his father.

'No. I don't think they're right to be concerned about stock prices. But what I think doesn't matter. They are going to vote on it at the next meeting.'

A meeting that Anäis had called. The reality of it simply blanked his mind. It stopped all thought. As if Benoit simply couldn't comprehend how she, of *all* people, could do that to him—could betray him like that, could threaten to take away the one thing—

'And what is this by-law?'

'It requires me to get married or step down as CEO.'

'That's crazy,' she replied.

'No more crazy than searching for a one-hun-dred-and-fifty-year-old map of secret passageways and hunting for missing jewels,' he bit back angrily, mentally at war with the need to defend his great-aunt whilst also cursing her. He was the only one who could do that.

'No, I mean what's crazy is the assumption that marriage would suddenly stop you being a philanderer.'

'Philanderer?'

'Would you prefer another description? Playboy, wom-aniser, Lothario, rake, libertine—'

'You're having too much fun with that,' he growled again. 'You'd think they'd have learned their lesson last time. It's not as if it worked with my fath—' He bit off the word, clenching his jaw, shocked that he'd even half said such a thing.

After a pause, he heard Skye ask, 'So when does this marriage have to happen by?'

'My thirty-second birthday.'

'Which is…?'

'Two weeks.'

'And if you're not married by then?'

'The company goes to my brother, who *is* married. And I'd rather see the whole lot burn in hell before I let that happen.'

Once again silence descended, occasionally punctuated by the thrash and thwack of Benoit's machete. Skye had been surprised by the anger in his voice when he'd spoken of his brother. No matter what had happened with her sisters, no matter how hard she'd had to push them to do their home-work or go to school, no matter what she'd given up for that to happen, she could never imagine feeling that much anger or…*hatred* towards either of them.

She checked her watch and realised that it had been twenty-four hours since she'd last spoken to them. Without a signal she hadn't been able to contact them last night, and this morning her phone's battery had died. The thought of being out of contact with them, with her mum…it was like a thousand spiders crawling all over her.

Were they worried about her? Would they try to call the hotel that she hadn't checked into? Would they try to contact the Costa Rican consulate? She thought of Summer, probably nose-deep in one of Catherine's journals. Of Star, daydreaming about exotic far-flung places. Of her mother, who knew nothing about the journey they were on. They'd decided against telling Mariam any more than that they were stuck in Norfolk sorting out the terms of the will, not wanting to get her hopes up, or remind her of painful encounters with her father. But, beneath the rambling roll of her thoughts, Skye had buried deep the fear that they weren't worried about her. That perhaps they weren't even thinking about her at all.

Benoit began to cut off to the left and soon Skye realised why. She felt an inconceivable amount of excitement when she saw a crumbled concrete road through the dense foliage and jogged to meet him. They shared a victorious smile as they reached the tarmac and pressed on. Without the protection of the rainforest the sun's heat was unbearable but the prospect of his home spurred them on. He pointed out the glimpse of a dark roof off to the left, but it wasn't until they rounded the last twist in the road that Skye finally saw the house.

Wow.

Nestled into the side of a hill within the rainforest, the building sprawled in deep mahogany lines and large planes of glass reflected nothing but the shapes of leaves and trees. It had two tiers perching along the hill's gradient, framed above by a large flat square of concrete that looked suspiciously like a helipad, the shape mirrored harmoniously below by an azure blue pool lined with trees to provide shelter and seclusion.

It took her the final fifteen minutes of their walk just to take it all in. It was the most beautiful construction she'd ever seen. The use of materials perfectly blended with the setting, but not just that…it was the detail. The finish. It was flawless. Rob would have probably dropped to his knees and wept to have seen such a thing. She was on the verge herself with the prospect of finally getting to a phone and speaking with her sisters. Once she knew they were okay, that Mum was okay, then she could talk to Benoit about the map.

She followed him through the front door, her eyes wide, expecting magnificence. She wasn't disappointed. She took in everything—the incredible mezzanine floor book-ended by the most breathtaking floor-to-ceiling window she'd ever seen, creating a wall of green trees, leaves, plants and wildlife. The ground floor was large and open-plan; the kitchen and dining area were along one side and the sitting area was set at a slightly lower level. Skye couldn't help but spin in a slow circle, trying not to feel overwhelmed by its opulence.

The furnishings were modern classic with touches of industrial materials mixing well with the natural wood and glass. Somehow the monotone shades suited the bright rich greens from the rainforest surrounding the house, ensuring that the natural artistry of the location was displayed to its fullest. Skye was drawn to the side wall of the sitting area—the entire length and breadth covered in rows and rows of book-covered shelves all the way to the ceiling. A stair ladder hung from rungs along the very top shelf. She had so many questions. But there was only really one to ask.

'Can I use your phone?'

Benoit stilled just as he was putting his bag on the kitchen countertop, his whole body taking on the solidity of the concrete beneath her feet.

'You cannot use yours?' he asked.

'My phone died last night, and my charger is in my suitcase back at the airport. Look, if you don't want me using your phone, that's fine. I'll just borrow your charger.'

She frowned as she realised that he was looking at her oddly.

'You don't have a charger,' he repeated slowly.

'No,' she said, unsure why he suddenly seemed so… weird.

'When I said I come here to get away, I meant to Get Away. From everything.'

'And?' she demanded, beginning to feel a little irritated.

'Everything includes phones, mobiles, internet…and phone chargers.'

'What are you trying to say?'

'I'm not trying. I'm saying. There is no way for anyone to contact me here. No way for you to call—'

'We're stuck here?' she demanded, the realisation finally sinking in.

'Until the helicopter arrives in four days' time to pick me up? Yes. We're stuck with each other.'

Forty-five minutes later and Benoit's ears were still ringing. He must have told her one hundred times that it couldn't be kidnapping if *she* was the one who'd got in his car. And the suggestion that her panic might be down to hunger had apparently been akin to saying that she was hormonal. She'd screamed. Actually, it had been more like a growl. Though, Benoit thought, that must be an English thing because he was starving and it was making him as angry as she appeared to be and he had no problem admitting that.

He winced as he heard the slam of one of the bedroom doors as she tore through his house, refusing to believe that his house was 'off-grid', as she had taken to calling it, or that he was that 'irresponsible', as she had taken to calling *him*.

'What if there was an emergency and your family needed to contact you?' she'd demanded.

His reply that they would send a helicopter hadn't appeased her.

'What if *you* had an emergency and needed help?'

His suggestion that he'd deal with it had been met with scathing disapproval.

'What if you fell down the stairs and couldn't move and were unconscious?'

He hadn't liked the way she'd looked at the long set of stairs to the first floor—as if she'd like to push him all the way down and test her theory.

He watched Skye come down the staircase and without a word pass through the large glass door that led out to the patio. And then he sighed. Because he did feel a bit bad for her; he wasn't a complete monster. She'd survived a car accident, a night in the Costa Rican rainforest, himself in the morning without coffee, only to arrive at their destination and discover there was no escape.

He picked up the cafetière cups and took them out to the table on the patio. He sat, trying to focus on the peace his garden usually brought him, but his attention snagged on the hunched shoulders of Skye Soames.

'I don't have time for this,' she said, facing away from him.

'I know the feeling,' he said grimly, thinking of the days counting down until his birthday.

'No, I mean I really… I can't be here right now. I need to be back home. I was supposed to be back home by now.'

Once again, Benoit couldn't quite shake the feeling that there was something that she wasn't telling him. Usually he wouldn't care, but there was something about her tone, something that snagged in his chest.

'What back home is so important?'

Everything. But Skye couldn't tell him that.

'Your sisters?' he asked.

She nodded, knowing that it was only half the reason she felt so panicked. She turned and joined him at the table. He tentatively pushed a cup of coffee in her direction, as if worried she might throw it over him. But she gratefully scooped up the china in her hands, her mouth watering at the rich scent and hopeful that it might help stimulate a few more neurons so that she could find a way out of here. She'd been surprised to find that Benoit had been telling the truth.

No phone. No internet. Nothing.

Her heartbeat thudded heavily in her chest as she battled with the panic in her mind. She couldn't be stuck here. They didn't have the time. Her mum didn't have the time. Each hour, minute even that she didn't have the map, that they weren't closer to finding the key, or the passageways, felt like a minute stolen from her mother's life—and that thought was paralysing.

'How old are they?'

'Twenty-four and twenty-two.'

He huffed out an incredulous breath. 'From the way you were speaking, I thought they'd be much younger. They'll be fine,' he said, instantly dismissing her concerns.

'It's a lot for them to deal with—' she tried to justify herself '—and Star? Well, she'll probably fall into some romantic notion about whatever the next step is to find the Soames diamonds and Summer will probably forget to eat because she'll be lost in Catherine's journals.'

'Skye, Star and Summer?'

'Mum's choice.'

'Not your father's then?'

Skye shrugged, ignoring the ache suddenly blooming in her chest, blotting out some of the panic, not quite sure which was the lesser of two evils. She drew her coffee cup to her chest as if it could ward off the question.

'Mum left him when I was about thirteen months old. She didn't like his normal, mainstream lifestyle.'

'And he just let you all go?'

'Well, he let me go. Star was born after an affair and Summer doesn't know who her father is. Don't get the wrong idea—it's not that Mum was…like that.'

He frowned. 'I'm not judging,' he said, raising his hands in defence.

'Everyone judges,' Skye assured him. 'I learned that pretty quickly.' Teachers, parents, school friends.

I don't want her playing with my child.

But Margaret, she's my daughter.

And that's fine. For you. But she runs around here like a wild thing, with barely any clothes or care, and it's not the way I will raise my son.

Skye hadn't thought about the conversation she'd over-heard between her father and stepmother for years. It sent a shiver down her spine, despite the thick damp heat of the forest around her.

She'd stopped talking about her childhood and her sisters when she realised a woman with three children by different men was called names. And the children? Her and her sisters? They didn't escape either. But with Benoit she genuinely hadn't felt such censure and it was an odd feeling.

'Look, why don't you have a shower? I'll leave a towel and some clothes out—they'll be mine, but better than what you have with you. I'll stay inside until you're done,' he offered, standing up from the table.

A shower sounded amazing. She was contemplating the opportunity to get out of her two-day-old, sweat-soaked, muddied clothes, when she registered his words fully. 'Stay inside? Where's the shower?'

He nodded over to the corner of the patio. Of course this man would have an outdoor shower. *Of course* he would.

She heard him disappear into the house while her mind registered the implications of showering outside, naked amongst the elements where anyone—or Benoit—could see her.

It's just a shower, Skye, she told herself sternly, disliking the way even the thought of it made her feel exposed, vulnerable...but hating the way it also sent a thrill rushing through her. As if it were something illicit, guiltily pleasurable. A thrill that she welcomed for blocking out all thoughts of her father, of her mother, her sisters...

She cut a glance to the shower and slowly pushed back her chair and made her way towards it, staring at it as if it were a challenge to her 'conservative' lifestyle—something her mother always bemoaned. Mariam Soames would have loved it.

Benoit returned with a towel and the clothing he'd promised before leaving again, but Skye waited for a good few minutes before she made her way across the decking towards the stunning outdoor shower surrounded by huge green leaves offering a sense of privacy. Small mosaic stones and turquoise-coloured tiles covered the floor in a beautiful pattern.

Toeing her shoes from her feet, her heart was racing to a different rhythm, a lighter one, faster. The idea that Benoit could—at any moment—catch a glimpse of her naked under the jets of water made her feel...*alive.*

She peeled her jeans from her legs, half fearful, half desperate to get rid of the clinging denim. Now that he wasn't in front of her, her mind raked over and indulged in memories of Benoit by the fire without his T-shirt on. The way his shoulders had seemed like organic boulders, large and powerful, the sandy blond trail of hair dipping below the waistline of his trousers.

The blush that rose to her cheeks stung in its intensity and she doused her heated skin with an icy blast of water from the shower. Only instead of soothing her fevered imagination, it inflamed. As she ran her hands over her body, in her mind they belonged to Benoit and it was making her want things she never had before. Certainly not with Alistair, her one and only boyfriend.

She turned beneath the spray, the sight of something glinting in the forest further down the hill cutting off the direction of her thoughts. She frowned. That couldn't be right. Benoit had said there was no one around here for miles. But then again, he hadn't mentioned the motorbike she'd found in the garage either.

Had he lied to her?

Skye turned back to the rooftop she'd seen glinting in the distance. It was definitely a house. Surely they would have a phone. Knowing there was no way she could stay here for four more days, she reached for the towel and fresh clothes before she could change her mind.

Benoit was hiding in the house from the temptation that was Skye Soames. The house wasn't very big but it was definitely clever. His ears strained for the sounds of the shower and he realised he hadn't heard it running for a while. In fact, he hadn't heard anything for a while now.

Frowning, he risked a glance outside his bedroom window and couldn't see her. Unease stirring in his chest, he scanned the spare rooms on the mezzanine floor and made his way downstairs. Not seeing her on the lower floor, he went out into the garden towards the shower, where the floor was still wet from use.

He looked about and, catching sight of the roof of his neighbour's house, he ran to the garage. His motorbike was gone.

He cursed out loud. She was going to get herself killed. Or worse—ruin his damn bike.

CHAPTER FIVE

THE WHEELS SPUN on the hot tarmac and Skye grappled with the evil machine as it threatened to shoot off once again without her. She was shaking with fear and it wasn't helping her control the bike, but she was determined to master the thing.

She'd made it at least two miles before she'd had to wobble to a stop when she'd hit one of the many cracks in the road and nearly toppled the whole thing over. It had been half that distance since she'd last seen the roof of the neighbour's house but the road kept twisting her in the wrong direction and she was beginning to worry now.

How on earth did people ride these things? Underneath the shower she'd felt rejuvenated and determined but the road was dusty and having a go on Alistair's moped seven years ago hadn't seemed to have given her any real ability to handle Benoit's motorbike.

She took in a shaky breath and told herself that she could get control of this blasted machine, of this damned situation. She had to. She desperately wanted to speak to her sisters but, more importantly, she didn't want to turn back, humiliated and shame-faced, and see that *I told you so* look on Benoit's face.

With trembling hands, she twisted the bike's handle, her heart momentarily soaring as the engine spluttered into life, only for it to buck and stall beneath her, knocking her off balance. The weight of the machine pulled her downwards and she and the bike crashed to the ground, hot metal digging into her calf muscles and pressing her skin into the gravel on the road.

She slammed the floor with her free hand and let loose a curse. 'What am I doing?' she demanded of herself.

'I was about to ask you the same question.'

She gasped out loud as she saw Benoit bearing down on her, his body so imposing it blocked out the sun. How could she be both relieved and terrified at the same time? Except she couldn't quite put a name to what she was scared of.

Benoit hauled the bike off her, righted it and, putting it on its stand, checked it over for damage. He remained silent but she could see the way he clenched his jaw, the muscle flaring again and again. She didn't have to justify herself or her actions to him, she thought defensively. Only…she had stolen his motorbike, probably damaged it, just like she'd damaged the Jeep.

Oh, God, the repair costs! She hadn't even thought of that. She was barely covering rent, let alone the contributions to Summer's university expenses. If they didn't find the map and the diamonds she'd be in debt to Benoit up to her eyeballs, and her mother…

Skye bit back the sob that was about to rise in her chest.

'I'm sorry,' she said, to Benoit and to her sisters. She'd let everyone down. She felt the hot press of tears behind her eyes and blinked desperately, hoping they wouldn't fall. 'I'm sorry,' she said again. 'I don't know what—'

'You saw the neighbour's house and the bike and thought I'd been keeping it from you. *Chérie*,' he said, finally turning to pin her with a gaze the colour of frost, 'do you think I want you here? Do you think I like the idea of sharing these four precious days—the *only* days in my whole calendar year that I'm not at the beck and call of emails or meetings or contracts?'

She bit her lip to stop it from trembling. Benoit spun around but barely spared her a glance before pacing back and forth with clenched fists.

'If I'd thought my neighbour was there I'd have taken you. If I thought there was enough gas in the tank of the bike to get us anywhere near a phone or civilisation I would have taken you. If there was any way I could have got rid of you, Ms Soames, I swear to you I would have taken it.'

Benoit was furious. But he was also relieved not to have found her in any serious trouble. The fear and anger he'd felt when he'd found the house empty... A shiver worked its way up his spine, and only now was the tension beginning to ease. Scouring the house for any sign of her had reminded him of the way his brother had run through the house the morning after his mother had left them. The slicing pain in his heart as he'd seen the moment Xander had realised that their mother had gone and left them behind.

Something Benoit had already known since the night before.

'Are you sure they're not at the house?' she whispered, making him feel bad. Which made him feel angry all over again.

'He's never at the house. But I can see that you don't trust me, so come on,' he said, ignoring the twist in his gut as he realised it was true. 'Let's go.'

She frowned, casting a glance over his sweat-soaked shirt and the rapid rise and fall of his chest. 'How did you—?'

'I ran,' he growled forcefully, slowing his breathing, its rapid pace having nothing to do with exercise or his anger. The moment he'd seen the bike on top of her... It just didn't bear thinking about. She ignored his hand and got up by herself, so he turned and swung a leg over the seat of the bike, pulling it to standing. 'Get on.'

'What?'

'Get on. We're wasting daylight hours and I don't fancy another three-hour walk in the rainforest, do you?' he asked pointedly.

Benoit held the bike in place as she tentatively stepped towards the machine she'd nearly destroyed. She was dressed in the clothes that he'd laid out for her. She'd rolled up the sleeves of the white linen shirt; the smallest one he could find was still large on her. It was tucked into the tan cargo shorts, which were cinched at the waist by the belt she'd worn previously, but the legs hung so low that they looked like culottes on her. There were a few inches of creamy, delectable calf and slender ankle on show before her tan Oxford brogues. How on earth she'd made the out-fit look even remotely stylish was lost on him.

He felt her settle into the seat behind him and couldn't help but roll his eyes as he waited until her hands were around his waist. Finally, when she'd exhausted every other option, he felt them, but she'd pushed herself as far back as she could get, which would topple them the moment they took the first corner. He reached behind him, hooked a hand behind each of her knees and tugged her against him, holding back a curse as he felt her slender thighs encase his own, the press of her breasts against his back. It wouldn't be for long. He could control himself in the less than ten-minute ride to his neighbour's. He had to.

He glanced at the fuel tank and prayed that they'd make it back home. He was done with trekking roads and jungle with this woman, especially when there was no whisky to make it at least a little enjoyable.

The thought reminded him of her missing jewels. The

search for a map that had brought her out here in the first place. Last night it had seemed amusing, like a campfire fairy tale. But now, with the sun beating down on them and Skye's desperation as clear as day...

Something strong and sure told him that if the map existed then Anaïs would have it, would have kept it all these years. He could recite the words she often said by heart. *We have a duty to the past. A responsibility to bear for future generations to come.* He felt them as if they were written on his soul, had always been.

He hadn't worked eighty-hour weeks for nearly fifteen years just because he wanted to prove himself better than his father, or to fill the devastating sinkhole he'd made in the company's finances. He'd done it because he'd felt the weight of the ancestors *before* his father. The ones who had given blood, sweat and tears for Chalendar Enterprises. Because they deserved more than his father. He'd done it for Anaïs and even now, when she was threatening to take it from him, he'd do it all over again. Because Chalendar Enterprises was the only thing in this world that—unlike people—wouldn't let him down.

The company that in two weeks he'd have to hand over to the brother who'd betrayed him because Anaïs no longer trusted him. Benoit revved the engine, momentarily forgetting his purpose until he felt Skye shift slightly behind him.

Skye, who was so desperate she had flown halfway across the world, stowed away in a stranger's car, stolen a motorbike she clearly didn't know how to ride...

A desperation he could use to his advantage.

Skye shielded her eyes against the rays of the sun as if that would suddenly allow her to see signs of life in a home that looked more like a prison. It was a foreboding concrete block of a house, so different to Benoit's. Instead of sympathetically echoing the surrounding nature, it stood out like a sore thumb. Angry and out of place.

As Benoit leaned the bike on its stand she rested her hands on his shoulders to lever herself from the seat and wobbled unsteadily on aching legs before finally coming to stand on her own. No. A second look did not reveal any more signs of life, other than a red blinking light next to what looked like a security camera. Perhaps...

'Don't even think about it.'

'What?' she asked innocently, as if she wasn't considering criminal action to get what she needed. Maybe she *was* going crazy. That, or she'd inherited a little more of Catherine Soames' adventurous nature than she'd realised. But there was a thin line between adventurous and reckless.

'If you do that you'll end up in jail for breaking and entering—which, I assume, was the next stage of your plan. And as much as I resent your presence here, I don't think I'd like to see you in a Costa Rican jail cell. Because that's what will happen. And then you and your sisters really will be in trouble.'

Anger spiked through her then. 'Don't use them against me.'

'Why? It seems to be the only thing that will get through to you.'

'It's just that I'm... I'm...'

'Feeling out of control and hating the fact that there's nothing you can do about it,' he cut in.

'Would you not finish the end of my sentences?' Her shout was consumed by the dense concrete and live green foliage surrounding it.

'Fine,' he replied, tight-lipped and grim-faced.

She knew that he was right. She couldn't break into someone's house to see if they had a phone. She might have ticked reckless behaviour, theft and destruction of private property off her criminal to-do list, but she couldn't add breaking and entering to the list. Even for her sisters.

Benoit was right; the neighbour wasn't at home and he really hadn't exaggerated the situation. There was no way out. Not until his helicopter arrived in four days' time.

'It is only four days,' he said, his tone for the first time neither mocking nor angry.

Four days.

Just four days. Skye knew that in the grand scheme of things it wasn't a lot of time. Even with her mum sick, it wasn't long. And really, what could Summer and Star get up to in ninety-six hours? She couldn't fight it, couldn't carry on like this. It was exhausting and damaging. She had to trust that they would all be okay. She *had* to.

'Are you done?' Benoit asked Skye the moment the res-olute energy holding her up seemed to drop away and she sagged in defeat.

'Yes,' she replied as a wave of exhaustion threatened to pull her under and she dropped onto the seat behind him. This time she put her arms around Benoit's waist without a second thought, her body sinking against his as the speed of the bike picked up and the air rushed through her hair.

She allowed her mind to completely blank, to simply rel-ish the sensations around her. The cool rushing air against her skin, the feel of Benoit's torso beneath her fingers, the shift and sway of the muscles of his back against her chest, her thighs reflexively tightening around his as they turned a corner... She closed her eyes and leaned a cheek against his shoulder blades, losing herself to the sensations of the bike's movement, rather than those of her fevered imagi-nation. When she next opened them, Benoit was slowing the bike at the gate to his home.

He walked the bike into the courtyard and leaned it on the stand. He waited for her to slither off the seat before he gracefully swung his leg over and stalked off into the house. His silence was beginning to really eat away at her and she hurried after him, having gone from wanting to flee to feeling as if the only safety she had was when she was with him.

'Where are you—'

Her question stopped short as she watched, eyebrows at her hairline, as he started to strip off his T-shirt.

'Shower,' he growled, looking at her as if daring her to comment.

She bit her lip and watched as he stalked through the French windows, grabbing a towel he must have left there earlier. She pulled her eyes away the moment his hands reached for his waistband.

Instead she turned to the kitchen and, with her back firmly to the garden, she focused on the contents of the fridge and not what was happening outside. In the shower. Where, in the gathering dusk, stood a very naked Benoit.

Food. They both needed to eat. And although she wasn't completely comfortable rummaging around in a man's fridge, it was the least she could do. The list of debts she was accruing with Benoit was getting longer and longer by the minute.

As she marinated steak and chopped cucumber, lettuce, tomatoes and whatever else she could find to go in a salad, the twist and turn of embarrassment that gripped her like bindweed wouldn't quit. She was embarrassed by her actions, by the train of her thoughts. By the way she'd reacted to the feel of her hands wrapped around his waist. A low thrum at her core reminded her that it hadn't just been the vibrations from the bike she'd felt, that the heat hadn't just been from *his* body, and…

And then Benoit walked through the French windows, emerging from the shower with just a towel around his waist and water droplets darkening the sandy blond hair curling around his head. She nearly dropped the knife she was using to cut the tomatoes.

Her eyes drank in the sight of him, the ripple of his muscles as he stalked towards her, her mind thankful for the barrier of the breakfast bar between them, her body crying out in frustration. The power of him, the predatory look in his gaze as he allowed her to take her fill of him unabashed, unashamed. Her skin sizzled in response; the thin flame of need turned into a wildfire storming through her body. She yanked in a jagged breath.

'You should not look at me like that unless you have every intention of finishing what you're starting.'

His words hung between them, the challenge ringing loud, clear and utterly undeniable.

Skye looked away, pretty sure she heard him say, 'I thought so,' as he made his way up the staircase to the second floor.

By the time Benoit was dressed he told himself he was back in command of his libido. She'd clearly had no idea what that look had done to him and he wished *he* didn't. Because it was interfering with the now fully formed plan in his mind. The one that said Skye Soames was the answer to his problems. And the reason that she was perfect was not just because she desperately needed the map that he was convinced his great-aunt had hidden away, but also because nice girls like Skye Soames didn't go for bad boys like him. In fact, he fully expected her to find his proposal so outrageous it would cut that attraction dead. Which was good, because he had absolutely no intention of messing up the only decent solution he'd found to this entire situation with something as fleeting as sexual desire.

Feeling a familiar sense of complete self-belief in his

plan and its success, he snagged a bottle of wine before
heading out into the garden where Skye had laid the table
and placed the steaks.

She had waited for him but when he took a seat she
barely met his eye.

'Would you like a glass of wine?' he asked.

'I don't think—'

'Not that I want to pressure you into drinking, but it's a
light wine and you can stop at one glass. You'd be drinking with food so…'

'The effects won't be as potent as the whisky?'

'Pretty much, *oui*.' He smiled, hoping to put her at ease,
and to completely ignore the passing comment he'd made on
his return from the shower earlier, even though the words
still burned his tongue. 'This looks delicious, thank you.'

After he took his first bite she seemed to gingerly approach the steak and spear the smallest piece with her fork.
She stared at it a long time before putting it in her mouth.

'Is something wrong?' he asked. She shook her head,
slowly chewing and eventually swallowing.

'No, it's just… I…haven't eaten meat in five years.'

Benoit nearly spat out his wine. 'What? You're vegetarian?' he demanded.

'It's not that shocking.'

'I'm not shocked by the vegetarianism, but that you'd
suddenly decide to eat steak!'

'Well, it's not me that's the vegetarian. Summer became
vegetarian five years ago and Mum's been vegan for years,
so it just seemed easier if we all did.'

'Skye, there are plenty of vegetables in the fridge!'

'I know. But you missed out on your steak last night.
You said so… And, given how much trouble I've been…
the Jeep, the bike… I can't even imagine how much I owe
you,' she said, still not meeting his eye.

'You don't owe me anything,' he said sincerely, not once having given thought to charging her for the damage. Instead, he was searching Skye's face for traces of the determined, no-nonsense woman who'd trekked through the jungle covered in scratches and bites. He rubbed his forehead, appalled that she had just broken her principles to appease him.

'Please, Skye, don't eat any more of it,' he said, the small bite he'd already managed sitting heavy in his gut.

She looked up then, gold flecks flickering in her brown eyes. 'Actually,' she whispered as if confiding a secret, 'I really like it.' And she took another mouthful of succulent meat. And another. And another.

She groaned in appreciation and Benoit fisted his cutlery in his hands, trying to shake off the realisation that this woman had spent years denying herself pleasure when he never refused it.

'I'm sorry. I genuinely support vegetarianism. I wholeheartedly believe that it's both better for our digestion as well as the environment,' she explained, eyeing up another forkful.

'These were sustainably sourced, I assure you.'

'Thank you. I appreciate it, I really do. But every once in a while…it makes you appreciate and value the meat you do have.'

'Will you regret it tomorrow?' Benoit asked, genuinely curious. Rather than fobbing him off with an answer she seemed to give the matter some thought. She looked into the distance over his shoulder, squinting a little as if working through possible consequences. Once again, he was struggling to fathom how she had put her own wants—something as simple as the occasional piece of meat—aside for her sisters. As a man who had luxuriated in giving into his every selfish want in the last two years it was a strange notion.

'No. I don't think so. It doesn't mean that I'll call my sisters and tell…' She trailed off, clearly remembering that she couldn't just pick up the phone and call them. 'But I knew what I was doing when I chose the steaks for dinner,' she pressed on.

'So the vegetarianism was…?'

'My mum,' she supplied. Benoit couldn't be sure but there was something in her eyes…as if she both wanted and didn't want to carry on the conversation. 'Mum's lifestyle is…*alternative*. It's a wonder we all survived childhood.'

Benoit was thinking that it probably had more to do with Skye than a wonder.

'What's she like?' He was clearly tired as usually he would never have allowed himself to voice such a personal question. But he couldn't deny that he was curious. Something about this woman was niggling at him. Like a puzzle that he wanted to solve.

Skye smiled but again that smile… It was…sad?

'She's loving and enthusiastic and creative, but not the most down-to-earth. She is truly a free spirit.'

'And you're not?'

'No, it's just that when you're a child, school and homework and clothing are actually mandatory, not just *governmental interventions on parenting and free will*.'

'She's a nudist?' he asked, the image of the self-contained, conforming Skye in front of him and the free-living and loving picture she was painting jarring in his mind.

'No—' Skye laughed '—not really. She just values her freedom to be how nature intended, freedom to love who she wants, be how she wants. But in reality that doesn't quite work when you have three children to drag into adulthood.'

Or two. Because Benoit had the distinct impression that

it wasn't her mother who had nurtured her children into adulthood but Skye.

Anger ignited in his gut and it took Benoit a second to get a hold on his feelings. The power of them had taken him by surprise while Skye seemed oblivious. In his mind's eye he saw his mother, the look on her face as he had caught her packing her bag that last night.

'Is it cooked okay?'

'Yes. Very okay,' he said, forcing an answer to numb lips as he returned to the present. He smiled belatedly and she cocked her head ever so slightly as if sensing something was wrong.

'I've been thinking about your map,' he said, forcing a change in subject and his mind onto the goal he should not have strayed from. 'The only person who might be able to help is my Great-Aunt Anaïs.' Even if their last parting had been heated, Benoit knew her love for him was as undeniable as his love of her and not even Chalendar Enterprises would change that. Especially if he found a way to keep it, despite her attempts. 'Anaïs is all about family duty, honouring the past to secure the future. She's also devious enough to have kept something like that a secret from me this long,' he said, a smile pulling at his lips.

'You love her,' Skye noted.

'You sound surprised? Of course I do. Anaïs took care of us after our father's death. Two orphaned teenage boys, as wilful as we were wayward.'

'Were?' she said sceptically.

'You think I'm wayward?' he replied, trying to avoid the truth of his past but knowing he couldn't. 'Our childhood was different to yours. My father might not have left, but sometimes I wonder if we would have been better off if he had.'

'Don't say that.'

She was right. He shouldn't have said that. Shouldn't have revealed as much. If there had been a thought that she might have understood…it disappeared like smoke.

'When the helicopter arrives,' he said, getting himself back on track, 'it will take me back to France, to the Dordogne where Anaïs lives.'

'And you'll take me?' The hope shining in her eyes was startling. For a moment he didn't want to douse that hope. But he had a company to save.

'That's up to you.'

'Why?'

'Because I have a proposition. One that you'll need to think seriously about before agreeing,' he said, his eyes locking with hers, confirming the seriousness of what he was about to say.

'What proposition? You know I have nothing to give you,' she said, frowning. 'And I doubt you need money.'

'Not money. I don't need that. But I do need a wife.'

CHAPTER SIX

SKYE STARED AT Benoit, waiting for him to laugh and tell her it was all a joke.

'You can't be serious,' were the only words to escape her lips.

'I am,' he said, his blue eyes hardening like ice. 'I have something you want—' the dismissive shrug of his shoulders just plain irritated her '—and you could be something I need. It's a simple exchange.'

'Exchange? It's not an exchange, it's a *marriage*,' she couldn't help but cry, her mind scrambling to process everything, her mind racing as he offered the one thing she needed and then pulled it from her reach. 'You're barbaric.'

'No, it would be barbaric to kidnap you and force you to marry me, but I'm not. I'm offering you a deal—'

'A deal?' she demanded, horrified at how quickly Benoit had turned from someone sharing confidences to contracts.

'You don't have to take it.'

'But we need the map,' she insisted.

'And I need a wife,' he said determinedly.

'Find someone else,' she begged.

'I don't have time.'

'But you *did* have,' she accused.

'Honestly, marriage is the last thing I ever wanted, and I truly thought I'd find a way to manipulate the board.'

'And instead you manipulate me?'

'It's easier,' he said as if he really didn't care.

She'd been about to tell him about her mother. To explain why it was he shouldn't have wished his father had left, no matter what. To try and share how precious life was, even if that relationship was flawed... And now? There was no way. This was not a man whose mercy you could hope for.

Her heartbeat pulsed in her ears.

Thud, thud, thud.

It felt like the seconds marked by a clock. Time running out. For the jewels, for her mother. And, horrifyingly, she could already feel herself wavering—her mind running over the possibilities, the steps that could be taken.

'This is crazy.'

'You want a way to control the situation—well, this is it. I'm offering you a way to take back that control.'

'By handing it over to you?'

'I wouldn't be that kind of husband.'

'And I refuse to be that kind of wife,' she said mulishly.

'Then the helicopter will drop you back at the airport, where you can get a flight home and you can explain to your sisters why you will never have access to the map.'

'Now that definitely sounds like blackmail,' she said, pushing back from the table, her half-eaten plate easily discarded now that her stomach was in turmoil. She stood and walked to the edge of the pool, casting a look about the dark shadows of the rainforest but not seeing it. Instead, she imagined her sisters in the library at the Soames estate, poring over Catherine's journals, trying to find the next clue in the search. She saw her mother in her friend's back garden looking over the New Forest, counting down sunsets that she had left. All the while Benoit waited. Waited for her to come to the same conclusion he had. That there was no other option.

She shook her head as if trying to deny what she knew she had to do. There must be another way, she thought. 'Why do you want the company so badly?' she asked in the hope that his answer might offer one. 'Surely it can't be the worst thing for your brother to—'

'I'll never let him have it. He's taken too much from me already.'

Once again Skye registered the darkness behind his words when he spoke of his brother. And for the first time since he'd dropped this shocking proposal like a bomb between them he wouldn't meet her gaze. This time *she* felt like the predator, waiting and watching, looking for signs of weakness. He had used hers against her and she was determined to repay the favour.

'Explain,' she demanded.

'No,' he scoffed.

'It clearly has something to do with this "deal" of yours and I would like to consider all angles—'

'There are none,' he growled.

'I'm sorry if this dents your ego, but if there's a way I don't have to marry you I'll take it,' she returned angrily.

His eyes turned even more frosty and a chill ran down her spine as if it had been touched by an icy finger.

He glared at her one last time before looking out at the rainforest over her shoulder. 'I was engaged once before,' he said, his voice grim and his jaw tight. 'Camilla was the daughter of a business associate. We met five years ago and within weeks it seemed like the perfect match. She was impeccable, poised, understood my need to focus on the company. Or…that's what I thought at the time. For three years we courted, Camilla reluctant to move in with me until we were married. I had proposed, but I was holding out on the wedding—I wanted everything in place, everything perfect. Xander and I were selling off one of the subsidiary companies to focus on the research and development side of things.

'Research and development was something I'd always wanted to do. My father had no head for science, nor finances, and under his tenure the company had gone to the brink. I wanted the company to get back on track, to work on building a foundation that was more than just about supply and demand of building materials. I wanted us to be *leading* the demand. There is so much that can still be done, different ways to make the materials. Cheaper ones that could be of benefit to the world as well as the environment, instead of mindlessly using what's already there despite now knowing the impact and the harm.'

She heard the pride and ambition in his voice. The passion. In some ways she felt it was the truest thing she'd heard him say. Felt it call to her because it met a yearning within her that she'd never been able to fulfil. Not while looking out for Star and Summer. And when he returned to the story of what had happened in the past, the light went out of his eyes.

'I'd been distracted by a big new contract and Xander had been distracted by something else. He'd grown withdrawn and uncharacteristically antagonistic. I was relieved when a trip to Hong Kong had been cancelled at the last minute so that I could see him and get to the bottom of what was going on. I wanted to make sure he was okay.'

Benoit huffed out a bitter laugh. 'I went to his apartment…' His words conjured memories he hadn't allowed himself to examine for two years and in his mind he retraced the steps up towards his brother's door. He watched himself retrieve the spare key to the apartment from his pocket, knowing that he should knock, perhaps even then sensing unconsciously that something was wrong.

As he'd walked down the hallway he'd known, he thought now. Because why else would he have pressed on, why else would he have rounded the corner to his brother's bedroom, when any sane person would have turned back? He'd ignored the signs in the kitchen and dining room— the glasses, the empty bottles of red wine…

'I found them. In bed.'

Even now bile rose to the back of his throat. The sight of Camilla in a red lacy body suit dressed for seduction churned his stomach. He remembered how she'd shifted, leaning back, and the moment that he'd locked eyes with Xander. The pain, guilt and anguish he'd seen there lost to the horror and outrage exhibited by Camilla.

'Rather than owning any sense of shame, she became a harpy, screaming and accusing.' For some reason all Benoit could call to mind was the flash of her bright red nails— the colour matching her lingerie—nails that had seemed more like talons that night. 'She told me it was my fault. That I had taken too long to get married. That Xander was everything that I wasn't.'

'And your brother?' he heard Skye ask, her voice filtering from the present into the past.

'He didn't say a thing. He didn't have to. He knew. I knew.'

Knew that the trust had been broken. And they would never get it back. Even now Benoit hated that the anger was mixed with an agony he daren't name, let alone acknowledge. And he would certainly not dig deep enough to investigate why it also made him feel a little less guilty.

Turning his back on the past, he looked at his future. Skye.

'I'm truly sorry that happened to you. I can't imagine what that kind of betrayal would be like,' Skye said. 'But is marriage really the right way to ensure the company stays with you?'

'I didn't tell you this for your sympathy,' he bit out. 'I told you to make you understand that there is no alternative. My hand has been forced by my family—something I believe you are familiar with—and I will not let you near the map unless you agree to be my wife. Now, it's getting late and I, for one, am looking forward to sleeping in a bed tonight.'

Skye looked around as if she'd only just noticed that the sun had set, the stars had risen and the day had turned to night.

'I don't have an answer for you, but I won't forget that you twisted my arm into this.'

'Good. You shouldn't. Don't forget, *never* forget, the one thing that can be trusted in life is that when everything is on the line, selfishness will always win out.'

Skye woke to the sound of Benoit's words on a loop in her mind, his accent and the softly spoken words at complete odds with the sentiment.

Selfishness will always win out.

And then she remembered his other words. *I need a wife.*

And I need the map, she thought.

She couldn't see a way round it. Benoit was the only person who could give her access to Anaïs, who *had* to have the map. And they needed the map to find the jewels to sell the estate if they were to have any hope of raising the money for the treatment Mariam needed so badly. For just a moment she had considered telling him about Mariam. About the cancer that was ravaging her body and how the only treatment they could get was freely given to others but would cost them the earth.

Or her hand in marriage.

Selfishness will always win out.

She just couldn't trust him not to use it against her. So no. She would *never* tell him about her mother.

She pulled back the covers of a bed so comfortable it had been like sleeping on a cloud. She went to stand in front of the window that formed the entire wall of the bedroom, just as it did below. The night before, the view had been a dark velvet cloak punctuated with silver sequins. Now the sight of the rainforest was magnificent, an endless stretch of green, making her feel like the only person on the planet.

She found her bag in the corner of the room where she'd dropped it yesterday, beside another shirt and a pair of lightweight trousers she *hadn't* seen yesterday. She'd have expected to feel outraged at the idea of Benoit in her room while she slept, but the image of him looking down on her while she'd been unaware... She shut down her errant thoughts.

This was a man who was trying to coerce her into a marriage she didn't want.

As she showered, she realised it didn't matter. Even if he wanted her to stay with him in France and never set foot back in England, even if she never saw her sisters again, Skye knew without a shadow of a doubt that she would do *anything* if it meant her mother would get the treatment she needed. If it helped the girls to find the jewels that would also secure their futures.

Even marry a complete stranger.

Only Benoit didn't *really* feel like a stranger. The only thing that had seemed strange about him was how cold he had become the night before. It was as if telling her about his ex-fiancée, about his brother, had drawn all the warmth from him. And she couldn't help the part of her that wanted to give him the benefit of the doubt. Because he was the man who had dismissed thousands of pounds in damages, who had been worried about her when she'd disappeared with his bike, who had been almost distraught at the idea she might have eaten meat on his account. And he was also a man who was clearly devastated by the hurt caused by his brother two years ago.

Dressed in the clothes that Benoit had left and the set of clean underwear she always carried in her hand luggage whenever she travelled, Skye followed the scent of coffee all the way to the patio outside.

Benoit was sitting in the same chair as the night before and if he wasn't wearing different clothes she might have thought he hadn't moved. His eyes were closed, his face turned up towards the sky and the sun. He seemed truly relaxed for the first time since she'd met him. There were slight crinkles around his eyes, but not as if he spent a lot of time laughing; rather that he spent a lot of time squinting—as if suspicious, or calculating.

The short beard was getting a little thicker, tempting her to wonder what it would feel like beneath her fingers. Soft? Rough? The way it framed his bottom lip, the full flesh casting a shadow from where it crested seemed carelessly sensual.

'Do you want some coffee?'

Skye jumped and couldn't help the cry of laughter that escaped at her own silly reaction. Her heart pounded in her chest and she felt tingles running all over her skin in relief as the spike of adrenaline crashed out of her system.

'You scared me,' she accused, taking the seat opposite Benoit, who still hadn't opened his eyes.

'You shouldn't sneak up on people.'

'*I* wasn't the one sneaking around.'

He opened one eye and peered at her. She gestured to her clothing, which she instantly regretted because the heat that burned beneath the places where his gaze raked was indecent.

'Would you rather have gone about naked? Or, worse, in yesterday's clothes?' he queried.

'I'm not sure you have that in the right order.'

He shrugged as if he didn't agree with her.

Despite having rolled up the dark blue linen trousers, the material kept unwinding to fall about her feet. But they were cool in this humid heat and, as Benoit pointed out, clean. She'd used her belt again to hold them in place, but somehow doing so had made her think about him, about the way his torso tapered down...

'Terms,' she said out loud, startling them both. 'We need terms,' she reaffirmed.

'So you agree? To the deal?'

'On one condition.'

'Yes?'

He'd nearly said, *Name it*, but that would have told her how much he needed her to agree. He hadn't realised how unsure he'd been of her answer. The night before, memories of the past had made him overly harsh and some alien inner voice told him to stop now before it was too late. But a darker one was already relishing victory.

Skye Soames was too sweet for this. She'd probably already rationalised his behaviour, finding some reason to justify his ruthlessness. But he had given her fair warning. *Selfishness will always win out.*

'I get the map first.' Skye's demand cut through his thoughts.

'No.'

'Yes. I have time constraints.'

'Which are...?'

'Immediate,' she replied, not answering his question as

he'd have liked, nor meeting his eye. She clearly didn't like being evasive. He could use that.

'How immediate?'

'More immediate than your birthday.' This time she was looking straight at him. In her eyes he could see a firm line. This, she wouldn't budge on.

'*D'accord*. When we return to France I'll take you to Anaïs and we will attempt to find this map of yours. Then we will marry.'

'Wait? France? No. I have to get back to England.'

'Not until after we are married.'

'Hold on—'

'Skye, let me make this incredibly, painstakingly clear to you. There is no way I'm going to let you have the map, should it exist, and leave, just trusting that you'll come back.'

'But I give you my word.' Her insistence was sweet, but definitely naïve.

'Sadly for you, that is not enough,' he said. 'For all I know you could be an axe murderer,' he replied, throwing her once hotly issued words back at her with a shrug of his shoulders. 'So. You can have the map, photograph it and send it to your sisters. You can courier the thing for all I care. But you will not leave France until we're married.'

He could tell she was buying time. She managed to stretch out pouring a single cup of coffee. Then she spent an inordinate amount of time picking her breakfast from the feast of fruits, pastries and yogurts he'd assembled before she'd come down from her room.

He watched her hand sway over a *pain au chocolat*. It went back and forth and, curiously, eventually back to her lap, leaving the pastry where it was. There was something about that he didn't like. It frustrated him that she would refuse to allow herself something she clearly wanted. It angered him, he realised, as he reached across the table, picked up the *pain au chocolat* and put it decidedly on her plate.

'I—'

Benoit cast her such a look—he might even have growled—that she immediately stopped what she'd been about to say. 'If this is another thing, like the vegetarianism, I don't want to hear it,' he commanded.

Skye folded her lips between her teeth and picked the corner of the flaky pastry, popping it into her mouth. She chewed slowly at first and then reached for another piece, then another until finally she picked up the whole pastry and started to take proper mouthfuls.

He picked up his coffee and looked out into the distance, away from where Skye's slender throat was working, clenching his jaw *again* against her gentle groan of pleasure that sent sparks down his spine and made his stomach curl. He cleared his throat, trying to block out the sound and restore his equilibrium.

'I have terms of my own,' he managed to bite out. As she was still enjoying the croissant, he took her raised eyebrow as an invitation to continue. 'This,' he said, gesturing between them, 'will not evolve beyond this deal.'

She blinked. Then she swallowed. Then she squinted. 'You mean…?'

'No romantic notions, no daydreams of a happy ever after, no—'

'I get it,' she interrupted before he could say any more. 'That won't be a problem,' she went on as she removed a flake of pastry from the corner of her mouth with her thumb. He watched every single second of her doing so. 'So what would this actually look like?'

'Real,' he replied more quickly than he'd have liked.

She locked her gaze onto his. She seemed to bite back a sigh. 'How do you see it working?'

In all honesty, Benoit wasn't sure he *had* seen it working. He'd fully expected her to tell him to go to hell.

'I need to be married before my birthday, which is two weeks away. I know that you have business to attend to, so afterwards I wouldn't expect you to be chained to my side,' he said, his vivid imagination stumbling over the image of metal loops and wrists and… 'But the board would need to believe that the marriage is real. And my family are the board of Chalendar Enterprises so it will have to look good. There is, however, not a length of time stipulated by the by-law. Perhaps because it was written when marriages were expected to last.'

'So we would divorce?'

No, he thought, but couldn't quite explain to himself where that had come from, so instead replied, 'Yes.'

'How long?'

Benoit shrugged, aiming for a nonchalance he really didn't feel. 'Three years.' He'd meant to say two.

Skye choked on her coffee. And not just a pretty throat-clearing for effect. Flakes of pastry and coffee caught in parts of her throat they shouldn't have been in, produced a considerably violent outburst.

Three years seemed impossible. She didn't even—

The thought stuttered to a halt, but Skye forced herself to face it. She didn't even know if her mother would be here in three years. The almost constant sob caught in her chest, throbbed. But if Mariam Soames wasn't alive in three years, then did it really matter what Skye's world looked like then?

'Water?' Benoit offered as if he didn't know that he had been the cause of her choking.

'No,' she said, clearing her throat. 'No, thank you. Three years…' she said, turning over what that might mean in her mind. 'You'd be celibate for three years? Really?' she said, her errant thought escaping before she could stop it.

Now it was Benoit's turn to look shocked.

'Explain,' he demanded.

'It might not be a real marriage, but I'm assuming there will be a fair amount of public scrutiny at the news that a well-known international playboy…' she pushed on past the scoffing sound he made '…is getting married. And I have absolutely no intention of being humiliated while you are repeatedly photographed with your latest plaything.'

'Plaything?' he repeated.

'*Not* the point, Benoit,' Skye replied, knowing that she would stand firm on this.

'And you?'

'What about me?'

'All things being equal, you would also be celibate for three years.'

'That…that's fine,' she said, suddenly not liking the way the focus of this conversation had turned back on her.

'There's nothing *fine* about it,' Benoit returned hotly. Honestly, Skye really didn't know what he was getting so worked up about. The one time that she'd had sex with Alistair had been…had been…well, *fine* and she just didn't really know what all the fuss was about.

He was staring at her now as if there was something wrong with her and she didn't like it. It was the same way she'd felt when she'd overheard women talking about sex as if it was something incredible—as if she were missing something. Life was so busy that she'd not really had a chance to make close friends and there was *no way* she was talking to her sisters or mother about it. Her mother, who thought that sex was a divine right, that bodies should be worshipped and that love was something that was better shared with as many people as possible.

Oh, God. She wanted to put her head in her hands. She was a twenty-six-year-old prude.

'We can talk about this later,' she said evasively.

'Oh, no. We're talking about this now. We'll have other things to talk about later,' he warned.

'Why—are you going to demand that I share your bed if you're not allowed to find others to do so?'

'Don't be crass. I wouldn't do that to an innocent.'

He said the word with such distaste that it took her a moment to realise what he was saying.

'Wait—you think I'm a virgin?'

'You're not?' he asked, just as shocked.

'No!'

Skye didn't know why she was so offended. There was absolutely nothing wrong with being a virgin; it was just that she wasn't and she didn't like him thinking that she was. Was that really how she came across? But now he was looking at her as if he couldn't quite work her out.

'Who was he?'

'No one important.'

'Clearly.'

'I didn't mean it like that. And I have no intention of sharing that with you.'

'Skye, we're going to have to get to know each other *very* well if we're going to fool my family and the Chalendar board that we're in love and getting married. And if you can't even tell me about a boyfriend then—'

'Fine, but not now.'

'You have something better to do?' he asked, as if amused.

'Yes.' *No.* She just had to get away from him. She didn't like the way she felt when he looked at her like that. As if he saw…*into* her. She pushed the chair back from the table, stood and nearly tripped right back into it when her foot caught on the long hemline of Benoit's trousers.

He reached out an arm to steady her, the muscles of his forearm corded and powerful; she looked from there to his face and his eyes…frosty blue shards flaring in the sun. She pulled herself back upright, rubbing at the spot on her arm that prickled from where he'd held her.

He'd let her off. She knew it and he knew that she knew it too.

CHAPTER SEVEN

It should have been easy to get lost in a house several times the size of the one that Skye shared with her sisters, but it wasn't. She was acutely aware of Benoit the entire day she tried to hide from him. First, she'd gone back to her room but there was absolutely no chance of her falling back to sleep again. Then she'd wanted to go for a shower but Benoit was still outside, having been for a swim, just soaking up the sun like a seal. Sleek and wet and…

Stop it!

Then, when she'd ventured downstairs to the bookcase that stretched all the way up to the ceiling and ran the entire breadth of the house, she'd been overwhelmed by choice. There were thousands of books. She ran her fingers along the spines, awed by the sheer number of crime novels, biographies and architecture and design books. She found a thriller she hadn't read and turned to go back upstairs but Benoit was cutting through the open living area so she dropped, sinking into the plush sofa, hoping that she hadn't been seen.

She lost herself in the story of a misanthropic British secret agent two years from retirement, stalking his arch nemesis through Westminster and London to Moscow and eventually Paris. She missed the sounds of Benoit making lunch in the kitchen, missed the sounds of her stomach growling as she turned each page. She couldn't remember the last time she'd had the luxury of getting lost in a book, without worrying for her sisters or her mother.

An ache she'd been ignoring for far too long rose within her. Usually she was too busy with work, with the house, with checking on Star and Summer and her mother to pay any attention to it. But here in the stillness of Benoit's Costa Rican paradise, with no distractions, it was getting harder and harder to ignore.

The suspicion that she hid behind all those things swirled like steam within her, thick, damp and sad. Sister, daughter, secretary, *parent*… The suspicion that she hid in those roles because they gave her purpose. They gave her a sense of identity, something she had lost when she had been torn between two vastly different households and ended up feeling as if she quite fitted into either of them.

She'd been so young she'd barely even had a sense of who she might be when it had seemed far easier just to be something else. The perfect, well-dressed daughter for her non-confrontational father, the stand-in parent for her half-sisters, the sensible, practical daughter for her mother—the mother who did exactly what she wanted, was exactly who she wanted to be, not having to conform to the rules because Skye was there to do it for her.

But who did Skye want to be?

'It's a good book, Skye, but it's not *that* good,' Benoit announced, cutting through her thoughts and the sob that had half risen in her chest. He placed a glass of wine on the table in front of her that looked red and rich and her mouth watered.

She looked up, startled. Night—it was night again?

'You've been reading for about eight hours.'

'Eight?'

'Yes. Hungry?'

'All I do here is eat and sleep and—' She broke off, looking at Benoit's broad, encouraging smile. 'What?'

'That is the point.'

'Of your escape here?'

He gave a deep sigh as he sank into the corner of the large L-shaped sofa, the breath expanding a chest clearly defined by a lightweight dark wool sweater over a white linen shirt. 'Yes. To completely switch off and recharge. There isn't always time in France.'

'Why Costa Rica? Why not the Caribbean or Monaco or…?' she asked, genuinely curious.

'Some other generic playboy destination?'

'Yes! That, exactly,' she replied, enthusiastically warming to the teasing, perhaps too much, desperate for a distraction from her thoughts.

Benoit leant his head back against the high arm of the sofa so that he was looking up at the ceiling. She hadn't meant it to be a probing question, but she realised in an instant that she had pushed his thoughts to a part of his past that he didn't want to go.

'My brother and I used to play forts. Anaïs would pack us lunch and we'd run off to the woods for the entire day, building fires, exploring. I loved it. I thought I'd be an explorer one day. But every time I'd ask where Xander wanted to explore next. It was always the same—'

'Costa Rica,' they said together, Skye smiling at the sweet story.

But it was a sad smile he offered her in return. 'I think even then we were making ourselves scarce from our father. He was…' Benoit struggled to find the right words to describe him. 'You never knew what mood he'd be in. He was charming and irrepressible when he was in a good mood, but most of those good moods were spent with other women, outside the home. And when it was bad he would rage through the house, berating us or our mother for some imagined slight.' The memories of those times rose up around him. His father's spiteful shouts, red-faced rage and fury were something he rarely dwelt on. 'He could be paranoid and furious. It's partly why he was so dangerous as CEO. The board thought that a wife and family would settle him, but I think we only made it worse. He had a marriage of convenience with my mother. I'm sure that she didn't know what she was getting into, which is why she chose to run away.'

He had spent so much of his childhood protecting Xander from his father, from his mother's absence. So yes, he knew something of what Skye felt towards her sisters. But he also knew what it had felt like when all that sacrifice, all that protection was turned against him, betrayed. Since the night his mother had left he'd always tried to protect Xander, to look out for him, to bear the brunt of his father's fury. Only for him to sleep with Camilla.

'What happened to your mother?' Skye asked.

'She died about two months after she left—a car accident in Italy.'

'I'm sorry.'

'Don't be—the family will expect us to know things like this about each other.' He knew that wasn't what she had been apologising for, but it made it easier to circumnavigate the solid ache in his chest. 'It's good; we need to know more about each other, so keep asking.'

He looked up at her. She had her feet tucked under her and a light throw over her lap. She seemed to fit, as if she'd always been here at the house. The reds in her hair blended with the dark wood and the paleness of her skin echoed the pale walls. She was a thousand textures. Smooth, soft, sharp, strong...

'Why did you think I was a virgin?'

His eyes snapped to hers in surprise. That was *not* what he'd expected her to ask. Her fingers were playing with the throw and it was clear she found the question deeply uncomfortable. He could lie to her. It would have been easier, for her and for him. Less…dangerous. But that wasn't his style.

'You don't seem that in touch with your sensual side,' he said, wondering if it was a trick of the light that made her cheeks seem to flush. 'You don't seem very aware of that part of you. You dress like a secretary.'

'I *am* a secretary. Well, office manager, but…'

He smiled. 'But you weren't working when you came out to Costa Rica to meet me. It's more than the clothes though. It's…' he waved his hand towards her and shrugged '…it's the way you are,' he said, avoiding the simple truth he felt to his soul.

'What is it? Just tell me,' she said, finally meeting his gaze.

He clenched his jaw. 'You don't behave as if someone has given you pleasure.'

Skye clamped her teeth together to prevent whatever reaction was welling up within her from escaping. Because she didn't know what would come out. Embarrassment, anger, hurt, arousal, cries, screams, sobs. She felt it all.

She might as well have been a virgin.

'Alistair was…we were young.' Why was she defending him? Because they had been young. They hadn't known better. Not really.

'How young?' Benoit demanded hotly.

'Not *that* young,' Skye said with a small smile at the strange kind of protectiveness that seemed to be on display. 'He just…'

'You were pressured?' Benoit had gone very still.

'No. Not in the way you think. We'd been together for the last two years of school. I don't even know what he was doing with me, even now. We hardly saw each other; I was so busy with Summer and Star and school. And he'd been patient and kind and understanding.' Sweet. It had felt sweet. 'But when it came time to leave school, to move onto the next stage in our lives, he thought I was going with him to London.'

'You didn't want to?'

'I did. But Summer was starting GCSEs, Star her A-levels. I couldn't go. He was hurt, sad. And...' She shrugged, unable to find the words as an adult, the ache in her chest, the awkwardness clogging her mind.

'You slept with him because you couldn't go with him to London?'

'I wanted him to have something that he wanted,' she said, heat in her cheeks. It seemed wrong, looking back over the distance of time.

'But did you want to?'

'Yes,' she replied. She'd wanted *him* to have that.

'You shouldn't make a gift of yourself like that. Your sexuality, your pleasure—that's not something to give away. You can share it, but you must have it for yourself at the same time.'

'Do you need to know anything else about him or are we done?' Skye forced the words out.

'You can ask me anything you like,' he said, his tone immediately lighter, for which she was eternally thankful. Because what he'd said had made her warm, ache, hurt and happy all at the same time.

'Your girlfriends? No, thanks.'

'Really? You don't want to ask me *anything*?'

'Not particularly. Though...the headline about the sisters... No. Actually, I don't want to know,' she said, laughing as she reached for the glass of wine on the table. It tasted dry but fruity on her tongue and she wondered whether it was just because he had an exquisite wine collection or he'd chosen it for her.

'What about your parents?' Benoit asked, studying her gently over the rim of his own wine glass. 'You said your mum is a free spirit?'

'Yes. The full package—tie-dye flowing skirts, flowers in her hair, the festival circuit. Her head is in the clouds but her heart is bigger than anyone's I've known,' she said, smiling at the memory of Mariam Soames dragging them out of school to play with them in a wildflower field, but feeling sad that she hadn't been able to fully enjoy it because she'd been too worried. About what the teachers would think. About what her father's new wife would think. She had been so torn. She ached to think of what she had missed. If only she'd been able to fit in with her mother and sisters just a little more.

'And your father?'

'A professor.'

'Of…?'

He clearly wasn't going to let her get away with one-word answers.

'English Literature. They met at university in London and had a passionate affair before Mum decided that "university education was riddled with the not always unconscious bias of male upper-class oppression".'

'She too doesn't like the patriarchy?' Benoit teased.

'Etymologically, patriarchy means a structure of rulership distributed unequally in favour of fathers,' Skye explained, slightly wincing at the tone of her own voice, but unable to stop. 'So I'm with Mum on this; universities are not skewed in favour of fathers, so I didn't mean patriarchal.'

His smile at her response hit her square in her chest. 'Where did you go to university?'

'I didn't,' Skye said, frowning and pulling at the thread on the beautiful throw covering her lap. She really shouldn't, she told herself. It might completely unravel.

'Really? Why not?' The surprise in Benoit's voice stung as much as it pleased. She liked that he'd thought she'd gone to university.

'We didn't have the money.'

'A university professor couldn't put his daughter through school?' He sounded half confused, half outraged.

'Dad remarried and he and his wife wanted to…decided that…' She hated that she was stumbling over words. It shouldn't be this hard just to say it. 'They put their money towards their son's education.'

'What?'

'It's fine,' she said to him in the same way she'd said to her mother, and to her father when he'd told her that he wasn't able to help. Even though he was able to; he and his wife had just chosen not to.

'It's not. What kind of mother is she?'

'Good, from what I can tell,' Skye replied honestly. 'She's a loving, perfect, stay-at-home mum who was on the PTA. The kind of mother who packed her son's bag the night before school, never forgot lunch, helped him with his homework and always remembered indoor shoes as well as outdoor ones.'

'Did you spend much time with them, growing up?'

'Some,' she said, remembering the way it would make her feel when she would leave home to spend the weekend with her father and then the way it would make her feel to come back home. Awful, awkward and not fitting in at either house. 'I didn't exactly make the best first impression. I was a bit of a wild child, running around naked, making a mess and ruining things. Margaret, Dad's wife, couldn't handle it and, no matter how much I tried to be the kind of daughter she might have in her house, it didn't seem to help.'

'Why bother?' Benoit demanded arrogantly, full of the self-assured confidence she'd never possessed.

'Because I wanted to spend time with my father?' she replied hotly. 'Because I would have liked to have got to know my brother? Because there's half a family out there that is mine and I'm cut off from them? It's not as simple as not caring what other people think, Benoit,' she said, fearing that the tears she felt pressing against the back of her eyes might escape.

She could feel the weight of his gaze on her face, on her skin, warming it, and then it cooled, as if he'd looked away.

'So is that what you'll do with the money?' Benoit asked, purposely changing the subject. They might need to get to know each other, but he didn't want to press any further than he had already. Because there was something about the way she had described being cut off from her family, the hurt there that called to his own, to the way he felt without Xander in his life.

'From the jewels?' she asked, as if needing clarification at the giant shift in conversation. 'No. I think I'm too old to go to university.'

'Oh, I didn't realise that they refused to allow people to attend university after the age of what, twenty-five?'

'Twenty-six.'

He rolled his eyes. 'So young.'

'And you're positively ancient,' she mocked. 'I wouldn't know what to study,' she said, not quite sure that was true.

He laughed. 'Really? I'd have thought it would be obvious.'

She frowned at him and Benoit wondered that she couldn't see it, how intelligent she was. Her mind was quick and she absorbed information like a sponge. And she was most definitely opinionated. That beat half of the people Chalendar employed and he employed some of the best.

'Sociology or politics. Definitely something to do with gender studies, though you really will have to stop using words like mansplaining and—'

He dodged the pillow she threw at him and laughed while rescuing the glass of wine before it could spill.

'No, university is for Summer. She has the brains; she's applying for her Masters as we speak.'

'And that stops you how?' Benoit asked, unsure as to why she would think any less of herself than her sisters.

'I just…it's not something I'm willing to get into debt over.'

'But we're talking about what happens if you find the jewels. Surely money won't be an issue then and you can spend it on whatever you like.'

'Yes. Of course,' she replied blankly and Benoit had the distinct impression that Skye wouldn't put herself first even if she had all the money in the world. It would go somewhere else, to someone else. And suddenly he was angry with the parents who had made her feel that she was not worthy of wanting such things for herself.

'It's late, so…' she said, unfurling herself from the sofa with an unconscious elegance that drew his gaze. Until she nearly tripped on the hem of his trousers again. She was going to hurt herself in those. He sighed. He'd liked those trousers.

'Come here,' he said, gesturing to her and hauling himself into a more seated position. He patted his pockets for the miniature Swiss army knife on his key chain. In the shadowed room, Skye looked at him with watchful eyes.

He glared up at her and she came close enough for him to snag her hip and pull her in between his legs. He didn't miss the way she flinched, nor the way she had bitten her lip between her teeth as if to stop herself from asking what he was doing. And he was thankful because for a second his mind went blank. He could feel the heat of her cresting over him like the gentlest of waves. His palms itched to feel the back of her thighs, her skin beneath his palm. His pulse jerked and he held his breath so that he couldn't be tantalised by the simple scent of her. No perfume or hair products, or gels or lotions. Just pure Skye.

He made the mistake of looking up. She was watching him, her neck bent so that her hair fell over her face like a waterfall. It reminded him of the plane, of her standing between his legs then, but this was different—*more*, somehow. Large brown eyes with golden flecks watching him, embers flaring, just waiting for a spark to ignite, to burn them both. He heard it, the hitch in her breathing, and warned himself to stop this, but seemed unable to.

He clenched his hand to prevent himself from pulling her towards him and felt the heavy ridged metal shape of the army knife in his palm. He broke the connection of their gaze and knew that he wouldn't look back at her again. Instead, he pulled out the scissor attachment, picked up one loose leg of the trousers at her mid-thigh and snipped.

'What are you—?'

Rip.

The tearing sound cut through the quiet of the room like a scream. He pulled the two edges of the material wide. She started and almost stepped back but, because he still held the material in his hands, couldn't.

'You were going to fall and break something, constantly tripping over the ends of these,' he said, turning his attention to snipping where the material had refused to tear on the inner seem. It had sounded like a growl. Like anger, as if it were her fault his trousers didn't fit her. He had to bend his head to see where to slip the scissors, only he felt a tremor in his hand. And that had nothing to do with anger, but it did have something to do with heat. It was spreading thick and fast over every inch of his skin. Invisible vibrations rattled him. He was always in control, but this? It was testing him.

Finally, he freed the first trouser leg and turned his attention to the other. She took another breath, as if she'd been about to say something, but he focused on the trousers. He felt her relax; the hands that she'd held up at her chest as if to protect herself dropped to her sides and he wished they hadn't. She needed to be on guard around him. She needed to protect herself.

He lined up the shortened leg with the hemline of the second and snipped. Skye's body swayed slightly as he tore the linen, the sound making him think of tearing other clothes from her body, and he made the mistake of looking down at her long shapely legs. The skin so smooth, and barely inches from his mouth, his tongue, his teeth.

'Go to bed,' he commanded without looking up.

She stayed for a moment, as if intending to defy him, but thankfully thought better of it. He sat there for a long time after she went to bed, wrestling with the bindings of the terms he had placed on their agreement.

Skye just didn't know what she was going to find when she came down to breakfast the next day—the charming, at ease playboy or the dark, brooding ruthless magnate. Both felt like an extreme of his personality and she couldn't help but feel that naturally he lay somewhere in the middle. But she was surprised to find him packing a bag when she rounded the corner.

'Going somewhere?' she asked.

'Oui,' he said, tight-lipped.

'Without me?' she asked, instantly wishing she could eat her words.

He paused ever so slightly before pressing a towel into his rucksack. That he'd planned to leave her alone made her feel...something she didn't want to examine too much. But, as much as she didn't like the idea, she wasn't going to force herself even more on a man who'd come here to be completely alone.

'Have fun. I'll...see you when I see you,' she said, cringing as she stuttered over the words that made it clear she didn't want to be left alone.

He sighed and she felt even worse.

'Get yourself a towel,' he threw over his shoulder. Only now she really didn't want to go, but couldn't say so because he'd have to insist that she came and it would be even worse.

Ten minutes later they had left the house and, rather than following the road, they'd cut down a worn path through the rainforest. Unlike before, their footsteps were meandering and the hacking of the machete was not as regular. Bathed in shadows and beams of light, she couldn't stop looking upwards at the way the impossibly tall trees stretched into a canopy high above them. Every single different shade of green she could imagine cocooned them, making her feel oddly safe in this huge expanse. A warmth that was faintly damp and the smell of the rich earth was so very different from the sprawling English forests she was used to. Skye felt alive and present in a way she had never done before.

Benoit looked back at her for a moment, and she wondered what he could see. She knew that the information they'd shared last night had been necessary to fool his family that they were engaged.

Engaged.

The word hit a wall in her mind and fell to the ground with a *thunk*. It still didn't feel real. Neither had last night.

You shouldn't make a gift of yourself like that.

Was that what she'd been doing? Offering herself to Alistair as some kind of thank you for his relationship with her? So desperate for affection or attention because of her parents, so *thankful* that she'd...

Benoit had stopped and she had to pull herself up short to prevent herself from running into the back of him. When she looked up over his shoulder she couldn't help the gasp that fell from her lips. How she'd missed the sound of the stunning waterfall before her she had no idea, until she realised that the dense foliage must have protected them from the gentle roar of the cascade.

A jagged rocky outcrop reached high above them, covered in moss and spindly trees that clung to the stone. Water poured off the edge of the cliff and rushed headlong into a clear blue pool at the base of what must have been a twenty-foot drop. The pool was surrounded by flat rocks, joining the forest floor. It was like something out of a fairy tale.

'It's incredible.'

She felt the heat of his gaze against her cheek, but when she turned to look he was staring at the waterfall.

'I come out here as many times as I can when I'm in Costa Rica. It's so far off the beaten track that only my neighbour and I can access it. But, as we've established, my neighbour is away,' he said, stalking off down the path before she could respond.

'I don't have a swimsuit,' she called after him, mildly frustrated.

'Neither do I,' he growled.

CHAPTER EIGHT

BENOIT HAD STOPPED on a grassy outcrop beside the pool and dropped his bag. He pulled off his shirt and toed off his shoes and socks, his fingers going to his waistband before his hands fisted at his sides.

She forced air into her lungs as she took in the powerful shoulders and sculpted chest that tapered into Benoit's lean hips. Good God, did people really look like that? Alistair had been a young tangle of limbs and the majority of the men working at the construction site had beer bellies that they joked were 'bought and paid for'. In the blink of an eye, Benoit dived into the pool, plunging beneath the surface, not emerging until he was far on the other side, as if he was desperate to put some distance between them.

He was pushing her away. The realisation hurt, tapped into deeper issues that she'd long covered over with roles and duties and responsibilities. But it also unlocked something within her, because if he *was* pushing her away then it meant she had come too close. It meant she wasn't the only one feeling…feeling…

She looked back to the other side of the pool, shocked to find Benoit half walking and half climbing up a pathway that she couldn't quite make out. The way the muscles on his back moved, rippling over strong shoulder blades, the powerful width of his arms looking as if he might tear the jagged cliff face down rather than scale it was hypnotic.

By the time he reached the top, Skye had to shield her eyes from the sun and the blush of her cheeks from his gaze because, standing atop the jagged outcrop beside the edge of the waterfall, he looked…like a conqueror—proud, exhilarated. And for just a moment she saw it—*felt* it—the entire weight of his gaze, his focus, his attention bearing down on her like a physical thing. Her heart stopped, her breath caught in her lungs, and then he soared into the air, his perfect dive slicing into the crystal blue pool below. It was over in a matter of seconds, but her quick mind had captured every detail, every movement his body made, her ears barely hearing the break of the water beneath him.

She didn't release her breath until he emerged from the water, shaking dark golden tendrils of hair from his face, sending droplets scattering across the surface of the pool. His mouth was still a thin line, but his eyes…they were electric. Zipping and zapping sparks of adrenaline and excitement that were so tempting.

'Your turn,' he said. He didn't have to shout, to project his voice. She heard it as clearly as if he were standing next to her.

'I don't think so,' she replied, only the words felt like a lie on her tongue.

He stayed where he was in the pool, just staring at her, holding his gaze on her as if he could tell, as if he knew that she wanted to take that leap as much as she needed her next breath.

'I have no intention of repeating myself,' he warned.

Skye looked up at the waterfall, the pathway that Benoit had made look easy, and she wanted it. Wanted to know what he'd felt, what he'd experienced that had made him look so *alive*. The yearning in her stomach reminded her of how she had felt last night, standing between his legs, so close to him. The thrill, the fear, the excitement rippling from her core outwards over her body.

An ache formed in her chest, one of pure want, like nothing she'd ever experienced before. As if she were building towards something that only leaping from the top of the waterfall could satisfy.

Without another word, she pulled her shirt over her head and Benoit turned away as if it had nothing to do with her modesty and more to do with a lack of interest. And it stung. It stung because she couldn't deny how much she wanted him any more. But the hurt didn't stop the aching need; it simply made it more obvious.

She kicked off her shoes and the shorts, ignoring the embarrassment she felt about being in her soon-to-be wet underwear. She dived into the water and reached the other side before she could change her mind. She dragged herself out onto the rocky outcrop, where Benoit was already standing. He barely looked at her and it only made her more determined.

'Follow where I put my feet and hands.'

She didn't bother replying. If he was going to be a monosyllabic brute then so be it.

She had expected the climb to be much harder, to hurt her feet, but the stone had been worn away by years and years of people doing exactly what they were about to do. As they got higher, the roar of the water was deafening and the spray flicked against her skin, making her feel hyperaware.

They reached the top and for a second the sudden absence of sound and spray was disorientating, but not as much as the view. The pool at the bottom looked a million miles away and she backed away from the edge, right into Benoit's chest.

The adrenaline in her body turned to fear, her legs trembled and her stomach twisted. She'd been wrong; she couldn't do this. She suddenly wanted to go home. Not back to his house or the estate in Norfolk, but to her little house in the New Forest. To life before Costa Rica, Benoit and the search for the jewels. She wanted to live in the bubble that she'd been happy with until she'd exposed her life to Benoit and found it wanting.

His hand was on her shoulder, steadying her but also keeping her literally at arm's length.

'I can't do this,' she said, the trembling in her legs getting worse.

'Why not?'

'It's not who I am. I don't do this kind of thing,' she said, leaning forward a little to peer down at the pool below and wondering how difficult it would be to climb back down. Gently, he pulled her back and turned her to face him. The way his eyes bored into hers, the icy blue depths glinting not with charm but determination struck her to her core.

'I don't want you to be something you're not. I want you to embrace who you are.'

Skye had to work so hard to keep the sob that rose in her chest from escaping. It felt as if in three days Benoit had unearthed the cornerstone of her entire being and it hurt. It hurt because she knew that he was right. That she needed to heal that part of herself that was always trying to be whatever other people needed her to be and not what she needed for herself.

'What do you see when you look at me?' she asked, unable to prevent the question falling from her lips and unwilling to meet his eyes.

'That's the point, Skye. It's not about what *I* see, but what *you* see.'

And with that he stepped past her and jumped, soaring into the sky and over the edge of the waterfall. Skye counted the rapid heartbeats fluttering in her chest until she heard the splash of water and knew that he was safe.

She expected her pulse to slow, but it didn't. Because it was her turn. She knew she could climb back down. After all, it was up to her and that was just as much a part of the point he was making. But she didn't want to. She remembered the thrill in his eyes just after he'd jumped the first time, the excitement stirring in her own body, the desire to feel that for herself. She approached the area where Benoit had jumped from. What was the worst that could happen? She could fall and break her heart. Arm, she corrected; she'd meant arm, obviously.

Before she could change her mind, she bent her legs and launched herself away from the grassy bank at the edge of the waterfall, shaping her body into a dive. It was as if everything she felt rushed through her in less than a second. Fear, happiness, excitement, pleasure. She was pretty sure she screamed, but by the time she rose from the depths of the water below she knew one thing about herself for certain.

She was someone who jumped off waterfalls and loved it.

Now she wanted to know what would happen if she took a different kind of leap.

Benoit let the spray from the shower clean away the sweat and traces of dirt from the return journey through the rainforest. It pummelled his skin but it wasn't enough. He switched the temperature to cold, then freezing. Anything to shock his system into clearing the kaleidoscope of erotic images of Skye from his mind. Skye in her wet underwear, climbing up the side of the waterfall like a sprite, emerging from the water and sweeping her hair from her face, her strong legs and arms holding her steady in the water.

Just like he'd dreamed the night before. At first his dreams had been intense and mouth-wateringly erotic; he could have slept for ever with dreams like that. But then, just before dawn, they'd changed. In his bedroom, in his *bed*, he'd found Skye in a red negligee with a faceless man and he'd woken with his heart pounding and a cold sweat over his entire body.

Was it a warning? Not about Skye—he didn't think for a second she would do such a thing. But for himself. He, of all people, knew that his judgement was unsound around women. Camilla, his mother—he should never forget that. So that morning he'd planned to go to the waterfall alone to get his head straight. But the way she'd looked at him at breakfast... And then, at the waterfall, the diamonds in her eyes after she'd jumped... It was as if he felt what she did—the adrenaline rush, that power. She'd jumped the very first time. Her strength was something he'd never questioned about her, but she seemed not to realise it about herself and that was a tragedy.

It had been getting dark by the time they'd returned to the house and now the patio was lit by the moon and stars overhead. He wrapped a towel around his waist and stalked back into the house, feeling angry. Angry at Skye, angry at himself. No, he corrected, not one for self-deceit, it wasn't anger—it was frustration. He wanted Skye with an intensity that he'd not experienced before, even with Camilla. And he had been stupid enough to make a deal that involved keeping her in his life for another three years. Once they were married he'd let her return to England. He simply couldn't be this close to temptation all the time. Because he was certain that he would destroy her. As he'd nearly destroyed his brother the night his mother had left.

He walked through the house and up the stairs, seeing no sign of Skye as he made his way to the bedroom. But he couldn't shake the feeling that she hadn't gone to bed. In his room, he threw the towel into the basket in the corner and pulled on a pair of loose black cotton trousers, the material for the first time awkward against his skin. Something was tearing at his insides to get out, something he'd not wanted to face for years.

The door to his room opened, drawing his gaze from the window to where Skye stood outlined in a halo of light. He ground his teeth together. She was wearing his shirt. Nothing else. The image was seared into his brain in the time it took to realise that Skye was unaware of what the light behind her revealed. He could see the shape of her hips against the thin linen material, the dip of her waist, the slight shadow of the curve of her breast and the seemingly endless expanse of the smooth pale skin of her thighs.

He clenched his hand to stop himself from reaching for her.

'You haven't spoken a word to me since we left the waterfall.'

'And you think coming here, now, you'll find what you're looking for?'

'Yes.'

He turned his back on her, on the temptation that she presented, and looked out across the dark shadow of forest beyond the windows. He shouldn't have pushed her at the waterfall. He just… He'd just wanted her to know. How amazing she could be if she stopped letting other people dictate who she was.

He heard her take another step into the room and closed his eyes. This could ruin everything. They had a perfect deal. Each would get what they wanted and walk away.

'Why do you cut yourself off from everything here?' she asked, her English accent so clear and unwavering.

It wasn't the question he'd been expecting so it took him a moment to shift mental gears. A moment in which she took another step forward. He felt it.

'Because it's completely cut off from the rest of my life.'

She nodded as if she not only understood but had expected the answer. 'It's contained.'

He frowned, but yes—it was contained.

'As if,' she said, coming another step towards him, 'what happens here doesn't affect what happens there.'

He stilled, realising where she was going with this but not sure he wanted to follow.

'Does it work the other way round?' she asked, and her simple question raised the hairs on his forearms. She was asking too much.

'No one else has ever been here to find out,' he said. He was losing the fight because he wanted something in his mouth other than the taste of guilt and regret. He wanted her.

Skye stood by his side and as she looked out through the window she let him study her, take her in; she felt his gaze against her skin, where his eyes roamed across her face and back.

'We have a deal,' he snarled, not scaring her in the least. She knew he was struggling with this. Knew that he wanted her as much as she wanted him. 'You've agreed to be my wife—for three years. If this gets—'

'You think because I'm inexperienced I won't be able to separate this night from our deal? Or do you think because I'm a woman I won't be able to separate my emotions from—?'

'It's not you,' he growled. 'It's me. It's me because I know, deep down, I am my parents' child—selfish and always one step away from doing whatever the hell I want. And, believe me, I want you. But it can't happen.'

He finally turned to face her and the look in his eyes stole her breath. She could see he was fighting it and it made her angry.

'Really? You spent all day pushing me, probing my emotions and hurts, demanding that I accept myself just as I am. You tell me to go for what I want and then tell me I can't have it?'

His eyes flared in the dark room, the moon shooting stars across his icy blue irises.

'One night? You just want one night?'

'Yes,' she breathed, not caring about the longing in her voice.

'It will never be enough, Skye.'

'Your arrogance is astounding,' she breathed, outraged.

'I didn't mean for you.' His voice was dark, angry with warning. It matched the fire he'd started within her and there was only one way forward now—to let it burn.

'It will have to be,' she said on a shaky breath. Because she wasn't ready for more. She wasn't sure she'd ever be ready for more.

She looked up at him to see if he'd heard, or even understood. He watched her for so long she was ready to turn and leave, when finally he nodded. Once.

And that was all the warning she had before his lips crashed down on hers, his hands coming to frame her face, pressing against her hair and anchoring her to him, angling her to him in a way that she couldn't resist. She opened up for him, his tongue plunging deep within her, filling her in a way that she felt she'd missed her entire life.

Her hands flew to his shoulders, holding on as he feasted

upon her, but also taking something for herself. His smooth, hot skin was perfect beneath her palms, her fingers flying over his collarbone to the stretch of his powerful traps, around his shoulders and down his sides. She felt like a sculptress, learning the figure she wanted to create by touch.

Each inch of skin she discovered was incredible but not enough. *More, more, more.* It was like a mantra turning over again and again in her mind. She wanted absolutely everything he could give her. He walked her back a step and she felt the coolness of the glass at her back through the thin linen shirt covering her fevered skin. He left her lips swollen and ravished as he bent his mouth to her neck, pressing open-mouthed kisses beneath her jawline down to her shoulder, where he gently bit down on her flesh. Her core clenched in reaction, desire and heat pooling low and throbbing.

Unable to help herself, she arched her chest to his, needing to feel him against her body. Benoit threaded an arm behind her in the space she had created, hauling her against him, and she lifted her leg, shamelessly hooking it around his hip and pressing into his erection.

The feel of it, of him, between her legs was indescribable. Her head fell back in pleasure as he continued to kiss, suck, lick, bite his way across her shoulder. His free arm came up in between them, his hand angling her head back so that he could lavish attention on her body. His fingers traced downwards, finding the central notch with his index finger, then her sternum, following the motion with his tongue until he veered off as his fingers found one nipple and his mouth the other.

She cried out. She couldn't help it. Never had she felt so utterly devoured and sure. Sure that there was even more pleasure to be had. An impatience was building within her, a need that she couldn't control. She curved into the hardness of his arousal and he growled against her breast, clenching the hand now fisting her bottom.

Nothing. She'd felt *nothing* like this before. Thoughts flitted through her mind at lightning speed. Benoit's dark glare…showering outside in the garden…swimming in the pool beneath the waterfall… Benoit hauling himself out onto the rocky outcrop…

You don't behave as if someone has given you pleasure.

Standing between his legs as he tore the linen trousers…

I want you to embrace who you are.

Jumping off the cliff…

Each thought merged with the way he touched her, the way he pulled desire and cries of pleasure from her soul. He pursed his lips around her nipple and she bucked away from the pleasure, pressing back against the glass. At the release of her breast she looked up and met eyes that were glistening like freshly formed frost beneath the moon. Intent, dark and devastating, he didn't take his eyes from her once as he tore at the button of the shorts and thrust them down her thighs. He was daring her, challenging her to stop him.

In that moment she knew she never would.

Still without taking his eyes from hers, he hooked his thumb beneath the waistband of her briefs, giving her a chance to stop him every step of the way. The power that hummed beneath her skin, the complete assurance that she was in control, that she could stop this at any point, the knowledge that he would stop, was intoxicating.

He seemed angry that she didn't. A look of resignation crossed his features for a second before desire blotted out everything and, finally, he broke their gaze as he turned his attention to where his thumb was pulling down the thin material of her briefs.

* * *

Benoit cursed. He cursed himself, cursed her, and cursed the fact that she looked, smelt, felt, tasted like everything he'd ever wanted. Slowly, inch by inch, he removed her panties, teasing her, teasing himself, he just didn't know any more.

You don't behave as if someone has given you pleasure.

He wished he'd never said it to her, because now it was all he could think of—giving her so much pleasure it overflowed. The delicate cross-hatching of curls at the apex of her legs was perfect to him and he anchored his hands at her hips, coming down onto his knees. She wriggled in his grasp and he couldn't help the spike of pleasure that flared, knowing that she was just as affected by this as he was—affected, tested, delighted. There were such fine lines between the range of feelings surging through him.

He brought his hands down around the curve of her bottom, cupping and tilting her pelvis, causing her legs to splay slightly—enough. Enough for him to bend his head, to press his mouth to her core. He ran his tongue the entire length of her, loving the way she parted for him, thrilled by the taste of her, delighted by the sobs of sheer pleasure that fell from her mouth into the air about them.

He found the soft nub of her clitoris and she trembled in his hands, her pleasure heightening his to an ache, throbbing and hardening and roaring for release. The shakes cascading through her body edged her closer and then further from his mouth. And it wasn't enough. He wanted her completely at his mercy, just as he felt at hers.

He released one hand from the back of her thigh, bringing it round to lift just behind her knee and place it over his shoulder, giving him greater access. His tongue fastened against her clitoris, he pressed a finger to her core and heard the sound of her back hitting the glass; faster and faster he heard her inhale, filling her lungs with air as he continued to fill her with his hands and mouth.

Until that moment—the moment where everything stopped…breath, thought, heartbeat…and he felt her come apart against his fingers and tongue. He consumed it all, everything she had to give and more. He held her through it all.

When the trembling in her body finally stopped, he picked her up and took her to the bed, laying her gently down on the mattress, her skin flushed and eyes closed.

'You were right,' she whispered. He wouldn't do her the disservice of asking what she meant. He knew. No one had given her pleasure before.

He stayed at the end of the bed, looking down on her. No matter how much he wanted to move, to lean over her, to touch her everywhere, to taste, to fill her completely, he wouldn't move until he was completely sure.

'We can stop now,' he said, even though he knew what her answer would be.

'More.'

'What?' He wasn't sure he'd heard the word that had escaped her mouth; her eyes were still closed in bliss.

She slowly opened them, leant back on her elbows, levelled him with a stare and said, 'More.' Her voice was strong and clear, her cheeks were flushed; he could tell that it took a lot for her to say it, but he knew she meant it.

Skye watched him climb onto the bed, over her, surrounding her completely, with an anticipation that rivalled any she'd ever experienced. Her heart was still beating a wild tattoo from an orgasm that had felt as if it had been trapped within her for years. Benoit came so far up the bed she had to cranc her neck to look back at him, arching her back, feeling utterly surrounded by him. He smiled down at her, but it was one of pure wickedness and she loved it.

He leaned back on his haunches, bringing his lips to hers and kissed her like she'd never been kissed before. It wasn't forceful, desperate or even lazy; it was…consuming. Her hands went to his head, to hold him there, but he reached for them and pushed them above her head, holding them there with his free hand while the other trailed an open palm down her neck, sternum and over her breast.

'If you keep touching me, Skye, I won't last,' he said but, rather than sounding weak, it only made her feel strong. She moaned into his mouth and he took it. He took everything.

His hand dipped lower, around her hip and to her inner thigh, gently moving it so that he could come between them. He broke the kiss and locked his eyes with hers. There was no challenge this time, no warning, no anger. This time she felt…assurance. Once again he was giving her power, only this time it felt as if he were trusting her with it.

He entered her slowly and she gasped for air as the length and width of him gently pushed at her muscles, filling her bit by bit but so completely. He never broke eye contact the entire time. Her eyes drifted closed as she got used to the incredible feeling of him within her. And when he pushed further, closer to that indefinable place that she both craved and wanted to delay, her eyes burst open to see him watching her in wonder.

He hadn't been talking about an orgasm, she realised— what Benoit had said about pleasure. It wasn't about an end goal, some point to achieve, but the feeling of luxuriating in ongoing pleasure—*that* was what he'd been talking about and *that* was what he was doing now. Unfurling a seemingly endless wave of pleasure and delight, filling her, overwhelming her, building within her until it poured over and out of her.

For what felt like hours Benoit moved within her, slowly, deeply, incredibly. Sweat slicked their bodies, the air was heated with cries and moans of delight, building a fire within them both. Her hand slid down the side of his body, around the curve of his ass, his hip, and a thread of excitement lit within her as she found where they were joined together.

Her only warning was his growl and then all she could do was hold on in utter glory as he thrust into her again and again, deeper, faster, harder, and her mind could barely register the pleasure that was raining down over her. Her panting met his growls, her fingers flew to his shoulders and her nails dug into his skin; his grip on her hips became an anchor until her breathing began to stutter as she got closer and closer…

'Skye—'

'Oh, God.' She couldn't help the words falling from her mouth. Encouragements, pleas, demands, threats…all were uttered as he drove them off a cliff face into bliss.

CHAPTER NINE

THUD, THUD, THUD, THUD...

At first Skye thought the sound was coming from her body, her heartbeat still erratic from her night with Benoit. But when she lifted herself onto her hands, his plush mattress cushioning her wrists, she realised it was something else. She was about to ask Benoit what was going on when she saw the door to his bedroom swing closed.

The rhythmic sound continued for a little longer before slowing to a stop. The sun had risen and soft beams of light were filtered through the thick foliage outside the windows.

She sat and turned, bringing the high thread count sheets to her chest, the motion making her aware of a pleasurable ache between her legs and she felt...amazing. A flush rose to her cheeks at the memory of what they had shared the night before—the way Benoit had held her as she had come apart in his arms more than once. Even thinking of it brought echoes of the pleasure she had experienced and she fisted her hands against the memories.

One night... It will never be enough.

She had been so sure of herself when she'd only had Alistair as a reference. But now she knew. She knew better. He'd been right. One night was not enough.

Benoit pushed into the room, the door bouncing back against the wall, and she sat further up in the bed.

'What's going on?' she asked, shocked at the sudden transformation.

'The helicopter. It's here. Apparently someone found the car, contacted the police, who alerted my great-aunt. I have to—' He stopped himself. Took a breath. '*We* are going back to France. Now.'

The helicopter ride was incredible. Much like the jump from the waterfall, it was over in what seemed like even half a second and she couldn't shake the feeling that she was hurtling towards an ending she wasn't prepared for. Even though, surely, if she was marrying Benoit then she had another three years? But the speed with which she found herself being led up the ramp of a private plane at Limón Airport made her feel slightly nauseous.

She frowned as she saw Benoit handing over a key. It was the key for the locker where she had left her bags and, more importantly, her phone charger. Her sisters. The map. She was horrified that she'd almost forgotten them.

A flight attendant, picture perfect with bright red lipstick and an immaculately clean pressed uniform, asked if she would like a drink. Skye shook her head, feeling completely out of her depth. She must have looked a fright in torn linen shorts and a clearly Benoit-sized white shirt. She was led to a seat she was afraid to use in case her clothes were too dirty or that she would damage it. She had known that Benoit was rich, but this? She shook her head.

'*Ça va?*' he asked.

She leaned her head to one side, not quite sure how to answer the question.

'My clothes; they're…'

'You're worried about your clothes?' he asked as if he too was finally considering all the things that they *did* have to worry about.

A gentle laugh fell from her lips. 'I'm not sure that even my luggage contains clothing suitable for...' *what is about to happen*, she finished silently. She wasn't sure *she* was suitable for what was about to happen.

'I'll arrange for you to have suitable clothes upon arrival in France.'

'You know my size?' Skye instantly regretted the way her voice squeaked at an unreasonably high pitch on the last word.

He simply looked at her. The old arrogant, monosyllabic Benoit was back, but this time she saw memories of last night dance across the icy blue depths.

Benoit went to check in with the pilot and complete the necessary paperwork, and all Skye was left with was a sense of foreboding. As if soon being able to turn on her phone had conjured the fear that something awful had happened, that her sisters had been trying desperately to contact her, that everything had gone wrong in her absence. So by the time Benoit's assistant rolled her luggage along the jet's small gangway she was ready to burst.

'Mademoiselle?' he offered.

'Merci, merci.' She batted the small man aside and dragged the case onto the table in front of her, unzipped the hardened top and thrust in a hand to retrieve her charger. She plugged it into the socket she had already identified and scrabbled for her phone in her handbag. She probably looked like a madwoman but Skye didn't care. She had to wait another infuriating two minutes while her completely dead phone registered enough charge to turn on, but finally the flashing green battery image appeared and it sprang to life in her hands. She quickly turned down the volume, expecting a barrage of twenty or more beeps from a series of increasingly worried messages from her sisters... But there was nothing.

She checked the socket, and the input port for the cable. Frowning, she turned her attention back to the screen as it vibrated just once.

Hey sis, hope you're having FUN! :) Have sent you an email with latest journal info and relevant sections. Catherine travelled to Arabia! After scandalous rel with Benoit forced her out of England. Long story! All in email. Love S&S

And that was it.

Skye had disappeared from the face of the planet for more than three days. And nothing. Her sisters hadn't worried—hadn't contacted the British Embassy, the coastguard or anyone else. They'd hoped she was *having fun*.

She fell back against the seat and stared out of the window. It hurt, she realised. Hurt that they hadn't worried about her in the same way that she worried about them. Guilt sliced through her. Of course she hadn't wanted anything bad to have happened to them, but…but it was clear that they didn't need her. All this time, for as long as she could remember, that was what had driven her—the conviction that without her they wouldn't be okay. She had made almost her entire life about them and she couldn't blame them for not having the same focus on her, because that was what she'd intended when she'd decided to step up to the role that her mother had stood back from. She'd *wanted* them to have their lives and live them. But…

'Are you not going to call them?' Benoit asked from where he stood at the top of the walkway in front of the cockpit.

Skye forced a smile to her lips. 'We're so close to finding the map, I thought I'd wait until I know where I…where *we* stand.'

Instead, fighting back the sting of tears, she fired off a text.

Lots of fun. Will tell you all about it soon. Just off to France (!) to see if the map is still with the Chalendars. Will take a look at email asap. Love S

Given just how desperately she had tried to escape in Costa Rica, Benoit was a little surprised that Skye had barely touched her phone. He couldn't take his eyes off her as she put her phone down and looked out of the window. His fiancée...

A fiancée he'd spent the entire night before thoroughly ravishing. In an instant he was hard and was forced to pull his laptop closer so as not to embarrass the flight attendant. He took a deep breath to calm himself, deeply resentful of the way even just the thought of her raised his pulse and blood pressure. He was thankful that she'd had the presence of mind to insist on only one night. Because even just one more night and Benoit was almost one hundred per cent sure that he'd never be able to let her go, let alone out of his bed. Never had he experienced anything like it. In the past, his tastes had been wide, varied and thoroughly investigated. But Skye...seeing her fall apart, feeling it in his hands, against his mouth...

He cursed out loud, drawing a frown from Skye before she resumed her watchful gaze at the window. He needed the flight back to the Dordogne to get himself under control. Because if he didn't he could lose everything.

Just over eleven hours later the jet taxied on the small private landing strip near the chateau in the Dordogne. He'd spent the entire flight furiously countering demands, threats and coercive emails from the family board members about the upcoming meeting in two days, tight-lipped and grim-faced while Skye slept and drifted to her phone during her waking moments, reading, frowning, smiling...her face so expressive as she reacted to whatever she was reading.

As the jet finally came to a stop, he stood and walked over to where Skye was, once again, asleep. Just before rousing her, he saw the petite frame of his great-aunt through the small circular window, swathed in layers of silk tugged about her on the wind, holding an impossibly tiny creature in her arms. He bit back a curse. The chihuahua had hated him on first sight and ever since had made numerous attempts to destroy any kind of footwear he possessed.

'Benoit?'

He looked down at Skye, who was slowly blinking her eyes open in a way that he'd missed that morning in Costa Rica before the helicopter arrived. He felt an urge to smile, to soften the edge of concern he saw in her gaze—which was precisely why he didn't. 'We're here.'

'The map,' she exclaimed eagerly.

He was thankful that at least one of them had some last thread of common sense.

'We have a welcoming party.' He gestured to where Skye would be able to see Anaïs through the window, hoping that she was ready. Because he sure as hell wasn't.

The wind that whipped about her took Skye by surprise. But not as much as the look on the older woman's face the moment she locked gazes with Skye. A sharp, high pitched *yap* drew Skye's attention to Anaïs' folded arms where something struggled within the swathes of pink and cream silk covering the woman's diminutive frame. With a sigh, Anaïs bent to the floor and released a tiny dog, straining at its lead as if the small animal was determined to break free and ravage… Benoit? Yes. Most definitely the chihuahua's focus was fixed on the man behind her on the steps leading down from the small jet.

Clearly, he and the little dog had history. But when Skye's gaze met with Anaïs, once again she felt an unusual sense that the woman was pleased to see her. There was an unaccountable look of recognition in her eyes but Skye wasn't quite sure how that could possibly be.

'Benoit Chalendar, the first thing you are going to do is get rid of that beard,' Anaïs said in English as he hugged her, her hand reaching for the jawline Skye now knew intimately.

'It is lovely to see you too, Anaïs,' he said, leaning into her hand and pressing a kiss into the palm. 'I am well, thank you for asking,' he said, somehow managing to dodge the chihuahua without inflicting damage on the small dog trying to devour his leather shoes. When Anaïs bent to pick up the yapping dog, Skye was sure she heard Benoit chide her for encouraging 'the little beast'.

'And your hair needs a trim. You look like a hippy,' Anaïs stated firmly whilst managing to convey a heart full of love within the words.

Benoit cast a look to Skye before replying. 'I promise to address the situation, once we've had refreshments and time to catch up.'

Anaïs followed Benoit's look and nodded. 'In the library, I think.'

'We don't usually meet in the library.' Benoit frowned.

'This time we will,' she said assuredly, leaning past Benoit and holding out an exquisitely jewelled hand. 'Anaïs Chalendar. It is nice to finally meet you.'

As Anaïs led them back through the jaw-dropping grounds of a chateau that looked as if it had come straight out of the fairy tales she used to read to Summer and Star when they were young, Skye turned over Anaïs' words in her mind, trying to make them fit. *Finally?* Did Anaïs already know that she was to marry her great-nephew?

Finding no sensible answer, Skye turned her attention to the surroundings. The chateau was beautiful and in a way, cast in the soft setting sun, it seemed everything that the dark, downtrodden Soames estate in Norfolk was not. Gorgeous light blond-coloured stones made up the brickwork of the large two-storey chateau. Little balconies wrapped around tall double-fronted windows, some of which were open, and glimpses of expensive curtains billowing in the breeze made the building feel lived-in and welcoming.

But Anaïs, despite her small stature and what must have been considerable age, was leading them along at a brisk clip. It might have been less ostentatious than the Soames estate, but this building felt more welcoming and loved. As Anaïs led them into the cooler, darker interior, Skye barely had time to take note of the hallways and corridors she found herself in.

'You grew up here?' she asked Benoit in awe.

He nodded. 'My father and mother had the east wing, and after he died…well, Anaïs moved us to the west wing, nearer to her living quarters.'

It was imposing and impossibly grand, but every now and then she thought she could see traces of similarities to the Soames estate. Neither, of course, was anything like the little house that she, her sisters and her mother had shared when they were younger.

Anaïs held the door to the library open and the moment that Skye stepped into the room the air whooshed from her lungs on a sudden, *'Oh!'*

Skye turned to see a large smile across Anaïs' lovely features.

'I thought as much,' the older woman said with a satis-fied nod.

'Thought what? Anaïs, what is going on?' Benoit asked from behind Skye, clearly out of the loop of the unspoken back and forth between her and Skye.

It was an exact replica of the library at the Soames estate. There were slight differences in the décor, but essentially it was the same layout. Skye's eyes flew to the window on the left-hand side and she didn't need to go into the hall-way to know that the room was the same mis-sized shape as Catherine's library.

'Ms Soames, I have been waiting quite some time to meet you,' Anaïs said, holding out her hand. Skye took the warm delicate hand in her own, channelling as much of her emotions as she could into the simple gesture. 'I believe you know where to find it?' the older woman said with a smile.

'May I?' she asked, permission the only thing holding her back.

'Of course.'

'What is going on?' Skye heard Benoit demand as she went to the shelves to find the hidden release she knew would be there. As Skye retrieved the package contained in the recess, Anaïs began her story.

'Years ago, my grandfather, Benoit, entrusted me with a secret, a responsibility that I have had for nearly my entire life. He told me about Catherine and their relationship in England,' she said, smiling towards Skye, 'always ensuring that I knew he loved his wife and children. But Catherine had been his first love. She had written to him just before her marriage to her cousin and explained that she needed him to keep the map a secret. That one day someone from her lineage would come looking for it and that he was the only person she trusted to keep the map of the secret passageways and rooms of her English estate safe. She swore to burn her copy and leave the rest to fate.'

'But how did you know that was Skye?' Benoit asked.

'My dear boy, do you really think I would just sit around and wait for some stranger to turn up? You're not the only one able to hire a private investigator, you know.'

Thankfully, his great-aunt turned back to Skye before she could see or hear him choking on his tea.

'You're the oldest, are you not?'

'Yes, Madame Chalendar.'

'Mademoiselle,' Anaïs corrected. 'I traced your mother to the south of England and when I discovered that she had three daughters I hoped that you might be the ones to finally follow the path that Catherine laid out all those years ago.'

Benoit frowned, the suspicion growing that *this* was the family duty that Anaïs had often referred to throughout his childhood—not the family business—shaking him to his core.

'Had not Ms Soames arrived within my lifetime, then I would have passed the responsibility to you,' she said to him.

Benoit was distracted from further thought as Skye took a seat beside his great-aunt with the cloth bundle in her lap. Fingers trembling, she reached for the strings that bound the package and began to release the contents.

There was a thickly bound old-fashioned map which could only have been the plans for her grandfather's estate, something that looked like a letter bearing the name Soames in strong handwriting and a ring. He watched as she held it up to the light, three citrine stones sparkling and set within a gold band.

'Is that one of the Soames jewels?' Benoit asked.

'*Non, chéri.* My grandfather gave Catherine this ring, but

she returned it with the map and letter,' Anaïs explained. It was beautiful and he was surprised to see Skye so easily discard it. Instead, she turned her attention to the map and began to unfold it. It looked ancient, the paper having aged into a beautiful golden colour over the hundred plus years it had remained hidden. The map was a study in fine detail, clearly outlining the design of a sprawling estate with secondary passages and chambers within the walls.

'There are so many of them. Surely they can't all be intact?'

'It would take a long time to search them all,' Benoit realised.

'Time we don't have. The will stipulates only two months before the entire estate is given over to the National Trust.'

Benoit watched as Skye snapped a few pictures of the map with her phone, then she was lost in attaching them to a message to her sisters.

Both Benoit and Anaïs were quiet as she did so, but he couldn't shake the watchful eyes of his great-aunt. There was something she wasn't telling him. But whether that was connected with Skye or not he couldn't quite tell.

'My sister emailed me transcriptions of Catherine's journals. I wondered if you might like to read them,' Skye asked Anaïs.

The older woman's face melted into a smile. 'I'd like that very much. I only had Benoit's part of the story all these years and have often wondered about Catherine.'

'I think she loved him greatly, even though she knew it would never be possible for them to be together.'

Anaïs patted Skye's hand. 'Now, my dear, I'm sorry to ask, but there are a few things I need to discuss with my great-nephew. Perhaps you would like to freshen up? I'll have someone show you to a room.'

Benoit registered Skye's response and intention to update her sisters despite the discomfort that had entered his chest.

'"We have a duty to the past. A responsibility to bear for future generations to come." I always thought you meant Chalendar Enterprises, but *this* is what you really meant, isn't it?' he said when Skye had left.

'Yes, I'm sorry that you misunderstood,' Anaïs replied, the pity in her eyes too much.

'You've kept secrets,' he accused.

'As have you. What's going on with the girl?'

'She's not a girl, Anaïs. She's my fiancée.'

Benoit tried to hold her gaze as it felt as if Anaïs peered into his soul. He fought the anger in him that cried that she had forced this on him. That the board would have given up the by-law without her interference.

'Are you sure? She seems like a lovely young woman.'

'She is and I am.' He couldn't quite understand why Anaïs seemed a little sad. Surely this was what she wanted? Disappointment hung heavily in the air between them.

'This is what you wanted, isn't it?' he demanded.

'Not like this,' she said, cupping his jaw with her delicate hand.

'I'm not like him,' he said to himself as much as her.

'In so many wonderful ways you are not like him, *mon coeur.*'

'Then why?' he asked, his voice barely above a whisper, not quite sure he was ready to hear the answer.

'Because I do not have many years left and when I'm gone I don't want the company to be all you have left. And that *would be* like your father. He cut himself off emotionally from everyone and I don't like to see you do the same.'

Something cracked in Benoit's chest—a tendril of grief and loneliness bleeding out at the thought of it.

'But actually,' Anaïs pressed on in a voice stronger and

more determined than a woman half her age, 'I wanted to talk to you about another matter. Xander is coming to the family gathering tomorrow and you should know that he has filed for divorce from Camilla.'

Benoit spent an hour walking around the grounds of the chateau with a bottle of whisky as his only companion. He'd failed to notice how the sky had darkened into night, how the seconds had slipped into minutes, which had crept towards an hour. He knew that he should get back to Skye, but couldn't quite bring himself to do so yet.

Too much was swirling around in his mind. That he'd taken on the mantle of the company because he'd misunderstood Anaïs' cryptic words about duty to the past. That she had forced the vote on the board because she wanted more than the company for him? And more, the argument he'd had with her about Xander still rang in his ears. The first thought he'd had—and had the misfortune to voice— was to wonder whether Xander's divorce would rule him out of the running for CEO.

Enough, Anaïs had commanded. *When did you start to lose your human decency?*

Camilla is a viper, he'd replied.

Yes, one who chose to bite Xander instead of you—and have you given no thought to the effects of the poison?

No, he hadn't. For two years Benoit had refused to allow his thoughts to settle anywhere near his brother and his ex-girlfriend. He was well practised in shifting his mind away from the painful betrayal and now, when he might have wanted to look slightly closer at it, his mind would still not allow it.

Unthinking, his feet had turned in the direction of the chateau, had led him down hallways and up staircases that led to the room he knew his great-aunt had put Skye in.

The entire time, the small object in his pocket had found its way into his palm, then onto the tip of his finger. He pulled his hand from his pocket now to knock on the door, inexplicably desperate to see her, unbelievably hopeful that somehow she'd soothe the raging beast within him.

When he heard no answer Benoit turned the handle and opened the door, but his mind couldn't quite work out what he was seeing. Skye's travel case was on the bed but, rather than her taking clothes out of it, she seemed to be in the middle of putting them back in. The rage he'd only just managed to suppress built within him.

'What are you doing?'

Skye looked up, shocked to see him standing in the doorway, filling it completely. She wanted to curse, to scream and cry out. She hadn't wanted him to catch her running away. She hadn't even wanted to run away. Not really. She had given him her word and that meant something to her. But her sisters came first. They always did and they always would.

The moment she'd got to the room, excitement coursing through her veins at finally having found the map, she couldn't wait to speak to her sisters. It was as if she'd jumped from the top of the waterfall all over again. She'd called them instantly and Summer had been just as excited, squealing in delight.

But when Skye had asked about Star, Summer had gone very quiet...

'It's not what you think. I came back to my room and called my sisters and... I can't stay,' she said. 'I *have* to go. Star has run off to some desert kingdom in the Middle East, chasing down the key to the room where the jewels are hidden, and she's just not equipped to handle that. She's too innocent, naïve. I can't let her...' There were no words left.

She couldn't put them up fast enough as a barrier between herself and the man staring at her with an intensity and emotion she didn't want to name. 'It's only for a few days.'

'Really? A few days? Come on, Skye,' he said as if he really wondered whether she was lying to herself as much as him. Perhaps she was. 'Once you're there you'll find a way to convince yourself that your sisters need your help, that they're unable to do what needs to be done. Because for some reason you don't think that they're capable of coping without you. You're going to rush back to England so that you can…what? Fly off to the Middle East instead of Star? Arrange for the sale of the house instead of Summer?'

Every single one of his words hurt, sliced into the thin excuses she had drawn about herself like a cloak.

'No! I just need to find out what's going on. And then I'll come back,' she said, her voice weak to her own ears.

'We both know that's a lie.'

He let the accusation stand between them and finally she tossed the shirt she had gripped and scrunched in her hands into the travel case.

'Were you even going to say goodbye?' he demanded.

'Of course I was,' Skye replied, barely managing to choke past the lie that fell so easily from her lips.

'There's no *of course* about it. My mother didn't.'

CHAPTER TEN

THERE WAS AN awful matter-of-factness about his tone that pulled Skye up short.

'Benoit—'

'I saw her that night,' he said, staring at some distant point in time just over her shoulder. 'I was eight when she left. I'd gone to her room because there had been a horrible storm and I'd woken up from a nightmare. I just didn't realise that I'd gone from one to another.'

Skye's heart lurched in her chest. She knew that there was only one way this story ended but she wasn't sure that she was ready to hear it. But Benoit pressed on.

'Usually her door was locked, which was why I was so surprised, why I entered the room.' Benoit shook his head against the memory, as if wondering at his own actions that night.

'Just like I came into this room just now,' he scoffed angrily. 'She looked almost exactly as you did. A half-packed suitcase on the bed, something in her hands and a guilty-as-sin look on her face.' He couldn't stem the tide of acidic bitterness.

'I knew, even as I asked my mother the question, I knew. That she was leaving my father, leaving us. I begged her, *begged* to take me with her. Pleaded and cried like the little child I was. And do you know what the worst thing was? In that moment I would have left Xander behind. I would have abandoned *my brother*,' Benoit spat, hating the memories of that night, how cowardly he had been, how desperately he had begged his mother to take him with her, to love him enough to want to.

'I told her that I hated my father, and that I just wanted to be with her. That I didn't care about Xander. But she kept shaking her head. Kept saying that it was something *she* had to do. That she couldn't take me with her. And then she made me promise not to tell anyone that I'd seen her. Not to say a word to anyone—my father, Xander or Anaïs. Not to cry in case it alerted one of the staff. I was to show no sign that I'd seen her that evening at all.'

Skye's heart was breaking for the little boy who'd not only watched his mother leave, but asked, begged her to take him with her and been refused. She felt fury on his behalf, even knowing that she had nearly done the same thing to him.

'She had no right to ask you to make that promise,' she said to Benoit.

'But I did. And it was the last time I saw her. I went back to my room and waited for the sun to come up, I waited for someone else to make the same discovery I had, but if I'd known that it would have been Xander I...

'I heard him calling for her when he couldn't find her.' He'd watched as Xander tore through the whole house looking for someone who wasn't there any more. He'd watched as Xander's heart had broken. Their father hadn't even looked up from his morning newspaper and coffee, but Xander? He'd cried for two whole weeks.

'I'm so sorry, Benoit.'

'I'm not. It taught me a very valuable lesson. That when it comes down to it, Skye, we *all* become selfish. We all take what it is that we need. So believe me when I say I'm not surprised by your actions. You have the map and you might even be able to find the jewels and do whatever the hell you want with them. But for me? The company is all I have left. And I'm going to make damn sure that I get it.

'Perhaps you think, because of the intimacies we've shared, that I'm someone whose finer feelings can be played upon. Well, don't. Let me be clear—all intimacies are over but the agreement is not. So you'd better still be here tomorrow, because we *will* be announcing our engagement at the party.'

Benoit speared her with a stare, as if to make sure that Skye understood his warning, before throwing something onto the bed beside her case and stalking from the room.

Skye felt as if the earth was shifting beneath her feet. She hurt for the little boy whose mother had abandoned him, who made him make a promise not to cry. A boy who grew into a man who was betrayed again by his girlfriend with his brother. And then by her.

She had done exactly as all those people who had hurt him had—taken what they wanted and left. Or planned to.

As much as she wanted to deny it, she *had* been about to run away.

Because, if she was honest, she'd never thought she'd actually find the map. Yes, she'd desperately hoped and prayed for her mother's sake. But the reality of it? Actually finding it? It had been inconceivable. Because that would mean not only that they might be able to find those jewels, but that she would actually have to marry Benoit.

And in some ways *not* finding the map had made that easier. It had been her get-out clause. It meant that she'd never have to face the fact that she'd marry a man who would never love her. So no, Benoit was wrong. She wasn't running away because of her sisters. She was running from her feelings for him. Because they terrified her. More than anything.

She crossed the room to her bed and picked up the object he had thrown there earlier. It was the ring they had found with the map. The citrine crystal that Benoit had given to Catherine before he'd left England all those years ago glinted in the low lighting of the room.

It had been meant to be her engagement ring Skye now realised as she sank onto the bed, the strange synchronicity touching her heart and breaking it at the same time. Tears gathered at the corners of her eyes and as she leaned back against the headboard she felt paper crumple in her back pocket.

The letter from Benoit's great-great-grandfather. As carefully as she could, she retrieved the aged envelope and with shaking hands began to read.

Dear Ms Soames
Please forgive the assumption of the address. I can only assume that Catherine is right in her faith and belief—as she has been in so many things—that it will be a female member of her family who will eventually unearth what she has hoped to have hidden. It is a hope we both share.

How does one explain such a thing to someone who is not yet born, and may not be for some years? It is almost unimaginable. But safe to say that this hope is one born of love. For Catherine, love of her future family, and for me... Love of her.

I have been truly blessed with my wife and family and would not change a single step on the path that led me to them. But Catherine—her strength, her determination, and the joy that shines through those two qualities... She was an incredible person and I feel lucky to have known her.

Ours was an impossible love. We knew it before we acted on it, during and most acutely after we were forced to part ways. Perhaps in the future, society's decrees will be less rigid, marriages will be less confined by duty and class, and love will be less judged. I hope that will be the case, so very much.

For Catherine, the Soames jewels have been a heavy weight to bear. They have brought only cruel, desperate men to her door. Her wish—our wish—is that you find the jewels that are rightfully yours and that they bring you great peace and true love.

You are our hopes and our dreams.

Always,
BC

Noticing the use of the same code that she and her sisters had seen in Catherine's diaries, she traced her fingers over the underlined letters on the page. And the message ran over and over in her mind as she put aside the letter and retrieved the ring. She was humbled and overwhelmed by a message over one hundred and fifty years old that was full of love, compassion and understanding.

And as her heart was torn between what she felt she should do for her sisters and what she wanted to do for Benoit, it broke a little. He was right. Her sisters would be fine. They would *always* be fine because she had done that for them, given them a security she had never felt herself. A small part of her realised then that the instinct to go to them was learned, was ingrained and habitual. She thought of the way Benoit had drawn her out in Costa Rica. Just one day, and over five thousand miles ago.

She slipped the citrine ring onto her engagement finger, a surprised sigh escaping her lips as it fitted perfectly. Her sisters had the map; they had what they needed to take the next step to finding the Soames jewels. It was Benoit who needed her now.

As she shifted back onto the bed, the message from Benoit's letter settled into her heart.

Go with love.

Skye hadn't seen Benoit all day. She'd slept late, grabbed some lunch and wandered the garden, looking for traces of Benoit's childhood and not quite finding any. Wandering through the beautiful chateau had only made her feel more in the way and uncomfortable as uniformed staff members hustled and bustled about in preparation for what looked to be a spectacular event. So eventually she'd retreated to her rooms and pored over the pages of Catherine's diaries that Summer had typed up and emailed.

Her heart ached for her ancestor, who'd loved a man she would never have been allowed to marry. And here Skye was, about to marry a man who might never love her. To marry a man she was beginning to fear that she really did love. Because the Benoit she had seen in Costa Rica, the incredible man who had drawn her out and shown her what she could be, the man who only hurt here at the chateau, a man convinced that selfishness was at the root of everything, yet he had only given to her...*that* man deserved her love.

Skye cast a glance at the dresses magically procured by Benoit's assistant, and she frowned. They were all perfectly fine, gorgeous even, but not quite...

A knock sounded at the door and her heartbeat picked up.

Benoit.

But as she opened the door to find Anaïs standing there Skye forced down the disappointment and hoped that it didn't show on her face. The little dog yapped a greeting from where he was nestled in her arms and, with an amused eye roll, Anaïs released him to explore Skye's room, dotingly watching as he raced about searching for invisible treats.

'I wanted to see how you were.' Anaïs looked beyond her to the selection of dresses hung in a row across the top of the dresser and scoffed. 'Benoit's assistant is a man with no taste. Business acumen, yes, but absolutely no taste. Trust me, Benoit would *never* have chosen any of these.'

Skye couldn't help but smile at the thought that Anaïs wanted to assure her that her great-nephew had better taste in clothing. But when the older woman's eyes turned back to her, taking her in from head to foot and then narrowing suspiciously, the first stirrings of excitement began to spread in Skye's chest. Because she wanted this evening to be perfect for Benoit. Wanted him to have a fiancée he would not only stand by but be proud of. And she had a feeling that Anaïs wanted that too.

Pulling at the neck of his shirt, Benoit wondered for the hundredth time how the ballroom had managed to get so hot. For nearly twenty minutes now, his frustration with Skye's absence had grown into a physical thing. He'd barely been able to utter a few civil words to his extended family, resenting each and every one of them for putting him in this situation.

A small rise in volume near the entrance alerted him to a new arrival and he bit back the familiar bitterness that coated his tongue when he finally saw his brother. It took a moment for the image he'd held in his mind and the actual reality of Xander to merge into one. Over the last two years he'd allowed betrayal to morph his brother into a monstrous presence at the back of his mind. But now that Xander was here, greeting members of his family, Benoit was struck dumb. Shocking sentiment clashed against hurt and he didn't know which one would win out. Xander, nearly as tall as his own six foot three inches, bent to greet some of the older generation before casting a glance directly towards him, as if he'd always known where Benoit was in the room.

A set of blue eyes pierced the isolation he had found himself in. Xander's familiar jawline, angular and as determined as his own, clenched as if ready for a confrontation. The murmurs in the room rose once again as the expectation of a showdown increased. Benoit bit off a bitter laugh. As if he'd give them the satisfaction.

The moment his brother made a move in his direction, Benoit purposely turned his back on him, scanning the crowds for any sign of Skye. But he couldn't ignore that he'd felt…not angry, but actually happy to see Xander. For a moment he'd forgotten everything and relief had spread through him at the sight of him. Was it the memories that he'd shared with Skye that had conjured this strange disjointed feeling? He'd admitted to Skye that he would have turned his back on Xander and gone with his mother without a second thought all those years ago, and with it had come the realisation that he'd actually been thankful for Xander's betrayal. Because it had—for the briefest time—overshadowed the years of guilt Benoit had felt. Finally, they were once again equal in their betrayal of each other.

But the ache forming at this thought overshadowed the night. Instead of the guests in the ballroom, he saw trees and branches. Instead of murmured conversations and gentle music, he heard the sounds of boyish laughter. Instead of the rich heady scent of perfume, damp, peaty forest earth filled his nose. Memories of building forts with Xander consumed him, the thoughtless ease and love of their bond stretched through him. The way they had stood together, side by side, with cardboard swords and tea-towel capes, as they faced down imaginary armies. And suddenly what rose up from the last two years wasn't betrayal or bitterness, but loneliness without his brother by his side. The brother he had consulted with each and every business deal, the confidante he had discussed almost every thought and feeling with.

As if pulled up by his own realisation, he was about to turn back to Xander when he noticed each of the guests turning towards the grand circular staircase at the head of the room. Expecting to see his great-aunt, his breath caught in his lungs unexpectedly and his chest seized.

If Anaïs hadn't been holding onto her arm as they rounded the balcony that looked over the huge ballroom, dotted with round tables as if it were a wedding reception, Skye would have stopped in her tracks. A soiree, Anaïs had called it. She was pretty sure Benoit had called it a gathering. This was something *entirely* different.

It reminded her of a ball described in Catherine's diary and, for just a moment, Skye felt the past and present merge. The notion was most definitely helped by the incredible dress that Anaïs had found for her. It had taken her breath away when she'd first seen it. The oyster-coloured silk was floor-length with a small silver waist detail at the front which closed in a ribbon at the back. From the shoulders, two drapes of chiffon veed down to the centre of her waist over the lace detail of the bodice beneath. Skye was thankful for the cap sleeves that left her arms bare in this heat. The lace at her back, exquisitely detailed, crossed her shoulder blades and met at the waist, but it was the skirt that Skye loved most. The silky chiffon fell away from the waist to the floor in thousands of tiny layers, making her look and feel like a princess. The easy glide of it against her skin took her by surprise each time she took a step and it made her feel feminine and sensual in a way she never could have imagined.

As if Anaïs was her fairy godmother and had planned it all, Skye's dress matched the ballroom filled with tables covered in creamy linen tablecloths and pale-coloured dinner sets, the room lit with white candles that hung in wall sconces and from the largest chandeliers she had ever seen.

Everywhere she looked, gold and diamonds twinkled. Music played by a real quartet at one end of the room softened the hum of the quietly spoken conversations rising up from the floor below. Some of the older guests were using fans to cool them from the surprising heat and Skye half expected a footman to be waiting at the top of the stairs that led down to the ballroom to announce her and Anaïs' arrival.

As she scanned the ballroom, looking for Benoit, her eyes snagged on a tall, sandy blond-haired man—the jawline familiar. But while her mind hooked onto the man, her heart knew that this wasn't Benoit and she paused, studying the person who could only be Xander, Benoit's brother.

In an instant Skye wanted to be beside Benoit because she knew that this would be difficult for him. And no matter Benoit's machinations, excuses even, for demanding that she wear his ring…it wasn't about the company. It wasn't about what was rightfully his. Beneath that, Skye had seen the hurt and anger swirling beneath the surface and, no matter how painful his parents' betrayal, Skye knew, *knew*, that the deepest hurt, the deepest guilt, had focused around his feelings for his brother. So she pushed aside the nervousness she felt within her chest and answered Anaïs' shrewd assessing gaze as they stepped towards the top of the staircase with a firm smile. She was ready.

She picked up the skirts of the dress so as not to trip on them or catch them with her heels, casting a look down the stairs to where they were heading. From the corner of her eye, the citrine ring caught the light and sparkled, as if to remind her, *Go with love.*

As they began to descend the staircase, finally her eyes found Benoit and her chest constricted as if she needed his permission to breathe. He was…marvellous. She swore she could feel the power resonating from him. The tuxedo he wore clung to his broad shoulders, dropping to a narrow V just above his waist. The starched white shirt clashed beautifully with the bronze tan of his skin and she couldn't take her eyes off his jaw. Clean shaven, he was even more handsome. As if the beard had softened his impact, it was now painfully clear that he was almost insolently sexy.

Desire shivered across her skin as she refused to drop her gaze, her eyes locked with his with each step that brought her closer and closer to him, with each glide of her silk skirts against her skin, wishing fervently that it was his hands rather than the material of her dress that covered her body.

A blush rose to her cheeks, she could feel the heat of it, not because every single one of the guests had fallen silent at their approach, but because of the sensual magic weaving between them. He stalked towards the bottom of the stairs, the look in his eyes as intense as she felt.

'Thank you for lending Skye to me for the day, but I feel it's time that I returned your fiancée to you.'

Skye registered the few gasps and murmurs that greeted Anaïs' decree, absently wondering if perhaps this was the first time that Benoit's family had heard the news. But everything paled into insignificance as Anaïs moved Skye's arm from hers to his. It felt…ritualistic—as if she were being presented to him as an offering. As a prize.

Anaïs disappeared and all Skye could see, could think of, could feel was him.

'I didn't think you would still be here.'

'I am. But not because you told me to be, but because I want to be.'

She kept her eyes on his, trying as much as possible to express her meaning, to imprint it upon him so that he would understand the truth behind her words. There was so much she desperately wanted to tell him—her feelings for him, why she had done what she'd done, about her mother—but the guests had now turned to crowd around them, questions on their lips and suspicion in their eyes. So she stayed silent as he led her towards the head table.

As she sat in the chair he pulled out for her, staring down at the sheer number of knives, forks, plates, side plates, first and second course plates, the four glasses—*four*—she tried not to flinch as a uniformed man poured champagne into the flute beside her.

It was only when she felt Benoit stiffen beside her that she realised Xander Chalendar had taken a seat opposite. For a moment the guests around the table seemed to take a collective breath until Anaïs launched into a topic of conversation Skye tried very hard to keep up with.

Noticing that Benoit had barely touched his starter, Skye couldn't help but sneak out a hand beneath the tablecloth, to reach for the clenched fist he held against his thigh. The fierce stretch of skin over knuckles told her how difficult he was finding this and she smoothed her palm over his fist and hoped that it would somehow relax him. She hadn't realised that she was holding her breath until slowly his hand unfurled and his fingers gently threaded through hers. A small smile pulled at her lips and finally she turned her attention back to the delicious food, enjoying the one-handed eating style that they were now both engaged in.

The easy conversation that covered the first and second courses, all the way to dessert, had lulled her into a false sense of security. So it took her a moment to realise that she was being pinned by a stare from Benoit's brother, as if he were waiting for her to make eye contact, demanding it even. When she finally did raise her gaze, she purposely left it open. She wasn't quite sure what she'd expected—suspicion, anger? But instead…truly? She thought she saw some kind of protectiveness in his eyes, recognising it as something she felt for her sisters. And that kind of protectiveness? It was dangerous and she was immediately on edge.

'So, Miss Soames,' Xander said, as if it weren't the first thing he'd ever uttered in her direction, 'how long have you known my brother?'

Skye wasn't quite sure what angle he was playing here, because she didn't really know enough about Xander to assume anything. She knew how Benoit felt about him and she didn't need the way he had clenched her hand in his to tell her that he was suspicious of his brother's motivations. Perhaps Xander wanted to disprove their relationship to the family so Benoit wouldn't be able to secure the CEO position permanently, perhaps not. She could hardly ignore the question, but neither was she going to leave Benoit open to any kind of suspicion or doubt.

'It feels like years,' she simply replied.

'I'm sure you could forgive us for thinking that this engagement is oddly fortuitous.'

So he was trying to undermine Benoit. Everything in her rose to his defence and she wouldn't let this go quietly. She didn't know these people, she didn't care about these people, but she did know Benoit. He had shown her time and time again that, despite his hurts, he wanted the best for his company, his family. He didn't want to make the same mistakes as his father or his mother, and not only had he led her to the map, he had shown her a part of herself she had long forgotten.

'I could forgive you for thinking that, but perhaps not for saying it,' she replied.

Xander nodded, accepting the criticism. 'But, with so much at stake, I'm sure that you can understand the family's concern. We would all love to hear how your relationship came into being.'

'Well, you could say that we crashed into each other's lives quite suddenly,' she said, a small smile pulling at her lips. 'And now I couldn't imagine mine without him in it,' she pressed on, surprised at how the sentiment rang true within her.

'I'm presuming the engagement will be short?'

'There's certainly no need to wait,' she fired back, finding strength in the way Anaïs' smile warmed her, while she tried to ignore the brooding anger vibrating from where she touched Benoit.

'I just find it hard to believe that you know each other well enough in such a short space of time,' Xander replied, his eyes flicking between her and Benoit.

Skye let loose a small laugh. 'Ask me anything,' she said, relishing the feeling of power that glowed within her. Because she did, she realised. She did know Benoit. And, for just a moment, she saw doubt spread across Xander's features.

Holding his gaze now, and refusing to look towards Benoit, she pressed on. 'How he likes his coffee? Black, strong and he doesn't stop until he's had three cups—and please, don't try and talk to him before then, he's impossible.' A small laugh rose from the other guests at the table. 'Benoit likes a very rich red wine, but prefers whisky after dinner.

He's proud and hates to admit he's wrong, which, admittedly, is rare but does happen on certain occasions. He has a penchant for crime fiction and autobiographies, likes print books instead of E-readers, and once a year travels to Costa Rica to switch off from the world. No phones, no internet, no neighbours and, more importantly, no contact from the company that every other day of the year he gives one hundred and ten per cent to.'

She saw the moment that surprise entered Xander's gaze, didn't miss the way that Benoit's hand had fallen slightly slack beneath hers and knew that she was about to cross a boundary, but she also knew instinctively that what she was about to say needed to be said. For Benoit and, yes, even for Xander.

'As a child he wanted to be an explorer, but gave it up for family duty. He still misses the forts that he once built with you in the forest here and, although he probably wouldn't admit to it on pain of death, he bitterly regrets the distance between both of you now. Something that may be undermined by your rather uncouth assertions that my relationship with him is built on nothing more than a desire to control the family company.'

Silence met her declaration until Anaïs shifted beside her, a sheen of tears glistening in the older woman's gaze.

'You love him,' she stated rather than asked. 'Why?'

'Because he saw me when I couldn't yet see myself,' she answered simply and honestly while her heartbeat raged within her chest. 'Now, if you'll excuse me, I think I'll retire for the night.'

CHAPTER ELEVEN

NEARLY AN HOUR later and fury still roiled within Benoit's chest. Just when he had been softening towards his brother, Xander had gone on the attack. He cursed as he stalked back to his room.

For the first time he'd actually wanted to strike his brother. Camilla's betrayal hadn't even affected him like this. The only thing that had prevented him from launching across the table at Xander had been Skye. Her words. Her declaration.

And that had floored him. She'd left not only him but the entire table in shocked silence as she'd regally retreated from the ballroom. But, once the shock had faded, the fury he felt towards his brother was nothing.

You love him.

Even Anaïs had been able to see it. Clear as day. And Benoit knew that Skye wasn't that good a liar.

She had shown her vulnerability. And he knew himself. He would take it and use it. His selfishness meant he would bend her to his will. His mind showed a kaleidoscope of his misdeeds, countless broken hearts, his brother... Even before, when he'd been fighting his selfish nature, he could hardly pretend that he had offered Camilla a proper relationship. He'd not been there at all, working all hours for his company, selfish even then. And he would ruin Skye. He simply couldn't let that happen.

The betrayal this time was not Xander's—it never had been. It had been his own.

He pulled up in front of his bedroom door, knowing that she would be there, needing to steady himself. To push down the roiling emotions that were making him nauseous. It was all her fault.

He found her perched on the end of his bed, waiting for him. The smooth silks of her cream dress presented her as the perfect package. But Benoit knew there was no such thing as perfect.

'I've arranged for the jet to take you anywhere you want to go,' he announced, his tone bland and completely emotionless.

'And why would I want to go anywhere?' Her tone matched his and it infuriated him.

'Because our deal is done,' he growled, unable to keep the leash on his feelings he'd been so proud of only moments ago.

'What do you mean? We aren't married, the company—'

'The company is a family matter and you are not family.'

He could see that his words had struck home and hard, exactly as intended, but it didn't make the slash of guilt slicing into his heart any easier to bear. But bear it he would, because he was going to have earned it by the end of this night.

'So they're just going to change their minds?' she asked, suspicion shining up from the dark depths of her brown eyes.

'I'm done with being manipulated from beyond the grave by my own ancestors. Aren't you?'

'I don't have much choice,' Skye said, this time something unreadable passing across her gaze. He ignored it, he had to focus. 'I—'

'You have what you need. You have the map, so you can go.'

'What if I want to stay? You might not be ready to hear it, but will you let me show you?' she asked. He knew what she wanted—wanted it himself—but he couldn't let her touch him. He knew that if she did that he'd be lost. And he'd already lost too damn much.

'I said that this part of our relationship was at an end.'

'I know what you said, and I understand why you said it—' sympathy and desire warring in her eyes. 'You were right when you accused me of running away, but not about the reason why,' she said, standing up and stepping towards him. 'And I think that you are also hiding from the very same thing, trying to control it, by denying this.'

She pressed a kiss against his lips—lips he refused to move, no matter how every single cell in his body rioted with the need to take her in his arms.

'Because this is terrifying,' she said, pressing yet another kiss against his lips, her hand coming up to claim his clean-shaven jaw. 'Because it makes us both feel out of control,' she stated, pressing her chest against his, firing need and desire deep within him. He feared that the internal tremors shaking him would be seen, the fierce battle between his desire for her and his need to reject what Skye was saying, reject what she was feeling, raging in his chest.

The softness of her lips met the firm, immovable line of his own. 'But, with you, I find that I like it. I want it. And I want you. Because I...'

And then it was too much. He had to stop her before she said it again, before she could claim him as hers, as she had done at the dinner. Because he didn't think he could survive it. He didn't think he'd be able to let her go.

His lips opened to hers, cutting her off mid-sentence and, as if he'd opened the floodgates, she poured into him, his mouth, his lungs, his veins, all he could sense was her. It blocked out all thought, all of the chaos in an instant; all he knew was her touch, her scent...*her*.

His hand flew to the back of her neck, cradling her head at an angle where he could feast upon her. His fingers tightened in the silken strands of her hair as she moaned her desire into his mouth. Her hands went to his chest, pulling, pushing, grasping him to her as he was pulling her to him. Every thrust of her tongue met the demands of his, as if suddenly all the power they both contained was coming together in a clash of thunder and lightning.

It wasn't enough. This kiss, this raw, feral thing within him, wasn't easing, wasn't satiated; it demanded more— *he* needed more. But more was absolutely impossible. He would ruin them both.

He broke the kiss and turned away, but not before he'd seen the shock and hurt across her painfully expressive eyes. It was something he would never forget for the rest of his life.

'Repeating past mistakes, Skye? Making a gift of yourself? Thanking me for the map?'

She reared back as if she had been slapped. 'Don't say that. Don't do that.'

But he couldn't stop. The words were like ash on his tongue, the pain in her eyes burning his heart, but it was the only way he could make sure that he didn't destroy her completely.

'Then don't belittle yourself by thinking that one night and one sexual awakening means you should beg to be with me.'

He watched her clench her jaw against the numerous terms of abuse she could throw at him, none more colourful or worse than what he was throwing at himself. But still she didn't move. His gut twisted in a knot he thought would never come undone as he forced the words he knew would hurt the most to his lips.

'It's time for you to leave, Skye. I don't need you any more.'

I don't need you any more.

Three weeks, three days ago even, that would have scarred her, scraped at deep hurts that she'd hidden from herself for years. It would have devastated her, would definitely have her running for the hills, no doubt as Benoit intended.

Oh, it hurt. Very much. But not enough to make her leave. Because in the last few days he had opened a door within her. A door that should have been opened years ago. He had made her really look at herself. At what *she* wanted from life. Now and in the future. It wasn't the dependence of her sisters, or approval from her father and his wife. It wasn't the fairy-soft wistfulness of her mother's acceptance either. But neither was it Benoit's money, his Costa Rican holiday home or the vaguely intimidating wealth she saw here in France. It was what she saw in his eyes when he looked at her every time she embraced who she was a bit more. It was the encouragement, the pleasure she saw— *knew*—he got from her being even more of herself each and every day.

No one had ever cared for her like that before. And it was precisely that sense of empowerment that allowed her to see through the walls that Benoit had built up around his heart, causing her to say, 'That's a lie.'

'Really, Skye, all this is making you look a little desperate.'

'And you scared,' she replied quickly before his verbal strike could draw blood. 'Beneath it all, you're just a coward. Because it's not me, Camilla or even Xander that you don't trust. It's yourself. That's why you disappear off to Costa Rica with no access to the outside world. Why you jump from impossibly tall waterfalls. You're seeing if you can trust yourself to be completely self-sufficient, because you're scared of depending on or needing someone again.'

'Don't you dare bring her into this,' he warned, his body physically trembling from the effort it was taking to hold himself in check. No matter. It was all or nothing—Skye knew that the moment she'd told his family that she loved him.

'Benoit, for so long the thing you've clung to from the night your mother ran away is your *almost* betrayal of Xander. You hold it to you as if it's evidence that you're a terrible person. But you were just a child who wanted to stay with his mother, no matter what. Because it was something you could control, the guilt you felt. Rather than what you couldn't—the fact that your mother left. And you've spent so long focusing on that guilt that when Xander betrayed you, *that* became your sole focus.'

'You don't know what you're talking about.'

'You think I don't know how painful it is to be abandoned by a parent and not just once, but again and again? My father chose his new family over me every chance he got. So yes, I do know what I'm talking about.'

She wanted him to see. Not for herself. She had very little hope now that he would relent, that he would keep her with him. But she did want him to see what was shaping the decision he was making. If only to stop him from doing the same in the future.

When she looked into his eyes for a moment she saw unfathomable hurt swirling dark inky streaks into his crystal-blue eyes. Until it passed and she saw…nothing. Complete absence.

'Are you so desperate to forge a connection between us that you will dig out our deepest hurts to compare them? *Mon Dieu*, Skye, how much more do I have to hurt you before you'll just leave?'

She knew then that she'd lost him. His eyes were dark, his jaw determined. Determined to refuse to see the truth of her words.

'Keep the ring,' he said to her. 'It was always meant for a Soames.'

With her heart trembling in her breast, she asked, 'Do you know why Catherine gave the ring back to Benoit? Despite the fact that she loved him then and always would?'

'Because she knew she had to set him free.'

With that he left and took Skye's heart with him.

Benoit didn't care that the tree stump he sat on was damp and it was seeping into his trousers as he took another swing of whisky from the bottle. It had been three days since Skye had left and it had rained almost constantly since then, as if the heavens were punishing him.

An ache had opened up in his chest the moment she'd accused him of covering over the hurt from his mother's abandonment with guilt, with misdirection, with almost everything other than the realisation of the damage his mother had done that night. It was as if all the years of suppressing it had magnified it, compounded it, and Skye had unlocked a door and it was escaping on one long scream of pain that seemed unending and only grew louder and louder with each passing hour.

All this time he'd been focusing on the pain of betrayal by others, by Camilla and his brother, even his own act of betrayal, and he'd not once thought about the little boy who had promised not to cry. Not to tell anyone. Had he kept that promise all these years? Was he still keeping that promise?

He looked up at the remnants of a fort long ago forgotten by two boys and wondered what on earth he was supposed to do now. His musings were cut short when he heard the soft crunch of wet twigs and he knew, without even having to turn, that Xander had found him.

'Leave,' Benoit said from behind closed eyes. 'Leave now or you'll regret it. It's not an empty threat this time.'

'I'm not going anywhere. I'm not letting you push me away. Not like last time.'

'Are you kidding me? You slept with Camilla! You betrayed me,' he shouted, desperately clinging to a source of anger that pointed outward rather than in. Because, honestly, he feared that this time he'd break.

'Camilla was a monumental mistake. I knew that even before I did it, but she was relentless,' Xander said, sitting opposite him on a fallen tree. 'And I was weak...' The words fell from his lips as if in defeat. 'You were so much to live up to, big brother. *Too* much. For almost my entire life you did everything for me. Looked after me, guided me. Protected me,' he said, the words almost painful for Benoit to hear. Because they were true. Benoit had done almost everything and anything he could, attempting to make up for his unknown betrayal.

'When I said it had to stop she told me she was pregnant.'

'What?' Benoit was yanked out of his introspection with an almost electric shock. Pins and needles dragged along his skin. *They had a child?*

'That's why I married her.'

Confusion spread through Benoit, short-circuiting his brain.

'But she lied. It was *all* a lie,' Xander said bitterly. 'She only wanted to be married to the CEO of Chalendar Enterprises and when I told her that it would never be me she left.'

'What do you mean?'

'I came here to tell you that I'm leaving the company,' Xander said, swiping a hand over his face, that now revealed an incredible amount of exhaustion. But, instead of sympathy, Benoit felt anger.

'Then what the hell was all that about the other night? Interrogating Skye about her feelings for me.'

He was surprised to find the ghost of a smile playing at the edges of his brother's mouth.

'At first I thought your relationship was just a marriage of convenience. And I wanted to ruin it because I didn't want you repeating the same mistakes our father made.' Benoit was pierced by his brother's fierce gaze. 'I didn't want you to sacrifice everything for this damn family company. I wanted to free you from it. Benoit, you've given everything and more for it, but it will never give you what you need and it will never make up for what we lost. And when I realised that she loves you—well, I didn't think you'd be stupid enough to push her away too.'

Benoit felt sick, a nausea that mounted as he scanned over the events of the past. Xander and Camilla, her evil machinations that had severed their connections more easily than his pleas to his mother had done. Meeting Skye, and the times that they had shared, the hurt in her eyes as he had thrown the ring on the bed, the shock on her face as he'd turned to leave. Had he really thought that becoming CEO was worth all she had to offer him?

Finally, he looked at his brother and deeply regretted the years they'd been apart, regretted how he'd let the hurt and betrayal overwhelm him to the point where he'd lost his closest friend. And he'd worn that loneliness around him like a cloak, as if that would protect him from what was worse…love. And the deepest, greatest pain that love could bring.

A pent-up breath escaped his lungs. 'I had no idea about Camilla. I can't even begin to imagine…lying about pregnancy like that. It's unspeakable.' He watched as Xander shrugged it off, but could only imagine the pain that his brother must have felt when he'd realised how Camilla had lied. 'For so long,' Benoit said, finally ready to admit his failing, 'it was easier to blame you, to be furious with you, than to admit the truth.'

'What truth?'

'The guilt I felt because of our mother. For allowing her to leave that night. I saw her. I knew what she was doing. I…begged to go with her. I would have left you,' he admitted, shaking his head and unable to look his brother in the eye.

'And, had it been me, I might have done the same,' he heard his brother say as he felt his hand on his shoulder. 'Benoit, our parents made their own decisions and were solely responsible for them. I think that we've spent too long focused on the past and not enough focused on the future. Because you need to get your head on straight if you're going to go after the woman you so clearly love.'

Benoit shook his head. 'I can't…' He gritted his teeth until his jaw ached. Everything ached. 'It's too much.'

Xander reached for the bottle hanging loosely in Benoit's hands and took a long mouthful. 'I'm surprised you haven't figured it out yet,' his brother said. Benoit threw a frown his way in query. 'That the pain of losing someone is absolutely *nothing* compared to hurting someone you love.'

Skye looked out across the stubble of the harvested fields behind the little cottage that Anaïs had taken her to, letting out a jagged breath that caught on the edges of the pain that had speared her chest since leaving Benoit.

She'd done as he'd requested, collected her things and packed a bag—but, as her hand had reached for the door knob, she'd realised that she didn't want to go back to England to see her sisters.

Not until she'd worked out her true feelings. Because there had been a horrible kernel of truth to what Benoit had said that night. So she'd tracked down Anaïs, who had somehow understood the garbled words Skye had managed to form around the lump in her throat and the ache in her chest. The older woman had simply smiled, patted her hand and led her to a car. Skye smiled through the hurt at the memory of Anaïs dismissing her driver, and soon understood the panic in the chauffeur's eyes as she recalled the dangerous driving that had brought the two women to this gorgeous little country cottage.

Anaïs had ensured that the cottage was stocked with enough food and supplies for as long as Skye needed it, and left only once Skye had assured her that she would be okay. It was a lie. She knew it. Anaïs knew it. But they both tacitly agreed to believe it for the moment.

The cottage was surrounded by fields which, aside from the beautiful garden, were the only thing to be seen for miles around. Which was a good thing, because Skye had done nothing but cry for the first two days. She cried for herself, for Benoit, for what they might have had.

She hadn't answered her sisters' calls, texts or emails. How ironic it was that they had begun to worry about her *now*. She'd called each of them two days ago, explaining a little about what had happened, a little of what she had managed to work through and a lot about how much she loved them, saying that she just needed some time and space. She'd promised to be in touch soon.

All the while, Benoit's words rang like accusations in her mind and she knew that he was right. That she had to let her sisters go, to stop focusing on them and live her life. She wondered now at the person who had found her strength with him in Costa Rica. The taste of it had been addictive and truly life-enhancing. But she knew that she needed to find that within herself, rather than borrowing it from Benoit. And that would take time.

When the sun dipped below the horizon Skye had taken to lighting the wood-burner in the small living room of the cottage. She knew it was a luxury—the summer's warmth was still enough to keep the cool nights mild—but each night she looked for the heat from the flames to draw out the cold ache she felt in her heart.

She had been reading the journals that Summer had typed up. This morning a new section had appeared in her inbox, a note reassuring her that her sisters loved her and were there if she needed them. And Skye was beginning to wonder if it might be about time for her to lean on them for a change. It wasn't easy and it wouldn't seem natural, but it was right.

At first, she'd thought she'd find it painful to read about Catherine and her Benoit. And it was. She'd cried with Catherine over the loss of Benoit Chalendar. At how, once Catherine's father had discovered the affair, he'd forced her to let him go. Benoit's family had been no way near a match for a peer of the realm. Skye had found some kind of solidarity with Catherine's feelings of hurt and anguish as they'd echoed her own. And felt the determination ring within her own breast as Catherine had forged a way forward, to the Middle East with her uncle, determined to put the pain behind her. The Middle East, where Star was now searching for the second part of the puzzle—the key to the hidden room.

And yesterday she'd called her mother. Skye knew instinctively that she wasn't yet ready to confront her feelings about her father, the pain was too raw. But her mother…they needed to talk. Skye hated that this was over the phone, but the need to speak to her had become urgent, an almost physical need, so that when her mother asked her if she was okay, the simple relief had her crying nonsensically down the phone for about fifteen minutes, while her beautiful, kind, generous mother poured equally nonsensical words of comfort and love back until Skye's sobs subsided.

Even now, a lump formed in her throat, thinking of the pure unconditional love of that moment and the sadness not only of what she had missed out on as a child by trying to fit in halfway with her father and halfway with her mother, which had made her feel like an outsider in both homes, but of what she was surely to miss out on in the future, even if they did manage to find the jewels.

Mariam Soames had offered to get on a plane and they had both laughed, knowing that neither had the money and that Mariam wasn't well enough to go anywhere. So instead her mother had promised Skye that she had a cup of camomile tea, a large blanket, a comfy chair and was ready for her to start at the very beginning.

And although Skye's story had started at Elias Soames' funeral, jumped to Costa Rica and back to her own childhood, touched on the overheard conversation between her father and his wife, about Skye's wildness and about her university education, moved on to Benoit and Anaïs, Catherine and her Benoit, and finished at Skye's little hideout in France, Mariam Soames was there for every single minute of it, offering comfort, kindness, understanding and sympathy. Not once did she ask why Skye hadn't told her any of this before, or chastise her for secrets and hurts kept hidden. Until Skye had worked herself up to the worst hurt, the worst confession—that she'd been keeping her mother at a distance because she'd been ashamed of her.

The second of silence from her mother was the longest moment of her entire life.

'My love, in my eyes it is the responsibility of a child to form their identity against that of their parents. I did it with Elias. And you did it with me. It doesn't make me shameful, or you boring.'

'And Elias?' Skye half joked.

'Well, he was always a nasty piece of work,' replied her mother sadly. 'Skye, I know that my…lifestyle was difficult on you. Difficult for our neighbours and your teachers and the parents of your friends. I am sorry for that—I'm not apologising for my choices, because I stand by every one of them. But I am sorry for the hurt and confusion it caused you. I don't like speaking for your father, because it has been a very long time since I knew him well enough to do so, but…his character is simply not as strong as yours, mine, and most especially his wife's. He does love you, Skye. He was just never that in touch with his emotions to be able to show it so well.'

Skye let that sink in. Truly sink in to a depth that she hoped might begin to bring acceptance. They'd spoken some more and Skye had promised to call in a few days when she knew what her plans would be. It hadn't been an easy conversation and there would be harder times ahead, especially with her father, but, whatever happened with the jewels—if she and her sisters did somehow manage to find them, and sell the estate to help pay for her mother's medical bills—Skye knew that the healing that had come from their conversation would sustain her throughout her life.

Just before hanging up, her mother had asked why she hadn't told Benoit the truth about what she would use the money for if they found the jewels. There was no censure in her mother's voice, but Skye had felt it all the same. She'd told herself one hundred excuses since that moment, all of which had been both simultaneously true and false. That at first she hadn't trusted him and then later he hadn't trusted her was true...but not reason enough.

And while she had intended to tell him the night of the ball...in some ways it had been a relief not to. Because, deep down, she knew that revealing this would make her the most vulnerable she'd ever been. How he responded to that could break her into a million pieces.

'And it could also give you the support you would need.'

'Mum, please don't talk like that.'

'I don't mean about me. Well, not *just* about me. You were doing yourself a disservice by not letting him be there for you, by not letting him be the man you believe he is.'

'But what if he's not, Mum?'

'I don't see how that's possible,' Mariam said confidently. 'You wouldn't have fallen in love with him if he wasn't.'

And that was it. As if it were that simple. The thought of the raw vulnerability of telling him about Mariam made Skye's heart quiver in her chest. But the hope that her mother had given her, the fact that she *did* know Benoit, *did* believe him to be good at heart soothed some of her fears and for the first time since leaving the chateau she considered the possibility of seeing him again.

Whether they found the jewels or not, whether they were able to do so in time for her mum's treatment, whether she would actually go to university or not, Skye knew that there were some big changes she wanted to make in her life. And they wouldn't cost a thing.

She would not be torn any more by what people expected or wanted from her. She would work hard to listen to herself, to find what it was she wanted to do or be. And, although everything screamed within her that the answer to that was inextricably linked to Benoit Chalendar, she knew that was something she had no control over.

Skye pulled the shawl around her shoulders as the first bite of the evening's chill edged into the air. She turned to head back into the cottage but pulled up short when she saw the figure standing in front of the back door, believing that she was simply imagining it.

For a second, her eyes drank in the sight of Benoit, as if starved by the lack of it in her life. She thought then that it was one of the most marvellous sights she'd ever seen. Until she looked closer and saw the dark hollows beneath his eyes, the shade of stubble across his jaw.

He took a step towards her and Skye stepped back to keep the distance between them. Because she wasn't sure that she would be able to resist the desperate longing to reach out to him, to touch him, pull him to her.

'What do you want?' she asked instead.

'I would like, very much, for you to hear me out, if you will?'

She nodded, because it was all she could do, her entire body and brain short-circuited by his presence. He gestured towards the old wooden bench beside the rosebush at the edge of the garden and, on stiff legs, she made her way to it. Finally, he sat beside her, leaning his elbows against his knees and looking out across the same field that she had previously been studying.

'Xander and I went to the shareholders' meeting two days ago,' Benoit started to explain, knowing that it was perhaps the wrong place, but the only place he could begin. 'We told them that they could enforce the by-law if they wanted, but that they didn't have to. It was their choice and both Xander and I were willing to abide by that choice. I told them that I should be CEO of Chalendar Enterprises not because I was married, but because I am damn good at it and I want it.' He tried to ignore the way she stiffened beside him and pressed on, hoping that she'd see the truth of his words. 'I do, but not badly enough to bind a kind, loving, amazing woman to me for the sake of it. So I need you to know that I would walk away if needed. Either way, Xander is stepping down from the company and...' he let out a small surprised laugh of his own '...we're going into business together,' he finished, smiling ruefully. If anything good had come out of the awfulness of the last few days it was that he had started to forge the kind of relationship he'd always wanted with his brother, not based on perceived guilt or debt but an honest one. It was interesting and a little like walking through a minefield, but they were getting there.

'I need you to know that before I tell you what I came here to say,' he said, still staring out at the fields as dusk began to draw over them. He clung to that view, a view he'd never seen before but would remember for the rest of his life. 'That you were right. I have spent years throwing distraction after distraction at the hurt my mother caused by leaving. It was so much easier to do that, to blame myself or others, than to recognise that hurt. Which was why I thought it was easier to push others away before they could inflict more of that hurt. But, as someone disturbingly wise pointed out, that pain was nothing compared to what I felt when I hurt you.'

He couldn't look at her. Not yet. He needed to finish what he'd come here to say, otherwise he'd lose it.

'I will never be able to apologise for...' He could barely force the words out through the terrible memory of the words he'd used against her that day. 'What I said was unforgivable. I belittled the time we spent together and I undermined you and everything that is powerful, glorious and incredible about you. Skye, please know that I will bear the scars of that hurt, that pain I caused you, on my heart for the rest of my life,' he promised, for the first time in his life not caring that his vision had become blurred from the threat of tears.

'You were also right when you said I was a coward. Even when I was hurting you, saying cruel things to push you away. I thought I was doing it to protect you from me, but I was wrong. It was because I was scared of the strength of my own feelings for you. You fought against me and *for* me. I was…scared because I've never been as happy as I was in Costa Rica with you, because I love you.'

Finally, he turned to look at her and his heart nearly broke in two when he saw the tears gathered in her eyes. 'I love you,' he said again. He might even have said it another time before she put her fingers to his lips and his heart dropped. He reached for her hands as if to hold her to him, but she pulled back and looked out at the same view he had just been desperately clinging to.

'Thank you,' she said, tucking her hand back under her thigh. 'I…thank you for apologising for what you said that night.'

He felt nauseous all of a sudden, only now realising that he might have truly lost all hope.

Skye hadn't missed the way that he had blanched before she had turned her attention to the horizon. But she'd had to turn away or she would never be able to say what she needed to. Shaking her head, blind to the beauty of the setting sun, she just marvelled.

'How can it only have been eight days?' she whispered, feeling the weight of his eyes on her face, neck, hair. 'In Costa Rica you made me see things about myself that I'd not even thought were possible. You helped me… No, you *made* me confront things about myself that I'd never told anyone. You were also right. I think, because of the way I grew up, I would make myself into what I thought people wanted from me so that they would…' she breathed around the sob welling in her chest '…so that they would keep me.' A tear dropped from where it had grown thick and round at the corner of her eye. She hastily swept it away.

'But you?' she said, a laugh in her voice this time. 'You didn't want me in the first place.'

'Skye—'

She couldn't help but laugh properly now. A sense of joy was building in her.

I love you. I love you. I love you.

She'd remember his words for the rest of her life.

'It's okay. Who would want a complete stranger literally crashing their one and only holiday, where they got to go off and be all—'

'Mancenary?'

'Exactly!' she said, her eyes turning to him, flashing bright with fun and love and everything in between. For the first time she saw a glint of hope shining amongst the icy shards of his blue eyes like a diamond. 'You must have thought me completely crazy, getting drunk and talking about missing jewels and secret passageways.'

'Never,' he said so sincerely she knew he was joking.

'But Benoit,' she said, finally looking at him, all the love she felt for him rising up and pouring out of her, knowing that she was safe, that her love was safe because she could see it shining in him. 'Who knew that, beneath all that mansplaining,' she said, reaching up to cup his jaw, running her thumb against the stubble he'd allowed to grow since the night of the ball, relishing the way he captured her hand in his, holding her to him, 'and all those terse monosyllabic replies, was the only man I would ever truly love?'

He took her hands in his then, his eyes open and expressing every single thing he felt. Pain, guilt, but also hope and love.

'I'm so sorry that I caused you such pain.'

'The pain was always there, you just exposed it to sunlight, allowing it to heal. Allowing me to really embrace my love for you without giving myself away. I *do* love you because you allowed me to have that control in my life, you showed me that I can be strong and powerful and allow others the freedom to love me for who I am and not what I can be for them.'

Skye took a deep breath, her heart full with happiness, sadness, a little bit of grief and a whole lot of love. 'But I also need to talk to you about something before I can say anything else. Because I'm going to need you to love me through this.'

He frowned and took her hand as if sensing the gravity of it. Slowly and with halting words, Skye explained how her mother had been diagnosed with stage three cancer and how they had just missed out on the most successful treatment the NHS had to offer because of where they lived. He held her hand as the tears fell and Skye confessed that the sisters only wanted the diamonds so that they could sell the estate and pay for Mariam's treatment, he held her—shaking in his arms—as she revealed that she'd been scared of telling him because if he did this, if he supported her, loved her through this then she wasn't sure that she would ever be able to let him go.

He told her that she'd never have to let him go as he wiped the tears from her cheeks. He promised her that together they would find either the treatment or the jewels, whatever it took to keep Mariam healthy for as long as possible, as he pressed gentle kisses to her forehead, eyelids, cheeks and mouth. He took her hand and placed it over his heart and told her that it belonged not just to her, now and always, but to her family, her sisters and mother, and that she would never face a hardship alone ever again.

'Then I will marry you tomorrow, or any other day before your birthday if that's what you want,' Skye promised him, feeling as if she were soaring into clouds with the love that she felt within and around her.

Benoit gazed at her, moving so slowly that she almost hauled him to her—and, as if realising that, a smile curved the corner of his lip upwards and she'd never seen him look so devastating as he was in that moment.

'You are so beautiful,' he said, placing a kiss on her cheek. 'So perfect,' he said, kissing her neck. 'So incredible,' he said, his lips gently pressing against hers. 'I have done nothing to deserve you,' he said. 'But I promise to spend the rest of my life trying to do so.'

He kissed her then, a slow building, powerful roll of lips and tongues and heat and love that threatened to take her breath away. They stayed there, kissing like teenagers until the moon came out and the stars twinkled as if laughing with them.

'We should go in,' Skye said reluctantly.

As if suddenly realising that inside there were many more options, like beds, and sofas, Benoit's eyes brightened. 'We should! We definitely should. But,' he said, his eyes growing serious, 'before we do… I won't be marrying you tomorrow.'

Skye pulled up short in confusion as his words seemed to contradict each other.

'I do want to marry you, more than anything I've ever wanted before. But I also want you to know that it's not because of any possible connection to the company. So, Skye

Soames, would you do me the honour of waiting until a year from today to marry me on my thirty-third birthday?'

She laughed, shock and a happy sort of surprise soaring in her breast. To know that, no matter what happened with the company, this was his gift to her. To know that he truly did love her, no matter what.

'A year?' she asked.

'Yes.'

'Well, I suppose that will give you plenty of time.'

'Time for what?'

'For you to teach me how to ride a motorbike.'

EPILOGUE

THREE HUNDRED AND sixty-five days later and Skye was standing in front of a floor-length antique gold mirror in the most beautiful wedding dress she'd ever seen. Delicate lace detail smoothed over silk that draped perfectly over and around her incredibly large baby bump, making her smile even more.

'Oh, Skye,' her mum cried from behind her, tears of joy glistening in her eyes. 'I never thought…' Skye watched as Mariam Soames pressed her lips together, holding back the words as Star reached for her mother's hands and Summer placed her head on Mariam's shoulder.

All four women knew the end of that sentence. Knew how close they'd come to not having this moment. So much had happened in the last year, highs, lows, fraught battles and hard-won victories, each one bringing them to a love and happiness that they never could have expected. Skye turned and was instantly wrapped in the loving embrace of the women she shared her life with.

'If you start crying…' Star warned through her own tears.

'It will ruin your eyeliner and that took me almost ten minutes to get right,' finished Summer, with the same sheen of tears as her sister and mother.

'You know weddings are supposed to be happy, right?'

Skye chided. 'And that you're not supposed to cry until the end?'

'But it's—'

'So *romantic*,' Skye, Summer and Mariam Soames finished for Star, before they all descended into gentle giggles.

There was a knock on the door and Xander, Benoit's best man, called out the time, alerting the girls to the fact that the ceremony was to start shortly. Skye ushered them all from the room with a smile, just wanting a moment to herself. With promises that she'd be down in a minute, she turned back to the mirror and took in the glow in her cheeks, the shine to her hair—a nice boon from her pregnancy—and the glint of the citrine ring on her finger the most magical of all. In some ways, it was even more special than the diamond necklace that hung from her neck, dropping low into the V of the bodice of her wedding dress. One third of the Soames jewels, the other two with her sisters, making it feel—as it always had done—as if some things were meant to be.

Life had changed so much in the last year. The moment Skye had returned to England with Benoit and been reunited with her sisters, to hear the accounts of their own fantastic journeys, her mother had been rushed into treatments that had dramatically changed everything. It had not been easy and, a year on, the only thing they knew the future held for certain was hope. And that wouldn't have been possible without Catherine Soames.

During that time, Skye had grown in confidence, had let go of the responsibilities she had placed upon herself and started to embrace her inner thrill-seeker, all of which had been down to her future husband—even if he did regret showing her how to ride a motorbike. She had fallen in love with the Dordogne and her French was improving every day, which was invaluable as they now split their time between England and France. But the love, the certainty and security she had found with Benoit was something she marvelled at the most, never imagining how powerful a thing it was to love and be loved without measure.

And, no matter how long she lived, she would never forget that she wouldn't have met Benoit without the Soames jewels. Wouldn't have rushed headlong into an adventure that—she now knew—had only just begun when she slipped into an unlocked car. And she hadn't been the only one, as Star's part in finding the Soames' jewels had been just as magical and exciting as her own, but that was a story for another time.

Downstairs, more than two hundred guests were taking their seats on the white chairs with large white bows on the beautiful green lawn in front of the wildflower arbour beneath which she would declare her love for Benoit. She bit down on her bottom lip when she thought on the fact that her father wasn't amongst them. It didn't hurt as much as it would have a year ago, but she wouldn't deny herself the moment to honour that feeling, before letting it go.

Frowning, she felt something draw her to the window and she had learned in the last year to pay attention to her instincts. With a smile already pulling at her lips, she pulled the curtain across her body to cover her dress, conscious of the superstition about wedding gowns and thankful that she had. Down on the grassy bank, as people made their way towards their seats, stood Benoit, staring up as if they'd arranged to meet like this.

He looked at her with wonder, as if he'd never seen anything more beautiful than her, as if he'd never stop looking at her. She watched as he covered his heart with his hand and then pressed it to his mouth. She would swear until her last day that she felt his lips against hers in that moment. But, in truth, they didn't need words, they didn't need touches, or kisses—they were, of course, welcome and wonderful—but unnecessary because she felt more than his kiss. She felt his soul entwine with hers, making her more than just herself, making them greater together. Skye no longer feared being herself, no longer feared past hurts or future pains because, whatever storm would come, they would survive it.

Because they would always *go with love.*

* * * * *

CROWNING HIS INNOCENT ASSISTANT

MILLIE ADAMS

For those who feel small, or timid.
You have more strength in you than you know.
Remember it was a mouse who pulled the thorn
from the lion's paw, not with great shows of strength but
with the courage of her character.

CHAPTER ONE

MATTEO DE LA CRUZ, King of Monte Blanco, sovereign leader of all he surveyed, from the deep green trees to the white mountains in the distance, strode into his well-appointed office in the very highest tower of the Monte Blancan palace, where he found his assistant, just as he had expected to find her: sitting at her desk, tapping away on her laptop.

She had four paper planners laid out in front of her, and pens of different colors sitting on each one. She was neat and orderly, it was true, but when she worked, she kept all resources handily at her fingertips.

Livia.

No last name, as she had no family. She was simply Livia. Though, he often called her by the preferred nickname. Mouse. He didn't know if she preferred it, but when it came right down to it, it didn't matter.

He preferred it.

He did not, though, call her Mouse for the reasons his brother, Prince Javier, supposed. It was not because she was gray or small. Not because she was timid or plain. No, he called her that because as king, he was a lion.

And there were times when he felt as if she, with all

her small delicacy, had removed a thorn from his paw when she had come into his life.

A stunning admission for a man such as himself to make, it was true. But if he were honest, and he was, bracingly so, he had been told many times, then he had to admit that he had most certainly changed Livia's life for the best as well. His mouse had been utterly and completely without resources when he had found her, a thin, pale guttersnipe who had been weighing in on the brink of starvation when he had discovered her.

It had been just after the death of his father, and he, the newly crowned king, had been taking in the sights of Monte Blanco, a country in much need of rehabilitation after being beneath the iron fist of a cruel dictator.

That was when he had seen her in the snow. Huddled in an alleyway and shivering.

He had picked her up and brought her into the limousine. And she had regarded him with wide, wary eyes. He couldn't blame her. It was clear that the world had not been kind to the shivering little thing he had brought inside his car.

But he had purposed, then and there, that he would be.

She was a symbol.

A symbol of the reform that he planned to bring to Monte Blanco. He had given her work at the palace, after giving her a place to sleep and making sure that she'd been given adequate food. But he had never found it... Well, she didn't have family. And he had not wanted to install her in the servants' quarters on the property. She had seemed too vulnerable to him at the time. Instead, he had given her a bedroom in the palace, which was highly unusual. He had noticed that she had an eye for organization, because he was very good at recognizing the talents of other people in implementing them to his greatest advantage. And that was when he had hit upon the idea of her being his assistant.

Over the years she had become a great deal more than that.

When his father had died, Matteo had expelled each and every advisor that had ever been in the old man's ear from ever setting foot in the palace again. He had started anew.

And so, Livia had become his assistant, his major-domo, his advisor, all rolled into one.

Livia was… Quite simply *his*. In every way.

His assistant.

His mouse.

And after today, very soon to be something else.

"Livia," he said, "I've been looking for you."

"I am exactly where I am always at this time of day, Your Majesty, unless we are off at another scheduled engagement, which you know we are not."

"True," he said. "I have something to discuss with you."

"Go on," she said, without looking up from her computer.

Her delicate features were placid, a round pair of glasses perched on the end of her nose. Her light brown hair was piled atop her head, wispy strands escaping around her face. She had such fine little features. Very large eyes with pale spiky-tipped lashes hiding behind those glasses. A nose that pointed upward with decisiveness.

Her mouth was unique. Her upper lip larger than her lower, curving dramatically upward toward the center before sloping down at the edges, giving her a permanent pout. Her hands were delicate, finely honed, and efficient as they moved over the keys.

And if her strange sort of beauty had bewitched him at times over the years, he'd become good at ignoring it. For he was a king. And she was...

Her.

And he knew that the computer in front of her held less information than her mind. For she remembered every detail of every single thing. In fact, Matteo himself had to remember nothing because it all resided inside of Livia's brain.

He was a king, and as such had a great many important things that must be thought of at all times. He had to remember how to keep the entire kingdom running.

He could not bother himself with details. Livia was the keeper of the details.

He kept the world spinning, she kept the day running. Between the two of them, it was quite perfect.

"Now that Violet and Javier have wed, I find myself quite without a fiancée."

"That's true," she said, her eyes not so much as flicking up from the screen.

"And I have been thinking."

"Mm," she said, the noise vaguely disinterested.

"You should be my wife, Livia."

"No." Her face did not budge, her fingers did not pause in their keystrokes. She acted as if he had said nothing half so remarkable as giving her a report on the weather.

"No?"

"No," she reiterated.

"It was not a question."

"Traditionally," she said, her tone maddeningly patient, her focus still on the computer, "such things are phrased as questions. As it is helpful to have the other party's permission."

Matteo waved his hand. "I do not need permission."

"*Indeed.* All the same, no." She continued typing away.

"It makes sense," he countered.

"So does the rather popular candy combination of chocolate and peanut butter, but I find it abhorrent nonetheless."

"I need a wife."

"And I can find you one. But I will not be your wife."

Men trembled in the wake of his disapproval. She did not so much as bat one spiked lash.

"Livia, surely you must acknowledge the great honor that I extend to you."

She did look up then, her enormous, violet eyes filled with disdain.

Disdain.

Not only had she outright refused him, an event he could not remember experiencing ever before in his life, she now disdained him. His mouse. The woman he had lifted from a gutter. He was offering her a chance to become Queen.

Queen.

To rise above the position of secretary, and she'd said no.

"I do not wish your honor. If it is such a great boon, extend it to someone else and they will no doubt be thrilled. For I will not reach out and grab *that* particular royal scepter. As flattering as it is to be offered the position after you have been denied by someone else, as wonderful as it surely is to be given a hand-me-down title rejected by another, I would think that you were much better off handling this the way most royals do."

"And how is that?"

"Well, I'm not royal, am I? So I'm not entirely sure. Political intrigue? A magical ball where all the young ladies of the land are invited to show off their wares? Inviting them to spend the night atop the heap of twenty mattresses and seeing who can feel the pea at the bottom. I don't know."

Matteo had a will of iron and he'd yet to find anyone who could meaningfully test it. Somehow, she was. "You do not have the right to refuse me."

"Will you throw me in the dungeon?" She stared him down blinking slowly and she did indeed put him in the mind of a mouse, but not as many people might imagine one of the small rodents. No. For she was not skittish and easily spooked. She was bright-eyed and immovable. And he had the feeling that if he made the wrong move, she would slip through his grasp completely.

"You don't think I will?"

"No, I don't. Because you and I both know that you're not the sort of king who leaves people to rot in dungeons, are you? That was your father. And you're not your father. You do a very good impersonation of an arrogant ass, but you're not a cruel man, and we both know it."

"I could've left you by the side of the road."

"You couldn't have. Your great tragedy, Matteo, is that you have a heart. Encrusted in coal though it may be."

"Livia, I have thought this over extensively. I am a man who knows his duty to his country, to his people. I'm a man who understands the office of Queen, and what will be required of her. And I have decided that you are the one to fill that office."

"You are mistaken, with respect, Your Majesty."

"Mouse…"

Her gaze sharpened. "I'm not a seventeen-year-old girl. Not anymore. I cannot be swayed by the fear of losing all that you've given me. Nor will I be swayed by the fear of losing the great blessing of being in your presence. You cannot threaten me. You cannot manipulate me."

She looked back at her computer screen. And Matteo was confronted by the fact that he might very well have met an object he could not move.

Livia wished, very much, that she could say she was surprised by Matteo's proposal. But no. In fact, by her calculations he was almost a full day early in his proposal from her original estimation, which was maybe the only surprising part about it.

She had known it was coming.

She had known it with a strange, depressing sort of certainty that really didn't bear mulling over much. She had been counting on this, from the moment that she had found out his marriage to Violet King was off because she had taken up with his brother, Prince Javier.

Yes, she had known that Matteo's proposal would be coming.

The worst part was, when Matteo's engagement to Violet had been dissolved, she'd experienced a moment of absolute and complete joy. She had let the rush of all her girlish fantasies come back and flood her, fill her with the kind of hope that women with her background simply couldn't afford to have.

But she had allowed it for a moment.

Just for a moment.

She had allowed herself to wonder. *What if.* To dream. It was so easy for her to conjure up the image of her perfect wedding. A royal one, large and lavish—not so much because it was what she wanted, but because it came with loving a king.

And she did love him. She had from the time she'd been a seventeen-year-old girl plucked out of the gutter by his royal hand. How could she not?

He was the most devastatingly handsome man she had ever seen. Of course, she'd been terrified of him at first, for he was not a safe sort of beast. No. He was a lion. Regal and majestic, and utterly capable of devastating any foe that came his way; willing and able to flex his unparalleled strength if need be. It had been obvious to her from the beginning, no matter that he tried to affect the posture of a civilized man, that Matteo was anything but. He had made a concerted effort to show the people of Monte Blanco that he was not his father. That his rule would not be marked by the same scorch that his father's reign had. There would be no dungeons. There would be no imprisonments. No more people disappearing in the dead of night for an imagined whisper against the King. No. There would be none of that. He had promised it would be so.

But she had known, always, that the same sort of danger lurked beneath the surface of Matteo's skin. And she didn't think it was simply because she had spent years out on the streets avoiding the dangers all around her.

Not *only* that, at least.

But in spite of the danger he represented, or perhaps

because of it, she had found herself becoming utterly infatuated with him.

And she had known there was no way the two of them could ever be together.

She was an urchin. And a rather plain one at that.

And he was... He was the King.

At least, that was what she had thought then, with all her silly, girlish hopes. But over the years, she could see that Matteo had started to think of her as a sort of Swiss Army knife; a woman who could, and did, perform any task he so desired. And as a result, she had realized—after the high of her joy over his broken engagement had worn off—that there was no chance at all he wasn't going to seize the opportunity to have a Swiss Army wife. It was just the sort of man he was.

And she knew that had nothing to do with the way he felt about her, not personally. It had everything to do with how she could serve him. And the idea of being in a perfunctory, passionless marriage with Matteo honestly made her wish she was dead.

Because she had spent years living beneath his notice. Years sending breakup gifts to the various mistresses that he had cast off. Coming up with excuses for why he couldn't meet them, and in general, dealing with discreet rendezvous. She had seen the women he liked. Even Violet King, Javier's wife and Matteo's former fiancée, hadn't been quite his type of beauty.

She had a modern sensibility about her. Curvy and vivacious, and incredibly beautiful as far as Livia was concerned. But the women that Matteo preferred were icy, statuesque. Women who matched up to his imposing frame. Who had the same sort of sophistication that he carried with him.

Yes, those were the women that Matteo loved. *Socialites.* Human icicles with platinum hair, wrapped in couture. Livia, for her part, barely came to the middle of his chest. When she wore heels, she could acquaint herself better with the bottom of his chin. She did not possess the sort of vapid wit that seemed to come as a standard feature on those particular models of women. Smiles that would cut with the accuracy of a knife while externally appearing to be the advertisement for a gum commercial. Saccharine and white and altogether pristine.

None of the women were airheads, of course, for if they had been Matteo would not have been able to bear them. But they all did a strange sort of half-giggle, before sharpening their words into spears and aiming them at the unsuspecting targets who truly did think that blondes had more fun and less brain cells.

They were to be commended in that way, Livia hated to admit. For they were women who had managed to take both the advantages and disadvantages given to them by society and turn them into something useful.

Livia had two assets. Two very real assets. The first was that she was stubborn. Utterly and completely. It was that stubbornness that helped her deal with heads of state who were trying to elbow their way into Matteo's schedule. With ex-girlfriends who wanted an audience with a man that Livia knew didn't want one with them; with party planners and media personnel; and with any other number of people who had to pass through her in an attempt to get to Matteo.

The second was that she forgot *nothing.* And so, could remember without fail whether Matteo had actually said he was waiting for a particular person's call, or suss out if they were lying. She could remember if he had ended things with a particular blonde model or not. If there was credibility to her claim she could be bearing his child based on timing... Yes, she was the keeper of all manner of trivial knowledge and an excessive amount of stubbornness. But none of those things made her think that Matteo had suddenly grown an intense attraction to her. No. But why did he have to be *quite so predictable*?

She would have been pleased if he would've come in and asked her to help arrange a ball. It was that she did know him quite so well, that she was this right about him, that distressed her. Because she knew what he liked, and it wasn't her. And she had also known that he would go for convenience before he went for anything else.

"You will not be able to retain your position if you do not comply, Livia."

She looked up at him, at his face that had become so dear to her. At this palace that had been her home these many years. Matteo paid her well. Generously. She did not stay on because she had to. She had also learned any number of valuable skills while in his employ. She had compiled education enough to have several degrees and had vast experience as an assistant. She was discreet and had worked with the highest level of state in Monte Blanco. Yes, she did not fear for her future should she choose to leave. It wasn't what had kept her here. But this was the end point, she could see it now.

"Then I quit."

She stood up from her desk and looked down at the planners there. They contained...everything. Every detail about what Matteo would be doing for the next year. Everything planned absolutely down to the minute.

Along with what he would wear, whom he would speak to, where cars would pick him up from.

She had coordinated all of it.

Where his private plane would fly, where it would refuel, which places he might pass through to make the most of the political opportunity. Even what she would wear. For she was always on hand at public events. She always wore black. Always blended into the background. She treated herself like a member of serving staff. Hanging at the outside, in case he ever needed her. Unremarkable. Unnoticed. *His mouse.* A small dowdy creature who might as well live in the walls of the palace for all that he noticed her when he didn't need something.

And he wanted her to be his wife.

No. Just no.

For living with, and working with, Matteo knowing she could never have him was bad enough. Having him and still not having him would be even worse.

"You cannot quit."

She shrugged. "I have."

She would leave those planners. Leave them behind and never look back on them again. Never think about them again. The sudden surge of joy that brought her was indescribable. The only thing that it matched was the moment she had found out that Matteo was no longer going to marry Violet. And she had a feeling that it would be matched by a similar crash when the reality of everything hit her, but for now she felt… New. Empowered. She would not marry him. And she would not be his assistant anymore. Maybe she wouldn't even stay in Monte Blanco.

That determination had been beyond the girl she had been when he had picked her up on the side of the road.

That girl, that creature, hadn't been able to choose or decide anything. She had been cold and angry and bitter. She had a knife in her boot for the express purpose of stabbing men who had tried to take liberties with her. And she had used it.

And the men had not succeeded.

Starvation had made her mean. And when she had found morsels of food, she hadn't wanted to share them with anyone. Not even the visibly hungry people she shared the streets with.

That girl had not been able to imagine anything beyond the next sunrise. She had not been able to imagine anything that wasn't hunger, sadness or desolation.

She had not been able to imagine a future where she had become the personal assistant to the King. And then feel empowered enough in her own self to walk away from that same King, rather than accepting his offer of becoming Queen.

She wished she could go back and tell that Livia. The one that had been on the streets for years after being dumped there by her mother.

Unwanted.

With ease, she could remember the pain, the fear, that she had felt when she had stood alone in that busy carnival, holding a bunch of cotton candy and looking around, sure that her mother must be around somewhere. Sure that she would come back for her. It had taken days for her to accept that her mother had well and truly left her.

On purpose.

In a carnival with a last treat like it might mask the pain of having been abandoned. It hadn't. Nothing could. Nothing did. She had been on her own ever since, and she knew what it was to be in the care of someone who didn't truly want you. She knew how it ended.

So yes, all things considered, she would rather die than become Matteo's consolation wife. Because she would only end up dropped off in the middle of a carnival with cotton candy as a poor substitution for love.

But she wasn't a child with nothing. And she didn't need to wait for pity treats. She was a woman. With money. With a mind of her own.

"You cannot leave me," he said.

"I can," she said, feeling buoyant now. "I will. And I will not marry you, Matteo. Not for anything." She collected her coat, and her purse, and then she swept out of the office, a smile curving her lips.

And she had to wonder if Matteo had ever heard of the mouse that roared.

CHAPTER TWO

"WHAT DO YOU mean she's gone?"

All of her planners were still there. He had checked.
And every single personal item in her room, except a
shelf full of books, and a small jewelry box, was still
there.

"She's gone," Javier responded.

His brother was lounging indolently on the chaise in
his and his wife's rooms.

"How do you know this?"

"Violet told me. She saw Livia scampering about the
place and asked her what was happening. According to
Violet, she looked quite sad, but said she had to leave."

"She can't leave," Matteo said. "She's my assistant."

"Your mouse," Javier said, his tone mocking.

He knew Javier was disapproving of the nickname.
Found it demeaning. Javier didn't understand. *No one
could.* She was more than an assistant and had been
from the start.

"That too," Matteo said. "I gave her everything she
has."

"Clearly not *everything*, as she has backbone enough
to stand up to you, so she seems to have had enough to
recommend her all on her own."

"You know what I mean. She said she quit, but I didn't believe her. She left her planners."

Javier lifted a brow. "Well, she doesn't need them anymore."

"How am I supposed to know where I'm supposed to be, or what I'm supposed to do?" He waved his arm over the space. The space that was empty now. Void of schedule and direction.

Livia's organization was more than a convenience. It left him able to focus on what needed to be done in a world where his waking hours consisted of wall-to-wall work and his sleeping hours were not guaranteed because of the nightmares that often plagued him. Which meant half the time he didn't sleep.

Half the time he chose to spend the early morning hours in the gym, punishing himself. Because at least then the pain came from something real and not the deep dark of his psyche and memories of an old man long dead.

"She left her planners," Javier pointed out quite unhelpfully.

"I am aware. I'm the one that told you," he bit out. "I proposed marriage to her."

"You *what*?" That brought his brother up out of his lounge.

"I proposed marriage to her."

"I had no idea that you felt that way about her."

"*What* way?" There was no one way he felt about Livia.

"That you… You don't, do you?"

"I have said to you an abundance of times that a king has no room in his heart for love. As you well know. I do not have—I cannot have—softer feelings for anyone. Livia was a sensible choice. She already organizes everything in my life, she would be a fantastic asset to the country. Just imagine the sort of charity events she could pull off. She already does the essential function of a queen."

"Except warm your bed. And potentially provide you with heirs."

That stopped Matteo short. He had gone out of his way to deny any thoughts of his bespectacled mouse in his bed. And over the years…

He had little in the way of conscience, but he had a chosen code of honor. And being with Livia that way, given her position, would have violated it in every way.

But of course, if she were Queen, that would be part of the job description. Truly, it was the most important part of the job description. Because if he did not need to produce heirs, he would not need a wife. He would just as soon prefer to not have one, as a point of fact. His bloodline was tainted, and that he was Royal made it so he had to carry it on, and he found that… He did not care for it as a tradition.

His father had been an evil man. The things he had done to Javier, the things he had manipulated him to do… It was evil, pure and simple. That Matteo had not been able to protect his brother from his father's ill-treatment ailed him. But of course, he had endured his own trials.

Bedding Livia…

A kick hit him hard in the gut.

He had trained himself to find that response to her abhorrent. He had known her since she was a girl. He had rescued her.

He imagined her as she'd been earlier, those wide

eyes looking up at him, her mouth pink and lovely and disapproving. And he gritted his teeth.

"It is practical."

"I cannot imagine why she turned you down."

"She was being unreasonable."

"Livia is *never* unreasonable. And you and I both know it. You, on the other hand, have cornered the market on unreasonable, at least, when it comes to this palace."

"Says the man tasked with fetching my fiancée, and then stole her."

"And you didn't care. Just like you don't really care that Livia won't marry you. You're inconvenienced and that's what you don't like."

But that wasn't it. It wasn't. He was not simply reacting as a man inconvenienced. He was not half so petty.

"Yes, you are," Javier said.

He met his brother's gaze, and did not ask him if he had said that last thought out loud.

"She asked if I was going to throw her in the dungeon for refusing. And as you know, generally when a king issues a commandment…"

"*Issues a commandment?* I thought you said you asked her to marry you."

"I did. By which I mean I issued an order that she would. Which when you are king is the same thing."

"It is not. And you, my dear brother, are out of touch with reality."

"Well, the next time I want the opinion of my younger brother, I will ask for it. But I do not believe I asked for your feelings."

"No. And indeed, only one person wants those. My lovely wife, who also didn't want to marry you."

"I cannot imagine why. I'm a nicer person than you."

"You lie better than I do. That's it."

Matteo let that settle in his chest for a moment.

"It is not a lie to behave in an appropriate manner in the appropriate venue. I am simply a man who knows when to put on the mantle of king."

"And I imagine Livia knows you a bit too well."

"Did Violet say where she had gone?"

"No. But I do not believe she said."

"Well, I will track her down, then. She cannot leave without it being on record. And I will find that information quickly enough."

"But she clearly does not wish you to know where she went," Javier said. "Perhaps you should respect that?"

"I have cared for her for nine years."

"She has cared for you. And anyone with eyes can see that."

"I will find her." He turned around to face his brother. "Where is your wife?"

"Do not bother her," Javier warned. "She's tired. Pregnancy is taking its toll on her."

"Congratulations. But I need to speak with her. And I am absolutely certain that she's hardy enough to handle it. Your great tragedy is that I have met her."

Javier rose from the chaise and went to the door that connected the antechamber and the bedroom.

"*Querida*, my brother wishes to have a word with you."

"Well, excellent."

Violet emerged from the bedroom, beautiful as always. She did not stir him, though. She never had. In fact, his interest had been…low. He did not worry over it, as he did not spend a large amount of time questioning his own motives, if any. He had no need of introspection.

"You saw my mouse earlier. Did she say where she was going?"

"I did see her. And Livia did not say where she was going. Only that she was."

"And you didn't stop her?"

"No. She seemed very upset and I can only assume that you were responsible."

"Yes, I was responsible. By proposing marriage to her."

"What he means is," Javier said, "he commanded that she marry him."

"Same thing."

"It's not," Violet said. "Having been on the receiving end of one of your proposals, I can tell you that it's not." She frowned. "It does surprise me that she would refuse you..."

"Thank you," Matteo said. "I find myself shocked."

"Please don't encourage him," Javier said. "His ego already needs its own wing."

"And we have the room for it," he said, his tone flat. "Especially now that Livia has vacated. Though I find it unacceptable, and I wish for her to return."

"Well, what were her objections to the marriage?"

"She made no specific objections. She only said no."

"It seems to me that she does not believe that marrying you has sufficient advantage. If I were you, I would focus on ensuring that she feels there is an advantage."

"And how will I do that?"

"Go and find her."

"Go and find her?"

He did not chase after people. Not anyone. Much less his assistant.

"If you really believe that she is the best choice for Queen, then I think you should."

Yes. That was actually not a bad idea. For she would marry him. She would see that he was correct. She was the best choice. And now that he had hit upon her as the ideal Queen, he could see it no other way. It would be Livia; it would have to be. He had given her a home, a position. Now he would give her a title, a family name. And she would give him heirs. Yes, he was determined in this and he would not allow her to defy him.

If his mouse thought she could escape him, she had better think again. For while she might have an extraordinary backbone, she was still prey.

And he was, as ever, a predator.

Livia had never had a place of her own before.

Once, she'd had a box. It was entirely hers. Centered in the middle of an alley. It had lasted two full days until moisture had encroached in the material and rendered it soft and useless. She supposed that didn't count, not as something of her own. Not really. But this apartment...

She stood in the empty space. The wood beneath her feet was scarred, the ceiling high, the windows tall and slim, facing out over the Seine River.

She'd been to Paris many times with Matteo. As his assistant, his background accessory shrouded in black. But now she stood there in her Parisian apartment, quite her own person. It was a small place for she had money but didn't see the point in wasting it all on a massive dwelling that she had no use for. There was a living area, a kitchen, one bathroom and one bedroom. It was all she needed.

This felt very much like coming to the palace for the first time had. Oh, she could remember that well.

She had been so downtrodden. Angry, frightened.

For whatever Matteo had said, she deeply distrusted him. He was the new ruler of the country and he had done nothing to prove that he was anything unlike his father.

The former King of Monte Blanco had been a monster, and there was no other way to view that. He had made a game out of tormenting her people. A small cluster of indigents who lived in the old ways, who moved around, following the seasons. They had been poor. Hideously so. She wondered sometimes if her mother had spent the last of her coin on that cotton candy. A sugary sop for her guilt.

She also wondered if her mother had been able to return to their people. For abandoning a child in such a manner would be seen as beneath contempt. They had been a poor people, but proud and rooted firmly in family. That made it worse, really. She could remember trying to go back. She had walked for days. But her people had moved on, and there was nothing but fire rings to denote that they'd ever been there.

And she just hadn't had the strength to walk on.

During the warmer parts of the year, they went higher into the mountains. Children rode ponies and in the backs of carts. She had gone to check one last time, the next winter, and they had not gone back to their usual haunts. She had known it was the fault of the King. There were talks of uprisings within the community. Men had disappeared. And her people had slipped away, not to be easily seen, and certainly beyond the reach of a ten-year-old girl.

In spite of herself, in spite of all that fear, she'd had no choice but to hope when Matteo had first brought her to the palace.

"This will be your room."

"*My* room?" She was filled with wonder in that moment. And for that moment she chose to feel nothing but awe.

"Different arrangements may be made in the future, depending."

Her awe immediately shifted to outrage. "I will not share a room with you."

He laughed. And it cut her somehow, even as she stood there wrapped in nothing but old clothes, pride and indignity. "I would not dream of asking. For I do not share my bed with girls. Particularly not girls that look like half-drowned mice who have not seen a morsel of cheese for weeks. But I will find you work here at the palace. There is always work to be done. You will have a position here for as long as you may need it."

"I will?"

"Yes."

"I..." She looked around at the glittering, gilded walls, the plush bedding. She had never in all her life seen anything like this. It was beyond her experience. Beyond her wildest dreams.

And this man, who had the face of an angel, all sharp cheekbones and dark eyes, black hair pushed back off his forehead and a smile that could not be described as kind, but not wicked either, looked as if he had been pulled from other dreams entirely.

"What is your name?" he asked, an intensity to the question that burned right through her. How long had it been since anyone had wanted to know? Whatever his reasons, he was asking after her and that felt something of a gift.

"Livia."

"And have you a family name?"

Bitterness clamped down in her chest and she lifted her chin high. "I have no family."

"Livia," he said. "A nice name."

She kept that compliment and turned it over in her heart. Livia. He liked her name. Bit by bit, she grew in strength. She found that she enjoyed work at the palace. There was cleaning involved, of course, but she found that she quite enjoyed making things shine. She found she had a talent for catching small details. She knew that she sometimes annoyed the more senior members of staff, but she was just so very…happy.

That was what had marked the first weeks there. *Happiness.*

She had spent years, the tenderest parts of her childhood, into burgeoning womanhood, existing in a space where she could barely make any progress. Where the best she could hope for was survival. And here she had found an existence that allowed her to embrace beauty. There was a simple sort of joy in polishing silver until it gleamed. In the excess that she found around her. The luxury of making things beautiful just for the sake of it.

And somewhere in the back of her mind she knew that her people would scoff. That all of this excess and indulgence was somehow contrary to the life that they had forged for themselves, but she didn't care. She had been betrayed by them.

She had been betrayed by her mother. She had lived a life of austerity, so why couldn't she enjoy the clean, fine clothes she was able to put on every day. Nothing fancy, a simple uniform of black pants and a white shirt, but the fabric was not scratchy, and everything fit perfectly. She was never too cold, she was never too hot. She was no longer at the mercy of the elements.

For weeks, she avoided going outside at all. For why should she? She had lived outdoors for years. She was tired of it. She could stay inside where the man-made air could flow over her skin at whatever temperature she wished. Her room had its own controls.

Yes. She was bathing in luxury and loving it. The food that the staff at the palace ate was divine. It was the same thing that the King ate. She didn't mind that they were the leftovers off his table, not at all.

For the first time in her memory she went to bed, and her stomach was full. She was comfortable for the first time in years. She had forgotten what comfortable felt like. She was nearly oppressed by it. Because there wasn't a moment that went by that she didn't feel aware, that the fabric against her skin felt good; that she was not shivering; that she was not sweating.

And then there was the King. His presence. She felt it everywhere. Like a silken robe that she wore on top of everything else. She was simply aware of him, was in full wonder of him at all times. And she knew that the other maids—for they were maids, as easy as it was to try and think of her position as something a bit less servile—found her silly, that she was quite so in awe of the man.

But they didn't know what it was like to live as she had. And King Matteo was her savior.

"Are you finding everything here to your satisfaction?"

One day he stopped her in the ballroom, where she was shining the golden tiles of the floor on her knees, going over and over them until she could see her reflection in the brilliant surface.

"Yes," she said. "I find that I very much enjoy the work."

"My head of staff says that you always do more than is asked of you. But you spend a bit too much time on details for her liking. That you do not see the big picture."

Terror rang through Livia. "Oh. Well, I… The details make up the big picture, Your Majesty, with all due respect. You cannot have a glistening vista if the pieces that make it up do not sing."

"I agree with you, Livia," he said, the usage of her name sending a whisper of sensation over her body.

"But I can work differently if Mrs. Fernandez wishes."

"No. I wish for you to do whatever it is seems best. What sort of details interest you?"

"Oh. I don't know. I suppose it's just… The small ways the world is put together. I've always had an eye for detail. I've a very good memory. I'm quite fascinated by the way things come together, and I never forget. It has been useful to me in my life, living on the streets. I can remember faces, I can remember people, and avoid them if need be. I can picture an object in my mind, and try to figure out how I might re-create it with the things I have available to me. For I can simply see the way something comes together."

"Interesting. And when it comes to events? If you were to fill this ballroom with people, can you see how they would fill the space?"

"Yes." She looked around the room, this room that she

had learned from top to bottom in her time here. This room she had labored over. Every ornate piece of molding, every pane of crystal on the windows. Every tile. "Yes. I can see how you might furnish it for a function."

"Fascinating." He looked at her, with those too-keen eyes that made her feel seen. "What a strange little brain you have."

She looked away. "I've had nothing to do really but focus on the small moments for years. Thinking too far ahead when you live on the streets is only ever depressing. A long life of the same sort of thing looms ahead of you. So you must reduce it. You must take it down to small moments. If you don't, you'll go crazy. You have to find joy in small things because small things are all there is."

"Well," he said. "I can use someone to focus on such small things. For I must keep mine larger. I might find a *captain of small things* to be useful."

She brought herself forward to the present. It did no good to think about such things. Of those days, when she'd been his *Captain of Small Things*.

Her eyes filled with tears. It did no good to mourn Matteo. He had only ever found her useful. And that was it. He was scarred. Too scarred by his past to love. She knew that. And she was...

What was she?

She was a sad girl who had never truly grown out of her hero worship. Who had been given an extraordinary gift, and had focused on the wrong bit.

This was the takeaway. The ability to have this life. The ability to make something of herself. The ability to live in Paris if she chose. To be all that she could be.

This was her life and all that she carried inside of her. Matteo should never have been her focus.

Matteo.

She didn't even think of him as King Matteo. Hadn't for years.

Well, now she wouldn't think of him at all. She was free of him. Finally.

She took a resolute breath and turned, and then her heart stopped.

She had heard nothing. Not a sound. But there he was, as if spirited there by magic. Standing in her doorway, broad, imposing and angry.

He was wearing a black suit, cut perfectly to outline the muscular lines of his physique. Expertly tailored, practically sewn on to ensure that it fell along the perfect lines. She knew, because she had been in the room when he'd been fitted. Had watched as he stood there, bare chested with measuring tape going over each part of his perfect form.

Oh, that had been a study in torture.

That was when she had learned about desire, and desiring a man. In Matteo's untouchable, awe-inspiring presence. He was across a room from her but may as well have been in another galaxy.

Men, in her experience, had been sources of fear. But there, with his stunning male beauty on display, she'd learned that there was more to men.

And as a result, her feelings on the matter had taken root deep inside of her and refused to let go. She did not have an attraction to men in general.

She had one *to him*.

But she was in Paris. She should be able to find a rakish, disheveled-looking man who was dangerously handsome and looking for nothing more than a good time. A man who could teach her that any man's body would do so long as it conformed roughly with her aesthetic preference.

Thinking about that seemed laughable with Matteo standing there.

She blinked once, very hard, just to make sure that he wasn't a hallucination of some kind.

He was still there.

"Paris?" His lip curled. "I did not take you for a romantic, Mouse."

She crossed her arms and fixed him with her most formidable glare, over the rims of her glasses. "I didn't take you for a stalker, Matteo."

"Are we on a first-name basis again? It was all very *Your Majesty* the day you left."

She lifted her chin. "I no longer work for you. Not only that, I'm no longer in your country."

"Your country as well."

"Not really." She thought again of her people, who she endeavored to not think of overly much. But she had been. Had she ever truly been part of the country?

"You have emigrated, then?"

"Clearly." She sniffed. "What are you doing here?"

"I've come to collect you." He looked around the space, disdain writ large in his expression. "Your tantrum is unwelcome."

"Oh, it's not a tantrum. It's called moving, I see it."

"That is not how I see it." He walked farther into the room. "In fact, I take a dim view."

"I hate to break it to you, but you do not make the rules of the universe. You do not get to decide what I feel."

He leveled his disdainful gaze onto her now. "You are acting like a child."

"*I'm* acting like a child? You've chased me down across country lines to bother me more about a question I gave you a definitive answer to. Not even a question," she said, laughing in spite of herself. "You truly are an arrogant bastard."

"Not a bastard. Legitimate. Arrogant, maybe, but not a bastard."

"I meant in the colloquial sense."

His eyes went sharp. "What will it take?"

"What?"

"What will it take to get you to agree to be my bride? There is a price for everything," he said, taking a step toward her. "If you don't, I'll believe you're holding out for a better bargain…"

"I am doing no such thing," she said, horror stealing through her. "I am not in the market to trade my body for anything."

"I'm not suggesting you become the palace whore, Mouse, I am suggesting you become my wife."

"Queen Mouse, ruler of your schedule." She waved her hand in a grand gesture. "Grand Duchess of your daily routine. Chancellor of your meetings. How could I resist?"

"Mother of my children."

She felt like he had shot her in the stomach with an arrow. So deep and hard was the pain that ran through her body. It resonated between her thighs, around her heart. Oh, she wanted to kill him.

There were no weapons handy in this empty apartment.

This was a farce.

She had not anticipated him playing quite so personal. For she had thought that if anything, he would go straight into his brand of logic, as he was a big fan of his own reasoning. But no. He had brought up children.

Oh, she wished that she could...

"The fact you consider that an enticement says a lot about you."

"What life do you think you'll have here? You could be like everyone else, I suppose. But you're *not* like everyone else, and we both know it. You are gritty and strong, it's true. You are resilient. Brilliant. Far too brilliant for most men, don't you think? I do. I think most of them wouldn't know the first thing about how to handle you."

"Your concern for me and my future is touching. And you obviously think..."

"It has nothing to do with me. And everything to do with you. Don't you think that after everything, you're worthy of a position as Queen? What are your concerns, Livia?"

Her name. When he used her name she...

"My concerns?" She cut her own thoughts off.

"Come now, surely you must have them? You come from a very particular position in life. You must see flaws in the system that I don't. You're correct, I'm arrogant. I'm a product of my environment. Resolutely and deeply, and I have never pretended to be anything else. I am suited to my position. I spent all of my life training for it. But my father was not concerned with the plight of his people. He made it worse. He plunged them into poverty. And you were swept up in that. You well know it. So tell me, what things am I overlooking? What causes could you spearhead in your position that you would otherwise be unable to do? How much more would you contribute than a woman of a different sort?"

"Yes, you're very concerned about this now, but you made a card table bargain with Violet King's father for her to be your wife. She's the daughter of a rich man who has made herself even richer. Where was your concern for the sensibilities of the impoverished at that time?"

"I wanted her American sensibility. For they are a country with flaws to be certain, but the perspective of someone from a family of those who have been self-made... I thought it would be useful. But you... You, Livia, are even more self-made."

"I was plucked off the street by your royal hand, Matteo. Surely you don't truly mean that I made myself."

"I think you have. Because it was you who caught my attention, you who moved through the ranks of staff at alarming speed. You and your brain that inspired me to promote you to assistant. Yes, Livia, I would say that you are self-made."

"Careful, if you keep referring to me by my name, I might start to think that you see me as a *woman* and not a *rodent*."

He frowned, staring at her for a long moment. "Is that what you think? That I see you as a rodent?"

"You call me *Mouse*." Such a love/hate relationship she had with that too. For he had nicknames for no one else. No one but her. He had casual endearments for his women. He called his brother by his name.

Only *she* had a nickname.

It was just an ignominious one.

"I'm the lion," he said, his voice soft but firm. "Didn't you know?"

Something hollowed out in the pit of her stomach,

and this was where she despised herself. Because she was truly unable to resist that. Unable to stand firm in the face of such naked flattery.

His attempt to spin the interactions between them going back years. That somehow she meant something to him, mattered to him. Oh, she wanted to throttle him.

"Get out of my house, Matteo. For the first time in our interaction, I am not under your roof. And I do not need you."

"But Monte Blanco needs you."

"That's too bad. Because I need to become something else."

"Give me a chance." And for the first time in her memory…his arrogance broke and he had truly asked for something.

"Give you a chance to what?"

"Prove what manner of husband I will be to you."

And then, he closed the space between them, wrapped his hand around her neck and drew her forward. Then his lips came crashing down onto hers.

CHAPTER THREE

HER MOUTH WAS a revelation, and on some level, he must have always known that it would be. No matter how he denied it. Told himself it would be a base, treacherous act, he had known. For he had been fascinated by that mouth and the many moods that she could convey with a twitch of the corner of those lips. Amusement, disdain, irritation. He had learned to read that mouth, and now he was tasting it.

Feasting upon it.

Livia.

Livia, the one woman who had ever…

It brought his mind back. To that night.

Just before she had become his assistant. Still, then, she had been nothing more than a mere palace employee. And certainly he found excuses for their paths to cross, because he quite enjoyed speaking to the bright little creature, but they had not seen each other daily.

Until then.

He was in pain. Ferocious pain. He had never felt such pain. It was like knives being buried beneath his skin. And it didn't take long for him to realize that he was dreaming, to begin to try and push himself up into consciousness, from beneath the rolling waves of his sub-conscious.

Pain was all in his head. He knew that.

Unfortunately, the doctor that he had spoken to about the subject also made it very clear that pain—even when there was not a clear physical cause for it—was *real* because it always originated in the mind, and the body responded however it was instructed to.

And he felt it, keenly, when he had these episodes. A return to the torture that his father had subjected him to as a boy.

And when he awoke, he could feel a presence in the room. And he did not think. He did not bother to figure out the identity of the person in the room. No. He simply did what a warrior must do.

He attacked.

He launched himself from the bed, stark naked, as he always slept, and pushed forward to grab hold of the enemy. The enemy was soft and pale and small. The enemy did not break beneath his hands, but rather stood rigid, not running, not crying out, not begging for his life.

And then, it became clear that the enemy...was a woman.

"Your Majesty."

He knew that voice. He knew that voice well. Soft and measured, and no different than if he had asked her to report on the state of the palace.

"Livia."

"Your Majesty, I heard your distress. I was wandering the halls because I couldn't sleep and I..." Her breath pitched sharply. "If you wouldn't mind, could you remove your hand from my throat?"

He hadn't realized he'd been holding her thus. He released his hold on her and took a stumbling step backward, his chest heaving. "You do not have permission to enter my chamber."

"I know. And I apologize. It's only that I was cleaning. I know there's a big event tomorrow, and I didn't think that... There were things that I thought could be amended. And so I set out to do so. I was on my way to my room when I heard you. Are you all right?"

"Yes," he said, gritting his teeth. For the effects of the pain lingered. Psychosomatic though it might be, it burned.

"Can I get you anything?"

"Coffee," he said. He could send her away, but why? She had asked if he needed anything. And he would take her service. He was the King, after all, and he was in pain.

"Of course."

She scurried from the room, and he half expected her not to return. But she did. She was wearing her palace uniform, as if it was still the middle of the day, and not gone one thirty in the morning.

She turned the light on in the room. He was sitting with a sheet covering his lap, but he saw her eyes widen fractionally. She took two steps forward.

She was not trembling. Rather she met his gaze full on. But she did stop short of the bed.

"I will not harm you."

"Of course," she said, closing the distance and handing him his coffee.

"You did not make one for yourself?"

"I do not avail myself of the pantry outside of the hours the staff eat, sire."

"You should. You must. You're still far too thin."

Irritation twitched in her brows. "Forgive me, Your Majesty, but do you always pass judgment upon the physical form of those who work for you?"

"No," he said, "but I do find that I'm concerned for yours. You were quite poorly when I found you, I cannot forget it."

"No more poorly than I had been in any of the preceding years. I survived." She lifted a shoulder. "As one does."

"Unless one doesn't."

She frowned slightly as if considering this. "True. But I did. And continue to do so."

"Admirable."

"You have also survived," she said. And then she did something wholly unexpected. She sat down on the bed, not close enough to him that he would think she was making an attempt at seduction, but down at the end of it. A strange show of solidarity, he felt. Oddly unexpected and… He could not think of the last time a woman, a person, had sat with him in this way. Certainly not in a state of undress. Certainly not in the middle of the night.

When he was naked with women in his room, it was not to chat.

"I have nightmares," she said softly. "There were nights on the street when I did not think I would live to see morning. I slept with a knife in my hand, carefully concealed for I had to be ready. To wake up and stab an attacker if the moment presented itself."

His chest went tight. "And did it?"

"Oh, on several occasions. When the weather gets warm, things get difficult. When it is cold, people hunker down, go to their caves, certainly they avoid accosting women in alleyways. But summer… It was beautiful, and in many ways a more comfortable time to be homeless in Monte Blanco. For the weather here can be glorious. But… Yes, then you must worry about an increase of marauders in the street. And all that they might try and take from you."

"Did you ever consider living away from the city streets?"

She looked away from him, picking at thread on the blanket. "I did at times. But there you have the pressing concerns of wolves, bears. And my weapons, small as they are, are more effective against men. Men are much softer." She grinned, wide enough that he could see it through the darkness. "Though, I find wolves and bears to be less predatory, of a general rule."

"You do not have a high opinion of men."

"I didn't. But I had yet to see much of the good in them. You have given me something else to consider. I think you should be quite proud of that."

He didn't quite know how to react to that. It was a strange sort of compliment issued by such a low creature. He found that it warmed him. For it mattered, that he was not his father. For that man had been a monster; a man with no compassion in his soul.

And he had done his best to bleed Matteo of it as well.

Yet sitting across from Livia seemed to indicate that he perhaps had not succeeded. She was the first real indicator that perhaps his father had not had a complete victory in the war over Matteo's soul. Yes, he had purpose to be a fair leader, a good leader. One thing he had never understood about his father, though, was his comfort in being king of the trash heap. Would it not have been better to be king of a country with a thriving economy, with a reputation for caring for its citizens? Why hoard all the gold in your castle? Wasn't it better to behave as if the citizens of this nation mattered? He had never been convinced of his own goodness, he had merely determined, logically, to be different. Livia made him feel that perhaps there was more, and he wanted to hold to it.

"Tell me what you dream of."

"It is not a good bedtime story."

"Well, neither of us are sleeping. And neither of us are children. I wonder if I ever was one."

"I am the same," he said.

It was a strange thing, for he and his brother had both been raised by the same man, but they had been so very separate. Javier had endured his own form of pain brought about when he'd realized what a monster their father was. Matteo had always known. He had never been fighting the good fight of the king before him. It was the reason he had kept a wedge between himself and his brother, until Javier became suspicious of different war tactics he'd been asked to take, and his illusion of his father had been shattered.

Matteo never held such illusions. But Matteo had been the heir and his father had not been able to contain his cruelty in Matteo's presence. No. He had appealed to what he had seen as Javier's sense of honor, and had lied to him about the missions he led the military on. But with Matteo... He had sought to twist him in the same ways he was, and when Matteo did not comply, he was forced to endure physical torture.

His father had been so certain he could train into

Matteo the kind of ruthlessness that he possessed. But Matteo simply did not yield. He *would* not.

In his dreams, though, sometimes he did.

"I dream of weakness," he said.

"Whose weakness?" she asked.

"My own. I have…withstood torture." He leaned backward, so that she could see the knife slashes that went across his chest. Then he turned his shoulder, so she could see where he had tasted the sting of the whip on his back. "I did not yield. I did not break. But in my dreams, sometimes I cry out. Sometimes, I am broken. And that is the final indignity."

"I'm sorry."

"There is no reason to be sorry for me." He inclined his head. "I am a king, after all."

She nodded. "But a man as well. I can see that in your scars."

"Reinforcing, perhaps, your theory that men are flawed."

"Oh, I know they are. But you've made me think, maybe they're good too."

"And what if I'm only good to further my own selfish ends?"

She was silent for a moment. "Do you intend to hurt people?"

"No."

"Then perhaps it doesn't matter why. I have lived very selfishly for a great many years. Because I had to survive."

He nodded slowly. "I'm familiar with survival."

"Isn't it a wonderful thing, to live for more than that?"

He did not know how she remained so bright. How she had so much optimism.

"I never thought of it as such."

"I do. Every day. I think that's the real reason I get lost in the details of this place. It's wonderful to want something other than to not feel quite so cold. To not feel quite so hungry."

"Do you dream still?"

"Yes. That is something that's not quite fair, isn't it? The dreams are still there. But at least we both sleep in safety."

"Indeed we do."

And he thought of her then as a mouse, not because she was small, but because she was as the tiny creature who fearlessly approached the lion, and perhaps was the only one who could say what needed to be said or do what needed to be done. No one else had ever spoken to him quite like this. Perhaps because she was a street urchin who was so outside of everything that held the kingdom together, she was quite so effective. All he knew was that he had never quite felt as if another person had understood him so keenly. And there was something healing about sitting across from her, and seeing how she sat with strength. How she had not responded to him with fear. That this creature, so filled with an appreciation for life that he did not feel, so placid in the face of danger, but never truly placid. She made him feel like he could see the best outcome for a person who had been through such trauma. And he didn't think he would ever feel as she did. But he could see the merit of one such as her, a person who had endured all she had, and still had emotion. Still had hope...

He could see how it might be valuable to use her.

As the heart that beat outside of his body, for there was none to be found within.

* * *

Her lips brought him back to the moment, a shocked sound escaping her mouth. It was soft and sweet, and filled with desire.

Yes. He had known it then, and he knew it now. That she could be his heart. She could be the one who led with all that fierce conviction that she had.

She was the only one who could be his Queen, and if he had to seduce her to see it done, then he would.

Women enjoyed his body. He was not conceited about it, but neither was he falsely humble when it came to the assets that he possessed that women enjoyed. Why should he be? And so he kissed her. Kissed her until she cried out and stepped back. "What was that?"

"If you're going to be my Queen and produce my heirs, we do need to know if we are compatible on that score."

He was honestly shocked as the desire that he felt for her poured through his veins.

He had not expected to feel this deep, low pull of attraction, not for his mouse. But then, she had always had a way to the core of him. She had always seemed to know him. And perhaps there was something in that. Perhaps in bed they would know each other in a way that proved pleasurable for them both.

"What makes you think you can manipulate me with sex?"

"Perhaps I'm not trying to manipulate you, Livia."

"No, I think you are. You're a man who does not like to be told no. And so, you chased me down, not because you want me half so badly, but because you cannot stand that I refused you."

"That isn't true."

"Don't argue with me. Do you know… I knew you were going to propose to me."

That stopped him. Cold.

"You… You knew?"

"Oh, yes. From the day that your engagement to Violet King was broken off I knew that you would be asking me next. Because I am practical, and I am sensible, and you want nothing less than what you want at all times, Matteo."

"I am a king, I'm not predictable."

"Maybe not to other people, but you are to me. This isn't about me. It's about having your way."

Anger burned through his veins. "Perhaps you have forgotten. Forgotten what I really come from. Forgotten who I really am. I am a man who has had no luxury of ruling with his heart, for I know how deceitfully wicked a person's heart can be. Perhaps you don't remember."

"Our late-night conversations about torture?" Her voice was quiet then. "Of course I do."

"Then before you write me off as an arrogant ass, perhaps you should recall that reality. I will not apologize. I will not apologize for seeking to do what is best for my country, and I will not apologize for limiting the danger that I posed to the world by cutting out my own heart."

"You have never been a danger to the world…"

"Of course I have been. You know nothing, Livia. Nothing of me. Not really."

"Arrogant even in your self-loathing. That you think so highly of yourself that you suppose you could mete destruction out upon the planet."

"You forget that I grew up with a monster. The only arrogance is believing that you are incapable of turning into such a thing yourself. That kind of arrogance is dangerous."

"All right. If that's what you need to believe."

"Let me take you to dinner."

The look she gave him was mean. "We go to dinner all the time."

"No. We don't." He looked around the space. "Where are you staying?"

"I'm currently in a hotel down the road, though I'm sure you know that."

He looked at her. "Of course I do."

"Then why did you bother asking?"

"I can't win. I'm either too arrogant or not arrogant enough."

"How tragic for you," she said, her tone arid.

"I will have clothes and instruction sent to the hotel."

"By whom?"

He smiled. "By me."

CHAPTER FOUR

LIVIA WAS STILL reeling over the kiss, and brooding over his actions, when there was a knock on the door to her suite. She had only had two hours' reprieve from him, and lying flat on her back in a dark room with a lavender sachet over her eyes hadn't been enough to quell her disquiet.

She had never been kissed before.

She hoped he didn't know that.

She would be *furious* if he did.

Absolutely *livid*.

Of course, she had no idea when he would think that she had had a sexual interaction of any kind. Her entire life had been devoted to him. And before that, her entire life had been devoted to her own survival.

She was in a foul disposition.

She stomped to the door and jerked it open. And there he was, looking downright disreputable. He was not dressed in a formal suit as he had been earlier. Rather, he was wearing a white shirt and no tie, the top button undone.

She had seen him nearly naked before.

And in fact, that night when she had gone into his room... He had been naked when he'd grabbed hold of her, but the room had been dark, so it had limited what she had been able to see. Still, over the years she had seen him in a bathing suit, in various states of half-dress as he wandered around, and she never got used to it.

His body was stunning.

A finely honed weapon that made a hard pulse go off between her thighs. And then there were his scars… She couldn't see them and not think of that night. The night when she had found out the two of them, however different they were, might have more in common than she had with anyone else she'd ever met. And it was an impossible sort of thing, to believe that someone like her could be so like a king. But she felt as if she was. She felt as if they recognized one another. Though she did not feel particularly like they recognized one another now. Mostly, she just felt like he was being an ass.

"I brought you a dress."

"I have plenty of dresses."

Of course, she had left all but two back at the palace, and they were all black.

"I do not wish for you to wear your typical garb. You are not to blend into the background. You are going out with me as a date. Not as an assistant."

"I…" As she had quit as his assistant, she had very little to say on the subject. It was very hard to argue. "Why?"

"You know why."

"You're infuriating."

She took the bag from him and stalked into the bathroom. From there, she unzipped the bag, and frowned. The gown was red. Bright red. She never wore things that drew so much attention to her. When she pulled it out of the bag she saw that the fabric was slinky. Silky.

It would spill over her curves like water and offer barely any coverage.

She slipped the dress over her slight curves and looked in the mirror. It was a simple dress. Barely more than a slip, with a V-neck and thin straps. The cut was basic, skimming close to her shape, and she had to ask herself why in the world she had put it on. Her own worried expression looked back at her. She reached into her makeup bag and pulled out a tube of red lipstick she had never used before. She didn't really wear makeup.

She swiped the crimson color over her mouth, and then dusted a bit of glowing sparkle over her cheeks. She looked... Well, as ever like Livia.

She would not wear her glasses out tonight, however. She took them off, and put them in their case, then put her contacts in. She didn't often do that; she found she liked her glasses, they provided a barrier between herself and the rest of the world, and sometimes that felt good. Sometimes it felt necessary.

Her stomach twisted as she put her hand on the doorknob. And she was reminded painfully of the day when he had asked her a different question altogether...

She'd been at the palace for two years. For the first time in her memory, she'd celebrated birthdays. She had done her best to forget when her birthday was, so when Mrs. Fernandez had asked, it had been nearly painful to come up with the answer. But she had cakes and gifts, and it was such a wonderful thing to be surrounded by friends.

It was her birthday, and King Matteo had asked to see her.

A shimmering sensation radiated in her stomach. She was certain she was in love with him. It was a foolish thing, and she did know it. He was far too high above her for it to become anything, but oh, he made her soul sing. He had asked her to meet him in the garden. She was already dressed up, because she had her birthday dinner. With her wages, she had bought herself a pretty red dress and she hoped that he would like it.

She was not a girl anymore, after all. She was a woman now.

She had filled out a bit, both due to age and easy access to food, and she looked much nicer, much healthier.

She pinched her cheeks a little bit for good measure before stepping out of the palace, and into the gardens. It was a warm evening. Summer. She had hated summer once. But she loved it now. "There you are," he said. "Little Mouse."

He had taken to calling her that, and she didn't really know why. He didn't have nicknames for anyone else, so it felt... It felt almost special. He did pay special attention to her; it had been noticed by the other members of staff. She did not live with them in their quarters; rather, she kept her room in the palace. It caused tension between her and a couple of the girls, but everybody else seemed all right with it. Anyway, they were wrong about him. He wasn't keeping her to use her.

Would it be such a bad thing if he did?

Of course, she did not want to be any man's mistress. Nor did she want to be a whore.

But you could never be a king's wife...

"Yes."

She waited for him to say something about her dress. To wish her a happy birthday. He did neither.

"I have something to ask you," he said.

Her heart leapt up her throat, lodging itself there.

He was a dark, imposing figure out there in the night, backed by a black sky shot through with stars. She used to sleep under a sky like that. The vastness of night had been frightening for her, never beautiful.

With Matteo in front of it, it felt…different.

He brought the vastness down to earth. Embodied it. She could no more tame or touch him than she could one of those stars but… But he made her feel safe, too.

He made her want.

"Yes?"

"Livia," he said, his tone going grave. "I would like for you to be my personal assistant."

Her heart stalled, then started again, slamming inelegantly against her breastbone. "Oh?"

"Yes. You see, I've been watching you, and I particularly appreciate your attention to detail. Plus… I don't know. You… You see things. It's not just details. You see things, and I need someone in my sphere who does. I need someone strong. Strong of opinion, strong in action. You will be my assistant, yes, but also my…advisor of sorts."

"Oh."

It was an incredibly flattering thing. But it was very far away from what she had hoped, for one brief moment, he might ask.

"I will of course pay you handsomely."

He named the salary that nearly made her double over.

"I don't understand what I've done to merit this kind of favor."

"Just being who you are."

And that was the shiniest, most glittering thing anyone had ever said to her and she took it and she held it close. And it wouldn't matter what else came after that.

"Now, I have sort of an unpleasant job for you, for your first task."

"Yes?" she asked tentatively.

She had no idea what he would classify as an unpleasant task, and frankly, it was a little bit disconcerting.

"I need you to select a farewell gift to my current mistress. Have it sent to her along with a note. Say something kind, but firm."

"I… You want me to…break up with a woman for you?"

"Don't be silly. It's a business arrangement, nothing half so feeling as 'breaking up' with. I never stay with a woman for longer than a few weeks. There's simply no way around it. If I stayed with someone for too long then I would have to start taking them to events, and I've yet to meet anyone who I would consider to be Queen. I have a prearranged marriage, you see."

And that was when all of her fantasies well and truly turned to dust. And that glittering thing she held close to her chest turned into nothing more than garden-variety craft glitter, which mattered not at all, and merely got all over everything and couldn't be gotten rid of, making a mockery of that feeling she had only a moment before.

"That makes sense. Of course, all of this has already been decided."

"By myself," he said. "An arrangement I made with an American businessman many years ago."

"I see. Well…" She knew she had a decision to make. She could feel sad that none of this was about her. That it wasn't about her birthday or her dress. That he was going to marry another woman. Or she could recognize the opportunity she'd been given for what it was, and grab hold of it.

"I'll take the job."

He smiled, and her heart leapt. She was a fool for him, and now she was about to be around him even more often than she already was.

"I didn't think you would ever refuse."

Oh, yes, she had been disappointed by Matteo while wearing a red dress before. And she could recall his confidence then, that she would simply go along with what he wanted. That she would comply with his commands.

She wanted to think she wasn't half so foolish now. Wanted to think that she had him completely and totally nailed down, and because of that, that there was no mystique left to him; and if there was no mystique left to him, he could no longer hurt her. But here she was, in a red dress, because he'd commanded it. With ferocity, she opened the door to the bathroom and walked out into the seating area of the hotel room, feeling defiant.

"Do I meet with your approval, Your Majesty?"

But there was something in his eyes then, entirely different than that night in the garden, that night when he'd asked her to become his assistant. There was heat there, and she felt an answering longing unfurl in her stomach. Of course, longing after Matteo was nothing new.

He kissed me.

Something shimmered low inside of her, that glitter that she would like to think had faded away years ago. But it hadn't. And this time it was different, because this time he'd kissed her. At least this time he was actually asking her to be his wife. It was just...

She wasn't that desperate street urchin anymore, and she didn't like to be made to feel like her. She didn't like remembering how weak he could make her. She wanted him; but he was a man who didn't love.

"Shall we go to dinner, *querida*?"

He had never called her *that* before.

"Don't call me that."

"It is, I think, an elevated term."

She shook her head. "Call me Mouse. That's what I am to you."

"Don't you think we should move on to something more intimate?"

"I don't. I don't, because at least Mouse is honest. It's how you see me. It's what I am to you. A tiny creature you think you can put in your pocket and keep with you at all times. That's what you think I am. I'm not your *beloved*. All those blonde amazons you prance around with, *they're* beloved. For a night or two. I would have you be honest with me, at least. If you manipulate me, I'll know."

"And what?"

Ferocity boiled over inside of her. "I'll bite you. At the very least."

He took a step toward her, his dark eyes blazing with intent. "And what if I told you, Mouse, that I would not mind so terribly being bitten?"

"Don't tempt me, Matteo," she said, doing her best to raise her eyes and meet his.

Staring into those obsidian eyes now, she asked herself when that girlish love inside of her had heated to such an intensity, only to be cooled in such a way that it turned it into a hard obsidian.

Oh, it was still there. She couldn't deny her feelings for him. No matter that she knew better, it was just that she had learned to protect herself. It was the years as his personal assistant.

They had been instructive about the manner of man he was. He could put on a smile with the best of them—Livia had been the one to teach him to do so—but he was not truly a civilized man, and she knew it. She'd seen it. He smiled at all those women who passed through his life, passed through his bed, but it never reached his eyes. He was missing a heart, where other men had one. And she would do well to remember that.

"Come on, *Mouse*," he said, putting emphasis on the name. "Let us go to dinner."

CHAPTER FIVE

LIVIA WAS A VISION. On some level, he had always known she could be. Her hair was not demonstrably different than normal, tucked back in a low roll, with little wisps framing her face. But her glasses were gone, and he could see the stunning violet of her eyes with greater clarity. And that mouth...

Her mouth was a problem. Had been for years.

He had never seen it painted red.

It brought to mind a host of thoughts, none of which Livia would find appropriate. All the places on his body she might leave smudges of that lipstick behind. The way that her mouth might look if it was wrapped around his...

He shuttered those thoughts and put his hand low on her back. "Come," he said, "our car awaits."

Seduction was one thing, but he did not wish to overwhelm Livia with the depth of his depravity. He did not wish to overwhelm anyone with it. For he knew that a man such as himself had to remain in control at all times. A woman like Livia would demand it. She had lived through hell enough as it was.

One of the many reasons the attraction he felt for her was anathema to him for the last several years. She was vulnerable, and she was in his protection.

There had never been a moment where he might have found it fine to use her and discard her. Not after everything.

Proposing to make her his Queen was a different proposition.

She came with him willingly, but he could sense the reticence in every line of her frame. She was quite an elegant creature, really. He had appreciated a great many things about her, but he wasn't certain if he had ever appreciated that elegance. For she was small, and he tended to prefer tall women as he was quite a tall man himself. But every bit of delicacy that Livia possessed came together to create smooth, proud lines that shifted with grace as they made their way down to the lobby of the hotel.

The sports car he brought with him on his private jet from Monte Blanco was there, waiting in the front of the building for him. Livia looked at it, then looked at him. "Not our typical mode of transportation."

It was true. Typically, if he and Livia traveled together, he had a driver, and the two of them sat in the back of a limousine. This car was reserved for personal outings, and he and Livia were never on personal outings.

"No indeed. But I thought you might enjoy it."

"Some," she said, the sound an amusing one.

"What does that mean?"

"I only wonder why you think I would enjoy it."

"Why don't you get in." He led her to the passenger side, and opened the door for her. Then he got in on his own side and turned the engine over, the purring sound that filled the car one that never failed to send a thrill through his veins. He was a king, a ruler who had to keep his mind present at all times, and guard against the invading darkness left behind by his father. But when he drove, he was merely a man.

"I thought you might like it, Livia, because I believe that you secretly wish to go fast."

"Do you?"

"Have you ever ridden in a car such as this?"

She arched her brow. "I think you know I have not."

"Then trust me."

When he accelerated, he noticed her shift beside him, and he nearly smiled. The vibration of the car was sexual, it was undeniable. The way that the tires clung to the road as he maneuvered over the winding streets that led out of the city.

"And where are we going?"

"I see that you thought we might take advantage of one of the fine eateries in Paris, and while there are many to choose from, there is a private restaurant out here in the hills that I prefer. One that will allow us to indulge ourselves with a bit more privacy."

"Thus excluding you from the prying lenses of the paparazzi?"

"Not at all. They always know where to look for interesting photographs, don't you agree?"

"I suppose."

They continued the drive, the pastoral scenery blending into a green blur, and he focused on nothing more than the way Livia moved beside him, and the sound she made as he accelerated.

"You do like it," he said.

"That isn't fair," she said. "How could you possibly know I would like a sports car?"

"Because beneath all of your reserve, Livia, I do believe the heart of an adventuress exists."

"I've experienced a real fight for survival. I'm unmoved by these games played to feel like it."

"You are not, though. You are not unmoved by luxury, nor are you unmoved by a thrill, much as you would like to pretend you are."

"I don't see…"

"You are not the only one of us who knows the other. And I suspect you find that quite bothersome."

"Well."

"Well indeed."

Matteo felt thrilled that he had finally managed to silence the creature. Because of course he knew what Livia secretly wanted, down in her soul. She might pretend to be practical, but he knew otherwise.

He had seen her yearn for better things. For bigger things. He had watched her grow in confidence over the years. *He knew her.* Better than he knew anyone else. No point pretending otherwise.

Too soon they arrived at the château that would serve as a private dining area for them tonight. There were a limited amount of guests allowed in the château at any given time and, of course, heaven and earth had been moved to make way for him when he had indicated that he wanted to eat there. They served some of the finest food in France here, and given the culinary delights available in the country, that was saying quite a lot.

They pulled up to the front, and there was already a man waiting to handle the practicalities of parking the vehicle. Matteo himself went around to Livia's side of the car and opened the door for her, for he would not allow another man to attend to her in any way. Then he took her arm, and led her up the grand, cobbled walk into the ancient, stucco château. It was dimly lit inside,

rustic wooden tables set about in the front of the building as they went through darkened halls, to a room that
afforded maximum privacy. In there was an intimate
wooden table, laid out for two. The chairs were clustered
together, but there was ample space on the tabletop, for
they would be served a grand feast, and he knew that
the waiters made a habit of not interrupting, to the best
of their ability.

"This is beautiful," she said softly.

She could not be cynical with him, which made him
all the more pleased, because when Livia could not affect disinterest, he knew he had won. At least one small
victory. She had liked the car, too, and she could not pretend with that either.

"Have a seat," he said, pulling the chair out for her.
She complied, and he sat across from her.

There was something about the moment that brought
him to another time, and as the food began to come out
on ample trays—beautiful fruits and cheeses, homemade
baguettes, local honeycomb and house-made pickled
vegetables—it all faded away.

"The biggest issue that you have," Livia said, looking
at him earnestly through her round, gold spectacles, "is
that you come across as a bit of the beast. And if not a
beast, then disinterested."

"That's because I find most people uninteresting," he
said, leaning back in his chair at his desk.

Livia paced the length of the floor in front of him.

"But you want to begin to truly open up the country.
To change things from the way that your father ran them,
and that's going to require that you become a different

sort of diplomat. And *that* is going to require that you become diplomatic."

"I suppose. But I am royal, is not my presence enough to sufficiently engage those around me?"

Livia rolled her eyes. She rolled her eyes at *him*. As if he was not her boss and her king.

"You will have to attempt to be a human being, Matteo."

"I must be human enough, for you have just called me by my first name."

Her cheeks colored. "Forgive me. I forgot myself."

"You forget yourself quite often, I find. Constant demands from someone in my employ, when it should work the other way around."

"Trust me on this, if you can trust nothing else. Trust that my perspective is from one who is not Royal. People need to see some humanity. When you go out and meet them, you need to be engaged. You need to… Smile. You need to at least pretend to listen to what they're saying."

"I'm sorry," he said. "I wasn't listening."

"You are maddening," she said. "Absolutely maddening."

"All right. I was teasing you. And I apologize. I will make an attempt at this civility that you speak of."

"If you really want to separate yourself from your father, it's not enough that you have a good heart."

He felt a strange, painful feeling squeezing around his chest. "I do not have a good heart. I don't have one at all. I find that is the best way to make sure you remain uncorrupted."

"You rescued me. You can't be all bad."

"I'm not," he said. "As I said. If you have no heart at all, then you cannot love power either. You cannot love yourself quite so much that you would put your needs above those of your own people. That is what my father did, Livia. As you know."

"Then what drives you? What makes you decide to do the right thing?"

"The knowledge that doing the wrong thing causes more damage than you could possibly imagine. The knowledge that the alternative is a wasteland of pain for all involved."

"Then get very used to figuring out a way to convey what I know about you. Which is that you have integrity. Will you agree with that?"

He inclined his head. "I will agree."

"It is not enough to simply act that way in private. You must actually show that you're a good leader."

"Are the people not fed? Are there not jobs? Have they not ceased disappearing from their beds for daring to disagree with me, or uttering a whisper of malcontentedness?"

"Of course they have. But people forget, their memories are short. The more comfortable you become, the smaller your complaints must be in order for you to feel badly. It does not take much to forget where you came from. To forget how truly bad things were. Take it from me. I used to sleep on the streets, and now sometimes I cannot sleep if I get tangled in the soft sheets on my bed."

The vision of Livia, tangled in her sheets, created a strange sensation low in his stomach. His assistant was growing more and more beautiful, it was difficult to deny. She was much different than the usual women he preferred, it was true, but there was a sort of delicate, bookish charm to her that he found fresh and appealing.

But he could also never forget where she had come from and the way they had come to know each other. He could not forget the position that put the two of them in.

He was engaged to be married. Or rather, an arrangement existed. Violet King would be his bride someday, and it had nothing to do with his feelings toward her at all, but simply what she might add to the kingdom. When he had made the arrangement with her father, it had only been out of consideration for what was best for the kingdom.

And one thing he could never do to Livia was…

He would never touch her. Beautiful or not.

He was pleased, though, to see how she had grown with health. To see her confidence. He found her a compelling, intriguing creature. This, he could not deny.

"Teach me, then."

"All right. Pick a topic that you're not interested in at all."

"There are so many," he said.

"All right," she said. "I will pick one for you. I have found that collecting hobbies is a wonderful side effect of having both free time, money and a lack of fear over your surroundings. I have begun doing needlepoint. I find something very soothing about it."

He could feel his eyes beginning to glaze over. He could think of nothing that he cared less about. Though there was something striking about the way her eyes lit up when she talked about it. Something about her joy that made him *feel*… Well, he did feel.

"Don't you think?"

That was when he realized he had not been listening.

"Of course," he said.

"You think there is nothing quite so diverting as

watching golden thread slide through the muslin on a sampler?"

"Well, I imagine for you," he said.

"You weren't listening."

"No. But it's very boring."

She sighed. "And that is what you must not do."

"Livia," he said. "I appreciate that it means something to you."

"Okay," she said. "That's very good. So when you find yourself drifting off, perhaps you can find it in you to appreciate that."

And for the next hour, he did endeavor to listen. And when he found it difficult, he focused on what it meant to her.

"So much better," she said. "Now tell me about something you like."

"Archery?"

She laughed. "Archery. All right. Why do you like it?"

"I like the thrill of the sound of the arrow flying through the air, knowing it will land at the center of its target. Knowing that I never fail. There is something intoxicating about seeing that. Seeing it and knowing it is so."

"Arrogant, but human."

"I am not a human, though, I am a king."

"It isn't about what you think. It's about what people will think."

"Why do you feel this so strongly?"

"Because I know what it's like, to be vulnerable. To be on the street. The idea that somebody strong is in charge, someone who might actually care for you, who has the heart of someone who would pull a girl from the street, and give her a new life… Oh, knowing that would have given me something to hope for. You don't think it matters—emotion, connection—but it does. Even if you cannot feel it, if you could show it, that would make all the difference in the world to the people who struggle."

"You are not wrong."

"Is that your way of saying I'm right?"

"I wouldn't go that far."

"Well, however far you would go... I'm glad that we could come to an agreement."

"I'm going to need you to come with me to this event. In fact, I believe you should come to all of them. Monitor my performance. Tell me how I'm doing."

"You want me to give you notes?"

"Yes," he said, "I believe I do. I think I would find it beneficial."

"Well...if you would find it beneficial...then...all right."

"Make sure you wear black, you will match the rest of the staff."

Those parting words echoed in Matteo's mind. He had truly said that to her. That she made sure she blended in. The problem with Livia was that, in his opinion, she didn't blend in easily. She was a distinct-looking woman, and she had been staff. So, it had been fair enough. Right now, she was not blending at all. She was eating bread and butter and the absolute joy in her expression was impossible to downplay.

"You are not so unhappy with me now," he said.

"Well, it's impossible to be unhappy when you're eating bread and butter."

"Is it?"

"Remember when you told me that I could make use of the pantry whenever I wanted?"

"Yes," he said. For he remembered every detail about that night. About their first real conversation. When he had been naked and drinking coffee, and she had perched herself on the end of the bed.

"It was a revelation. To be able to have food whenever I wanted. My life was never like that. Growing up, I…" She hesitated.

"Tell me," he said. For he didn't know anything about how she had grown up. He knew about her time on the streets, but not how she came to be there. Not even really how long she had been there. They had spoken of that part of her life, but not the time before it, and he'd always had the sense that it was the before that was all too painful for her to cope with.

"My family were…"

"I thought you said you had no family. No family name."

She shook her head. "Well, I didn't. After I was left on the street, I had no family. And anyway, my people do not have family names."

"You are one of the people who live in the old ways," he said.

"Yes."

There were those who had resisted the move to modern technology in Monte Blanco. Those who had resisted the monarchy. Who had preferred to live as they always had, in large extended family groups governed by themselves. His father had done everything he could to stamp them out. For in these groups there were often whispers of revolution. And anything his father could not control, he hated. These people were beholden only to each other. They cultivated their own ground, they made their own economy. It left them difficult to govern.

A fact that did not bother Matteo, but they had been heavily persecuted under the rule of his father.

"You never said."

"I do not like to think of it, for what is more important to those of the old ways than family? It is who we are supposed to be governed by, in allegiance to. Above the King. But I was left. So..."

"Yes," he said.

"Anyway. There was not ample food. Not always. It was finite, and there was not really currency exchange. We bartered and traded with others like us, and we grew our own food, farmed our own animals and hunted the woods. Feast or famine, that's how it was. But there was no refrigerator to simply open and find within it food of infinite varieties. Still, it was luxurious compared to the time I spent on the streets. I have never forgotten that. That moment when... Food, whenever I wanted it, whatever I wanted, simply became available to me. I love food." She laughed, the sound expanding something in his chest. "I really do. I love bread."

"I am pleased to give it to you." And he found it was true.

He had given women diamonds and been on the receiving end of less gratitude. She still thanked him for bread.

It made him want to give her more. To shower her with things that he never had. Their relationship had always been...different. She had never been strictly his employee. But of course not, for she had been his advisor in many ways. He felt that all kings needed one, someone that they had some sort of accountability to.

And while his brother served, in part, that position, what he had always liked about Livia was that she was not part of their toxic upbringing. She came at things from an entirely different perspective than they did, and he found that to be beneficial. But the fact remained that theirs had been a professional relationship. Sort of. They had not sat like this, and he had not personally given her things. Not personally chosen a dress for her or sat in an intimate dining situation. They talked always in his office, with the exception of that night. And with the exception of their trip only a month ago...

"Think of all the other things I could give you access to," he said. "Think of that change. Being able to open the fridge and have food whenever. Being Queen would give you doors you could open that you cannot possibly imagine just sitting here now."

"You act as if I might be swayed by the offer of power."

"Not power. Opportunity. I know you well enough to know power does not appeal." The rest of the meal came, and it was as divine as what had preceded it, and they quit talking, just sitting together in a companionable silence while they ate.

When they were through, knowing that there would be coffee and dessert coming soon, he looked at her, and he made the determination that he would continue this, as he would with any woman he had taken for a date. "Shall we dance?"

CHAPTER SIX

LIVIA DIDN'T PARTICULARLY want to dance. Because she didn't want to be quite so under his spell. From the moment he had put her in the sports car, and they'd gone whizzing out of the city, whipping around the tight turns on the road that led up to the château, she had been... She was feeling weak.

That was the problem. Because he was right; she did love the speed, and it was something she had never experienced. Because he did show her things that she had never even thought she would like, and he made them into something that felt essential. The problem was, Matteo had been engaged in a slow seduction of her senses for the past nine years, whether he knew it or not.

She had practice shielding her feelings, but it became complicated when all these other things were woven in. The food had been beyond anything, and she ate well. The food at the palace in Monte Blanco was fantastic, as was the food served at all the events that they frequented. But she had never sat down at a gorgeous restaurant and been served in this way. There had always been a division, and here she was being treated as an equal. Being treated as if she was one of those fancy, beautiful women that had always been in his sphere.

Not with that slight difference in their station that had always been there. More than slight. The fact that she had been given weight to her opinions was a testament to her job, not to anything else.

She was a girl from the streets, and before that from the woods. And she had finally told him.

And now he was asking her to dance.

She should say no. She should. But she had not danced with Matteo since…

"It is likely that you will need to learn to dance."

"Why?"

"Because we are beginning to do more and more events. Because the nation is beginning to blossom. And as you do attend all these events with me…"

"As staff," she said.

"Yes, but I think it would be beneficial for you to have the skill. Part of being cultured, and all that."

Livia cocked her head. "Your father prioritized you knowing how to dance?"

"It was considered a skill of enrichment that all royals should have. Part of what our au pair instilled in us. Things my father issued edicts about." He let out a bitter laugh, and it made Livia shiver. "You know, between bouts of torture."

"I wish he were not dead," she said. "For I would dearly like to kill him."

He laughed again, this time with a bit more mirth. "I do not doubt you would, Mouse. For you are ferocious if nothing else."

"I do not like injustice. I've experienced too much of it in my life."

"Sadly, injustice is all too common in the world, is it not?"

"Yes. Very sadly."

"Come," he said.

He extended his hand, and she looked around the office. "What?"

"Dance."

"There is no music."

"You do not need music. For it is all run on a very specific rhythm, these traditional dances. You can feel it. You can count it by your feet."

"That is not very... I mean, that's definitely not how I think of dancing."

"Because you don't do it. You do not know of which you speak."

His hand was still extended, and she looked at it quite like it was a snake that might attack her at any moment. But she was skeptical and suspicious of all of this. And mostly afraid of what might happen to her if he actually touched her.

"Livia," he said, and it was her name that enticed her to move.

Damn the man.

She took his hand then and electricity zipped through her body, and she was grateful that he quickly pulled her up against the hardness of his chest, for it hid the flaming heat that flooded her face, that she knew would be visible if he were to look. "Like this," he said, beginning to move. "One two three four. One, two, three, four." And with each count, a step, and a sweep of movement. He established a steady rhythm that carried her over the floor as if she was flying through the air, and all the music that she would ever need was inside of her. Flooding her, filling her, and then, she could no longer hide her face, because she needed to see his. She looked up, meeting his gaze. "Just like that," he said, his voice soft. "One, two, three, four. One, two, three, four. Perfect."

"This isn't so hard," she said, her voice trembling. Betraying her.

"It will depend on your partner, of course. For not all men have quite the skill I do in leading."

"So arrogant."

"One, two, three, four. Good girl."

Pleasure poured over her. Oh, she badly wanted to be a good girl for him. To be what he needed her to be. The things she felt for this man were... Well, they were beyond anything she had ever experienced before. And really, she hoped to never experience them again. She could scarcely stand it with a man who didn't much acknowledge her as a human being.

Sometimes, she felt she did not want it to be more. Did not want to take it deeper, and sometimes she badly did. But it didn't matter. Because it would never be anything. It never could. He was not teaching her to dance so that she could dance with him, but so she could blend and not embarrass him at an event if the opportunity arose.

That was all.

"One, two, three, four."

It got lost, though, in that steady rhythm of his beautiful voice. Oh, she truly was a lost cause, finding everything about him so enticing. She suddenly became aware that she could feel his heartbeat. Steady, like the rhythm he counted. Her own was not so steady. It was bouncing around erratically in her chest.

"Very good," he said, and it took her a moment to

realize they had stopped moving, because everything inside of her was still spinning.

And then suddenly, as she looked up at his face, she felt something crackle in the air. Felt the thickness there, like a tension band being slowly stretched. And her heart jittered, slamming against her breastbone.

She could barely breathe. She could...

"I think that is enough for today," he said, turning away from her.

"Yes," she said, feeling dizzy and breathless and entirely out of sorts. "Quite enough."

"Shall we?"

"Yes," she said.

He took her hand, and led her away from the table, down the hall into a small, intimate room, where there were other couples. There was music playing and people were swaying together slowly.

He took her into his arms, and she felt that same thrill she had years ago, being held up against that big, solid chest. He had only grown broader and more solid with the passing years. A man who had grown exponentially in strength and character.

Of course, she would keep all that to herself, for it was a bit fanciful. But she never felt fanciful. Not really. But now, in his arms...

She just wanted to forget everything else for a moment. To forget the proposal, and why she had run. To forget that he didn't feel the things that she did.

To forget how much she feared being in a relationship where she was the one who loved, and the other one did not. Oh, why couldn't she just accept what he was offering? Accept the commitment, even without the feeling.

That made her feel strange and hollowed out and she decided she didn't want to think of it at all.

Not in the least.

So she pushed it aside and focused on nothing more than the precise feeling of where she was at the moment; the warmth of his body, the strength of his arms, the feeling of his suit jacket beneath her hands, and the heat and strength of the muscle beneath.

This wasn't a memory. It was now, and it was happening. He was dancing with her as he had done with any number of women over the years. With her dressed up, and with music. Not just counting off the rhythm in the privacy of his office while she was wearing her sensible uniform. Now, so much of her skin was exposed, and she felt every inch of it.

She didn't know how to feel about the fact that his touch didn't affect her any less now than it had when she was nineteen. That she could know all the many things she did about him, have years' worth of experience knowing him, living with him, caring for him, being hurt by him... How could she still be so enamored? She wanted to know better. Fleeing to Paris was her trying to know better. It really was. She had no desire to be a fool where Matteo was concerned, but there were times when she worried that there was simply no other way for her to be with the man, so it had seemed like the better part of virtue to leave. Completely.

But he had come after her.

And if she'd been thinking, really thinking, about the man that he was she would have realized that.

Did you not?

She ground her teeth together.

Really, Livia. You anticipated his proposal, but did not consider that he would chase you down?

Well, when she looked at it from the point of view of his arrogance, then perhaps she could see it. But truthfully, deep in her soul she had thought that his proposal would be born out of a sense of convenience, and chasing her down to Paris was not convenient. Not in the least.

Yet here he was, and here they were. And they were dancing. And his hands were warm and large, his arms were strong, and she wanted nothing more than to melt into him. Wouldn't it be wonderful to just lose herself completely this way?

Why did she have to think so much? Couldn't she just not think for a moment?

She thought all the time.

Remembered what she knew of Matteo's life, reminded herself not to fall too deeply under his spell, considered the optics of every interaction she had with members of state, and of the palace, and then Matteo's *optics* as well. Thinking had been what brought her here. Thinking had been the thing that had saved her.

And she had to credit it was quite a lot, all things considered.

But for a moment couldn't she just feel? Couldn't she just… Couldn't she simply be a woman in the arms of a man that she desired? Why shouldn't she have that? And really, when all was said and done, why shouldn't she have a little bit of…

Couldn't she have a little something for herself? Maybe she needed to leave him. She knew that she did. She knew that she needed to make a new life for herself. Maybe it would be at this apartment in Paris, or maybe she would move on.

Maybe she would go to Spain, or Italy.

Maybe she would go to the United States.

She loved America.

She loved California, and the endless coastline there. She loved New York, and the skyscrapers that seemed to build a glass-and-steel box all around you with just the barest window into the sky when you stood in the midst of Manhattan.

He had taken her to Wyoming once, to a ranch, to discuss some business deal or another, and she had been absolutely enraptured by the endless sky.

The world was opened to her.

She could not forget that to an extent it was open to her because of Matteo.

But it was also limited because of it. Because her feelings for him kept her in thrall.

You just thought it yourself. Your mind got you to all these places. All the things you did.

It was true. She had done a great deal of her own rescuing. She had needed to take his hand, and she had, but everything else she had fought for all on her own.

From the moment her mother had left her at that carnival she had been fighting for herself.

So why shouldn't she take the reward that she wanted?

Not his crown.

His body.

And so she let all of her thoughts fall away. Like the petals on a rose, wilting as time passed, inevitable, sad, but the way it must be. Shift, fall, as time marched on. The shape of all that beauty changing, passing away.

And yet at the center of it there was the truth: her feelings, her desire.

She wasn't a girl anymore, that much was true. Wasn't

a starry-eyed girl who would believe that the King might find it in himself to love, just for her.

A woman who wasn't even suitable to be his Queen.

And this was not about suitability, but about Matteo's own need for convenience. She knew that. Violet King had been about suitability.

Neither one was particularly romantic, but at least Violet wouldn't have cared.

For Violet did not love him.

Of course, she had fallen in love with Javier, who Livia had always known had a heart beating beneath that iron exterior.

Matteo's brother was a warrior, openly. He had been a part of the battalion that had led devastation against her people. But she did not hate him for it. For he was a man driven by the burning belief in what he thought was truth. And once he had recognized the lies, he had gone in search of the truth, because he cared more about integrity than about any ideology.

There was a passion to that.

Whereas Matteo... He had always seemed so much colder. Cut off. Matteo was a different sort of thing altogether.

But he felt warm beneath her hands. There she could sense passion. There she could sense a man.

She moved her hand from his shoulders, down to the center of his chest, and beneath her palm she felt the beating of his heart. She closed her eyes for a moment and simply felt it.

For whatever he said about the presence of his heart, it was very clearly there. And she knew that he had meant it in a metaphorical sense, when he said he didn't have one, but the incontrovertible evidence that it beat just like it would in the chest of any other...

It made her feel resolute in this.

"You have grown into quite a good dancer," he said, his voice rough.

"You have never had occasion to know."

"Other than our lesson, no. But you did always move with grace, even then."

"Years of running and dodging foes in the streets, I would imagine."

"Ah, perhaps that explains my skill at it. Years of dodging my father's wrath."

It was so rare he would ever speak of this pain in such a casual tone. She knew about his past. She'd seen him in the throes of his nightmares. But it wasn't just... something to be spoken of plainly. Out in the middle of a dance floor.

She stared at the pulse pounding in his throat. "Probably," she said.

"We are not so different." His words were soft, and they wrapped themselves around her like a blanket.

She and a king, not so different?

Except she felt that sometimes. Like he might be the only person who matched the innermost part of her.

And it was foolish.

"No. Not so different. Only from different worlds. Might as well be different planets, honestly."

"You know we are not."

"Does it matter?"

He shook his head. "No. It is not about whether or not we are alike or different. But I believe you would be a good queen."

"Well, I thank you for your confidence in me. It is truly flattering."

"Am I not always?"

"Rarely. Never."

"Such flattery coming from you, Mouse."

She sniffed. "You know I never flatter."

"No," he said. "It's true. At the same time, you're the one who taught me to do it. Remember how you told me I needed to be human?"

"Yes. I do."

"Is that something you had to learn?"

She shook her head. "No. I had to learn to pretend not to be. To put away concerns about whether or not I had truly hurt someone with my knife when I was defending myself. To eliminate any guilt that I felt over taking a loaf of bread from a bakery. For they had many and I had none. I had to unlearn humanity, and coming back to the palace allowed me to find it again."

"A difference," he said. "I think."

"Yes. I believe so."

"You left your family when?"

Matteo was treading on new ground somehow, with each spoken word. They knew these things about each other. Information dripped into conversations over years. But they didn't *speak* of them. Not like this. Not with intention.

"My family left me," she said firmly. "When I was ten. But you make a good point. For ten years, I was happy. For ten years, I felt a sense of security, a sense of love. The fact that it turned out to be a lie doesn't erase it. And whatever my mother felt or didn't feel, there was a time when I was surrounded by the warmth of that family group. There was a time when I felt…cared for. You never felt that, did you?"

It was her turn to push. Her turn to make him share.

He shifted his hold on her.

"Not until my father was dead. And even then, it's not a sense of being cared for, it's just being able to control the environment that I am in. And the environment all of my people are in."

Her heart squeezed. She didn't want to feel so much for him, but she did. This man who'd had to learn how to show an interest in others because he didn't know *how* to show, not because he didn't know how to feel.

Whatever he thought.

"You had to show a level of care that was never extended to you, to others," she said, wanting to lean closer to him as she spoke, "and it is to be commended."

He made a scoffing sound. "None of it is to be commended," he said. "It's basic human decency, and even without the ability to feel much of anything, I can show it."

"Many people would choose not to. Has anyone ever taken care of you?" she asked, meeting his gaze.

His answer came quickly, firmly. "You."

"Oh."

They continued to dance without speaking and she let her focus go entirely to the way his arms felt around her, the way his body felt. He felt that she had cared for him. And she hated the way that it made her chest feel like it was broken open. Hated how much it made her feel. How she would like to be free of this. This desperate yearning inside of her. Hadn't she just purposed to try and embrace her attraction to him only to fulfill a fantasy? Well, perhaps it would work if *he* were simply a fantasy.

But the knowledge that she, and she alone, was where he had experienced care…

Little moments of their life shared passed through her mind, from that night they had sat together on his bed drinking coffee, to the times that she had left him notes on his birthday, quite apart from the vast gifts that he received from heads of state, just personal things. The way that he had done the same for her, at least after that first, disastrous birthday, where she had dressed in red and he hadn't known. He had found out later. And why? He claimed he didn't feel, but that was… It was feeling. It was caring.

He was a man with shields erected all around his heart. And she understood that. But she could also feel that same heart beating.

So she knew it was there.

Don't do this to yourself.

You came to Paris for a reason. You came to get away from him.

But she found herself leaning into him. Found herself stretching up on her toes and kissing his mouth. All that mouth. It held so many of her most dearly cherished fantasies. He tightened his hold on her, angled his head, his tongue sweeping between her lips, sliding against hers.

Her heart was threatening to beat right out of her body. Her pulse thrumming at the base of her throat.

Matteo.

Oh, Matteo.

She didn't say it out loud but his name filled her like a prayer, like a promise, echoing in the chambers of her heart, making it feel too large for her body.

Matteo.

They stopped moving then, and he gripped her chin, holding her face steady as he kissed her harder, deeper.

It was as if the room around them had faded into nothing, the people around them dissolving along with it. Because nothing mattered but this. This moment.

Don't get caught up in it. You have to remember.

You have to remember.

"My brother tells me that he has made contact with Violet King."

"Oh?" Livia knew exactly who Violet King was. A makeup mogul, famous in the United States, and indeed the world over.

"Yes. She's my fiancée."

"What?" Her heart slammed against her breastbone.

"The woman that I have been promised to marry all this time, Violet King."

Livia felt her mouth drop open and close, and realized that she must resemble an indignant guppy and the last thing she needed was that kind of comparison floating around. She was already called a rodent half of her days. She didn't need to be a flopping fish. But she felt like one. Gasping and dry drowning in the air.

"Violet King is your fiancée?" The woman was younger than Livia. It was… Insulting.

Right. Because Violet King is a self-made billionaire and you are…?

A street urchin.

A street mouse.

Never, ever to be deemed appropriate to touch the sainted hem of Matteo's robe, let alone his body. Let alone… What did she even think? These fantasies that she had been so unsuccessful in staving off over the years.

But the problem was sometimes it was so easy to be-lieve that they almost were an old married couple. One that didn't exchange endearments or physical contact, but they were downright domestic at times. Except that he was filled with arrogance and she with acerbic come-backs for his nonsense. So yes. That was a type of do-mestic, or at least, she assumed so.

But sometimes it felt like…like their lives were theirs. Like nobody else truly shared time with Matteo the way that she did. She saw him in the morning, she saw him before he went to bed. Sometimes she saw him after. She saw him barefoot, which was a decidedly intimate thing, she had determined. For he was a king, and she saw him without his formality draped around him. Saw him wandering his bedroom shirtless, wearing nothing but a pair of black trousers, his beautiful, muscled body shifting and rippling each time he moved.

She had seen him *brush his teeth.*

This man, who was nearly immortal. She had literally stood in his hotel suite while he stood at the bathroom sink and brushed his teeth.

Violet King had never seen him brush his teeth.

And Livia may not have so much as kissed him, touched him, but surely she was the only one who truly knew the man.

And what kind of unfairness was this?

A twenty-one-year-old socialite? Who did… *Internet posts for her job.*

And yes, made makeup. So, it was a real thing. And Livia was just being bitter. But she felt entitled to her bitterness. To her disappointment.

You knew it was coming. You always did. He made no secret of the fact that he was promised to another woman.

Why it should gall so much that it was an American, a young one, she didn't know.

You don't know? Of course you do. Because he is yours, and this is your country. Because it isn't even Violet's country. She has no loyalty or allegiance to the throne, to the crown, not in the way that you do.

Even all that didn't really matter, because the real issue was Violet didn't love him. Not like Livia did. She couldn't.

But you're a fool, because he doesn't love you, and he has never pretended to. He has never loved you. He has never acted like he did. He has never so much as put a hand on you other than to teach you to dance.

To lift you from the gutter.

Her chest heaved with building disappointment, and she turned away from him to try and keep him from noticing. To try and disguise what was undeniably a sob.

"When will she be here?" she asked, pretending to be busy with papers on his desk. But her eyes were blurry and she couldn't see anything.

"Soon, I imagine. Javier said that she was not…amenable to the situation."

"What?"

"Oh, she didn't know, apparently. Which is the fault of her father…"

"So then… What?"

"Javier is bringing her here."

"Against her will?"

"Well, I don't know about all that."

"I think you do."

"Her will is not my concern."

"You…" She rarely fought with Matteo. She challenged him, but she did not yell at him, for he was the

King, after all, and engaging in something like that was not proper. But, here she was. About to completely and utterly lose it. No, not about to. She *had* lost it.

"You arrogant bastard. You uprooted this woman from her home, from her country and dragged her here?"

"Is it really any different than what I did for you?"

That was like a knife straight through her heart.

"Yes. You brought me here and hired me as a maid. I had nothing, and you remind me of it constantly. You act like you saved me. But you know, the virtue of your presence doesn't save anyone, Matteo. The people in this country were saved, not simply by your hand, but the fact that you declined to bring it down upon them the way that your father did. And what they have chosen to do with their lives is what will save them. They have lifted themselves up with their own hands. Your father prevented it, more than you have ever aided it. Violet is a billionaire, of her own authority and her own hand. Not yours. And you are uprooting her out of a life that she built for what?"

"Her father promised her to me."

"This is not the twelfth century. What about her choice? What about what she wants?" And suddenly, she did not feel that she was talking about Violet. "You don't care about any of that, do you? You just want to assign roles to the people in your life. And all the better that your Queen be a woman who didn't even know that she was engaged to you. Who has no choice. You don't know her, you can't simply slot her into the position that you see her filling. It doesn't matter who she is…"

"She is well-liked throughout the world. I have seen her photographs. She is very modern. She is the kind of person who will bring the image of rehabilitation to the country that—"

"Kidnapping an American girl is hardly going to rehabilitate the image of Monte Blanco. Or your image. I thought… All these years I thought maybe I had done something in… Not just teaching you to smile, but teaching you to feel it. Not just teaching you how to pretend to connect with people, but to actually… But I didn't, did I? I taught you nothing. You… You don't feel anything, do you? You're a monster."

"I never claimed to be anything but a monster," he said, reaching out and gripping her arm, turning her to face him. "Did I? I just claimed that I was going to do my best not to continue the harm that my father caused. But I told you, all those years ago, you know."

"About your scars? Yes. I know. I know all about your scars, Matteo. You've shown them to me. But what does it matter if you've done nothing to try to heal from them?"

"They do not heal. It has been years, and there they remain." He tapped his forefinger against his temple. "And the pain stays there. And I feel it here." He touched his chest. And she knew that he was indicating the knife wounds there, but she wondered if he actually meant somewhere deeper. Though he would never admit it. "I am what he made me. Do you think I would not like to be? Why do you think that I debased myself to go and see a psychologist about the pain?"

His pain echoed inside her. Along with the gutting realization that perhaps she had not done a thing to make him…better.

She'd hoped.

She really had.

But it was possible he wanted too much. Demanded too much.

"It pains you that you're just a man, doesn't it?" she asked. "You wish to be immortal, but you aren't. You are just a man. And you have to contend with the failings, the limits of your body the same as the rest of us do."

"It should not be."

He was impossible. He really was. He wanted perfection and without it he would see himself as broken and for some reason…it offended.

Because you wanted to believe you fixed him.

You wanted to believe you were special.

But Violet King is the one he thinks is special.

"It's not fair," she shouted. "But nothing is fair. You don't have to pass on the unfairness, though, and you are. But you're the only one making that determination."

"She is what's right for the country. And therefore, I will continue on."

"You utter, heartless…"

"I told you I was."

"I might hate you," she said, the word coming out a whisper. "I truly might."

"And I'm sorry for that. I would rather you did not. But it does not mean I can make a different decision."

"You're the King, you could do whatever you want."

"Isn't that just the thing you were telling me I should not do?"

"Now you listen to me. Wonderful."

"She will learn to adjust."

But would Livia? Would she ever heal from this? From this devastation, not just of his marriage finally coming into the present, but knowing just how void of feeling he truly was.

She didn't think she could.

Except, it would be better, if that had cured her of loving him.

The sad thing was, it did not.

She broke the kiss, and stepped away from him. She had thought that memory might bring her some clarity, and it had.

She couldn't marry him.

But since nothing had done the job of eliminating her feelings for him, eliminating her desire for him…

Well, she would claim that.

"Take me back to the hotel," she whispered. Shame flooded her, heat flooding her face.

"Be very certain of what you're asking me," he said, his tone a warning.

"I'm certain," she said.

"Then let us go."

He wrapped his arm around her waist and led her from the dance floor. And when they arrived, she could see that their dessert had been wrapped up to go. And she felt sort of silly, how obvious things were, even to the waitstaff.

Except, she didn't care. Because she would not have to deal with the fallout of this. Because this was a goodbye, whether he knew it or not.

"I'm very certain," she said, not to him, but to herself.

And then he took her arm and led her out into the night.

CHAPTER SEVEN

FIRE STREAKED THROUGH his veins as they drove down the mountainside, heading toward Paris. But they would not be staying in the hotel that she had chosen. Rather, they would be going to his suite. Of course, he was in the same hotel that she was in. He wasn't a fool. He had not only known exactly where she was, he had availed himself to her room and he had her things moved into it. That should have been done the moment they had gone out to dinner. The staff had their orders, and of course they had complied.

He was a king, after all.

She wanted him.

And he was a little bit wary of how quickly she had changed her tune, that a bit of French bread and kissing had brought her to the place where she wanted to go to bed with him.

But he would not question his good fortune.

Livia was just a woman, like any other, and she was being given the chance to have money, power, a title. And because she was Livia, he did imagine that his reminding her she had a chance to do some very real good had brought her to this conclusion as well.

But still, she was human, his mouse.

He didn't know why that disappointed him slightly.
That she could be so easily convinced.

But then, there was also the chemistry between them.

Chemistry he had worked for years to deny. If it had
become harder recently, he had done his best not to think
of it. He had been promised to Violet, and while he
would not claim to be a great man, he had intended to
keep his vows to his American fiancée. Who had not
kept hers, and had found herself in love with his brother.

She made no vows to you. You kidnapped her.

Technically, *Javier* had kidnapped her.

And Matteo had not been bothered. Not in the least.
From the moment his brother had said that he and Violet
were going to wed each other, Matteo had shifted focus.

It was his own fault after all, he had left Violet unat-
tended with his brother.

And he had been away with Livia.

It had been a very important political summit.

And he could've brought Violet with him, but their
connection was still very new, and she had been unhappy
and he had a feeling that she would have only damaged
any political outreach he was attempting, with her general bitterness at the state of things.

Fair enough.

So, it had been just him and Livia, who had been
angry with him, frosty.

Since their fight when he had told her about Violet
King.

"And when will you decide to speak to me again?"

"Not anytime soon," she huffed.

"You're putting on quite a brave face in the palace."

"Well, it's not good for morale for everyone to see what an ass I think you are."

"You forget yourself," he said, rolling his shoulders back and turning to walk the length of the hotel suite. Livia was sitting on the couch there, perched on the end, looking indignant, her shoulders rigid and straight, her legs crossed at the ankles. She looked everything good and proper, an admonishment of what she found improper in him.

"How good of you to think of morale. I have political alliances to make tonight, though, and it would not benefit me to have my assistant lurking in the background looking like she wants to stab me with one of the very tiny forks that we will find at this banquet."

"Why bother to have me lurking in the background?"

"You know I need you there."

"Oh. I see. So, you intend to keep me in the position I'm in even when you have a Queen?"

"All men keep their advisors when they marry."

"So she's simply decorative? Not your primary advisor?"

"No. She will not be my primary advisor. She's just a woman. From America. What does she know about politics? And, indeed, what does she know about Monte Blanco?"

"What's the point of it?"

"Optics." He shook his head. "Honestly, Livia, you are the one that taught me about such things. Told me how important it is. Shouldn't you be pleased?"

"I'm not pleased. I'm not pleased that you're acting like a marauding medieval barbarian."

"You are inconsistent." He stood in front of her expectantly.

"What?" she asked.

"My tie."

"You know how to tie your own tie."

"You do it better."

She looked up at him with furious eyes. She was wearing those big, gold spectacles she was so fond of. A strange choice, he had always thought. Exceedingly obvious, and not at all subtle. An announcement to the world, he supposed, that she was bookish. But she was beautiful, and those glasses couldn't hide it. Indeed, he found them quite charming, though he would never admit it to her.

He found her quite charming, even when she was furious, something else he would never admit to her.

"You're an ass," she repeated, her fingers moving resolutely over the black silk fabric of his tie.

"I'm not concerned about it."

"But then," she said, bristling, "you wouldn't be, would you? You're a beast."

"And yet, you remain."

"So I do. Call it a care for my country. Without me, we would be in true jeopardy."

"I see. So you see yourself as a rudder for our great nation."

"I steer the ship. To the best of my ability."

"And I'm the one who's arrogant."

"I never said I wasn't."

She disappeared, and emerged a moment later. Her hair was in a simple bun, and she wore very little makeup. She was wearing her typical uniform of black dress, though this one clung a bit more tightly to her curves. It was a dress that swept to the floor, flaring out like an unfurling lily as it fell past her knee.

It was not bright or obvious. She would not be quite so glittery as the other women in attendance.

But Livia always took pains not to set herself apart. He wouldn't have minded, as the years passed, if she made herself slightly more obviously a key player, rather than just waitstaff, but she never had. Had never shifted from the background to anything more.

She looked beautiful, though, he thought.

Perhaps it was her fury.

Nobody else dared challenge him in the way that she did. Only Javier ever did, and he was a prince.

It was the audacity of Livia that got to him.

It was expected for Javier to get angry with him sometimes. But not for his assistant.

It was a charming thing.

Charming.

Why was he feeling half so *charmed* by Livia at the moment? She was being a termagant.

"Let us away," she said.

They went downstairs, and a limo was waiting for them. Livia slid inside, her skirt fanning out around her, revealing a slit in the long, flowing black dress, showing off a length of pale leg.

Her legs were quite lovely. He had endeavored not to notice before.

He looked at her, and her profile, that staunch upturned nose, and the dramatic lips, her pert little chin.

The line of her neck, that curve at the back of it, was also quite something. She was a study in delicate lines, elegant swoops. She was soft. And yet… Not soft at all in her interaction.

"You're quite beautiful," he said.

She turned to him, and he found the anger that burned

in her eyes was even more pronounced now than it had been a moment ago. "Are you trying to flatter me?"

"I don't do flattery. I thought you should know."

"Oh, yes, I do know, but I find that all of your behavior of late is quite a bit outside the character of the man I thought I knew."

"It was not a leading comment, simply a statement. You're beautiful, Livia."

Her cheeks turned pink, and she looked away from him. "How lucky for me."

"I imagine no matter that you dressed in black men pay quite a bit of attention to you at these events."

"It wouldn't matter if they did. I'm working."

"Ah yes, always working, aren't you?"

"Yes. As my boss, *you* should know *that*."

When they got out of the car, he took her arm.

"What are you doing?"

"I wish you to stay with me tonight."

"I don't stay with you at these sorts of things, as well you know. We do not come in together. I go through the back."

"You're not going through the back tonight," he said, his voice hard. "You must endeavor to find a way to deal with that."

"This was not the plan."

"And I decide what the plans are. You may organize them, but I have the ultimate decision-making power. I suggest you find a way to cope with that."

"Inconvenient…"

But the beginning of her tirade was cut off by the fact that they had arrived at the entrance to the Grand Hotel. And then, she was far too good at her job to do anything but smile. As he had known that she would be. It was how Livia was.

The perfect assistant, the perfect advisor. She always had been.

In fact, it was difficult for him to recall how he had ever gotten along without her. He didn't like to think of it, not really. For she was the perfect partner in every way, and that was undeniable.

Even when she was angry with him.

She nearly vibrated with it now, but she kept it to herself.

"Just like you taught me," he whispered in her ear.

She turned her head, her face a scant inch from his. "What?"

"Smiling. Even when you don't feel like it."

She scrunched her nose up, and he could tell that it was a fury that contorted her expression thus, but also that no one else would recognize it.

No, all they would see was a small, beautiful woman, looking up at him.

"Careful," he said. "They might think that you're gazing adoringly at me."

She nearly hissed. "I'm not."

"I'm only telling you, optics."

"You and your damn optics."

"They're *your* damn optics, of a technicality."

They swept into the ballroom together, where he was announced, as was fitting his station. But of course, they did not announce Livia.

He could see the person making the introductions was quite put off by the fact that he had shown up with someone unexpected.

But whether anybody there knew it or not, Livia was not unexpected.

Livia was with him wherever he went.

He wondered why he had never brought her in with him like this before.

You know why.

Because it didn't matter that she worked for him, and nothing more. People would assume, of course, that she was more to him than that.

In point of fact, she was.

"I'm very sorry." A man came from the recesses of the room, melting into the floor in a suit that announced him as staff, rather than one of the dignitaries in attendance. "But Your Majesty, we did not know you would be bringing a guest with you. And we did not set the table as such."

"Then I suggest you remedy that."

"Yes, sir."

"And why is it you feel you must come to me with your concerns. Surely you can speak to someone else, and make it appear as if you magically did your jobs without having to apologize in such an obsequious fashion."

"Stop it," Livia said, in full view of the man. "You're being a terror."

The man's lips twitched, as he fought to keep his expression neutral.

"Perhaps I would like the lady to sit on the floor."

"That will make a wonderful headline."

"I will see to getting her place sitting right away."

"What is the matter with you?" Livia rounded on him.

"I might ask you the same question, as you have been acting the part of guttersnipe since…"

"Since you kidnapped Violet King and brought her to the palace? I don't approve. Was that not clear?"

"You don't approve. Yet all you do is move palely around the palace, looking for all to see like a serene handmaiden."

"I am nobody's handmaiden, as you well know. And you want me to yell at you in front of everyone else?"

"You seem on the verge of doing it here."

"Because I'm appalled at you. Shocked and appalled."

"So appalled," he said, moving his arm from her elbow, to her lower back. And she went stiff.

Her body was supple. It really was quite lovely. Lust tightened low in his stomach and he castigated himself.

Even attempting to cause her grief—as he was at the moment—he did not want to feel these things for Livia.

He had always been aware of what he must not do with her. Of what he must not feel.

His age, his position, her dependence on him…

It was all impossible. And what sort of impossible situation would it become if he carried on an affair with Livia while married to Violet? Though, granted, many men might find it convenient to have his mistress and wife housed in the same place.

But it was a recipe for disaster. And Livia would never quietly be a mistress.

She would likely crusade about, joining forces with Violet. Unionizing. That was all he needed.

Anyway, Livia had never evinced the slightest bit of interest in him in that way. She was nothing but brisk and efficient, and a woman who wanted him would scarcely yell at him and all other things that Livia did to him on a daily basis.

She did not conduct herself as a woman who wanted sexual attention from him.

He did not have the words for what that made him feel.

He could not have her preoccupied with such things if he expected her to do her job. That much was true. But...

A spark smoldered in his blood when he looked at her for too long.

And he was not accustomed to being near a woman who did not react to him as a potential partner. He did not know if he wanted it from her, or not. And it was the not knowing that frustrated as much as it intrigued.

"I suggest you get your emotions in order," he said. "For I am at the end of my patience. This is a very important event. We have inroads that we have to make at this summit tomorrow. And it begins tonight. You know how it is. I need you with me. I cannot do it without you."

"Why don't you think you can do it without me? You've been doing all of this just fine with me in the background for years."

"I know everything there is to know about the economy of Monte Blanco, I know everything that I must to make this alliance work. But I do not know how to do...diplomacy."

"You are much better at it than you used to be."

"But I need you there. I need you to help. And I need you to not be opposing me at every turn."

"You are difficult," she said.

"And so are you. It is what I like about you, and I assume on a good day, it is what you like about me."

"Who said I like you?" she said, looking up at him from beneath her lashes. "You sign my paychecks."

A harsh statement, and he was surprised at the note

of discomfort it left in his gut. For he did not care about things like that, like whether someone liked him. Least of all Livia. It had never occurred to him that she might not. For were they not, in many ways, two halves of one whole?

"You like me," he said.

But they didn't get a chance to continue their banter because the tables were set and they were ushered to them.

He had never had the chance to see Livia in quite this environment. And he was stunned by how easy it seemed for her. She was able to carry on conversations seamlessly. He introduced her as his advisor, and it was accepted that she was so. Her opinion given weight, just as he imagined it should be.

And as he watched her speak, as he watched her bring everyone at the table onto her side, he realized that she was so much more than he had ever given her credit for.

She should be promoted. Not just be an assistant or an advisor. Perhaps some sort of liaison. She was the diplomat; she knew everything about politics and Monte Blanco. Everything about the country itself.

He could remember her as she'd been. Skinny and tragic and bedraggled when he had first found her. And she was as far away from that now as a woman born to be queen might be.

Queen.

The talks the table continued for long hours, while other revelers that were not diplomats of one country or another enjoyed dancing, and desserts.

"Shall we take this conversation to the balcony?"

One of the representatives from the United States

asked that question, and Livia nodded eagerly. "Yes. I would be happy to continue the conversation outside."

"And you, Your Majesty?"

"Of course. If we have exhausted the table's goodwill for the topic."

"I fear very much we might have," the man said, laughing.

One of the leaders from the United Kingdom joined them, and they stood out there talking for many hours, about the ways in which each country could benefit the other. And he felt, by the end, that when they convened tomorrow for the actual summit, things would go well.

The diplomat from the United States left first, followed by the man from the United Kingdom.

And that left himself and Livia standing there out on the balcony. She wrapped her arms around herself, rubbing her pale arms. "I'm sorry about our fight earlier," she said. "It was pointless. You're right. This is what matters. Monte Blanco. And this went... Well. It went well."

"I would like to think so."

"I do feel sorry for Violet."

"I don't. She will be treated well."

"But without freedom."

He leaned against the balustrade that overlooked the grand gardens below. "Do any of us have true freedom, Livia?"

The words scraped raw against his throat and he disliked how deep a place they came from.

"I don't know how to answer that." Her tone was carefully bland. And it angered him. She had been charming inside, and here she was so careful with him.

She was like that sometimes. Fire and unguarded in a

moment, and then unreachable in another and he hated it. Because he could not figure out why. And he could not force her to change when she had her mind set on retreating as she had now.

"Think about it," he pushed. "We are all born into a certain position. And then life does what it will with us. Those who have control of us when we are children… They get to have so much control over what we become. As we discussed with my father… He may not have been able to determine what manner of king I am, but his hooks are in me that I have not been able to successfully remove. I still have nightmares."

Those nightmares she alone had seen. She had touched him then, without fear. Without a wall.

There was silence for a moment.

"So do I," she said softly.

The catch in her voice betrayed her. She was letting her guard down and he found he wanted that.

He felt, for some strange reason, like there was sand running through an hourglass. That if they did not have this moment, they would never have it.

Because of Violet? Perhaps.

Whatever the reason, he felt they had to speak like this now, or they never would.

It mattered, just then.

"Because of decisions your mother made. Because you were put out on the streets. Violet King has had a comparably easy life, at least as far as I'm aware. She has money, and influence. And now… Her father has made a decision that is impacting her. How is she any different from us? Except I will not be cruel to her."

"What if she wished to fall in love? To have her husband love her back?"

Those words made it feel like an avalanche had gone off inside him.

"Then she will be disappointed. But as disappointments go…" He looked at her, at her elegant profile. She seemed so solitary, his mouse. Right next to him and yet…very far away. "Did you ever expect to be loved, Livia?"

The only sound in the air now was the crickets, chirping from the garden below. She did not move. Did not look at him. "No. I didn't expect to be loved. Not even for one moment of my life. The greatest thing I could hope for was to live."

She looked at him then, her eyes brighter than stars.

"And have your expectations been surpassed now?" he asked, his voice that of a stranger's.

She nodded. "Yes. I must confess they have. For this has been better than any scenario I could have ever imagined for myself. I cannot pretend otherwise."

He ground his teeth together. "I never imagined I would be loved. I imagined having loyalty given to me by the people of my country. I imagined… Not in my wildest dreams did I imagine love."

"But perhaps she did."

The soft rebuke should have wounded him, and yet it wasn't feelings for Violet he had in this moment. But his soft, strong Livia….

Should she not expect more than mere survival?

"And Violet will overcome the disappointment, for there are many other things in life that are vastly more important."

"Yes, I suppose that is so."

"It will not be so bad for her. No doubt her business will increase tenfold, and from everything I've seen about her, her business is her life. As far as I'm aware she's never had a relationship. All my surveillance points to the fact that the growth of her company is her one true love. And I believe that her goals will mesh nicely with mine."

The silence between them filled with night air and crickets as they stood, saying nothing for a long while.

Then Livia spoke. Her voice puncturing his chest like a knife in the dark.

"What do you think it would be like?"

"What?"

"To be in love."

Such a simple question, and one everything in him turned away from.

"That sort of thing is the opiate of the masses, I fear. Nothing real about it. Nothing substantial."

"You don't think?"

He looked at her. "Have you ever seen it?"

She shook her head. "No. Sadly. My father was never around. I'm not even entirely certain who he was. But he did not love my mother. I do not even know where he was from or what he did. But there was no love there, clearly, or she would have spoken of him. And I thought she loved me, but it turned out not to be. And you…"

"My father saw me as a plaything." The words were hard and harsh. "Whether or not it was as an exorcism for his psychopathy, or a true belief inside of himself that he was training me to be a hardened leader, I don't know. But he seemed to enjoy hurting me. Javier and I have a loyalty between ourselves."

"And that's all?"

A muscle in his face ticked. "I would wish better for him," Matteo said. "Better for him than to be me."

"Do you think you'll find better?"

"I don't know." He hated that. Not knowing. This entire moment was full of not knowing.

"You *do* think there's better. Is it love, do you think, that makes the difference?"

"Perhaps."

"So you acknowledge that… That if it is real… It might be wonderful?"

"A great many things could be classified that way. It would not change the way things are." He gripped the railing. Hard. "I hope you find someone who loves you, Mouse."

She looked up at him, her eyes wide. Startled.

"Why?"

He moved toward her, suddenly compelled by her pale silhouette. "Because you've seen enough hardship, I think. Enough hardship to last you a lifetime."

The air seemed to disappear entirely.

"I certainly think so," she said, sounding breathless. "But why don't you want better for yourself?"

"Better for me is simply not being my father." It felt like the stone of the building behind him was sitting on his shoulders. For Livia assumed this was a simple task, and he feared it was not. To hate his father would make it simple. The reality… The reality was much more complicated. "And I'll take that. Unhappily. It does not grieve me if the future set before me is only as lofty as that."

"And me?"

He reached out, and did something he thought he might regret. He touched her face, and found it soft. Let his hand move down to her chin. She took a sharp, indrawn breath, but she didn't move away.

"You are the most singular creature I have ever

known. Even when you're being a harpy. In fact, perhaps especially then, because nobody dares challenge me the way that you do. You have fought diligently for our country tonight. You... You among all people deserve love, if such a thing exists."

"Even the façade of it?"

"People seem quite happy."

"Some of them do, yes."

"But you can never leave me," he said. "Whatever man catches your eye, you must stay with me."

"I don't think I could." She turned away from him.

"Why not?"

"I cannot be yours while professing to be someone else's, surely you must know that."

"Well, if he is from Monte Blanco, I don't think you will see a problem with it. I'm the King. So everything is mine first."

"Thank you for reminding me," she said, nearly laughing. "That even when you're being kind, you're still you. And still arrogant underneath it all."

"And you are still a feral little creature. Even underneath all that sophistication you put on."

"A compliment."

"And I take your insult such as well."

"Matteo..."

"Yes?"

But she turned away. And so he reached out, and gripped her chin again, leaning down as he turned her face up, bringing their mouths within a whisper of each other. And then, everything stopped. Time was suspended.

And held.

He had been on the verge of kisses before. Though

typically, he just took them, and the women he was with claimed them right back. No pausing. No hesitation.

This was not a hesitation.

It was a profound discovery. And he could do nothing but sit there in it. In this realization that what he wanted more than anything, right in that moment, was to taste her.

To taste her vile temper, her recriminations, her compliments. To drink them all in and somehow take them inside of himself. So that he could feel all that she did. That fire and passion. For he had just thought to himself how she was his other half in many ways. And this was the half that he yearned for. The one that contained all that bright, brilliant emotion that his body nearly refused to let him have. Pain, he had that. Anger, aplenty. But the rest... She contained all of that. A great mystery, a great certainty.

"Livia," he whispered.

"You will marry Violet King?" she asked, her voice sounding almost like she was drunk.

"Yes," he said.

She moved away from him. "Don't do that to me again."

"What did I..."

"Just don't. Tonight's been strange, and not at all like what we normally are. Let us not repeat it."

And then she turned and walked back into the ballroom.

They were at the hotel, and he pulled her out of the car and into his arms on the street. And he kissed her. With all the longing he had felt in that moment at the hotel in

Spain. That deep desire to be with her. He had held himself back then because she had asked him to.

Because...

Because he had been resolute in his course then, and he could see now that it had been the wrong one.

What was it about Livia that always made him have to confront his flaws? He preferred to labor under the assumption he had none. That by excising his heart, he had done away with the potential for mistakes. But she was ever a reminder that he was human.

And now he reveled in it.

For only a human, only a man, could enjoy the feel of a woman in his arms quite this way.

And he kissed her, right there on the streets for anyone to see. Claiming.

Because she was his.

From the moment he had taken her off the streets, she had been his.

She had tried to run from it, from him, but they were inevitable.

He could see that now. That night he had brought her to the gala, it had been a trial, for her being his Queen. It was as if something in him had known it before his mind had, and he had never experienced anything quite like that. But in many ways, it was like that thing inside him had known it from the moment he'd seen her out on the street. That she was to be taken in, for just this moment. That her destiny was to be the Queen of Monte Blanco. The country needed her. He was absolutely convinced of that now. She had been guiding him all this time, had been advising him and organizing him, and he could see now that the common bond—other than himself—when it came to all the growth in the country and the growth in himself, was Livia.

She was inevitable.

As was this.

Fate, if you believed in such things.

He did not. But how could he deny that there was something of a higher power at work here? It didn't matter. Because he was not in a position to deny it, nor did he want to. Tonight, he just wanted her.

When he could drag his mouth away from hers, he led her into the hotel, bringing her into the private elevator that took him to the top floor, to his suite.

His thumbprint allowed the doors to open, bringing them out to the luxury penthouse.

"I…" She sounded dizzy.

"Did you not realize we were not headed to your room?"

"I can't say that I noticed much of anything."

"I had us moved."

Her eyes flickered, and he had a feeling he was about to get a lecture on his arrogance again, so he silenced her with a kiss. And drunk her in deep. He could taste the notes of the wine she had at dinner, could taste the sun somehow, and something that was essentially her.

And he knew that there was no turning back now.

CHAPTER EIGHT

LIVIA WAS DIZZY with desire. The way that he held her, the way that he kissed her. She couldn't even bring herself to be angry at the high-handedness inherent in him moving all of her things into this beautiful penthouse. She had seen a great many spectacular hotel rooms, suites and apartments over the years. Had been living in a palace for nearly a decade. But still, she was never immune to the luxury around her. Because she could never forget to be grateful for comfort when she had been so uncomfortable for so long.

But this was all somehow different. Because it wasn't comfort in the way she understood it. There was a lushness to it, almost a sensuality. As if every texture in the room called out an invitation to sex, every surface a potential place for her to spend her desire for him.

She was not naïve.

She had known what sex was for a long time. Her people were earthy. And then on top of that, she had spent so much time on the street she had seen any number of women selling themselves to buying men. She had been groped and harassed and chased down by those seeking the same thing from her. Had been accosted by men in suits offering money in exchange for lewd acts. And while she had managed to escape any personal experience, she knew about sex. Both the violence that could come with it, and the pleasure.

Of course, knowing about and being prepared to experience were two very different things. But she was about to. With him.

It had always had to be this way.

He would have to be the first.

Because if she didn't know what it was to be with Matteo, then she would never be with anybody.

It just wouldn't happen.

Because he had formed her every thought about attraction, so he would have to be the one to introduce her to the pleasures of the flesh.

But all of her justifications went out the window when his mouth moved over hers.

And then, he kissed her neck, moved down to her collarbone, pushing the spaghetti strap of her dress off of her shoulder. And then the other. Her bodice fell, and her breasts were exposed. They were not particularly large. But then, they weren't small either. Just sort of unremarkable, she thought.

Everyday breasts.

But he let out a sound, a growl, that reverberated inside of her, and seemed to suggest something entirely different.

"You are beautiful," he said, his voice rough.

And it echoed that night three weeks ago, when he'd said that to her for the first time, in the limousine, before they went into the hotel.

"Do you really think so?"

"I do," he said, looking at her. "You know how hard

I fought to keep myself from ever... It would have been a grave sin against you, Livia."

"Tell me," she said, suddenly desperate. "Tell me how long you thought I was beautiful."

"It is a shame to me," he said.

"But it is water in a desert to me."

"Very well." He growled, lifting her up off the ground, and she let out an undignified squeak. Then he put his hand on one of her breasts, drawing his thumb slowly over her nipple, his gaze filled with intent concentration as he watched himself touch her. "I remember the night I first asked you to be my assistant. And you were wearing red. I do not know why."

"It was my birthday," she whispered.

"How foolish of me." He put his hand on her face, his eyes intense. "To not remember that. But I do remember your dress. I thought you beautiful. And impossibly young. So...vulnerable."

"I had stabbed men by then. I was hardly vulnerable."

"And then when I would catch you examining the tiles in the ballroom, as if you were looking for any speck of dirt there that might defy you."

"Why would you know something like that?"

"Because of the way your brow would increase when you concentrated. And I thought you beautiful."

"Oh."

"Then there was the night you came into my room, and I was naked. You brought me a drink and you sat with me. And it was tenderness in a way I had never known. And I thought you beautiful."

She closed her eyes and fought against the tears that were threatening to build.

"Then, you yelled at me in a wild fury in my office

when I told you about Violet. You were in a rage like I had never seen you. And I thought you beautiful. Like when I taught you to dance in my office and you looked up to me with trust and openness and let me hold you in my arms even though you and I both know the cost of trusting another person that way. And I thought you beautiful."

"Matteo…"

"So you see, this is not new. It is only that I said it for the first time recently. Not that I thought it for the first time."

"Make love to me."

"That's what I'm already doing, *querida*."

"Don't call me that."

"Mouse," he whispered. "But you must admit, it is not sexy."

"But it's mine."

And that was the end of that, for he kissed her again, his hand still playing havoc on her breast, causing showers of sparks to bounce around inside her stomach. Then he took his mouth away from hers, and moved down to her breast, taking one nipple and sucking it deep. She arched in his arms, the desperate need building between her legs undeniable.

Unstoppable.

He moved his mouth to her other breast, and she felt like she might die. He strode across the room then, depositing her on the center of the very large bed. And then he moved away from her, standing at the foot of it.

"Matteo," she said, not caring if she sounded as if she was begging. She would beg him. She would beg him for more, for his touch, for his possession. Anything, so that he wouldn't stop.

But then, his hands moved to his shirt, and he began to unbutton it deftly, dropping it and the suit jacket down to the floor and leaving him bare chested. Oh, she had seen his chest many times, and it always thrilled her. But this still felt like the first time. The first time seeing that broad, muscular chest covered with just the right amount of dark hair. Those perfect ab muscles, and the deep cut right at his hip bones.

Because now, she would actually get to touch him. Now, he was not just an unobtainable symbol, wandering around in front of her as if she wasn't there, the ultimate sign of her sexlessness, that he didn't even bother to dress completely to meet with her.

No. He had said he thought her beautiful. And he was there, half-naked and ready for her.

And she found she could not keep still. She launched herself to the edge of the bed and put her hands on his chest.

She was touching him. Finally. She had seen him up close over the years, but he might as well have been behind a wall of glass. Because that was how unavailable he was to her. Looking, but never touching. And she had been so certain that she never would.

But finally, finally she was able to put her hands on him. Matteo.

She nearly wept with it, but he kissed her again, swallowing the sob even as it rose up in her throat.

She kissed him, letting her hands explore his chest, his stomach, luxuriating in the feel of his muscles, of the body hair, the heat of his skin. He was such a man. The masculine to her feminine. Hard and beautiful and unparalleled. He was everything she had ever fantasized about, and more. He was a revelation in the form of a human. For Livia felt beautiful in his arms. Felt spectacular and unique, and nothing like the poor, sad abandoned creature she had felt like for most of her days.

Because nothing could really erase that. Not the success that she had found working at the palace, not the many intervening years. It wasn't so simple to just erase those years spent alone.

That abandonment. That trauma.

No, it would never be quite so simple. But right now, at least, she could feel something like healed. Something special, held in his arms.

He laid her down onto the bed, coming over her, a commanding warrior that made her shiver beneath his fierce gaze. She had always known that he was dangerous and had taken a great sort of satisfaction in knowing so. That she was protected by a man who was, at his core, dangerous.

But now he was hers to touch, hers to kiss. Now she could make him shudder with desire, and did, as she nipped his lower lip while he continued a bold exploration of her body. He pushed her red dress down, past her waist, her hips, drawing it completely off of her, then turning his focus to the waistband of her panties. He teased the delicate skin just beneath and she shivered. She couldn't have fathomed that it would be like this. That he would be like this. At least, not for her. All of the women she had to get parting gifts for, who had left his bed, had been very, very sad their association had ended, and now she could see why.

For he wove delicious torture wherever he touched, left behind burn marks on her skin with the heat of his hands. And then, he allowed his fingers to inch slowly beneath that flimsy fabric, finding her center between her thighs, finding her wet and ready and filled with desire for him. He stroked her there, the pleasure that she found white-hot and brilliant. She could feel the muscles in her thighs quaking as he stroked her, long and slow, drawing circles over the most sensitive part of her. She shifted, arching her hip, and he pressed a finger deep inside of her. She cried out at the unfamiliar invasion, but then nearly wept for the beauty of it. Matteo was inside of her. And it was brilliant. And there would be more.

So much more.

And this might be it. Her last night with him. Her first night with him. But she would pour everything into this. And she would hold nothing back. Because she would be broken by leaving him. Whether they had this or not. So she would seize this fantasy for the girl who had slept on cold streets. Who had held herself while she cried. For the girl who had loved a king knowing she could never have him. Who had cried herself to sleep when he told her about his engagement to another woman.

For *that* girl, she would have this pleasure.

Have this connectedness. She kissed him, reveling in the pleasure he created between them. And she let her hands roam over his body, let them move to the front of his slacks, as she undid the closure there, felt the hardness pressing insistently against her. He wanted her.

He really did. So regardless of whether or not he had asked her to be his Queen because of convenience, she could know that. That he was attracted to her. That he wanted this. His body could not lie about it. Which was good, because her own could not either. Because that slickness between her legs advertised her need for him, and as he added a second finger, she gasped, rocking against him, desperately seeking fulfillment. But she wouldn't be fulfilled. Not until she had him. All of him.

With fumbling fingers, she tried to get his slacks pushed off completely, but he had to assist, pressing his body against hers, completely naked, chest to chest, thigh to thigh. His skin was so hot. And his desire was pushing against her with ferocity.

In this moment, she was wanted. Gloriously and without boundaries. And she would take it. More than take it. She would use it to rebuild. Use it to create something new. For she would know what it was. And there was some deep, undeniable satisfaction buried in the truth that he wanted something from her she wasn't going to give.

That she would maybe be the one to leave him wanting more. And perhaps that was revenge against her mother more than it was anything, perhaps it had nothing to do with Matteo at all. But she had spent nine years wanting the man, so maybe it did.

A small, petty revenge that came with blindingly brilliant pleasure. She would take it.

He growled, kissing her, and then she could think of nothing more, as his fingers worked in and out of her body, as his lips played havoc with her. And then, he began to kiss his way down her body, blazing a trail past her belly button, down to the very heart of her, where he teased and stroked her with his fingers even as he consumed her with his mouth.

She gasped, rocking and rolling her hips, her head thrashing back and forth on the pillow as he brought her to new heights of pleasure she hadn't known were possible. And then, she shattered, broke into a million pieces of crystalline glass, and she had no idea how he still held on to her, how he still pushed her higher, farther, with his wicked lips and tongue, because she didn't think she was rooted to the earth anymore.

She was scattered in the wind.

She was all the glitter that she'd contained inside of herself. And she couldn't be distinguished from it.

Not anymore.

While she was still sobbing and gasping her pleasure, he rose up over her body and kissed her, the flavor of her own desire heady on his lips as he pressed himself against the entrance to her body.

And then he thrust home.

She cried out in pain, and he stilled, holding her tightly against him, making a low, whispering sound, as if he was quieting a frightened creature.

And she quieted. She felt the pain between her thighs begin to ease, felt her body begin to relax around him.

And it didn't take long for pleasure to begin to build again.

He moved back out slowly, then pushed back inside, and she moaned. And he took that as his signal that he could move.

And so he did. Establishing a rhythm, as he had done in his office when he had taught her to dance. She could almost feel it, echoing in her chest, in her soul.

One, two, three, four.

One, two, three, four.

It was a different sort of rhythm, but it lived inside her all the same. It rose up like a wave, wrapping itself around her, that rhythm, that sound, simply in her blood.

And it all made sense then, why she had been able to dance with him that way. Because it was always meant to be like this. Always. And impossibly, she felt another climax building inside of her, and she didn't think she could handle it. Honestly, thought it might destroy her.

But he held her tight. "Let go," he growled.

"Yes," she whispered, grabbing hold of his face and meeting his gaze.

Her lion. So fierce and powerful. But with a thorn in his paw.

He had said she had removed it, but she had not gotten to the one in his heart. She didn't think anyone could. Not even his mouse.

It was a terrible sorrow, but it was eclipsed by the desire that rioted through her like a storm. And then, she broke again, a horse cry of desire rising in her throat even as her internal muscles contracted around him, deep inside.

And then, he let go.

He spilled himself inside of her on a growl, his release making him pulse, making him tremble. And right then, she felt they were equals.

No longer the king and the street urchin. But two people unraveled, undone. Broken by desire and pleasure. Brought down to nothing but needed.

And need they had found sated only in each other.

And as she lay there against the mattress, breathing hard, her heart beating erratically, she felt that same rush of joy she had felt when he told her he wasn't going to marry Violet. When all seemed possible and new.

And it did. Like the sky had opened up. Right there over the bed.

"Apparently, Violet has fallen in love with Javier."

Livia looked up from her computer. "He… She… *What?*"

"While we were gone, it turns out. While we were handling that big important alliance for Monte Blanco, my brother was stealing my bride."

"You don't seem upset." She narrowed her eyes and examined him.

"I'm not. It is what I wanted for him, after all. I wanted him to find love, I just didn't assume it would be with my fiancée. But I suppose all's well that ends well. Monte Blanco could still have the benefit of Violet's influence, and she and Javier can be happy. And not even you can be angry at me anymore, Mouse."

"I think I'll find some new reasons," she said absently.

She sat there for a moment, her heart buoyant in her chest.

And suddenly, it felt like it might have burst open. He wasn't marrying Violet. She was going to marry Javier. She…

"Will you excuse me for a moment?"

"Certainly."

She left the office, and ducked into the nearest alcove of the palace, leaning against the stone wall and pressing her hand to her breast. "He's not marrying her."

She wanted to shout. She wanted to cry. For everything that had transpired on the trip had been… She had never felt like Matteo might have noticed her in that way, but during this trip she had. The way he had held her chin, the way he had looked at her…

Her foolish heart had begun to dream, and now…now he wasn't even engaged and he…

Then the cold hard dagger of reality stabbed into her.

He had seen how she was with diplomats on the trip. He had been impressed with her. And he had reiterated just how important she was to him. How he didn't want her to leave him even if she were to marry someone else. And she knew Matteo. Knew that his arrogance far surpassed just about anything else, and what he wanted, he went out and got.

Matteo was going to propose to *her*.

He would wait. He would wait until Javier and Violet had married. Until there had been a suitable lapse in time so that it was clear that he had not betrayed his fiancée in any way. And then he would... He would ask her to be his wife. No, he would demand it. Because that's who he was. It would never occur to him that she would say no. Not because he thought she was in love with him—thank God for that—but because he would simply assume that what he was asking was so logical no one would deny him. And immediately, her heart crumpled with pain.

She didn't know what to do. The reality of the situation was that things had changed. He was the same man. It didn't matter that the circumstances had shifted. He hadn't. He wouldn't. He was King Matteo of Monte Blanco, a man who considered possession of emotions to be a near crime as far as his own heart was concerned. That wouldn't change just because his circumstances with Violet King had changed. And she could see the path that he would take, and the reason he would get on it. She could see that he would choose her as a logical course of action, and it would be worse...

It would be worse than watching him marry someone else.

Because if she had to stand back and watch him marry Violet, then she would've had to watch that other woman be consigned to a life without love. And she wouldn't have envied her half so much as she might have otherwise. That would've been bearable. In a strange, small, twisted way, she found that she would have been able to bear that.

But she couldn't bear it for herself. She couldn't bear a life without love.

Not loving him the way that she did. If she hadn't loved him, it would be an entirely different story. If she hadn't felt the way that she did for him, cutting down deep into her soul, then it wouldn't be so painful. So impossible. But she did, and it was.

And she knew what it was like.

When someone else could drop you off callously, leave you standing there, alone and frightened and confused, with nothing but a sugary sweet to comfort you. Yes, she knew what that was like. She had endured it once, and she refused to put herself through it again. She refused to ever expose herself to such pain ever again.

Not for him. Not for anyone.

Not for king. Not for country.

And so she would have to steel herself. Because when he asked, she would have to say no. She would have to show no emotion whatsoever. She would have to tell herself every single day that he could walk into the office and propose marriage, any day. At any moment.

So that when he finally did, she reacted not at all. Didn't even bat an eyelash. It would destroy her. It would be as a knife, cutting across the vulnerable places in her soul.

But she would do it.

And then, she would offer to find him another wife. Because it was the only way. It was the only way she would be able to cope with all of this. The only way she would be able to be strong. Resolute in herself.

There was no other choice. *There was no other choice.*
She couldn't forget.

She could not afford to let emotion take over.

He never would.

And that was what she had to remember.

The joy that she felt inside of her chest deflated.

This was no different than that moment he told her that his engagement was off. Yes, everything bright and beautiful seemed possible for a moment. But only for a moment. Because reality remained. He was no different, and neither was she.

She got out of bed, her heart hammering.

"We will go back to Monte Blanco," he said, sitting up, the sheets sliding down and only barely covering any part of him.

"We will not," she said, panic rioting through her now.

"There is no discussion to be had," he said, frowning. "You are to be my bride, Livia."

"No. I didn't say that."

"You said that you wanted me."

"I did. And I had you. It was lovely, don't get me wrong. But… This was not an agreement to be your wife."

"The hell it wasn't."

"Do you marry every woman you have sex with, Matteo? Only, we both know you don't, as I have been responsible for shoving a great many of them out of your life. So what exactly did you think I would do when you proposed to me?"

"I thought you would say yes. Because I thought you had a brain in your head."

"I have spent years seeing the way that you treat women. As disposable, easily discarded things."

"That isn't fair," he said. "The women that I've been in relationships with have known full well how it was going to end. Quickly. They knew that I would offer a good time in bed, and a few hours of conversation. Civilized conversation. They knew that there would be nothing more than that. And they knew it from the beginning. I have never gone about being a breaker of hearts. No one has ever had their hearts engaged. Do not pretend now that you are responding to something you imagined."

"No. You're misconstruing what I'm saying. I have watched you have feelings for no one. Why would I consent to live with such a man? And what will happen when you tire of me? When you get bored? You will simply find yourself another lover, because your emotions are otherwise engaged. Or rather, not engaged at all."

"I will not. I will honor our vows."

"No. I'm not a fool. And you thought that I would be so grateful for your attentions that I would simply fall down onto my knees and accept. You thought that you could come in making demands and that I would comply. Because you thought that I was small and desperate. You can say whatever you want about why you call me Mouse, but I don't believe you. I think it is because you find me small and grateful, and you thought that I would still be that same desperate, grasping creature that you found on the streets. Oh, that I should be so lucky as to gain your attentions. As to be offered this elevation as your Queen. But no. I will not take it, and I do not want it."

"It is too late," he said.

"What do you mean?"

"It is too late for you to refuse. You made love with me."

"A commonplace act for *you*."

"But not for you," he ground out. "As it became abundantly clear when we joined."

"Are you truly shocked that I was a virgin? When would I have had the time to have a lover?"

"You have plenty of your own life, Mouse. If I had time for sex, I assumed you did as well."

She could tell by his tone the revelation truly stunned him but she couldn't fathom why. Or why he cared.

And in this moment she didn't much care. He was infuriating her.

"You know that isn't true. Because everything in your life is made easier by the actions conducted in mine. I am busy, while you are abed with any number of models."

"That isn't true. You paint a picture to appease the anger that you feel now, when you're simply indignant because you gave in. You can deny it all you want, and you can act ruffled of feather, but you wanted this, and you wanted me. Now you know it can't be hidden, and you're upset. Because you've been exposed. But your discomfort is not my concern. And you are coming back to Monte Blanco with me."

"I will not." She shimmied, slipping the dress back on. "I'm going back to my room."

"You don't have a room anymore," he said, his voice hard. "You are staying here. With me."

"I'm not. I'm leaving. I'll go back to my apartment, then."

"No."

"You cannot tell me what to do."

He picked her up off of the ground, handily holding her over his shoulder as he hunted around on the floor for pants. Somehow, he managed to hold her and put them on.

"You're coming with me. You are mine now, end of story."

"You…" She wiggled. "You have no authority to do this."

"Watch me."

"It's kidnap," she said.

"Oh, well."

"How dare you?"

"With surprising ease."

And then he walked into the elevator of the suite, completely shirtless, carrying her over his shoulder. It was late, and there was no one down in the lobby of the hotel other than an employee. Who didn't even look at them.

"You can't do this," she reiterated, hoping to get a response out of the employee, who only looked the other way. "This is outrageous."

"So it is."

"Put me down," she demanded.

She looked over her shoulder, trying to get a view of his face.

"No," he said, simply, and with no inflection.

"I said put me down."

"No," he repeated.

And suddenly she realized that he was echoing his proposal and her refusal of last week.

"Matteo…"

"I have told you from the beginning, Mouse, that a monster lived inside of me. That I was capable of all manner of things. And you told me… What did you tell me? That it wasn't true? That I had no need to be so vigilant?

That I was not my father? Let us test the limits of that, then. And your trust in me. All that you think I am capable of, and that what you think I am not. Let us plumb the depths of it, shall we?"

He bundled her into the sports car, and she was trying to gain her balance when he started the engine and began to pull away from the curb.

"You are...unbelievable," she said as he whizzed through the city streets, heading to God knew where.

"I am the King," he said. "I will have that which is mine."

CHAPTER NINE

An hour later he sat on his private plane with an angry Livia sitting across from him. Her dress was bunched up around her knees, which were pulled up against her chest, her mouth turned down into a sulky frown. Her hair was disheveled, absolutely wrecked from their love-making earlier. She had thought she would leave him? Incomprehensible. Inconceivable.

He had taken her virginity.

He had done what he had vowed never to do to her, without the offer of marriage.

With marriage on the table, it was acceptable. Without it was not. It was that simple. He could not—*ever*—leave her to take another lover. The very idea sent him into a black rage. So she was coming back with him.

And kidnap is somehow acceptable?

It was not stealing if the item belongs to you. Livia belonged to him. It was clear enough in his mind.

Something fierce burned in his chest and he did not wish to guess at what it might be.

It didn't matter.

He was set on his course. He would deal with the fallout later. Once they were back in Monte Blanco, everything would be simpler. She would not be allowed to leave. Things were more complicated when she had been in another country. A place where he did not have ultimate domain. But he did in Monte Blanco, and he would exercise it.

All would be well.

"Would you like a drink?" he asked, standing up and making his way over to the bar in the corner of the living area of the large, spacious cabin.

"I would not," she said.

"A good idea, though perhaps a bit premature. You could be carrying my child."

He had not used protection. And Livia had been a virgin, so he assumed there was a possibility that she could be pregnant.

Or on her way to pregnant, as the case may be.

"Oh," she said, the sound filled with distress.

"Things you did not consider when you thought you might walk away from me."

"I didn't think of it."

"Of course not. You lack the experience to think of such a thing. But you might be carrying my heir. Not a small consideration."

"You knew it though. You didn't use protection."

"There is no need. I assumed that your desire for me was your agreement."

"And here we are again, back to your ego. Wanting your body has nothing to do with wanting to spend the rest of my life with you."

"But it will be a royal marriage, Mouse. That means we might manage to see very little of each other. If you so desire."

"Why do you want to marry me?" she asked. "You

could have asked any woman. Any random woman on the street might have said yes."

"Because I need you," he said, the words coming out so rough they surprised even him. "I do not know how to be a man without you. I do not know what I would do if you were not in my life, and that trip we took just before Violet cried off our engagement only underlined that. You are what this country needs. They need you more than they need me. *I* need you." It was true, for he did not possess a soul, not a real one. But she did.

"Matteo, you don't need me. Not like that."

Her rejection of the honesty he had not wanted to issue enraged him. It was poison to admit his need and now she was telling him it was not real.

"Livia, look at us. Look at *this*. Are you going to sit there and defend my humanity even now? I'm a monster, but a monster who craves you nonetheless, and I will not leave you for another man to devour. That simple. That base."

"You're a stubborn ass, but that doesn't make you a monster."

"Even now you think so?"

"Yes, even now. Matteo," she said, feeling defeated now. "Don't I deserve a chance at a life?"

"I am offering you a life beyond any you could have had on your own. And no, not because I will be your husband. Because you will be Queen. Think of all that you can accomplish."

"I have accomplished a lot," she said, sounding weary. "I had thought that for a while I could just live."

The weary words settled between them.

"Some people are not meant for that," he said. "Some people are meant for greatness. It was always going to be us, Liv," he said, her name hoarse in his throat. "It was always going to be this, don't you agree?"

His chest felt painful with the truth of it. With the years laid out honest and clean behind him so he could see, truly, how inevitable it was.

"You were meant to be Queen, from the moment you were born. And it was a hard road getting here, but I believe you were born to it the same that I was. That from the very beginning, you were chosen, by fate, by the universe, to be the Queen, and it is why I saw you that day when I was driving along the streets. And it is why you came with me. Why you seemed fated to be in the palace, why everything you touched turned to gold. Perhaps it is why Violet and Javier think they are in love. Perhaps it is not they who are meant to be, so much as us. Because you are meant for great things. Greater than just living."

A tear spilled down her cheek. "What a very lofty thing to claim for someone else's life."

"Is it so very lofty?" he asked. "Compared to everything you do all the time? You are… You are an exceptional creature, Livia, why would you ever seek to be ordinary?"

"I've never been ordinary," she said. "I suppose maybe when you have never had the experience, it's what you dream of."

There was a need in her eyes that made him feel less than a king. Less than a man. He hated it. Hated that he had no idea what to do for her.

"I don't know that I have ever dreamed."

She looked up at him. "Never?"

He laughed. "How could I?"

"I don't know."

"Tell me, Livia," he demanded. "Tell me your dreams."

If it was a white horse, a white peacock, a closet of garments, he could make it so. He wanted to know that he could fulfill her dreams.

He wanted to know he could answer that need but he feared it would not be so simple.

"My nightmares are always being left at the carnival. My mother took me there when I was ten years old. A treat. The sort of thing we never did. For she had always taught me to be wary and distrustful of the outside world. We spent very little time in it. But I had seen a carnival one day, and I had told her I really wished to go. I was always asking for things. I think...in hindsight, I always wanted too much. And she felt defeated by such things, for we had nothing. Nothing. She struggled to feed me. Struggled to keep me happy. I did not go to school. What I learned, I learned on my own. Picking up books and asking those around me if they knew the sounds the letters made. And I wanted... I wanted more than the life that we had. I wanted too much. She used to tell me that. 'You want too much, Livia. The world does not exist to serve you.'" Livia blinked hard. "And one day, she took me to the carnival. I hadn't even asked. Not that day, and I was stunned. She bought me cotton candy, and it was the first time I had ever tried it. It was wonderful, and I was distracted, taken in by all the lights and colors and the sweetness of the treat. And then she was gone. I looked for her everywhere. I looked for her for days. I was thrown out of the carnival when they closed at night, and I stayed by the gates. Crying. Things were different then... There were no police particularly concerned with my plight. When your father ruled it was a military state, and the health and wellness of children crying on the street were hardly a real concern. But you know that. I waited. She didn't return. And I finally realized… I realized when I went back to our camp, after days of walking, and they were gone, that she had meant to leave me behind. I don't know what she told the rest of the people. If she told them anything at all. We are meant largely to govern ourselves, and so…"

Rage filled him. Fueled him.

She might not have told him her dreams, but he could work with her nightmares.

His lip curled. *Of course.* A monster could work much more easily with nightmares.

"Don't you think your mother deserves nothing less than for you to become her Queen?" he asked, anger on behalf of Livia burning in his gut.

How do you have the right to be angry for her? You kidnapped her.

Yes, he had. But only because it was for her own good. And surely it wouldn't take long for her to understand that. For her to see it.

"You can be the Queen your people deserve. And your mother will know. Don't you think she will recognize you? And if you tell your story, of how you were a girl abandoned, who became Queen, she will hear. She will know that's her daughter. The one she said wanted too much. Only to have it all. Only to have the whole world at her feet. The entire country. What do you think of that?"

"I think…" The words were choked in her throat. "I do not know that I can live my life for those kinds of motivations."

"Don't you think we could be happy in some regard? Don't you think…"

"I don't know."

"What were you going to do with your life if you did not marry me? You were going to stay my assistant until I proposed?"

She looked up at him, exhaustion on her face.

"I'm tired," she said. "I do not wish to be badgered. Leave me alone." And then she curled up on the seat as if he had been dismissed, and buried her face in the butter-soft leather. Whether or not she was actually asleep he couldn't tell, but she was certainly doing a great impression of a person who might be.

An hour later, they landed on the grounds of the palace in Monte Blanco. He had gotten dressed on the plane, and had arranged for all of Livia's things to be sent back to the palace. He had also dealt with her lease on the apartment. It was now in his name.

She would be furious. He hadn't wanted her to lose the place, if she wanted it as a little bolt-hole, or a vacation spot for them... He found it slightly underwhelming, but he was not going to take from her what she wanted.

When the plane landed, he woke her.

She gave him a mean-eyed stare, anger the first emotion on her face, even coming out of dreams.

"We are here."

She sat. Unmoving.

"If you don't think I will carry you into the palace, you are mistaken."

"I think you should have to do it. I think that everyone should know."

"Oh, Mouse, that you think I might balk at that shows that you do not know me half as well as you think. And here you made such bold claims about understanding me. No. You understood my civilized façade. Because it is the one you helped create. But you do not understand me. I have been cut open in the darkness. I have been asked to endure unimaginable amounts of pain. Do you know what sort of humiliation comes with that? It is endless. To be my father's own personal canvas of destruction. But I never gave in to his desire to see me weep. I never gave him what he wanted. The screams that he demanded. I withstood all the interrogation meant to simulate foreign invaders. Like I said, I just think he was a sociopath. A psychopath perhaps. Because he seemed to enjoy it. But I withstood all these things, and you think you know what created me? You think you know what will make me flinch? You think that you can shame me by forcing me to carry you into the palace?" He laughed. And then he picked her up from her seat and held her in his arms like a child, as the door to the plane lowered and their feet touched Monte Blancan soil.

Then, the two of them entered the palace, though she not on her own feet. Every member of staff looked away discreetly. He carried her back to her own bedchamber. "I will be back to speak to you. You have time to change and get yourself together. There will be instructions that you are not to leave, though, so I suggest that you not try. You will not be leaving the country. You will not be leaving the palace."

Then he turned and left her, heading straight toward his brother's offices. He found Javier sitting at his desk, with Violet perched on a love seat, taking a picture of herself.

"I have returned," he said.

"So you have," Javier responded.

Violet looked up at him. "Did you leave?"

"I brought Livia back."

"Did you?" Javier asked.

"Yes. We are to be married."

"She said yes?" Violet asked.

"Not exactly."

"What do you mean not exactly?" Javier asked.

"Oh, I've kidnapped her. She is shut in her rooms, and the entire staff will be given strict instructions not to allow her to leave. Also, she is on a no-fly list for the country."

"Madre de Dios," Javier said. "You know you can't do that."

"But I have." He shrugged. "So it seems that I can."

"That is not the way to start a marriage," Violet said.

"Well," Javier said. "Actually, that is how we began ours. With kidnap."

"Kidnap should not be quite so common," Violet said grumpily.

"It is how we solve our problems."

"Perhaps you should try *talking* about your feelings," Violet said.

Matteo and Javier exchanged a glance, and both of them chuckled.

"That is silly," Matteo said.

"That is rather silly," Javier agreed.

"We talk about our feelings all the time," Violet said.

"I might talk about them with you," Javier said. "But I will go to great lengths to not discuss them with my brother more than is humanly possible."

"I do not have feelings."

"Clearly you have some, or you would not have gone to such an extent to bring Livia back."

"She is the best choice to be Queen of the country. Actually, it's perfect. Because she is better at diplomacy than you will ever be, no offense," he said, directing that at Violet.

"None taken."

"And we still retain the benefit of your presence here in the country. Truly, I could not have planned it better. And you know that pains me to say it. That fate might have better plans than I do. I like to fancy myself as being supreme director of all things. But sometimes, you simply must acknowledge that a twist of fate has produced something even better."

"Wow," Violet said.

"I expect your support in all of this," he said, addressing both of them.

"I will not support your kidnap of your assistant."

"Neither will I," Javier said.

"You have to," he said, directing that at Javier. "Because you kidnapped Violet. And look how you ended up."

"We are in love. That's different."

"Livia was going to stay here at the palace anyway. She is simply out of sorts over the marriage aspect. God knows why."

"It's as if you're impossible and frustrating," Violet said sweetly.

"Is my brother not?"

"Well…"

"That's what I thought. Anyway. She is here. And the marriage will proceed. Whether she says yes or not."

"And when it comes to actually exchanging vows? What do you intend to do then?"

"I am a king. The marriage can be binding however I choose it to be. I could write up a document that I signed myself stating that I married her, and it would be done."

He supposed he ought to feel…something. About the

fact that he was being quite such an autocrat. But he would not be bad to her. In fact, he would treat her as if she were… As if she were Queen. But she would be. So there was no reason for guilt. None whatsoever.

And for him, control was essential.

"I'm sorry," Javier said. "But I will not allow it. And I am second in command in this country, and the head of your military, and I will have to see that Livia has agreed to the marriage before I will allow it to proceed."

"Or you will start a war with me?"

"Yes. To prevent you from engaging with an even bigger one inside of yourself. You do not wish to be this leader."

He growled. "Do not tell me what I wish." He turned and stalked out of the room, going straight back to Livia.

She gasped when he opened the chamber door, and held the T-shirt to her breast. She was wearing a pair of sweatpants, and a bra.

"A bit late for belated shows of modesty, don't you agree?"

"What are you doing here?"

"I'm here to speak to you of marriage."

She let out a growl, and jerked the top over her head. "Be reasonable."

"Why should I marry you?"

And somehow, even with all the reasons, all the logic that existed inside of him, there was only one answer that came to him. Only one that resonated in his soul.

"Because I want you."

And then Livia let out a cry, closed the space between them and flung herself into his arms.

CHAPTER TEN

THIS WAS FOLLY. It was disastrous. And she couldn't stop herself. Because what he had said, so ragged and raw, was the first thing that had actually resonated within her.

Oh, yes, it had been very tempting when he asked her about her mother. When he had asked if she would enjoy it if the woman knew that Livia was now her Queen. She was only human. And it was an enticement to a girl who had spent a great many nights dreaming about all the ways she might show her mother she had never needed her.

And he'd known that. Had known of a way to cut down deep into her soul.

He was good at that. Unfortunately.

But this.

Raw and honest, this was what she could not deny.

She had thought that she could make love with him once and walk away?

She had been a fool.

And not because she had imagined he would pick her up and fling her over his shoulder and kidnap her, but because she was bound to him. Whether he had done it or not.

She hadn't made a very good sport of trying to escape him. And in truth… He could've taken her hand

and led her down to that car, led her onto the plane, and she probably would've gone.

Because she was only human.

She was only a woman. A woman who had loved one man for a very long time. Who'd had to flee a country in order to keep herself from capitulating to him too easily.

But he had come after her. She had run away, and he had been right there behind her. And she had given in. Folded herself into him with no great resistance at all.

And she had told herself all kinds of lies.

But now, with him holding her like this, she could see them for what they were.

It was all such a farce.

As if she could ever refuse him. She loved him too much. And this was far too close to a perfect dream than anything else Livia had ever had.

She had never been able to find her people again. She had never seen her mother. She had never known her father. She had spent nine years in fear, yearning, and then…

He was offering her a chance to be Queen. He was offering her his hand, even though he was not offering her his heart. So she kissed him. Like she might be drowning, and he was there to save her. Kissed him as if her life depended on it, and in the moment, it felt like it did.

Kissed him until his hands created all manner of pleasure and fire that consumed the uncertainty inside of her.

She had known this man for years, loved him. But there were still dark places in him she could sense but could not see.

And she wanted to see them. Wanted to see him.

For better or worse.

"Say yes," he growled.

"Yes," she said, tears pouring down her cheeks.

She had lost. She had lost the battle inside of herself but she had won him, so wasn't that fine? Wasn't it okay?

What she was tired of was fighting. Pure and simple. Of wanting and not having. Of being in a constant state of deprivation.

So yes, the idea of being Queen, of being his wife who would never have his heart, had notes of exhaustion buried inside of it, but so did this. A life spent without Matteo. The nine years that she had carried wanting him, needing him, and never having him… It was not less exhausting. And if she could not have him now, then it would all have been for nothing. So she had lost at some things. And perhaps it was not so bad to surrender.

She thought of him reaching out his hand when she had been a girl. Seventeen years old and alone on the streets. Refusing him then would have been foolish. Was refusing him now any better? Sometimes you had to take the offered hand, even not knowing where it might lead. Because otherwise you would simply stay in the same spot, and that wasn't always good either.

Maybe that was all fanciful justification, but it amounted to the same thing. She could not turn away from Matteo. And more to the point, she didn't want to.

So, she kissed him. Kissed him until she couldn't breathe. Luxuriated in the feel of his mouth against hers, his gorgeous, hard body the sheltering place she had never had while living on the street.

He gave her so much. So much more than she could have ever hoped to have. Why did she insist on asking for everything?

Everything was…

She was a girl who had come up from a place of wanting only to survive.

She did not need more than being Queen.

She was selfish. And she was fanciful.

Because you look at him and he makes you believe that you could have everything.

No. This was everything. It was all she needed.

He stripped her comfortable clothes away from her body, and she made quick work of his. She'd not had the time to examine the full glory of his male form last night. Last night had been frantic, and it had felt like the end of something.

This, this was just the beginning. This really was a promise she was making, not only to him but to herself.

That she would be thankful for what she had been given, that she would do her best with what fate had set out before her. Because it really was sort of a miraculous thing, and there was no purpose in keeping herself from it.

He laid her down on the glorious, velvet bedspread that she loved so much—she had left it behind when she had gone to Paris. She had been willing to leave so many things behind—for what was a preferred bedspread when she was leaving behind the only man she had ever cared for?—and covered her body with his.

She moved her hands over the muscles on his back, the raised ridges of scars there. And when he raised up slightly, she ran her hands over the scars on his front too. Then she leaned in, kissing them. Tracing the line that she knew his father's knife had followed across his skin. As if she might heal it with her touch.

With the love that burned in her breast, whether she wanted it to be there or not.

Perhaps it would be easier to simply not love him. She knew that Javier and Matteo loved each other as brothers. She knew that they cared, but they did not show that caring in an effusive way. She was the only one that could ever love Matteo like this. And she did not want to hold it back, not now.

All of a sudden, she wanted to pour it out over him. Make him feel it. For hadn't he brought her into the palace and into a sense of safety that she had never known possible? She had spent all these years trying to earn her place, but perhaps she simply needed to be thankful for it. And she was. She was so immensely grateful for all that he had given to her, and it made her want to give no less than she had received.

She wished she could heal him. She really did. Wished that her kisses would penetrate not only his scars, but the hardness of his heart.

But she would take the feel of his body trembling beneath her touch, she would take the apparent arousal that he felt as she moved her hands over his skin, her lips.

She kissed a path down his chest, down his stomach, down to that most masculine part of him. He was glorious. Beautiful.

She had not been prepared to think a man's body was half so beautiful as his was, but it was. A glorious work of art. Carved from the white mountains of their country. Carved from the hardship that he had endured. Weakness. That was the thing he feared most. Not pain. Not death or defeat. Weakness.

That his father might have found a way to make him weak. And what hurt her the most was that she knew that he had.

Whether Matteo could ever see it that way or not...

He had taken away Matteo's ability to feel. Because he had made his son fear that that might be the biggest weakness of all. No. Matteo would never be weak in that way. He was a good man. It was only that he feared himself so deeply.

But when you had been shaped and formed by a monster, how could you do anything else?

She knew that. She knew him.

She worried enough about her own value, her own worth, because of what her mother had done.

And it hurt.

You did not simply unlearn those things, you did not simply unfeel them.

It was not half so simple.

But this was, at least. This desire that she felt for him. And this was an easy way to show him. Because he could understand this. He could feel this.

She caressed him, running her palm over his hardness. Luxuriating in the feel of him beneath her hand.

Oh, but he was a glorious man. Truly wonderful and miraculous in ways that she could not express fully. Not without touch.

So she squeezed him, tested his length. He was large. If she had examined him too closely prior to their first joining she might have been terrified.

But then of course, Matteo de la Cruz could never be anything but exceptional. And he was.

Then she leaned in, his musky, masculine scent tormenting her, enticing her. To greater exploration. She pressed her lips to his shaft, then tasted him tentatively, before taking him fully into her mouth.

He jerked beneath her, and she took control of this moment. Of their pleasure.

All the while, he reached between her thighs and began to test her wetness. Her desire for him. He pushed two fingers inside of her as she continued to taste him, and she let out a low moan of pleasure, which made him growl out his own.

Then he grabbed hold of her, his large hands spanning her waist and easily lifting her up, bringing her down to straddle his body.

"Go right ahead, Mouse. Show me what you can do."

Her heart pounding hard, she shifted, and felt the blunt head of his erection against the entrance to her body. And with shaking thighs, she lowered herself onto him slowly, achingly so. And he filled her, inch by delicious inch. She gasped as he did, her head thrown back on a sigh of pleasure.

"Show me," he growled. "Show me what you want, Livia."

She shifted her hips tentatively, finding a slow and steady rhythm until pleasure began to build inside of her to an unbearable degree. Her core ached with need, her body so slick, the friction it created driving her near to the brink. And then, he seemed to lose his control entirely. He thrust up into her, arching up off the bed, the ferocity of his movements pushing her over. Her internal muscles pulsed around him, and she couldn't hold back the scream of her release, didn't want to. For she wanted him to know. Wanted him to know just how deeply she was affected by this. By the intensity of their joining.

His own feral growl of release was not far behind, his blunt fingers digging hard into her hips, and she was certain there would be bruises there.

Good. She wanted to be marked by it. Wanted to be changed by it. She wanted to wear it.

For she had wanted this, wanted him for an untold number of years.

And when it was done, she lay, spent and breathing hard against his chest.

And she felt... Happy.

For all that this was imperfect, for all that they were imperfect, there was a deep sort of satisfaction to this that she had never known before.

"Would you like anything?" he asked, his voice rough.

A smile curved her lips. "Coffee."

And that was how she found herself naked, sitting in her bed drinking coffee with Matteo. It was a direct echo of that night she had found him dreaming.

And it was a relief, because it was something other than the fighting and all of his autocratic behavior from the previous few days. This was where he was human. She liked him something more than human too. It was part of his charm after all. Perhaps charm was overstating it. But it was part of him. A man who was bigger than life. A man who was nearly a god. A rock. A mountain.

But also a man.

"When you were a child," he said, "what did you dream? Before there were nightmares. Before... Before everything. What was all that *too much* that you wanted?"

"I dreamed of education. I dreamed of a world where we didn't have to be afraid of the King. Where we did not have to hide from soldiers."

"I'm sorry."

"It isn't your fault. My people are freer now than they've ever been, and that is because of you."

"And you will continue it," he said. "I'm confident in that."

"I hope so. I hope I will be a good queen."

"You will marry me, then."

"It enrages me to say, since I know you were nothing but confident in it this whole time."

"I was not," he said softly. "I questioned it. The thing about you, Livia, is that I have never been able to anticipate what you would do. You are a constant source of surprise, Mouse. And very few people are that to me. If anyone. For I realized when I was very young that no matter what façade a person presented to the world, they could be anything beneath it. My father never looked like a good king, but I'm not convinced he looked entirely like the sociopath he was behind the scenes. I don't think anyone would have ever guessed that he would play havoc with the body of his heir, for example."

She shook her head. "No. I don't suppose. You would think that he would have valued you. That he would've protected you above all else."

"Perhaps that was what he told himself. That he was building me into a resilient super soldier of some kind. Though I doubt it."

"And what of your dreams?"

"I did not have any. I was born into darkness, and I felt as if I would continue to live in it no matter what. That there would be no escaping it. After all, my father was my blood. And he told me, repeatedly, that I would be the same manner of king that he is. He made it clear that his goal was to transform me into another part of him. He said his father before him was the same, and his father before him. So why would I have any chance of being different? I knew that I had to make a choice. And it wasn't a dream. It was simply… Determination. I saw the suffering of my people and I regretted it bitterly.

So I bided my time. I gave no indication that I might be different. And then… And then when it was my time, I set about to change things. But you are right, I didn't know how to interact with people. I mostly still don't. For I had to learn to hide everything, to keep it hidden, to keep it pushed down, otherwise… What my father could see, he would exploit. What he could touch, he would damage. What he could fight against, he would. And I cannot allow that to be so."

"How do you know? That there is something else out there in the world when you are born into a specific environment that does not allow you to see a reality that's different from yours?"

"I might ask you the same, Livia. You certainly didn't know that there was a world out there where you could have education. You must not have known your own potential. Here you are, on the verge of being Queen. Surely you could not have known that, and yet dared to want better. And you fought to survive on the streets, not even knowing if you would ever find a different sort of reality than the one that you had been thrust into. How exhausting it must be, to fight so hard to simply survive."

"Yes. I didn't just dream of that. I dreamed of candy and cake and living. Of gowns, of parties. A birthday party. I had my very first birthday party that I can ever remember here at the palace. It was magic. I wanted so many pretty things, and I do worry…"

"What is it?"

"That part of me wishes to be Queen because I will have beautiful dresses and I will be pampered and cared for and I will have all of the sex that I could ever want, and I will be so comfortable. And isn't that quite selfish?"

"There is nothing wrong with wanting all of those things. Particularly not when you have been deprived as you've been."

"Well. Now you know. I am quite only human."

"You are quite the most amazing human."

"Thank you. Matteo… What about children?"

"I must have them," he said.

"Yes. But you have told me, many times over the years, that your heart is stone. That you cannot feel emotion because of what happened to you. I understand that. I… I do." She might not accept it, but she did understand it. She might not think it was right, but she could understand it. "But what about *our* children?"

She wanted to cry. Admitting, accepting that this would mean having children with Matteo. Having children at all, when that was a dream that she had never even thought to entertain…. It was wonderful. Wonderful and emotional and terrifying all at once.

"I will be good to them. And I will show them the path that they should walk on. And you… Livia, you are the only person who has ever given me the sort of care that you did. You will be the best mother. My mother vanished from my life when I was too young to remember her clearly. And I always feared asking what had become of her. Now I will never know. But you… You will be there for our children. A gift that neither of us had. That is enough for me."

Her heart felt like it might burst. And she knew that she should be suspicious of this, knew that she should be on her guard, knew that she should protect herself, but she didn't have the energy to do it. In this moment, she simply wanted to sink into it. Simply wanted to revel in it and be.

"I will do my very best," she said. "To treat them as neither of us were."

"We will be married as soon as possible," he said, resolute.

"Yes," she agreed.

"I will go back to my room now," he said.

"No," she said. "Stay with me."

He looked at her, his dark eyes unfathomable. Then she saw in it an emotion, so deep and raw that it was nearly terrifying to look at directly.

"Being married does not mean you have to share a room with me. That is not how royal marriages typically work."

"No. But I should like for us to share a room. What do you think of that?"

"Then we shall," he said.

He took the coffee cup in her hand and set it along with his own on the nightstand. "Come to me, my Queen."

And she thought, as she gave herself over to him, that being Queen Mouse might not be so bad after all.

He awoke in the dark. Gasping, sweating. The pain was unbearable. But then, cool hands were on his skin, a soft mouth pressed to his scars.

He had never fallen asleep with a woman before. Never. For this reason. But she was there. And she comforted him. And he knew immediately who it was. Livia. His Mouse.

His Queen.

Comforting him in the way that only she could.

It had been so from the beginning.

It was a weakness, perhaps, to need this the way that he did.

But he wasn't sure he cared.

For he was too caught up in it, in her touch, and the soothing words that she spoke. He pulled her to him, and kissed her. Kissed her with all the rising, angry emotion in his chest.

No. It was only in his dreams that he ever felt this. During the day, he walked around with the rock where his heart should be. During the day, he remembered who he was, what he must be.

It was only now, only now at night that things became muddled and fuzzy. But she was so soft, his Livia.

Livia.

For it had always been her. *He would've married another woman.*

Right then, in the darkness of their room, in this shared bed, with his nightmares fresh on his heels and his body burning from the pain woven out of his dreams, he felt destroyed by that thought.

That he might've made another woman his Queen.

Livia was his Queen.

On this line between sleep and wakefulness it seemed so clear. She kissed him, matching his desperation. And when he turned her over and sank into her welcoming body, everything seemed bright. Everything seemed to make sense. Everything seemed to be as it had never been before. His chest felt like it might burst, and he found that he could not breathe.

He felt as if she might have answers. And she might have had those same answers on that night so many years ago, when she had first come to him.

Livia.

His.

His woman.

CHAPTER ELEVEN

MATTEO MOVED ALL of her things into his chamber shortly after that.

And the plans for the wedding were proceeding at pace. Livia couldn't deny that she felt a certain amount of disquiet over the whole thing. Mostly because… Well, she was used to fading into the background. And now… She wouldn't be.

Matteo had made an announcement to his people, that Livia was going to be Queen. And it was all done now. There was no turning back. She'd said yes to him. She would've been disappointed in herself if she were not quite so satisfied in other ways.

She was sitting in the dining room, having an afternoon espresso, when Violet walked in. Violet, who would be her sister-in-law. Violet, whom she had resented so much not that long ago.

It was strange. How much things had changed so quickly. She had liked Violet almost immediately, that had been difficult, when she'd been mired in her jealousy.

Jealousy she'd gotten over immediately when she'd seen how Violet loved Javier. It had been easy for them to find a friendship after that.

"Hi," Violet said.

"Hello," Livia responded.

"How is everything going with the wedding plans?"

A staff member came in, and Violet requested her own espresso, and some cake.

"I might have some cake," Livia said.

"Of course," the woman responded.

"Is it strange?" Violet asked. "To go from…working here to…"

Livia blinked. "Well, yes. Though, honestly it's all happened so slowly. I've been with Matteo for nine years. I mean, not *been* with… I… I've been here at the palace. And things have evolved."

"Yes," Violet said. "They truly have. I haven't been here very long. And things with Javier moved quite quickly. But… That wasn't the case for you."

Livia looked away. "I loved him… For a very long time."

"You must be happy, then. That it has worked out this way."

"I'm not sure anything is worked out yet."

"Why not? You're marrying him."

"Yes. I'm marrying him." Javier and Violet were in love. In love in a way Matteo said they could not be. But somehow Javier loved. She was desperate to know more about that. "You know… Javier must've had a very difficult time with his feelings."

"Yes. He did. Did Matteo not tell you how things were for Javier?"

"Some small things. I know about Matteo's experiences, but not Javier's. He guards that relationship. Between himself and his brother. I think it is the only lifelong relationship he's ever had that meant anything to him. No, I don't think that, I know it. He cares for Javier very much, but showing feelings is hard for him."

"He has always seemed…" Violet looked thoughtful. "Granted I don't know him that well, but he has always seemed easier than Javier. I was quite annoyed of myself that it was Javier who captured my attention. Considering he was my jail keeper, and a grump."

"Matteo hides it. But he's very…" She thought of his scars. She thought of his nightmares. All of those things she would keep to herself. For it was his story. And it was not hers to share. She would never uncover him in such a way.

They had trust between them that he didn't share with anyone else, and she would never do anything to violate that.

"You know about their father. Their mother was gone before either of them could have ever known her. And their father was not a good man. Javier trusted him, Matteo never did. But Matteo saw the worst of him. And he is… It's like emotion doesn't touch him. As if everything glances off. It's why he seems an easier man. He does not easily feel anything half so intense as anger."

But things between them were intense enough, and there was no denying that. They felt plenty for each other. At least, in bed.

"He believes it is how a king must be."

"I see. And so… His view of love…"

"Dim," she said. "Actually, I don't think he believes he can feel it."

"And you?"

"I know I can," Livia said.

"Are you happy, though, with the prospect of marrying him?"

"I am… I would not be happy had he married anyone else, that much is certain. But I… I'm afraid."

"You don't have to marry him," Violet said softly. "I know he wants you to, and I understand that you love him, and that you want him, but you don't have to simply take what's on offer."

"But what other choice do I have? I would be miserable without him." She sighed heavily. "I already tried to leave. I didn't stay gone."

"Sure, but you deserve to be loved," Violet said. "Not just to give it, but to get it back."

"But he deserves to be loved," Livia said. "And I think I'm the only one that can love him the way that I do."

"He should become the only man who can love you as he does. And as much as I care for him, as he is my brother-in-law, and I do know that he and my husband had a terrible time in their youth... I really do think that he might have to work for something, for feelings, to ever be able to heal. It would not be good for him to simply be given everything he asks for, and not be required to change at all."

"He's changed," Livia said, feeling defensive.

"If you say so. I don't want you to leave, Livia, to be very clear. I like having you here, and I think now we have become friends. But should you not have everything?"

"Some people just can't have everything."

She repeated what she had told herself only last night.

"No," Violet said. "That isn't true. Somebody who loves as ferociously as you absolutely deserves to have everything. It doesn't matter what happened in your past. It doesn't matter what other people have made you feel about yourself. How small they've made you feel. How insecure it's made you feel. None of it is true. It doesn't get to decide what you become. The only person that can decide to accept less is you."

"What if it isn't less?" she whispered. "I mean... I was nothing. I was on the streets. He's going to make me a queen. And I... I love him."

"The real concern is if you are allowing him to accept less. What if he could feel more? Not for another woman, don't mistake me. But if you asked for more, what if he had to dig inside himself and heal?"

She didn't know what to say to that. "But I want to marry him," she said, after their cake had been left sitting in front of them.

"Then you should."

"Well, you just made it sound like you thought I shouldn't."

"No. It's only that I want you to be happy. That I want both of you to be happy. That's all. I'm really not telling you what to do. Maybe it's hormones. I should probably be ignored. Anyway," Violet said, a slight smile curving her lips. "There is a very interesting Royal wedding night tradition in Monte Blanco."

"Is there?"

"Yes. It involves jeweled handcuffs." Violet made eye contact with her as she took a sip of her espresso. "If nothing else, it's worth getting to that point just for the experience."

"Only on the wedding night?" Livia asked.

"No," she said. "Javier finds excuses to use them whenever he is of a mood. Which is often."

Was it so wrong to want this? Violet had made her question it, and yet Violet's presence was part of what made Livia want this. She could have a sister-in-law. A friend. Right here in the palace. She could have... Royal wedding nights complete with handcuffs. She could have so much here.

But not love.

Maybe love was overrated. Maybe it didn't matter.

It was all fine for Violet and her American sensibilities to feel like it was something that Livia should be fighting for. But maybe she could just... Maybe she could just have this. And it would be enough.

It was time for the pre-wedding festivities to begin. All of it was a bit much for Matteo's taste, but he also did not see why he would change the protocol. He did not want to offend Livia in any way, and he had the feeling that were he to back off on the festivities, she would take it as a sign that somehow she was less important to him than another queen might have been, and not simply that he did not care for seven days' worth of pageantry.

Which was the truth of it.

He had not seen her all day. She was being treated, royally, in order to come out gleaming and wrapped in velvet, and worthy of her position as Queen, though in his opinion, she was already far beyond worthy. It wasn't until it was nearly time to go into the ballroom that he saw her for the first time. Uncharacteristically, her hair was down, falling in soft waves just past her shoulders. Her makeup was light, illuminating her face, rather than covering it. As much as he had liked the red lipstick she'd worn the other night, he liked this version of her. This one that was familiar but gleaming and special all at the same time.

She was wearing green. A strapless, velvet gown with a neckline that plunged down between her glorious breasts, and he wanted to cover her, because he did not want anyone else to see what was his.

"Hi," she said, looking almost shy. She looked down, her pale lashes fanning across her cheekbones.

"I would rather take you to our bedroom, than into the ballroom," he said.

"Oh," she answered.

"I heard… I did hear… That is to say… Violet said something about handcuffs?"

The idea warmed his blood. He had thought little about the tradition in Monte Blanco of binding the bride's wrists and ankles on the wedding night, but he was thinking of it now. And found it quite overly appealing. Oh, yes, he would enjoy exploring those sensual delights with Livia. The games that could be made out of restraints would be lush, and the very thought sent a kick of desire through him.

"I used to scrub these floors," she said, as they stood before the ballroom doors.

"And you never will again," he said.

No. He wished to elevate her and keep her there. This beautiful, incomparable woman who was his in every way.

His.

The doors opened for them, and they entered the room. It was already filled with peacocks, guests dressed in finery from head to toe. Laughing and drinking and dancing. His brother was there, and he was actually smiling, with Violet on his arm, looking stunning in the color that was her namesake. But he could not imagine her on his arm. And he could only be grateful, yet again, that she and Javier had found each other, so that he could stand here with Livia.

As they walked into the room, a hush fell over it, and he found that even the members of staff in attendance were staring at them. At her.

But of course, it must be notable, that she was among them, not so long ago, and now she was to be their Queen.

He wondered how that would be for her. But then, if there was even a whisper of disrespect among the staff, he would have them removed at once.

Livia had suffered enough in her life, and there was no need for her to suffer anymore. He would see to that. He would never allow anyone to make her feel like she was less, not ever again.

They moved deeper into the room, and it took a while, but soon Livia began to loosen, began to warm, and the way that she had been on their previous trip started to come into the fore. He could see that she would do well at this. He was confident in it. And he was prouder of her than he had ever been of anyone or anything in all of his life.

She was an amazing creature. And she was his.

He was waylaid by heads of state, and Livia kept on walking, greeting others in attendance. He kept watch on her out of the corner of his eye, but trusted she would do well.

And she did. She was not shy, nor was she unaccustomed to many of the guests.

Suddenly, she jolted, as one of the men in attendance bumped into her and spilled a drink over the bodice of her gown.

"Oh," she said. "I'm sorry... I..."

"Perhaps you should clean it yourself," the man said. "As you are only a maid, after all."

Matteo found himself moving toward her without thought.

He was across the space immediately, his blood pounding like a hammer. "Clean this up," he said to the man. "Who are you?"

"A reporter, Your Majesty."

"For?"

"Monte Blanco Press."

"And you are no longer employed there, I will ensure that. Now, see yourself out of the palace."

Everything had stopped in the room. Everyone was listening to him. Was watching.

"Your Majesty…"

"There is no argument. If this is not clean and you are not gone in the next few moments I will see you thrown in the dungeon. Have no doubts, there is still a dungeon here. Do you think I fear to use it? I may not be the same King as my father, but I will not tolerate disrespect. You will respect my Queen. As she *is* to be your Queen. And it does not matter where she came from, she is above you. She always has been. You are nothing. And I could destroy you with a mere word."

The man had gone pale, and Matteo didn't care. He wanted the man to be fearful. For his life. For he would pay for this insult to Livia.

"Matteo," she said, putting her hand on his arm. "Stop. Please."

"He dared insult you," Matteo said. "At your own party. And I will have it known this will not stand."

"And I appreciate it," Livia said. "But these are not medieval times, and he can say whatever he wishes. Does he not have the freedom to do so?"

"No," Matteo growled.

"He must," she said. "Or we are no better than we were. He must have the freedom to insult me, as I have the freedom to respond or not respond as I see fit. And I choose not to respond. For I have been through much worse than a few casual insults hurled at me by a man unhappy with his life. And I will endure more scathing commentary, I'm certain. It's true," she said, her voice rising above all other sounds in the ballroom. "I was a maid here. I was a street urchin and one of the forest people before that. I am nothing. And I am now to be Queen. And I will not forget where I came from. I am an advocate for those who do not have a voice, for those who do not have power. This I promise. I will never forget."

She turned to Matteo. "I beg of you. Do not take his job from him."

"He was not able to perform it," Matteo said. "He spilled a drink, on you, and insulted you."

"Yes," Livia said. "And one thing neither you nor I ever got in life was grace. You have a chance to extend it now. Please, Matteo, do it for me."

"No. Get out. It is a wonderful thing that my wife will not forget where she came from. It is why I'm marrying her. But I will not forget from what *I* came from. I'm not a man to be trifled with. You can say whatever you wish, but it will be met with consequences if it is in my hearing. Out."

He could not allow this. Livia deserved better. And there were things he could not give to her, but he could demand her respect.

And the man left. Nearly running out the ballroom door. "Resume festivities," Matteo said.

And as if he had flipped a switch, everyone went back to talking.

Livia looked at him with round, wounded eyes. "Why did you do that?"

"I will have respect. As will you. You are my chosen bride and…"

"And what? And *what*, Matteo? You will exercise your position as king to be a tyrant?"

His chest pitched, heaved.

"I told you already. I do not know another place to be. I was formed by a tyrant. A master manipulator, an evil man. Did you think that I would truly be above any of those things? I am not, nor will I be. I am simply a man. And men can be made into monsters."

Already, these things that he felt for Livia were far too intense.

"We will speak after this."

She was frosty to him for the rest of the evening, and it put him in a foul mood. And when they arrived back at their bedchamber, she rounded on him.

"If I did not wish for him to have such consequences, why did I not get to say?"

"I am the King. Not you. And allowing that kind of disrespect is setting a bad precedent."

"And what consequence comes of it? This is the kind of thing that signals you're an autocrat. That demonstrates to people that you wish to control not only their daily lives but the things they think, the things they say. People will disapprove of me. I did used to be a maid. There's nothing you can do about it."

"I am the King," he said.

"Listen to yourself. This is everything you said you did not want."

He looked at her, realization turning over in his chest. It was true. This was what he had professed he would never be. Not simply an action, but the fact that he had been caught in his own perspective for so many hours now. Deeply convinced of his own rightness. And this was how it began.

This was how it began.

"Matteo," she said. "I know what you came from. And I feel deeply for all that you have endured. But you have it wrong. You don't need to close your heart, you need to open it. You must. At a certain point, you must. If you don't, then it will always be hard like this, and when things happen, when people make mistakes in your presence, they will be nothing but horrendously penalized for it. And you will not be able to see... You won't be able to see. This is the problem. The problem is that you could not understand where his pain was coming from. And that is something I cannot teach you. It's not about putting a smile on your face, it's about learning empathy. He is upset because his own standing in life will not change. He is upset because mine did. It has nothing to do with thinking I am not worthy, so much as he thinks he should have been. It isn't fair. You can accept a certain amount of poverty if you look around you and see others suffering with you, but when someone transcends... It gives you false hope. And this is not a typical trajectory, it is not something other people can dream of. What I was given is not... It is not about my own cleverness. I am made by an act of great mercy shown to me by you. But will all the people get so much mercy shown to them?"

"He is not homeless. He has work. He is not suffering."

"It doesn't matter. It is a feeling of not being able to move positions in life."

"But I think you are wrong," Matteo said. "It is not because I feel nothing, it is because I feel too much."

The words were dragged from him, jagged bits of glass pulled through his chest, his throat. Feelings—good and bad—always existed alongside each other in his heart and he could never separate one from the other.

The trick for him had been to have none and here he was…bleeding with it.

"Matteo…" She put her hand on his arm and looked up at him. "Surely you must know by now how very much I love you."

His whole body went stiff, and his heart turned to stone. Everything in him rejected that simple, softly spoken statement. "No," he said.

"I do. I do love you and…"

"You were warned. You were told. There will be no love between us. Not ever."

Love.

Love was the greatest enemy.

For him, love was toxic.

He wished it didn't exist.

He wished it were so.

"It's too late. There already is. And love is what you need, you hardheaded ass. You need to feel something in that great, mountain of a chest of yours. You cannot be a rock forever."

"I must be a rock, immovable. For it is emotion that caused me to lash out at that man. A sense of anger. Of what I thought to be right, colored by the way I felt. It is not good. I must know what is right, and it must never change, regardless of the circumstances. You are right. I violated all which I had chosen to be in the way that

I behaved tonight, and I did it in a room full of people. No. You will not entice me to more feeling, Mouse."

"Then I never did remove the thorn. And I was never your mouse, not really. Because it's still there, festering away, creating a wound that will never, ever heal. You don't want it to heal. You wanted it to sit there, causing you pain, because it makes you feel good to know it's there, because you can protect yourself. And you can say whatever you wish about protecting the kingdom but it isn't the truth. You don't want to feel because then you have to cope with being human. With being vulnerable. And we both know it's the thing you fear most. Making mistakes. Being seen as weak. Crying out with pain. But… Perhaps Violet is right. Perhaps it is what you need."

"What does Violet have to do with anything?"

"Never mind. Just tell me… Could you love me? Do you think there is a chance you could, even a little bit?"

"It is an impossibility. I cannot love you."

"You cannot? Or you will not?"

"They are the same, for I am a king. And what I will is simply what is."

The look on her face was devastated, crushed, but she had known. There was not another person on earth who knew him half so well as she did. She should not be surprised. She should not be so wounded. And he… He should not respond to it. "We wed tomorrow," he said. "We have the rest of our lives to disagree."

"I don't want that."

"You're mine," he said. "Mine." And he pulled her to him and kissed her, fiercely. And she returned it. Giving back everything he gave to her. Matching him, with each and every kiss. He stripped her of her gown and allowed her to strip him of his suit. And then it was just the two of them, here in his room, this place where they had compared scars and nightmares. This place where they slept together, tangled up in each other, just enough that it kept the dreams away. And this was the only thing he could do now. The only thing that felt right. For he was a naked mass of too many feelings, and it was all her fault. This was all her fault. And tonight had demonstrated that what he was afraid of was exactly what would come to pass if he gave in.

Oh, but it was a short bridge, to firing someone and making threats of the dungeon to actually following through with it. To disallowing disloyal talk about the Queen, to demanding total control over a group of people who refused to live under the King's command.

Such a short bridge to what his father had become. And the vision of it now, the clarity there, was a rolling tide of horror.

But her mouth was not. For here things made sense. She made sense.

And so he lost himself. In her. In the softness of her touch. And everything she gave.

And he took.

Greedily. Drank from her mouth, lost himself in her body. And when he thrust deep within her, she let out a gasp. "I love you."

It washed over him like a warm wave. And he could feel it, reaching the parched places of his soul. Could feel how desperate he was.

No.

He could not accept it. He could not.

"I love you," she whispered again as he thrust back inside her. "I love you. I love you. I love you. I love you."

Like the counting off in their dance lesson. Steady and insistent and filled with all the need that he had tried to deny all these years.

He could feel that weakness. Shifting, eroding inside of him.

And suddenly, he felt like a boy. Enduring torture.

But not the kind his father had given out. No. This was like having a cherished dream held out in front of him, only to have it be just out of reach.

Then, he could no longer think. Then, there was nothing but the white-hot pleasure that erupted inside of him, and she cried out as he spilled himself inside of her, as she pulsed around him. And then he worked to harden himself, to go back to what he was.

For a moment, he had her and that would have to be enough. It would have to be, because it was all he could allow.

Livia was his. And she would be as she had been in the ballroom. His conscience. And she would love him.

I was never your mouse...

He shut that out, and he held her close.

Because she was. Whatever she said.

And he would allow no other reality to encroach.

For he decided what it was.

And he was set in this.

And so, it would be.

CHAPTER TWELVE

THE DAY OF the wedding dawned bright and clear, and Livia felt as if there was a storm cloud hanging over her head. She was dressed in a gown of the finest satin, a dream for the girl that she'd been, who had thought that she might have nice things one day.

This was beyond nice.

She was swathed in the fabric, which molded perfectly to her form, and billowed out around her feet. There were small, glass beads sewn into a growing cascade from the bodice down all the way to the floor, where it shimmered as if it had been put together with ice crystals.

She looked beautiful. She felt beautiful. Just as she had felt Matteo's desperation for her last night. But she could not forget what Violet had said to her.

She had nearly told him last night, but she hadn't the strength. Not when he had kissed her.

She had simply wanted to push everything away and be with him. Because it was better. Because it was easier. Easier than dealing with the sad reality of the situation she found herself in.

Everything. Absolutely everything was right at her fingertips except...

Matteo was breaking apart. She could see it. She could see it in the way that he had behaved last night. And she was not... She was not helping him.

She had given so much credit to the fact that she had healed him in some way, but what she'd said last night remained true.

She clearly had not healed him in any meaningful fashion, or...or he would not be so hard, not still.

But there were things that he refused to see. Things that he refused to accept. And that she could not do for him. However, she had a terrible feeling that she might be part of preventing the healing.

She couldn't take that final step for him, but she could certainly keep him comfortable enough that he never took the step for himself.

She looked at herself in the mirror. She was dressed as his bride. Ready to walk down the aisle toward him. Ready to be everything that she had ever dreamed. His Queen. His wife.

Except his love.

She would never be his love.

And she would never know what it was to be loved. She would just be an assistant who had undergone a very fancy promotion. She would not be the wife of his heart. Not really. Not for so long as he denied even having a heart.

She took a deep breath, and picked up her bouquet. And then she saw the time.

The wedding was about to begin.

The massive chapel on the grounds of the palace was filled to capacity. Everyone inside dressed in finery.

Women in hats and dresses that brought to mind an array of Easter eggs, the men in fitted suits.

And Matteo stood at the head of the altar and waited. And waited.

For Livia. Always for Livia.

His heart was like a bruised and battered thing, and had been since she'd told him of her love, and still he was here.

Because he could not imagine a future without her.

A future where you cannot give her the one thing she wants...

He was not strong enough to turn away from her.

That was his failing.

That was his shame.

And so he waited.

The music began, and then changed. But Livia did not appear. And even when he was certain that she had missed her cue, she still did not appear.

A hush rippled through the room as he strode back up the aisle and out the doors. "Livia," he shouted.

"Livia."

Then he walked to the room where she had been readying herself, only to find it...empty.

Her bouquet was sitting there on the vanity. But there was no note.

But of course, Livia wouldn't leave a note. She would simply do what she had always done.

And it was as if all the blood within him ran free of his body.

He wrenched his tie free and ran from the chapel, making his way toward the palace. Because she couldn't have gone. He would have been notified by the rest of the staff. There was no way she could've simply slipped away.

And when he entered the palace, he met her at the exit. She was wearing black. Her gold spectacles were back on her face. Her hair laughably formal for the attire she was currently garbed in.

"I'm sorry," she said. "But it is for the best."

"Why?"

"Because you don't love me."

"I cannot love anyone. You know that."

"No. It's a lie, and I know it is. And if you cannot love me, then it will be someone else, but I will not do us this disservice. I will not do *you* this disservice." She put her hands on his face. "I love you," she said with ferocity. "I love you." Her chest pitched in a sob, and it caught in his own. "I will never love another. But we deserve to share that. We do. We deserve everything. And we would give ourselves such a small portion of it. I cannot heal you. I tried to remove the thorn. The wound remains, and there's nothing I can do about it. Healing has to come from you. Please... Please understand. I have always wanted too much. My mother told me so. And that used to make me feel terrible. It's something I've been awash in these last weeks. I do want everything. It's not about being Queen, it's not about having nice dresses. It's about being loved. Don't I deserve it? Don't you deserve it."

"Livia," he said, his voice filled with torture.

"Matteo, please do not come after me for your pride."

"I do not give in," he said as she began to walk away from him.

"I know you don't."

"No. I will not be manipulated. Torture does not work on me."

"I'm not the one torturing you."

And as she took a step away from him, a sound rose in his chest that reminded him of a dying animal, guttural and filled with pain. The embodiment of everything he had ever been terrified to let out when his father had physically destroyed him.

"Do not leave me," he said.

"Can you give me what I want?"

Tears fell down her face, and he felt nothing but a blinding, stabbing pain.

"No," he said.

And then she was gone. One of his members of staff ran up to him. "Should we stop her? Shall we stop flights?"

"No," Matteo said. "No."

She was not his. And she never had been. She was *hers*. And unless he could give her even a fraction of what she was giving to him how could he...

Yes, his pride would be left in tatters by this. A second bride failing to actually follow through with the wedding, and this one in such a public way. But it didn't matter. What mattered was Livia. What an awful time to consider the feelings of another before his own for the very first time in his entire life.

But she was right.

She deserved everything. And his hands were empty.

He could offer her gowns and a castle, the world on a platter, but he did not know how to reach his own heart.

He could buy her anything she wished. He could buy

himself anything he wished, for that matter, but he could not buy her. Could not make her stay.

And for the first time since he was a boy, King Matteo de la Cruz felt utterly powerless.

CHAPTER THIRTEEN

"YOU HAVE BECOME a beast."

Matteo looked up to see his brother standing in his office.

"I have always been," he growled. "This is nothing new."

"It seems remarkable to me."

"Well, I know how I feel. There is nothing different."

"Except that Livia left you devastated?"

He growled. "Do not speak her name to me."

"You are truly going to let… You're going to let your mouse leave you?"

"She wanted the one thing I cannot give, Javier. What would you have me do?"

"And that is?"

"Love."

His brother laughed, hollow and flat. "All right. And this is the part where I remember you telling me to pursue the love of Violet, all while telling me why you cannot feel it. I should, but you cannot."

"I am the King, and I can't…"

"Your bitterness is hardly helping you with your powers as a ruler, my dear brother. And I am only telling you this because it is honest. You love this woman. You do. You are trying to pretend that you don't, you are throwing every barrier in humanity in front of it. But you have loved her for the better part of nine years, and anyone around you could recognize it. But you cannot."

"No," Matteo said. "Love is…"

"A weakness? I know you think this for yourself, but what I don't understand is why. Our father had no love in his heart."

"It allows for vulnerabilities. Too many gray areas."

"You're afraid. And you had no trouble telling me that. No trouble telling me that perhaps love is worth trying since it is the one thing our father certainly never made an attempt at."

"But I loved him," Matteo said. "And he cut my skin open. I loved him, and he was a monster. I do not trust my own heart."

Love. Love was the cruelest, most dangerous thing of all. And he knew it. He *knew*.

"And here we come to it," Javier said. "You're just like me. Just the same as me. And don't give me anything about how you're the King. It makes no difference. You and I are the same. Desperately afraid of trusting our own hearts."

"But you didn't know he was a monster. I did, and still…"

"The bastard did wrong by us. There is no getting around it. No denying it. What we endured, it was not a normal childhood. He tried to destroy us. Do not let him. We never had the chance of growing up without scars. That much is true. How could we not? But we can decide what we are now. Look at Livia. Look at what she's become. From where she started… You're a king, Matteo. If she can overcome in such a way, surely you can too."

"No," Matteo said. "She is better than I am."

"And Violet is better than I am. There is a gift in loving a woman who is that strong. Who is that certain."

"I am miserable."

"So stop."

"How can it be so simple?"

"It is that simple and that difficult. You have been trained to live on an island. You have been trained to let your soul be a wasteland. To not allow for anything to touch you. For anyone. And you have decided that all emotion is a weakness. But think of how much strength it takes Livia to love you."

"It only makes me feel sorry for her."

"She did not ask for your pity. I believe she asked for your love."

"I don't know how."

"Think of your life with her. I do not know your relationship with Livia. But I do know love. You share things. You carry each other's burdens. It is more than sex, though that is part of it. She completes you. She is your other half."

And he thought back, to these nine years that he had spent with Livia, and he knew that what his brother said was right. That it was true.

Livia was the one woman who had listened as he talked about his scars. She had seen him have nightmares and held him while he was in pain. He had taught her to dance and she had taught him to be human. She was the one he went to with all of his most pressing problems. She was the only person that he could see completing the way that he ruled the country. For she was his other half.

The one who made strength from all of his weaknesses.

His Livia.

He understood now, the manner in which she would allow him to approach. Not to claim her. But to make an offer. A real offer. For all he had done was make demands.

It was all his arrogance had allowed for.

But his love, which he realized had been there all along, hidden beneath the wall of rock… His love could humble itself. And it could ask—no, it would beg—for Livia.

"I must go."

"Of course."

"I can only hope she will still have me."

"There are some things," Javier said. "Some *people* that I believe are destined to be together. You and Livia are destined. Now you just have to go and claim it."

"I think I had better… I think I had better go and ask instead."

Livia was exhausted. She had walked around Paris all day and tried to feel something other than the crushing heartbreak that rolled through her chest in unending waves. She tried to enjoy the little magazine and art stands that were piled atop each other along the banks of the Seine. She tried to take comfort in the Arc de Triomphe and the glowing pyramid in front of the Louvre. She wandered the Musée d'Orsay aimlessly, expecting to find answers in the artwork and finding only echoes of her own sadness. She was utterly sick of herself by the time she got back to her sparsely furnished apartment. An apartment she had been surprised was still there waiting for her when she returned.

But it had been. Matteo had not taken it from her, and

in fact, had bought it outright. She would have to leave, or buy it from him, or something.

But you're still hoping he'll come after you.

Yes, but not as he had done before…

You would take that. Admit it. You are weak for him…

No. She was trying to be strong for them both. Because they both deserved better than a lifetime spent beholden to the past. Than allowing Matteo's father to determine how much happiness they might have.

She took out the baguette she had brought in from the boulangerie downstairs, and simply took a bite out of the end. It was uncivilized, and she didn't care. Her apartment. Her bread.

There was a knock on the door, and her heart stilled. Matteo did not knock.

"Yes?"

"Mouse."

It was him. She jumped up from her chair and flung the door open, and she didn't care if she had crumbs on her black top, or if she looked half so desperate as she felt. "What are you doing here?"

"I came to speak to you. I came to see you."

"Please do not tease me."

"No. This is not to tease you. Livia, I am a man in hell without you. And I have… I have turned over everything we have ever said to one another in these last years. I have thought of our life, for we have shared part of a lifetime together already. Is it not amazing?"

"It is," she said. "It is sort of amazing."

"I am flawed. Desperately so. And I did not wish to be, because I thought the only way to rule would be if I… If I somehow sanded away every vulnerability, and made myself into a cliffside. I thought I could decide to be the perfect ruler, and then I would be. But that is not to be. Livia, I told myself that a lack of emotion was needed in order to rule that way, but… You know I loved my father."

"Matteo…"

"It was so easy to say I hated him, but if it were so simple… Emotion would be black-and-white, then, would it not? I could choose good things, and turn away from the bad, but for me… It has all been one. I loved him. And he harmed me. Left me devastated. And mostly, I fear the pain that comes with this sort of feeling. I fear weakness. And I am weak standing before you."

"You are not weak," she said. "Matteo, you are the strongest man I know."

"I am weak for you. Weak now. But I would endure this weakness a thousand times over if it meant being able to have you. I would cry out in pain and think nothing of it, for I have nothing to protect if I do not have you. Nothing. I am a fool, because I had to ask my brother what love was, and what he described to me is what we are. What we had for years. It is a life shared. A burden shared."

"Matteo," she whispered. "I was very, deeply afraid to be trapped in a marriage with a man who did not love me, because I knew how easy it would be for you to abandon me. But it was my conversation with Violet that… No, you would not have left me, and I know that. But what I feared was that if I gave you everything you wanted you would never… You would never heal."

"You were right. You took the thorn out, and the rest was up to me. I had to reconcile my fears, my shortcomings. That it is not pretending I do not have them, but rather facing them head-on, and trusting that you,

Livia, are the answer for all that I am not. And I will do my best to be the same for you."

Her heart nearly burst. It was a beautiful thing, this revelation. She didn't have to do all the healing, he carried some of it all on his own. This love was not heavy. It was a gift. Not a burden.

They did not poison one another, they gave each other the tools to heal. To be the best they could be.

"You have been." She looked at his beloved face. "I was such a weak, bitter creature when I arrived here, and you gave me dreams again."

"And you have given them to me. I do not want you to be my wife for the sake of the country. I do not want to have children with you for the sake of producing heirs. I want them for my sake. I want you for the sake of my own heart. Because only then... Only then will I be healed. But I have to ask you... Will you marry me, Livia?"

A question. A question she could answer, and easily.

And in that question was his true change, his true growth. Because in the question was a willingness to be vulnerable. To admit he could not control her or the world. He gave her a choice, and in that showed he was willing to fail.

For her.

But she wanted only to say yes. And she would.

"Yes," she said.

And he swept her up in his arms and kissed her lips. "I love you."

"I love you too, Mouse."

And Livia knew him. Knew his heart. Had for all this time.

And she knew that he meant it, from the depths of his soul. And that his love would never run out.

EPILOGUE

QUEEN LIVIA DE LA CRUZ had a title and a name now. She had spent so many years of her life without those things. Without a family name. But she had one, and a family to go with it. And now they were completing the Herculean task of taking their brood of children, along with Javier, Violet and their children, to the carnival.

Of course, being royalty, it also required that they have a security team hovering in the background, but Livia had grown used to it. And for the most part, it felt like a regular family outing. Though, none of it was regular for Matteo, Javier or herself. For they had never had family outings, and what a family was had been based on nothing other than their own dreams. Certainly not experiences.

Matteo and Livia had become the parents they *wanted* to be. Not the ones they'd had.

Therefore children were scrambling about, playing with their two cousins, creating an exceedingly well-dressed kerfuffle wherever they went.

Royalty they might be, but they were children first.

"Camila, Byron, do not scream."

Her son and daughter looked at her sheepishly. Her two younger boys looked at each other, clearly satisfied that it was not they who were on the receiving end of the scolding.

"Just one moment," Matteo said. "I'll only be a moment." Then he slipped away, and she exchanged a glance with Violet.

"What is he up to?"

"Difficult to say," Violet said, stopping for a moment and breathing heavily. She was pregnant again, and considering her and Javier's youngest child was six, she was deeply irritated with the state of things, but Livia also knew she was pleased to be adding to the family. When she wasn't angry over being pregnant again so unexpectedly.

"It's the handcuffs," she said. "I am weak for them, and I don't think."

And Livia knew exactly what she meant.

Matteo returned and he had in his hand a large serving of cotton candy.

"Matteo…" He handed it to her, and then he pulled her into an embrace, kissing her firmly on the mouth as she held tightly to the pink sweet treat.

"This is for you," he said. "Along with my promise. That for ten years I have been your husband. And I will continue to be. Forever. That's what this means now. Forever."

Tears filled her eyes, and she felt some of the remaining, lingering bruises of her past fade away.

Matteo had shown her what love was. Just how enduring it could be.

"Forever," she agreed.

And they held hands and followed their children deeper into the carnival. And Livia had never been happier.

* * * * *

MILLS & BOON

Coming next month

HIS STOLEN INNOCENT'S VOW
Marcella Bell

"I can't," she repeated, her voice low and earnest. "I can't, because when I went to him as he lay dying, I looked him in his eye and swore to him that the d'Tierrza line would end with me, that there would be no d'Tierrza children to inherit the lands or title and that I would see to it that the family name was wiped from the face of the earth so that everything he had ever worked for, or cared about, was lost to history, the legacy he cared so much about nothing but dust. I swore to him that I would never marry and never have children, that not a trace of his legacy would be left on this planet."

For a moment, there was a pause, as if the room itself had sucked in a hiss of irritation. The muscles in his neck tensed, then flexed, though he remained otherwise motionless. He blinked as if in slow motion, the movement a sigh, carrying something much deeper than frustration, though no sound came out. Hel's chest squeezed as she merely observed him. She felt like she'd let him down in some monumental way though they'd only just become reacquainted. She struggled to understand why the sensation was so familiar until she recognized the experience of being in the presence of her father.

Then he opened his eyes again, and instead of the cold green disdain her heart expected, they still burned that fascinating warm brown—a heat that was a steady home fire, as comforting as the imaginary family she'd dreamed up as a child—and all of the taut disappointment in the air was gone.

Her vow was a hiccup in his plans. That he had a low tolerance for hiccups was becoming clear. How she knew any of this when he had revealed so little in his reaction, and her mind only now offered up hazy memories of him as a young man, she didn't know.

She offered a shrug and an airy laugh in consolation, mildly embarrassed about the whole thing though she was simultaneously unsure as to exactly why. "Otherwise, you know, I'd be all in. Despite the whole abduction..." Her cheeks were hot, likely bright pink, but it couldn't be helped so she made the joke, anyway, despite the risk that it might bring his eyes to her face, that it might mean their eyes locked again and he stole her breath again.

Of course, that is what happened. And then there was that smile again, the one that said he knew all about the strange mesmerizing power he had over her, and it pleased him.

Whether he was the kind of man who used his power for good or evil had yet to be determined.

Either way, beneath that infuriating smile, deep in his endless brown eyes, was the sharp attunement of a predator locked on its target. "Give me a week." His face may not have changed, but his voice gave him away, a trace of hoarseness, as if his sails had been slashed and the wind slipped through them, threaded it, a strange hint of something Hel might have described as desperation...if it had come from anyone other than him.

"What?" she asked.

"Give me a week to change your mind."

Continue reading
HIS STOLEN INNOCENT'S VOW
Marcella Bell

Available next month
www.millsandboon.co.uk

COMING SOON!

MILLS & BOON

THE HEART OF ROMANCE

A ROMANCE FOR EVERY KIND OF READER

MODERN

Prepare to be swept off your feet by sophisticated, sexy and seductive heroes, in some of the world's most glamourous and romantic locations, where power and passion collide.
8 stories per month.

HISTORICAL

Escape with historical heroes from time gone by. Whether you passion is for wicked Regency Rakes, muscled Vikings or rugg Highlanders, awaken the romance of the past.
6 stories per month.

MEDICAL

Set your pulse racing with dedicated, delectable doctors in the high-pressure world of medicine, where emotions run high a passion, comfort and love are the best medicine.
6 stories per month.

True Love

Celebrate true love with tender stories of heartfelt romance, the rush of falling in love to the joy a new baby can bring, and focus on the emotional heart of a relationship.
8 stories per month.

Desire

Indulge in secrets and scandal, intense drama and plenty of s hot action with powerful and passionate heroes who have it a wealth, status, good looks…everything but the right woman.
6 stories per month.

HEROES

Experience all the excitement of a gripping thriller, with an i romance at its heart. Resourceful, true-to-life women and stro fearless men face danger and desire - a killer combination!
8 stories per month.

DARE

Sensual love stories featuring smart, sassy heroines you'd wan best friend, and compelling intense heroes who are worthy of
4 stories per month.

To see which titles are coming soon, please visit

millsandboon.co.uk/nextmonth

JOIN US ON SOCIAL MEDIA!

Stay up to date with our latest releases, author news and gossip, special offers and discounts, and all the behind-the-scenes action from Mills & Boon...

 millsandboon

 millsandboonuk

millsandboon

might just be true love...

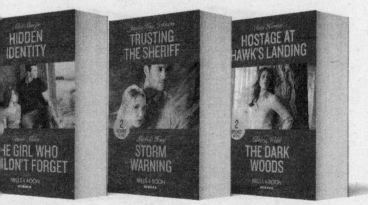

MILLS & BOON
Desire

Indulge in secrets and scandal, intense drama and plenty of sizzling hot action with powerful and passionate heroes who have it all: wealth, status, good looks… everything but the right woman.